HOLDING A
TENDER HEART

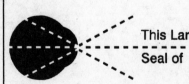

THE BEILER SISTERS

HOLDING A TENDER HEART

JERRY S. EICHER

THORNDIKE PRESS
A part of Gale, Cengage Learning

GALE
CENGAGE Learning·

Farmington Hills, Mich • San Francisco • New York • Waterville, Maine
Meriden, Conn • Mason, Ohio • Chicago

GALE
CENGAGE Learning®

LIBRARY OF CONGRESS CATALOGING-IN-PUBLICATION DATA

Eicher, Jerry S.
  Holding a tender heart / by Jerry S. Eicher. — Large print edition.
    pages ; cm. — (The Beiler sisters ; book 1) (Thorndike Press large print Christian romance)
  ISBN-13: 978-1-4104-6833-8 (hardcover)
  ISBN-10: 1-4104-6833-X (hardcover)
  1. Sisters—Fiction. 2. Amish—Fiction. 3. Large type books. I. Title.
PS3605.I34H65 2014b
813'.6—dc23   2014002183

Published in 2014 by arrangement with Harvest House Publishers

Printed in the United States of America
1 2 3 4 5 6 7 18 17 16 15 14

HOLDING A
TENDER HEART

ONE

Debbie Watson slowed her Toyota Camry as she neared the buggy ahead of her. She'd often done this, living as she did in Snyder County's Amish country. And after all this time, she still didn't resent the Plain people and their old-fashioned buggies. In fact, she wondered what it would be like to actually drive one.

Of course, she knew part of the answer. She'd grown up next door to an Amish family — the Beilers — and though she was *Englisha,* the Beilers had invited her to ride with them on more than one occasion. On a few Saturday afternoons she'd driven into Mifflinburg with Verna, the eldest of the three Beiler girls, to buy groceries for Verna's mother, Saloma.

Those times had been peaceful as she listened to the steady clip-clop of hooves striking the pavement as they drove along. The soft sounds weren't drowned out even when motorized vehicles passed the buggy — some of them accompanied by loud roars of their engines. Thankfully the locals and occasional tourists were mostly respectful of the area's Amish community and behaved accordingly.

When a car did roar by, Buttercup, one of the Beilers' driving horses, would shake her head at such rude interruptions, as if the noise were too much for her tender ears. She spent most of her life in a quiet barnyard or a pasture with plenty of grass, got extra feed when she had to work, and was fed delicious hay in the winter months. It was a life to be envied — as was the life of all the Beilers, as far as Debbie was concerned.

Life was hectic in her *Englisha* world — at least most of the time. Hopefully now that she was graduating from college in Lancaster on Saturday, her life might calm down a bit. But she had a job interview in Lewistown tomorrow. If she were hired . . . well, maybe her life wouldn't be as calm as she was hoping. The job interview was with a Mr. Fulton, a friend of Debbie's dad. Would Mr. Fulton really take her on? Would he think her qualified with only her college education? Wouldn't he ask about her lack of experience? It was hard to tell. But Mr.

Fulton had given her the best of wishes for her graduation and a warm smile when she'd dropped off the application.

Did she want a job that her dad arranged for her? Not really. But there were few other options, and she needed a job now that college was over — and they were scarce. Of all the applications she'd filled out, Mr. Fulton was the only one to offer her an interview. Had her mom pushed her dad to speak to Mr. Fulton? Had her dad pulled strings? It was possible since they were good friends. But she didn't dare ask Mr. Fulton or her parents such a thing. And what was so wrong if her dad *had* spoken with Mr. Fulton? Her parents loved her and only wanted to help out. She should be humble enough to appreciate their efforts and take the job if it were offered.

If her mom was behind this, she meant no harm. But even so, it made Debbie feel smothered. Even the decision to go to college had been more her mother's than hers. But now that college was behind her, shouldn't she make some decisions for herself?

Debbie grimaced as two vehicles behind her pulled out to pass her and probably the buggy ahead of her. Why were people in such a hurry? If the truth were known,

Debbie would have traded her car for the buggy she was staring at. She would trade her job prospects and even her college degree for the contentment she saw in the Beiler family and the other Amish within their community.

But how could that ever be? Her parents had their expectations of her. A college degree, a good job, money, and eventually marriage to a nice man who was a good social match. A man like Doug Williams. Oh, Doug was nice enough, but he didn't understand her any more than her parents did. The truth was that neither Debbie's parents nor Doug really wanted what she wanted. That too was a problem from her mother's point of view, along with Debbie's "lack of drive and motivation." Debbie didn't fit into the world her mother circulated in. The two were so different from each other. There was no question about that. Her mom had even said Debbie needed an awakening of some sort.

Debbie sighed. She knew she couldn't do much about being different. It wasn't like she hadn't tried. She'd gone to college. But even that was only a small victory for her mother. She'd wanted Debbie to go to Penn State or maybe even one of the Ivy League schools. Her mother had simply sighed and relented when Debbie had been accepted at Franklin & Marshall in Lancaster, one of the oldest colleges in Pennsylvania. Her dad had been on her side, reminding her mother how well esteemed the small college was.

What would either of them say if she told them the truth? That college really didn't matter that much to her. She wanted a simpler life — one like the Beilers led. She had never said those words out loud in her parents' presence, but she supposed she didn't have to. Surely it was evident enough in the way she lived. Conservative and quiet, she hadn't dashed around to wild parties on weekends like most of the high school and college students did. Her dad wrote this off to her religious life, which both parents knew was vibrant.

Out of politeness she did go to the Baptist church with her mother every Sunday when home from school. But even that she credited to the Amish and not to her mother. As for being a Baptist herself . . . well, her heart wasn't in it. Oh, they were fine people, but they weren't living the life Debbie wanted for herself. What she longed for was a faith to call her own. Something like the Beiler family's faith. From the time she was a small girl, the Beilers' lifestyle had made her feel the closeness of God. They did this by the way they lived and their simple trust that God would take care of them.

Debbie leaned back in the seat as the buggy turned off the road and she was able to speed up. Oh, if only she'd been born into an Amish family and had somehow been switched at birth. That would explain her longing for Amish life. But, really, the idea was ridiculous! Debbie Watson born into an Amish family? There were too many things that argued against it. Her baby pictures, her birth certificate, the family resemblance. She was *Englisha* born, but her heart was Amish. That was all there was to it.

No doubt the Beiler influence had something to do with it. Debbie had felt drawn to their farm ever since she could remember. She would head over there for any reason she could find. She'd always loved the smell and sounds of the place in the summertime when the hayfields were cut, the barnyard was clean, and the horses leaned over the fences. In the evening the cows mooed as milking time approached and they meandered up from the pasture. It was life as close to heaven on earth as she'd ever known.

She would often run over when Verna and Ida, the oldest Beiler girls, came out to chore. They would make sure she was comfortably seated on a three-legged milking stool while they bustled about the barn. Wayne and Reuben, the two oldest brothers of the family, had mostly ignored her. To them she was just the curious *Englisha* girl from next door who sometimes hung around . . . obviously having no chores to do at her own home.

Lois, the third Beiler daughter, had shown no end of fascination with Debbie's *Englisha* life. On Saturdays Lois would play with her in the yard and pepper her with questions about her world. What was it like to wear pretty dresses? Did it hurt to put holes in your ears for earrings? As the two girls grew up, questions had continually arisen, especially when Debbie neared the age of driving a car. Lois had almost swooned at the news that her friend would attend college. These were all things Debbie had talked about reluctantly, especially after she caught on that Lois only asked such questions when she was sure her *daett,* Bishop Beiler, was out of earshot. But that didn't keep Lois from asking more questions. And their differences didn't end there. Lois stayed inside during chore time so she could help with the supper preparations. She was a born cook and didn't like barn life as much as

Debbie didn't like kitchens. They couldn't have been more different if they'd tried.

Down through the years, Debbie's friendship with Verna and Ida had grown deeper. For several years all three Beiler girls had come over for occasional overnight visits, but those had stopped when it became obvious to Bishop Beiler how much Lois loved the *Englisha* life. Thankfully, the bishop hadn't blamed Debbie for Lois's fascination with all things *Englisha.*

Now Verna and Ida were out of their traditional *rumspringa* time and had joined the church. Whether this was from their father's orders or their own choices, Debbie had never been able to ascertain. Lois was at the tail end of her *rumspringa* time. She still hadn't joined the Amish church, even though she'd just turned twenty-one. And she showed no inclination to join either — at least that Debbie had heard of. The only thing holding Lois back from plunging ahead into the *Englisha* world was the deep respect she, along with her two sisters, had for her father's position in the community. How long that would restrain Lois, Debbie could only wonder.

Thankfully Bishop Beiler hadn't known everything that had transpired when Lois visited her house. She'd stayed up most of the nights listening to music, watching television, and trying her hand at using the electric kitchen appliances — all things never found in an Amish home.

Debbie slowed down to pull into her parents' driveway. As she parked the car, she paused for a moment to gaze across the field toward the Beiler farm. In the late-afternoon light the scene was peaceful, like it was always, the red barn still gleaming from last year's paint job. Emery, the youngest Beiler boy, had seen to that. He was full of youthful energy and well into his *rumspringa*. He likely didn't want his reputation tarnished by a fading homestead.

Wayne and Reuben were long married now and had children of their own, but sometimes on Sunday afternoons they came home for a visit. Marriage prospects for the Beiler daughters seemed less promising. None of the three had dated yet, but Debbie didn't feel comfortable asking why. Lois not dating, she could understand. The youngest Beiler daughter didn't want to settle down with an Amish boy — and likely never would. But Verna and Ida were another matter. Both of them were decent looking and nice, so the problem had to be something else.

Debbie sighed as her gaze shifted from

the barn to the well-kept Beiler house. Oh, what she wouldn't give to be there right now! If only she and Lois could trade places — that would make both of them happy. Perhaps she should march over to the Beiler farm and offer to switch places with Lois. That would provoke a hearty laugh from Bishop Beiler — until he thought her words through. His laughter would stop then. Bishop Beiler didn't plan to lose a single one of his children to the world.

It was enough for Debbie that he tolerated her visits all these years, apparently never seeing her as a threat. Did he perhaps understand her heart? Was that why he'd put up with her hanging around so much? She'd practically grown up with his children. She'd even picked up enough of the Pennsylvania Dutch language so she could get the gist of what they were saying part of the time, though she still couldn't speak it. She had to be careful lest Bishop Beiler see her as an interloper, Debbie mused. The girl who'd crept in where she didn't belong. Oh, if only she *could* belong! But that wasn't possible. She was who she was. She would continue to fail to fit in with her own world. She would continue to feel shut out, lonely, and different.

Debbie got out of her car and went into

the house. Silence enveloped her — only it wasn't the silence of an Amish home. In the kitchen the refrigerator rattled, and she heard a load of ice drop inside the freezer. The home's heating system whirred as it poured warm air into the room. But the starkest difference was the lack of people. Debbie's mom had a job and wouldn't be back until late. Her dad was working at their garage in town. He spent every weekday and even some weekends there. This was how it always had been and apparently always would be. There was a continuance of sorts, but a continuance of monotony, not the ebb and flow of life that happened over at the Beilers'.

Debbie walked to the back patio doors and looked toward the Beilers' farm. The wash line was empty. If this were a Monday, Ida would have laundry strung up, flapping in the wind until dry enough to take inside. Debbie could see it now in her memory. Mostly long lines of dark-blue and white clothing sprinkled occasionally with lighter colors. The bright spots would be Lois's dresses, no doubt. Lois pushed the *Ordnung* rules until they stretched like rubber bands. But Debbie knew Lois could take things only so far because she was the bishop's daughter. That had been confirmed once during an overnight visit. Lois had collapsed into giggles by the time she was done with the tale, but Debbie had listened in horror, which had only increased Lois's delight.

As Lois's story went, one afternoon after a shopping trip to Mifflinburg with Ida, Lois had snuck a few yards of light-green material into the house. She'd begun making a dress in secret down in the basement, working late at night after her *mamm* and *daett* were in bed. She'd draped the whole contraption, plus herself, in two of their thickest quilts to muffle the sound of the sewing machine. For light, Lois had set a gas lantern on the concrete floor. But her mother had discovered the project before Lois could sneak out of the house with the dress on and head for a youth social. Her *daett* had put his foot down, which had, of course, undone all of Lois's hard work.

Debbie's sympathies were clearly on Bishop Beiler's side, and she'd told Lois so.

That admission had provoked an outburst of astonishment from Lois. How could one not enjoy the *Englisha* life with such opportunities as dressing in beautiful colors at one's fingertips? Debbie's view was clearly beyond Lois's comprehension.

Well, it was beyond Debbie's understanding how one couldn't love the Amish world.

18

Especially if one had been born into it.

With one last glance toward her neighbors' farm, Debbie retreated to the kitchen and tossed her purse on the table. As if the bounce had made the cell phone inside come alive, it began to ring. Debbie dug into her purse and glanced at the incoming number. It was Doug Williams. She almost let the phone continue to ring, but Doug would expect an answer. She'd avoided him all week, but that couldn't go on forever.

"Hello," she said, holding the phone to her ear.

"Debbie?" Doug's voice sounded surprised.

She laughed. "Not expecting me to answer, huh?"

"Well, I never know with you."

"There's no law saying you have to call, Doug."

He sighed. "Look, Debbie, please stop playing games. You know I'd like to go out with you this weekend. Maybe Friday or Saturday night? Or after the graduation ceremony maybe? A nice restaurant back here in Lewistown. Or whatever you want."

"You leave plenty of options, don't you, Doug?"

"That's because I want to see you, Debbie. I really do."

Debbie took a moment to answer. "I don't know if I can, Doug. There will be a lot going on with me . . . you know . . . graduating."

His voice hesitated. "Debbie, are you seeing someone else? Is that why you're avoiding me?"

She laughed. "No, of course not! Who would want to see me?" Maybe that was a bit over the top, but right now that was how she felt. No one, including Doug, would want to be with her if they knew what she was really like. He'd hung around for a year or so now, taking her out on occasional dates. He said he wanted a deeper relationship, but she had stalled.

Debbie pressed the phone harder against her ear. Doug must have said something she hadn't caught because she could hear irritation as he asked, "Debbie, are you still there?"

She cleared her throat. "Yes, just thinking."

"What's so hard about going out with me?" he teased. "I'm a nice guy. Surely you know that by now. You'd enjoy yourself."

"Okay." Debbie sighed. "Where shall it be?" She sounded like she was giving in, and Doug would count chickens where they didn't exist, but that couldn't be helped.

Doug's voice brightened. "How about somewhere where we can talk? Perhaps Andrea's Pizzeria? At six on Saturday night?"

She didn't hesitate this time. "Okay, I'll see you then." When they hung up, Debbie wondered if it was fair to not just tell him flat out they had no future together. But how did one say, "It's not going to work for us" face-to-face . . . or, worse, over the phone? And yet she did care about Doug. He *was* nice, but . . .

Her mind went back to last spring. She'd caught sight of a young Amish man as he cultivated his corn crop, and she'd felt . . . drawn to him. But was it to him or to his Amish life? She'd seen him again during the summer and had experienced the same feelings as she watched him cut his hay. Then in the fall, she'd seen him hauling manure. His spreader had bounced across the rough, plowed ground. By then she knew his name was Alvin Knepp.

He was, as far as she knew, unmarried. She'd heard his father was the poorest Amish farmer around. "The Knepps," Lois had said, "are poor in both farming methods and in money." But Debbie didn't care about those things. Wasn't that exactly what she wanted to get away from? Was that why she often caught herself daydreaming about a certain Amish man?

Alvin exuded a rugged goodness that drew her heart in a way she didn't understand. And she didn't even know him! She'd had only fleeting glimpses every so often. What would it be like to speak to him? Debbie drew in her breath at the thought. Alvin wore a tattered and torn hat most of the time. Maybe that was all he could afford. Either way, he made a striking figure as he worked. How he appeared on Sundays she didn't know, having never attended an Amish church service. But it couldn't be worse than on workdays. Likely he cleaned up well. She laughed at the thought. What did it matter? He was clearly out of her reach.

How on earth was she supposed to tell Doug all that? He would think her insane, and he would probably be right. Somehow she needed to get past this fascination with a life that could never be hers.

Two

The next morning Debbie slept in later than usual. She arose to find that both of her parents had already left for work. After a leisurely breakfast, she changed into her gray-striped dress, affecting what she hoped was a classy business look for her job interview. She smiled at the irony that this clerical job was one she might have been able to get even without a college degree. Why did she even go to college!

The thought still rankled. Her mother's fingerprints were on all the major decisions of her life. "Purpose, my girl!" mother would say if she were here — just as she had during Debbie's four years of college. The truth was that getting a job and looking classy weren't the goals Debbie had in mind for herself. She glanced at her watch and shot up from the breakfast table. She couldn't be late for this interview! That would not go down well with Mr. Fulton, much less her parents.

Debbie tried to dull the stab of regret with a final rush through the house. She grabbed her keys and forced herself outside and into the car. She pulled out of the driveway and drove above the speed limit for the first mile. The trip into Lewistown soon slowed to a crawl as the traffic increased and cars had to make their way around the occasional buggy and horse clip-clopping along the side of the road. Since she was late, this should stir her angst, but it didn't. She felt more relaxed the more buggies she passed. They reminded her that the world she lived in wasn't all that important. Seen from the inside of a buggy, life passed in slow motion. The fields inched past buggy doors. Time stretched out, it seemed, and took its time to go by. Debbie smiled at the thought of how the Amish, despite their slow pace, seemed to have more time than anyone else. They savored each hour. They never seemed to rush about like she was at the moment.

She swung deftly around another buggy. She glanced at the horse as she went past. The animal plodded on with its nose close to the ground, looking tired from the uphill climb. She waved to the young woman and child inside. The woman responded with a smile and a wave. Who they were, Debbie had no idea. The Snyder County Amish Church Districts were spread over the long valley, and no one knew everyone, even among the Amish. The Amish had the time and the confidence to wave back — even to strangers. Debbie liked that.

Debbie fought the traffic for several more minutes and eventually arrived at the warehouse buildings of Destiny Relocation Services. They were the local branch of a national chain of movers that had more than 250 outlets in the United States. *What an appropriate name for my first job* Debbie thought as she parked her car. Destiny! Was this hers?

Mr. Fulton probably hoped people would find the company's name a comfort as he hauled their belongings across the country. Perhaps the name suggested that destiny had played a hand literally and divinely in a major and, no doubt, unsettling life experience. Perhaps she could also find purpose and meaning here. Wouldn't that be something?

Debbie entered the front door and gave her name to the young woman at the desk.

"Mr. Fulton will be with you in a moment," the woman told her with a smile. "I'm Rhonda Clemens."

25

"Good to meet you!" Debbie returned the smile and then took a seat in the small waiting room. Moments later Mr. Fulton appeared. "Hello, Debbie. Glad you could come in today."

"Good morning, Mr. Fulton." Debbie stood. "I'm sorry I'm a little late. I hadn't counted on the traffic."

"Ah, what does it matter for today?" Mr. Fulton waved her in. "You're the only interview I've scheduled this morning. So let's see what we can do for you. Please have a seat." Mr. Fulton motioned toward a chair. "How are your parents?"

"They're fine," Debbie replied as she sat down.

Mr. Fulton beamed. "Good, good. So I hear you're graduating this weekend? From Franklin & Marshall?"

Debbie nodded.

"Fine old school. I see you majored in sociology and anthropology. You earned good grades, I assume."

Debbie nodded. "An 'A' average I hope, but I haven't gotten my final grades for this semester."

"Now, now," Mr. Fulton chided, "don't be modest about it. I wouldn't expect anything else from Herbert Watson's daughter." He grinned. "What are your plans this summer?"

"Working, I hope."

"Anything beyond that? Any vacation plans?"

What was she supposed to say? Debbie wondered. No doubt Mr. Fulton expected answers like a Disney World trip or a church mission outing. Perhaps travel out West, a vacation in Yellowstone, or spending time in the Bitterroot Mountains. None of which she'd planned. What she really wanted was a summer spent on the Beiler farm where she'd get up at five o'clock each morning, eat breakfast as part of the large family, and then help with chores. But if she gave that kind of an answer, Mr. Fulton would probably turn her down on the spot.

"I'm staying in the area," she told him.

"Well, you might wish to spread your wings a little next year," Mr. Fulton offered. "Our company offers two-weeks paid vacation time. That's enough to get most anywhere folks wish to go."

Debbie found nothing to say in reply, so she just smiled and nodded.

Mr. Fulton went on. "I've looked over your application and, of course, knowing your parents, I have no qualms about your ability to do a good job here. The job is yours . . . if you want it."

"Yes, I do want it! That's very kind. Thank you, Mr. Fulton!"

"Well then, that's just fine. When can you start?"

"Whenever you wish! Sometime after this week, I guess." Debbie searched for more words to say. The interview had been so short, and she hadn't expected to be hired on the spot.

"Fantastic!" Mr. Fulton glowed. "How about next Tuesday then? You'll have your own office in the back. Sally Wells, from billing, will give you the basic training you'll need."

"Thank you so much!" Debbie gave Mr. Fulton her best smile. A little rush of joy ran through her. Her first full-time job!

Mr. Fulton rose. "Give my regards to your parents. I'll see you at eight o'clock on Tuesday. Don't run late now. Work begins at eight o'clock sharp." '

"I'll be here!" Debbie said as she rose and offered her hand. "And thank you again, Mr. Fulton."

"You're welcome, Debbie. Glad we can take you on. You'll do well with us, I'm sure."

Mr. Fulton showed her to the lobby. As she went past the front desk, Rhonda gave her a little wave. Debbie waved back and smiled. Next week she'd be a part of this place. Her destiny, no doubt! It warmed her heart yet also left an emptiness inside. Perhaps she expected too much from life. Perhaps she was being idealistic. A job was a job, and she was thankful to be able to earn a living. Interest in the work would no doubt grow as time went on.

As Debbie drove back toward Beaver Springs, an idea formed. She ought to celebrate! But with whom? Mom was at work, and so was Dad. Either of them would go out to eat with her tonight if she asked — tired though they'd be from their day's work. But no, there must be a better idea. Debbie thought the matter over for a moment. Yes, there were people she could celebrate with — if she dared.

Would the Beilers think her crazy if she stopped by for lunch? No, if there was a danger of that, it would have happened years ago. They were always glad to see her. For this moment, at least, she would pursue her dream. She would step into an Amish home and relish the feel of it. Lois and her mom, Saloma, might only have sandwiches ready for a quick bite to eat, but they would have plenty, and that would be enough.

Debbie drove faster and whipped her car around a few buggies. Now she was the one who buzzed past the slow-moving vehicles as she dashed around another buggy on Route 522. She pressed on, and a few minutes before twelve turned in at the Beilers' lane. She brought her car to a stop beside the buggies parked near the barn. There was no sign of anyone around, but that only meant they were inside the house or in the barn hard at work. Everyone was home. She knew the buggies well enough to figure that out.

Debbie climbed out of her car, walked up to the front door, and knocked.

Verna opened the door and wrapped her arms around Debbie's neck. "*Ach*, it's so *gut* to see you again! You haven't been by in a long time." Verna let go and stepped back. "I had begun to think you'd forsaken us."

Debbie laughed and stepped inside. "If you only knew! I've been busy, what with graduation this weekend and . . ."

"Oh!" Lois gasped from the kitchen doorway, her face almost glowing. "That's so *wunderbah*, Debbie. A real college education! You ought to be so happy you can't sleep at night."

"It's not that big a deal, Lois, really," Debbie said. But by the look on Lois's face, Debbie could see she wasn't convinced. As usual, Lois thought all things *Englisha* were the best things that could happen to a person.

Ida stuck her head through the kitchen doorway. "Hi, Debbie! You're just in time for lunch."

"I hoped you'd say that," Debbie admitted. "I've missed you all."

"So tell me about the college thing." Lois's face still glowed.

Debbie winced. "Like I said, it's not that big a deal, Lois. At graduation we all wear hats with tassels, some professors make speeches, we get our diplomas, and we go home. Then it's back to our normal lives."

"Oh, but that's so *wunderbah*!" Lois said. "So it's Saturday? May I come? I'd love to see the ceremony for myself."

Debbie hesitated. "I don't know about that, Lois. Your parents, you know . . ."

"I'll convince them," Lois said, though a tinge of doubt was in her voice.

"I have more news!" Debbie said. "I just got my first full-time job!"

Lois's hands flew to her face. "Now I'm so jealous I could turn green, Debbie. A real job!"

Debbie smiled at her friend's enthusiasm. "Work away from home is not all it's cooked up to be, I'm sure."

Lois didn't appear convinced, but before

31

she could say anything more, Saloma appeared.

"Debbie!" she said. "Surely you're staying for lunch? Or have you eaten already?"

Debbie smiled. "I'd love to stay if you don't mind."

"It would be a joy," Saloma told her. "You're almost part of the family, you know."

Oh, if that were only true! Debbie thought.

Lois announced in a loud voice, "Debbie found her first job today, and she's celebrating."

"That's *gut,*" Saloma said. "I'm glad for you, Debbie."

Debbie knew that Amish women seldom worked outside their homes. She'd heard they sometimes worked during *rumspringa,* but she didn't know if Saloma had done that. Except for *rumspringa,* the Beiler daughters would probably never work outside their community either. Saloma was congratulating her because she rejoiced with those who rejoiced. That was the kind of people the Beilers were. "Thank you," she said. "I'm grateful to have a full-time job in this market."

"So why are we wasting time then?" Saloma waved her hands toward the kitchen. "*Daett* and Emery just got in the washroom, and the sandwiches and soup are ready."

"Come then!" Lois led Debbie to the kitchen table. Debbie slipped onto the back bench. This was her familiar spot since childhood on those occasions when she'd eaten with the Beiler family. Debbie felt a tear slip down her cheek. She really shouldn't be this affected by a simple lunch. The emotion probably came because she'd thought too much about her future the past few days. And now she was thinking about her past at this house with this family. Since she was an adult with a job, there would probably be fewer occasions like this. No doubt meals with the Beilers would become just a memory in a few short years. Memories of the Beiler place would become ever more distant as the years rolled past. No wonder she was sad. She did the best she could to hide the tears. Who among the Beilers would understand such an emotion?

"Hi, Debbie!" Bishop Beiler boomed as he came in through the washroom doorway. Water droplets still clung to his lengthy gray beard. "What a nice surprise."

"It's good to see you too," Debbie said.

Emery nodded to her but didn't say anything as he sat down. He was much like his older brothers. Mostly they ignored this *Englisha* friend of their sisters who appeared

33

and disappeared at irregular intervals.

Bishop Beiler stroked his moist beard. "Well, looks like we only have sandwiches and soup, but let's give thanks nonetheless."

He only teased, Debbie knew, as they bowed their heads together for prayer. She reached up to wipe a stray teardrop on her cheek.

THREE

On Saturday morning the sunlight filtered through the campus trees on the lawn of Franklin & Marshall, the rays falling on the rows of tasseled students. Debbie straightened her chair, pulling up on one leg that had dug into the dirt. She twisted sideways a fraction of an inch. If these speeches kept on much longer, she would tip over and fall flat on her face. What a sight that would make on one's graduation day.

She glanced across the lawn and saw her mom and dad looking her way. They smiled and waved. They were thrilled with her accomplishment even if she wasn't. Lois, seated beside them, absolutely beamed — almost as if this were her graduation. It was a miracle she was even here. Bishop Beiler had raised his eyebrows when Lois had asked him if she could attend the ceremony. Debbie thought she'd even seen a look of fear cross his face. She figured the bishop was worried that if he wasn't flexible to some degree, his youngest daughter would defy his wishes, now that she was of age, and jump the fence into the *Englisha* world for good.

The bishop had looked at Debbie for a moment before he seemed to relax.

Did the sight of me comfort him? she wondered. Maybe he figured Lois was safe in her company. Maybe he hoped she'd be able to dim Lois's rosy view of *Englisha* life. Debbie knew that was doubtful. Still, it did warm her heart. She — an *Englisha* girl — had the confidence of an Amish bishop on such a grave matter.

Debbie jerked herself out of her thoughts. The president of Franklin & Marshall, Dr. Elmer Towers, had approached the podium. She turned her full attention to him. The professor had always impressed her as a man worthy of attention. At least in the brief contacts she'd had with him during the four years she'd attended classes.

Dr. Towers cleared his throat away from the mike before he began to speak. "I welcome all of you today. This is a moment of great importance, not only for our students who graduate today, but for their families and our faculty. I give a heartfelt thanks to all who have played a part in the formation of the minds of this graduating class. To you, to our professors, to our staff, and to the relatives and friends gathered here, I give my congratulations."

As the crowd clapped, Debbie's thoughts drifted. The Beiler family ought to receive thanks for her decent childhood. Her mom and dad had played their parts — very important parts, and she didn't wish to belittle that — but in the depths of her soul unseen hands from the farm down the road had always been active. Those hands had molded her into a creature who didn't fit into the world she lived in.

Dr. Towers continued. "We at Franklin and Marshall endeavor to continue the great traditions on which this university was founded. We seek the development of students in liberal arts and in life itself. No one is an island unto themselves. As we promote the growth of character and the love of learning in those who pass through these hallowed halls, we all in some measure promote our own well-being."

Another round of applause interrupted Dr. Towers. When it died down, he wrapped up his remarks. "With that being said, I will delay no longer. Congratulations to our fine graduates who have completed this stage of their journey in education. Let us begin awarding the much-deserved diplomas."

Dr. Towers stepped back. The graduating students formed a line, and several professors took assigned places on the platform. Debbie moved forward when her turn came. She approached the lectern and heard her name spoken over the loud speakers.

"Debbie Watson, with a BA in sociology and a minor in anthropology, with honors."

She marched up, shook the hand of the head of the sociology department, and whispered, "Thank you." She moved through the crowd snapping photographs and returned to her seat. The minutes ticked by until finally the last student was through the line. The ceremony wrapped up with a raucous cry from the graduating class and mortarboards tossed into the air. With a great heave, Debbie flung her cap upward. She'd earned this celebration with hard work and diligence. For better or worse she was now a college graduate! She was bound for a life of participation in the great American Dream. What that was, she had no idea, but it felt good to think it at this moment surrounded by her shouting fellow graduates.

As the crowd broke up, Debbie found her mom and dad and gave them both quick hugs.

Lois nearly squeezed the air out of Debbie's lungs with her embrace. "That was so *wunderbah!*" Lois gushed. "I've never seen anything like it in all my life. And those professors, Debbie! Did you actually study under them? They looked so wise and learned. I thought I was going to pass clear out."

Debbie laughed. "Life isn't always what things are cooked up to be, Lois. Remember that."

Lois didn't listen though. She grabbed the diploma from Debbie's hand and stared at it with wide eyes. "Oh, Debbie, you're such an important person now. Bound for a *wunderbah* life in the *real* world. Aren't you just bubbling over with joy and happiness?"

"I don't know about that," Debbie managed. She turned her attention to her father and mother. "Are we going out to eat?"

Her dad grinned. "Of course! We have to celebrate this great occasion. We're very proud of you, Debbie. You did great!"

"Thank you!" Debbie whispered, holding back the tears. Her accomplishment did mean a lot to her dad even if she didn't appreciate it fully.

"Let's go then," her mother said. "Enough tears for one day. I could use a good lunch myself before we drive back. I'm starving."

"What shall it be then?" her dad asked as he led the way to the car.

Lois, still excited, bounced up and down on her toes and lingered to look over her shoulder, as if she wished to etch the occasion deep into her memory.

"Anything's good enough," Debbie said, as she watched her friend's antics. Debbie mainly wanted to get out of this place. Now that she had her diploma, life had already moved on. Doug would pick her up tonight for their date. Well, sort of a date. And she needed to get things straight in her mind on what she was going to tell him. So far nothing she'd prepared would make him happy.

"Then why not a fast-food joint?" her dad suggested. "Then we'll be on our way faster."

No one objected as they climbed into the car and made their way to the freeway. Lois gazed starry-eyed at the passing buildings as if she'd never seen them before. A few minutes later as they sat eating hamburgers at Wendy's, Lois blurted out, "Do you think I could attend college, Debbie? Get a diploma like you just did?"

Debbie's dad spoke up with a wry look on his face. "College is expensive."

"Now, Herbert!" Debbie's mom said as she slapped him gently on the arm. "You know we gladly paid Debbie's college expenses. Don't make her feel bad about that. And don't disparage a young girl's dream — even if she is Amish." She gave Lois a soft smile.

Debbie's dad responded, "You're right, Callie. I'm sorry."

Debbie's heart sank a bit — not at the thought of the expenses her parents paid for her education but at the reaction Bishop Beiler would have when Lois announced her desire to attend college. That would *not* be a happy moment. So much for Bishop Beiler's trust in her.

Her mom spoke to Lois encouragingly. "College is a long, hard road, dear, though a worthy one. I'm glad you're so excited. We had to work on Debbie a while before she would enroll."

"You *had* to?" Lois sounded incredulous. "You have no idea how excited I am. I see now better than ever that there's a whole world just waiting out here to explore."

Have mercy on us all! Debbie groaned under her breath. Bishop Beiler would never allow her on his place again.

Her mom glowed and stared at Lois. "That's certainly a refreshing attitude for a young woman to have."

Debbie interrupted them. "Lois is Amish,

Mom. For crying out loud! Don't encourage such things for her. Bishop Beiler will be most displeased."

Her mother remained silent and glanced away.

Lois spoke up and fairly snapped, "I'm of age now. I should be allowed some decisions of my own. Look at Verna and Ida. They're both at home yet and still single. All because *Daett* won't approve their boyfriends. I'm not going to be like them. I'm going to strike out on my own."

Debbie tried not to gasp. She knew the family well, but even this was inside information she hadn't been privy to. The Amish usually kept such thoughts within the family and community. She was sure Lois wasn't supposed to spill information about their family conflicts in public.

Her mother looked horrified. "Your father oversees your sisters' dating habits . . . and yours? At such an age, Lois? Why, that's going a little far, I say."

Lois had sobered by now. She looked like she knew too much had been said.

Debbie's mom added, "I certainly encourage you to think about moving out, Lois. No child should hang around the house — not longer than is necessary. That's what I've always believed. Staying too long breeds dependency and destroys character, if nothing else."

Now Lois clearly tried to extract herself from her earlier outburst. "I'm sure that's right, Mrs. Watson, but *Daett* is very concerned about his children."

"Watch what you say, Callie," Herbert said, jumping into the conversation with a quiet laugh. "We still have Debbie at home with us."

Debbie felt a sting at her mother's words. Did she think she was being a sponge at home? That she was there only to live off them? In a way she did, but only because . . .

"Well," Debbie's dad said as he stood and brushed the crumbs off his hands, "that was good. Let's head on home."

Debbie didn't move. "What did you mean about children moving out as soon as possible, Mom?"

"Oh nothing, Debbie." Her mother waved her hand as if the thought had already vanished into thin air. She tidied up the table and then stood.

Debbie wasn't about to let it pass. "Mom, tell me what you meant. Do you want me to move out right away?"

"Debbie, don't be silly," her dad chided as he laughed. "I'd miss you if you weren't there. And of course your mom didn't mean it quite the way it sounded. She was pontificating in theory, in general terms."

Callie glared at him. "That's what you think I do, Herbert? Pontificate?"

Herbert grimaced. "Callie, dear, that's only an expression. Look, let's get back to the house. I have things that need to be done."

Debbie still didn't move although her dad was halfway to the door. Lois might be restricted from talking about family problems, but she wasn't. "Mom, please!"

Her mom faced her. "I'm not trying to hurt your feelings, Debbie, but I do worry sometimes. While you attended college I could rationalize you still living at home, but now . . ."

Debbie stood up. The pain her mom's words caused burned deep. And the worst thing was Debbie knew they were true. At least in their world. Now in Lois's world daughters stayed home past the time they came of age without any disgrace attached to it.

"Look, dear," Callie began again. "I'm sure you'll be on your own in good time. You just haven't mentioned it. Let's not quarrel on your graduation day."

Debbie allowed herself to be led out the door, with Lois tagging along. But inside her heart, Debbie realized she'd never be able to satisfy her mother. She itemized some of the reasons. She'd accepted a menial job that really didn't require a degree, she had no steady boyfriend, and there was nothing in her life that met her mother's standards. Debbie would always be playing catch-up to the way her mom thought her life should be.

Debbie turned her attention back to Lois. However badly she felt right now, she would feel a whole lot worse when Lois told her dad about her desire to attend college. Somehow she had to wipe that thought out of Lois's mind — and fast! But how? Her friend seemed as stuck on being different from the life she knew as Debbie was. Debbie climbed into the car and chuckled softly. It was funny . . . yet it wasn't.

"What's the joke?" Lois asked.

Debbie shook her head. "Just thinking, that's all."

"If you move out, you could come live with us," Lois said, all smiles. "I'd like that."

"I don't think that would work," Debbie said absently.

"I'd still like it," Lois chirped.

Debbie glanced out the window. Lois would indeed love it if someone from the *Englisha* world lived at her house, but it was out of the question. She couldn't move into the Beiler home. The bishop would never allow such a thing . . . or would he? Debbie pondered the question all the way back to Snyder County and home.

FOUR

Later that evening and still in her graduation dress, Debbie drove her car back toward Lewistown. The rest of the afternoon hadn't gone well — at least not since she'd taken Lois home. Bishop Beiler hadn't been at the house, but Verna, Ida, and Saloma were. Lois had wasted no time before launching into an excited recitation of the day's events, complete with the declaration that she wanted to attend college.

"I had nothing to do with this," Debbie protested. Beyond that, she didn't dare elaborate. Lois was still her friend, even with her over-the-top admiration of the *Englisha* world. So there Debbie stood in the Beiler house caught between two competing forces: Lois's desire to experience what Debbie had and the Beiler family's traditional way of life, which Debbie loved.

In a way, Debbie could sympathize with Lois. After all, didn't she harbor impossible dreams? And didn't she wish someone would give her encouragement in those dreams? The only difference was Lois's community had religious reasons for their objections, while her parents had only their personal preferences. Still, both were strongly held positions.

Thankfully, Lois hadn't repeated her suggestion that Debbie move into the Beiler household. Such an idea presented now might look like Debbie was scheming with Lois to bring such a thing about. Still, the more Debbie thought about it, the more the possibility appealed to her. If only the bishop could be persuaded . . .

Debbie sighed. It was complicated. Like the conversation that had continued at the Beilers' until she'd finally spoken against Lois's badgering. "Lois, you'd better listen to your mother's advice. You don't know what lies out there in my world. There are a lot of bad things, and life can be very hard. And you'd have to get your GED before you attend college. That's four grades to make up." She said this for Lois's long-term well-being and in defense of the rich Amish heritage Lois had grown up with. Debbie could tell Saloma was comforted by her words. Beyond expressing her opinion, Debbie couldn't do more.

"*Ach,* Lois," Saloma pleaded, "you're overly excited from the day's events. A good night's sleep will set your mind at ease again. The things of the world come and go. They might look good today, but tomorrow the glory of them passes like the flowers in the field." Saloma turned toward her guest. "Is this not true, Debbie?"

"Yes, it is," Debbie answered without hesitation.

Saloma ushered her outside then and smiled with gratitude on the front porch. "Thank you so much, Debbie. We'll talk more with Lois later. I know it's not your fault she gets these wild ideas into her head."

Debbie had left, but her heart was still troubled . . . and stayed that way all afternoon. For Lois and for herself something must change, but what? And now Debbie's own mother wanted her out of the house. She hadn't come right out and said it, but Debbie knew her mom well enough to know that she did indeed think it was time her daughter moved on with her life . . . beginning with leaving the nest.

As she drove the back roads toward Lewistown for her dinner date with Doug, Debbie was using this roundabout way to give her time to think. And no one would think

49

anything about it if she just happened to go past Alvin Knepp's place. Maybe he would wave to her if he were outside. That might be enough to cheer her up.

Thoughts from Lois's suggestion earlier in the day ran through her mind. Was there a way to persuade Bishop Beiler to agree to let her move in? Perhaps if she brought the subject up in the right context? Moving in with an Amish family would be the answer to so many things. If she needed to step out on her own, why not step out into the place her dreams led — being with the Amish? She probably could never truly become one, but why not indulge the fantasy for a few months or a few years and see what it was really like?

She didn't know that much about Amish dating habits — only the little pieces of information Lois and her sisters had dropped along the way. And she knew enough from them to recognize courting couples when she saw an Amish man driving his "courting buggy" with a young woman close beside him on the seat. What if she could stay at the Beiler place until she knew what she really wanted to do with her life? Oh, if only it could work . . .

Debbie's thoughts drifted to Alvin as she approached his farm. Did he have a courting buggy? She'd never seen one parked in front of his barn when she drove by. But that didn't mean anything. It could be inside the barn and all dust covered since Alvin hadn't dated — as far as she knew. She'd dared to ask Lois once. The question aroused less suspicion than she'd feared. Apparently Alvin wasn't considered a very desirable dating option within the Amish community. Lois didn't say why other than to mention that Alvin had been scorned by Mildred Schrock. Mildred had been a school crush of Alvin's apparently. Debbie hadn't asked for more details because Lois had turned up her nose at the very mention of Alvin's name.

Debbie slowed as she approached the Knepp driveway. Off the road was a white, two-story house set on a small knoll. Fields stretched out on either side of the barn. The corn was already a foot high in the section to the east. A wagon appeared drawn by a team of horses. Debbie slowed even more. It was Alvin! He stood tall on the wagon as it bounced and rattled toward her.

As she drew abreast of him, he waved in her direction. A friendly, noncommittal sort of wave, Debbie thought as she waved back. She was pretty sure he'd recognized her. She'd seen him once when they were both at the Beiler place. Her cheeks burned at the memory. Alvin hadn't even climbed out of his buggy that day, but he had smiled when she nodded to him on her way out of the driveway.

Debbie accelerated and drove out of sight. She could still feel the flush of heat on her cheeks. What was wrong with her anyway? Was she infatuated with this Amish man? Her mother would have a fit and a half if she ever suspected such a thing! She glanced at her watch and drove faster, soon approaching Lewistown. She glanced at her watch again. If she didn't hurry, there would be a call from Doug asking where she was. Well, that was something Alvin would never do. He'd probably never been to an *Englisha* restaurant in his life, much less did he own a cell phone.

Such a life — a life with such a boyfriend as Alvin — would be all about freedom. There would be no hurry to meet deadlines. Such a man would have no dates with women who didn't wish to see him. He'd pass the hours of his day peacefully until nightfall, when he'd gather with his family and everyone would enjoy each other's company. When was the last time she'd gathered with her parents at home? For anything other than Christmas or Thanks-giving?

Debbie pushed the thoughts of her parents and, especially, Alvin Knepp away. What chance had she to gain the attention of a decent Amish man? None.

She pulled into the parking lot at Andrea's Pizzeria and rushed inside to find Doug already waiting at a table.

"Good to see you, Debbie," Doug said as he stood. He appraised her with a quick look and approving smile. "How was your big day?"

"It was fine, Doug." She sat down. "I wish you could have been there."

Doug pulled up his chair. "I know. I wish I could have too. I had a work assignment that I couldn't get out of. You do under-stand?"

"Sure, I understand. To be honest, I really didn't enjoy it that much myself. I'm glad it's over."

"Really? I loved my graduation day. I knew it marked the beginning of a new life for me. A life of success and achievement. I'm well on my way to that goal. And you will be too, Debbie. You should be happy about the great things ahead for you . . . and for *us*."

Debbie ignored his remark, her mind

drifting. "There's got to be some way Bishop Beiler can be persuaded," she murmured.

"What? Is this some kind of riddle?" Doug stared at her as the waitress came up.

Debbie waited until they'd given their orders before she answered. "Sorry, Doug. I'm off in my own world right now. The truth is that what you think of as success, I think of as drudgery. A successful career and all that goes with it — the money, the ambition, the climb to the top — just don't interest me."

"Then what does interest you?"

Debbie smiled as she answered. "You'll never understand, Doug. But I think I'd like to move into the Amish community. I'm wondering if they'll let me."

"This is a joke, right?" Doug asked, his gaze piercing hers. "I'm not getting it. What's the punch line?"

"There's no punch line, Doug."

Doug leaned forward. "You're not serious are you, Debbie? I mean, all of us have our fantasies, but joining the Amish never was one of mine. And for you I never imagined it either."

"I probably couldn't join their faith . . . at least not at first," Debbie said, not looking at Doug. "Mom wants me out of the house as soon as possible. If I have to pay room and board somewhere, I'm hoping it can be with the Beilers. They have the rooms upstairs their two boys left when they married. It would be perfect for me — if they'll have me, of course. That's the big question."

Doug was dumbfounded. "Debbie, you're not making the least bit of sense!"

"Does my life make sense now, Doug?" Debbie leaned forward on the table. "Ask yourself that question. Do I really fit in with your world . . . your plans . . . your future?" There! She'd said it. Let the chips fall where they may.

The waitress arrived with their food, so neither of them said anything for a while.

Doug picked up his pizza, broke off a small piece, and popped it into his mouth.

For once Debbie knew what she wanted to say. "Would you mind if we prayed before we eat?"

"Whoa!" He wiped his brow of imaginary sweat. "What has gotten into you, woman? We've *never* done that before."

"Maybe it's time we did. Or time I did, anyway."

He laughed and put down his pizza. "I don't get you, Debbie. Really, I don't."

"Well, I'm praying," Debbie said, bowing her head. When she looked up moments later, she noticed Doug had done the same, although he appeared red in the face.

"You're really getting out of my league, Debbie. I don't know what to say. You've changed."

"Yes, I suppose I have," she said. "I guess finally finishing college and getting a job have made me change. Made me take stock of what I really want."

He touched her hand. "What do you really want, Debbie? I asked you to come here to talk about our future, hoping *that* is what you want. We go back many years. All through college I've waited for you, Debbie. I haven't dated any other girls because I like you. And occasionally you've given me encouragement to believe you feel the same way about me as I do about you. Has it all been for nothing? Is that how this is going to turn out?"

She met his gaze. "I honestly don't know, Doug. It's just that I've been thinking the past few days. Wondering how I can find peace with the way things are in our world."

"So you're serious about the Amish thing?" His fingers moved on her hand.

Debbie sighed. "I'm serious about finding out if I might fit. Although with me, who knows? I go up and down like a yo-yo. Scared of my own shadow. Afraid to step out and pursue what I really want. This morning an Amish girl embarrassed me. She has more nerve than I do, Doug. She's surrounded by a family and a community who oppose her feelings and beliefs, yet she dares to express them. Maybe nothing will come of it, but she at least speaks what she wants. And yet I don't dare say similar words to those I love. What kind of courage is that?"

Doug leaned back in his chair. "So where does that leave us, Debbie? Are you saying I'm wrong for you?"

"Doug, please." She touched his arm. "I didn't mean it like that. This really is about me."

"Sounds an awfully lot like you're sending me off gently into the night."

"Doug, I don't mean to hurt you. I'd never intentionally do that. I guess I've told you this because you were the closest person to me when it first wanted to spill out."

"Doesn't that tell you something?" he asked. "I'm you're listening ear. You need me."

"Doug, you're sweet." She tried to smile. "You've always been sweet to me. You *are* a good listening ear. But I think it's obvious we need to take a break in our relationship. I need the freedom to find out what I really want my future to look like."

He looked away and let out a long breath. "I wish we'd had this talk a long time ago."

Doug finished his pizza slice, and Debbie nibbled at her piece. Further talk seemed unnecessary. When they'd finished, they stood and walked to the counter. Doug paid at the register, and she waited until he was ready to walk outside.

"Thanks for the dinner," she said. "I'm sorry it worked out this way. You deserve better . . ."

"Thanks for the years we've known each other, Debbie. I don't understand what you really want, but whatever it is, I hope you find it."

"You've always been kind, Doug," Debbie said. She reached up and kissed him on the cheek. That it had turned out like this surprised her. She hadn't known what would happen, but now that it had, maybe it was for the best. At least she couldn't turn back now. She knew she had to pursue her dream. "Goodbye, Doug."

He nodded and turned and walked down the street. He gave a brief backward glance but kept moving.

FIVE

The following afternoon Verna Beiler stood in the kitchen tapping her fingers on the table. Outside, the late-Sunday-afternoon sunlight flooded the yard. Shadows danced across the kitchen sink as the branches of the old oak moved in the gentle breeze. *Why does Lois have to ruin everything?* Verna wondered. Handsome Joe Weaver had taken Verna aside at the youth gathering and asked if he could bring her home tonight. Her first decent offer from a man in a long time, and it came at the same time Lois was creating a *kafuffle* about attending *Englisha* college like Debbie Watson had done. Yesterday when she'd come home from Debbie's graduation, Lois couldn't stop beaming and going on and on about her plans to "make something of herself."

After that scene, *Daett* wouldn't be in any mood to hear Verna out. But at twenty-four, wasn't she old enough to make some of these decisions on her own? *Daett* kept too close a watch on his daughters, Verna told herself. She'd thought this for some time but hadn't dared say so. She knew his strictness was in part because he was the bishop for their community. If he wasn't, then he might not care about appearances as much.

Daett couldn't help that he was a bishop. He hadn't chosen his station in life. The responsibility had been thrust on him by *Da Hah*'s will, expressed all those years ago by the sacred lot. Neither must she hold ill will against the community when they expected their bishop's daughters to hold a higher standard than everyone else.

The problem was *Daett* went well above and beyond that standard. At least that's what her rebellious side whispered to her. *Mamm* reminded her often of the dangers of rebellion. That was why both she and Ida had stayed away from anything radical during their *rumspringa* and had quickly joined the church afterward. Lois hadn't done anything radical so far either. But neither had she joined the church. And she probably never would if her words about going to an *Englisha* college were any indication. But she shouldn't care so much about what Lois might do. Verna had her own life to live, and *Mamm* encouraged all her girls to seek having a heart that was submissive and graced with inner beauty. At least Lois was trying to heed those lessons even with her admiration for fancy *Englisha* ways.

So Verna worked hard to remember the words her *mamm* had spoken to warn her. She especially tried in the times when *Daett* had made her turn down another request of courtship from a man. This had been especially hard when Evert Stoltzfus asked last year for the privilege of driving her home from the Sunday night hymn singing. *He'd consider her consent a great privilege,* Evert had said. Her heart had beat faster at the very sound of such fancy words. How could it be that handsome Evert Stoltzfus considered it a privilege to have her in his buggy?

She should have said *yah* on the spot. Instead, she'd stood speechless, finally managing the words, "I'll have to ask *Daett.*"

From the look on his face, Evert hadn't liked that answer. Nor had he liked what *Daett* had told her. "You'd better wait a while on that one, Verna. Tell him *nee* — for now."

With *Daett* it was always "wait." He had a cautious approach to life, enforced on him, no doubt, because he had to lead the community through many difficult spiritual decisions. But Evert had no plans to wait.

She could tell at the following youth gathering by how he frowned when she told him her answer. Though to *Daett*'s credit, his evaluation of Evert's character had proven correct. The young man had left the community for the *Englisha* world not two months later.

It was *Daett*'s only clear victory. All the others — two boys who had asked before Evert (one of which she would have turned down herself) — had gone on to date other Amish girls. Mose Yoder — the one she wouldn't have turned down — would be married in this fall's wedding season if the rumors in the community were correct. And she might have been the one who stood beside Mose on his wedding day if *Daett* had been able to overcome his fears.

And *Daett* did the same thing to Ida. He'd turned down two boys already. Thankfully, both of them were boys Ida didn't particularly care for.

Lois, on the other hand, had received no offers so far even though she was twenty-one. Whether this came from *Daett*'s reputation or from Lois's own choosing, one couldn't be certain. With what the people of the community expected from them as the bishop's daughters, Lois didn't do anything to help her cause by blabbing all the time about her admiration of the *Englisha* world.

Last night, though, had been the worst yet. Never had Lois spoken so outright about her plans to take action. Hopefully her feelings would blow over before long and nothing would become of this. Verna and Ida certainly didn't need a sister who had jumped the fence to add to their already difficult reputations. If Lois did something wild like that, they might never find suitable husbands — and already the field was getting quite thin.

Not many men were left who hadn't either chosen girlfriends or were well on their way to saying their marriage vows. In fact, Joe Weaver wouldn't have asked Verna home if his girlfriend, Rosy — whom he'd dated for two years — hadn't broken off their relationship a month or so ago. Because of this, Joe's request had come as a total surprise. Verna hadn't even noticed him make eyes at her at the Sunday meetings. But then neither had she paid much attention, which only confirmed that her heart had been given over to despair that the right man would ever come along. At least someone *Daett* would approve of. So what exactly could *Daett* have against Joe Weaver? He lived north of the district, and he was the second boy in his family. The Weavers had been farmers for generations, and his family had a decent reputation. Joe was even *gut* friends with the handsome and loud-mouthed Paul Wagler, whose reputation no one doubted — at least when it came to whether he was a decent Amish man.

Surely *Daett* could find nothing wrong with Joe Weaver. And so when Joe asked her last Sunday, Verna had said *yah* on the spot. For this man she would put up a fight if necessary. And perhaps *Mamm* would give her support — if it came to that. But now she had to tell *Daett,* and her courage failed her. Verna thought back over the week and figured she should have approached *Daett* at once. But how did she know Lois would have her meltdown last night?

Verna turned toward the kitchen sink just as Ida walked in. She took a look at Verna and said, "You're still troubled over Lois, aren't you?"

"Why? Has she been saying anything more?"

"*Nee,* and I hope it's blown over."

"So do I," Verna said and then fell silent.

"So if it's not Lois, then what's really bothering you?" Ida asked.

Ida saw right through her, but that was Ida — always caring. "Oh, it's nothing really."

"You can't fool me. Now come. You should tell me." Ida pulled out a chair and motioned for Verna to sit.

Verna did so with a sigh. "Joe Weaver asked me home last week, and I said *yah.*"

Ida's eyes grew large. "Did *Daett* agree to this?"

"I haven't told him yet."

Ida's eyes grew even bigger thinking of another *kafuffle* ahead. Still, it might not happen. She whispered, "There's nothing wrong with Joe."

"That's what I keep telling myself. But I still can't bring myself to face *Daett.*"

Ida glanced toward the living room where both of their parents relaxed in their rockers, *Mamm* reading *The Budget* and *Daett* deep into his Sunday-afternoon nap.

Ida's face lit up with inspiration. "I know! Let's make popcorn and squeeze fresh oranges."

Verna clasped her hands together. "Why didn't I think of that? You're so wise, Ida."

Ida basked for a moment in the praise before she crept down the stairs to the basement. Verna had the popcorn popper warm by the time Ida came back with her arms full of ripe oranges.

Thankfully, *Mamm* had ordered their stock replenished only this week from the bulk food store in Mifflinburg. They didn't always keep the expensive treat around, but it would be put to *gut* use this afternoon, Verna decided. *Daett* must be brought to see the wisdom of allowing Joe Weaver's attention for her.

Ida squeezed oranges at the table while Verna twirled the popcorn lever. Soon the sound of popcorn popping filled the kitchen. Some of the kernels spilled onto the floor when Verna jerked off the cover. The prepared bowl caught most of the rest. She would sweep later. Right now she was so nervous it was a wonder the whole popper-full hadn't ended up on the floor.

Ida smiled her sympathy from across the room.

Verna returned the smile. Her sister was a jewel. Why didn't someone ask Ida home on Sunday nights? Someday surely some nice Amish boy would notice her. But right now Verna needed to be concerned about her own future. Oh, what if *Daett* said *nee* about Joe Weaver? There would be an awful fight inside of her — she just knew it. How much would come out, she didn't know. She had yet to be pushed to such an extreme.

Ida poured the orange juice into tall glasses, and Verna filled individual serving bowls until they almost overflowed with popcorn. They glanced at each other for a moment before they headed into the living room.

Mamm looked up. "I thought I heard something in the kitchen. Are we in for a treat this afternoon?"

Verna didn't say anything. *Mamm* might think this an innocent gesture, but it wasn't. And, in fact, from the look that crept across *Mamm*'s face, perhaps she already understood.

Daett's face beamed though. He boomed, "Oh! Now this wasn't necessary, girls!" But he took the popcorn eagerly enough.

Ida made sure a tall glass of orange juice was within his reach. With a quick sideways glance at Verna, she retreated into the kitchen.

Verna wished Ida had stayed, but perhaps she'd best face this on her own. She sat down on the couch and cleared her throat. *Daett* was already reaching for his weekly copy of *The Budget* when she began to speak. "I have something I have to tell you, *Daett*. Well, both of you, really."

Daett's bowl of popcorn teetered a moment in his lap. "*Yah,* Verna? Are you still troubled about Lois last night? I suppose I was a little too upset myself, but *Da Hah* has given me assurance that Lois will see the error of her ways. If we pray . . ."

Verna cleared her throat again. "It's not about Lois, *Daett.* It's about me. Joe Weaver has asked if he can bring me home tonight, and I told him *yah.*"

"You told him what?" *Daett*'s hand clutched his popcorn bowl. He turned to Saloma. "Do you know anything about this, *Mamm?*"

Mamm shook her head. "Verna has told me nothing. But please think about this before you say anything, Adam."

Daett didn't wait even a second. "I will have no heartbroken man bringing my daughter home. I don't believe in my girls playing second to anyone."

Daett *keeps an amazingly* gut *tab on what all the unmarried men do,* Verna thought. It was one of the inconveniences of a talk like this. As bishop, he always knew every fault and discrepancy that lay within any suitor's character.

"I have already said *yah.*" Verna tried to keep her voice calm.

Daett glared at her. "Have you thought about this, Verna? Joe Weaver isn't fit to ask any girl home until he gets over that Rosy of his. And I won't have you hang around him until a decent amount of time has passed."

Verna didn't hesitate. "He's not a widower, *Daett*. Girls drop their boyfriends all the time. It's not a disgrace. And I plan to avail myself of this opportunity. And I will not insult Joe by making him wait. It's not like I'm getting any younger. I'm twenty-four years of age. Do you want your daughters living at home with you all your life?"

Daett grunted and looked away.

She had obviously scored some points, but not enough yet. If *Mamm* would only help! Verna kept her voice steady. "He's bringing me home tonight, *Daett*. I think I'm old enough to make up my own mind."

Daett's gaze turned toward her. "I will not have you speaking like that, Verna. Lois is already causing enough trouble in this house."

"Please, Adam," *Mamm* joined in.

Verna felt relief rush through her.

Daett ignored *Mamm*. "Give the boy some time, Verna, and we'll talk about this in a few months."

But Verna dug in. "He's not a boy, *Daett*. Joe is a *man*. He's a year older than I am, and I intend to bring him home tonight, with or without your approval."

A kernel of popcorn flew from *Daett*'s fingers. "What is the world getting to, anyway? My daughters are all defying me in

69

my own house!"

"Adam, please!" *Mamm* tried again.

Verna tried once more. "I have a right to date the man, *Daett.* There's nothing wrong with him."

Daett looked at his popcorn bowl for a long moment before he sighed. "Okay, then, but don't come crying to me when you find out what a mess this boy is, Verna. You'll have to heal up from your own wounds."

Verna felt a flush spread over her face.

Daett turned his attention to his popcorn. Just like that, she'd won.

Mamm motioned with her hand toward the kitchen.

Apparently it was best if she disappeared for a while. Verna dashed off before another word could be said.

Ida met her in the kitchen, and the two hugged each other and danced a silent jig on the kitchen floor.

A small victory had been won, Verna told herself. They both knew it, and her sweet sister rejoiced with her.

"It's really going to happen!" Verna whispered in Ida's ear.

"He'll be so *wunderbah* for you," Ida whispered back and then did another little jump before they both collapsed into the kitchen chairs.

SIX

Later that evening, after the hymn singing had closed at nine o'clock, Verna slipped out the washroom door. She fell in with the line of girls who waited on the sidewalk for their rides. No one seemed to notice anything unusual about her, but she was sure they would soon hear the pounding of her heart. Here she was at twenty-four years of age, and a man would soon take her home for the first time.

She hadn't imagined things would turn out this way. Not while she was growing up, at least. A bishop's daughter was supposed to bring suitors out of the woodwork. At least that's what her girlfriends from schooldays had whispered at recess when the talk turned to boys. But no one had counted on *Daett*'s unreasonable fear. Even tonight he hadn't let up.

He admonished Verna before she left for the hymn singing, "Don't be too easy on the boy now, Verna. You can always tell him he's not coming back."

Lois, who overheard, had appeared ready to fire back some retort, but she must have decided against it. This added fuss over Joe would do nothing to ease Lois's negative feelings on all things Amish. If he really wanted Lois to simmer down, *Daett* would have to lay off his objections over such an innocent thing as a boy taking a girl home. That happened all the time. Unmarried men were supposed to take eligible women home from hymn singings.

Of course, dating wasn't all innocence and fun, Verna told herself. It could lead to kisses, and promises, and finally to marriage vows. Those would bind you to one man for the rest of your life, which was exactly what she wanted. And why *Daett* couldn't see that was beyond her. She would have to continue to work on him. He had to lighten up if she wanted Joe to ask her home again. And she already knew she did even before his buggy approached the walkway.

Girls climbed like shadows into the buggies, many of those pulled by prancing horses. This was the early crowd, the *steadies* who were in a hurry to get on the road and spend time with each other. That explained why no one paid much attention to her yet. But before long someone would notice she hadn't headed toward the barn like usual to get her horse. The Beiler youth drove two buggies on Sunday evenings. Emery should by rights drive his three sisters in the larger surrey because they couldn't all four fit into a single buggy. But Emery had always refused. He said no one would see him drive a married couple's buggy until he was married. So his sisters had given up the argument years ago, and they drove a single buggy themselves. Emery was worse than *Daett* when it came to stubbornness.

Tonight Lois would leave with Ida for the drive home, and Emery could ride alone as usual. That was suitable punishment for him, but likely Emery was happy for any time spent without his sisters. Some boys were that way, Verna supposed, and no one could do much about it.

Would Joe be like that? Verna asked herself as his buggy drove up. She hadn't thought that far, but what did it matter? Wasn't she used to stubborn and cautious men? Perhaps *Da Hah* had prepared her for marriage to such a man. "*Gut* evening," Verna said as she pulled herself up to the seat of the open buggy.

"*Gut* evening." Joe's voice was firm but kind.

He doesn't sound fearful or stubborn, Verna noted. But this was way too early to tell. Right now all that mattered was a man was taking her home from the hymn singing, and she was going to soak in every minute of the experience.

Joe's horse dashed out of the lane and onto the blacktop road. Joe offered her a share of the buggy blanket.

She took the edge, and tucked it between herself and the side of the buggy. Verna stole a quick glance at Joe. She couldn't see the features of his face in the night shadows, and she shouldn't stare up at him anyway. He might think her too forward. Perhaps Rosy had acted like that during their two years of courtship. If Rosy had, Verna wanted no reminders of her in his head tonight. Verna quickly pushed those thoughts away. Thoughts of Rosy weren't wise at the moment. That woman was in Joe's past and would stay there if she had anything to say about it.

"What's the name of your horse?" Verna asked. Her voice didn't tremble. *Gut.* Joe didn't need to know how much her heart was pounding.

"Isaiah," Joe replied, sounding surprised.

"Isaiah!" This came out more exclamation than question.

"Don't you like it?"

"I . . . I just hadn't heard that name before used with a horse," she managed. "Usually our *kinner* have such names, not our animals."

His laugh was soft. "I thought the name the *Englisha* from the racetrack gave him was wrong, so I changed it once I arrived home. I guess he just looked like an 'Isaiah' to me."

"What was his *Englisha* name?"

"Red Lantern."

Verna joined his laughter. "I suppose that wouldn't be a decent name, although I've heard worse from racetrack horses. Emery claims he once bid on a "Dainty Rose." Now imagine an Amish boy with such a horse. We teased Emery about it for a week, so he never told us any names from then on."

Joe slapped the reins gently against Isaiah's back. "Thankfully we're allowed as a people from the community to see things our own way. And not just with horses. We can thank *Da Hah* each day of our lives that we live in a country that allows us freedom without forcing their ways on us."

"That's so true," Verna agreed at once,

thinking how spiritual Joe must be to work in a comment like that. That should impress *Daett* — once she had a chance to tell him. It might even help *Daett* get past his fears. But the most important thing was that Joe's words warmed her heart. He was already a man she could look up to. Any woman who raised *kinner* with him would find it a great joy indeed.

She stole another glance at Joe's face. He looked straight forward as the wind blew across them. The silence was comfortable enough, which was another *gut* sign — as if she needed one. Already she liked Joe a lot.

Joe seemed to know where their driveway was in the darkness. He took the turn without slowing down too much. He stopped by the hitching rack and jumped to the ground with the tie rope already in his hand.

Joe was also efficient. Why had Rosy let this man get away from her?

With Isaiah tied up, Verna stepped down from the buggy and led the way to the house. She paused at the porch and motioned toward the swing. "Do you want to sit out here for a while?"

"Sure!" Joe plopped down without further ado.

They couldn't see each other's faces out

here, but that wasn't Verna's real reason for the request. The others of the family would soon traipse past and stare at Joe like he was a novelty from an *Englisha* zoo. Which he kind of was — the first man any of the sisters had brought home. Maybe next Sunday night she'd let them get a better look at this man of hers.

"Nice weather tonight," Joe said from his side of the swing.

"*Yah,* it is," Verna agreed. She was more interested in the buggy lights coming down the lane at the moment.

Joe also looked in that direction. Laughing voices floated across the lawn as Ida and Lois pulled in behind Emery, and the three young people unhitched the two buggies. Joe stood. "I should go help."

Verna reached up and pulled down on Joe's arm. "There are plenty of them; they can handle it. But it's nice of you to offer."

He sat down again.

"We're here on the porch!" Verna sang out, triumph in her voice, as her two sisters approached.

"What is this?" Lois teased looking at Joe. "Where can I find myself one?"

"You can go look for yourself," Verna shot back.

They all laughed, including Joe, who rose

and greeted the arriving girls with a "*Gut* evening."

"Run along now," Verna told the two once they returned Joe's greeting.

"Well, then, have a nice evening," Ida said, obviously impressed. Ida would have been impressed regardless of who sat on the front porch swing with her eldest sister. The two younger sisters went inside and shut the door.

Someday Ida will find a decent man, Verna thought as silence settled around them. She would pray and do her part. She would make her relationship with Joe a model of perfection. That way *Daett* would have no reason to deny either Ida or Lois the attentions of eligible Amish boys.

Moments later, Emery hollered a "*Gut* evening," as he went by. He paused just long enough to add, "Are you behaving yourself, Verna?"

Joe chuckled and Verna glared into the darkness after Emery. "Stop teasing, and get up to bed!" she said. She'd had enough of her family for this evening — as nice as they were. It was now safe to go inside once the sound of Emery's footsteps faded. Verna rose and held open the front door. Joe followed without a word of protest. He took off his hat once they were inside and placed it on a wall hook behind the door that Verna showed him.

"You can sit on the couch while I get us something to eat," Verna said with a smile.

The soft glow of the kerosene lamp filled the room as he returned her smile. "You don't have to bother. I had supper."

"Oh, come on!" she teased as she made a funny face. "Not even a piece of shoofly pie?"

"Now that I can't resist!" Joe sat down with a pleased look on his face.

Verna scurried toward the kitchen. Her neck burned red from the pleasure of a correct guess on the first date. Not all boys liked shoofly pie, even though it was a common enough dessert in Snyder County. Emery was one of those who didn't. He claimed he couldn't stand the sight of it.

Thankfully the kitchen was empty. If either Ida or Lois had stayed downstairs unnoticed, she would have chased them upstairs at once. No one need eavesdrop on this her special night. Verna slid two pieces of pie onto plates and filled two glasses with milk. She was on the first trip to the living room when Emery came back downstairs.

He wrinkled his nose when he saw what she carried. "Yuck! I'd go straight home if I had to eat that kind of stuff."

Verna gave the piece of pie and a glass of milk to Joe.

Joe looked at Emery and laughed. "Come on now! Don't tell me a Snyder County boy doesn't like shoofly."

"Maybe it hasn't been made right yet." Emery paused as if taking another look. He shook his head. "Don't think so. It's awful stuff."

"Get upstairs right now!" Verna ordered as she went back into the kitchen. "I already know your feelings about shoofly pie."

"But I'm enlightening Joe with my wisdom," Emery said, keeping a straight face. "And I need a cup of water."

"Get, my lad!" Verna ordered as Emery took his good old time at the kitchen sink with a glass of water.

Joe still had his grin on when Emery vanished and Verna came back into the living room with her own piece of pie and a glass of milk. "You have an interesting family, Verna," Joe offered.

"A little too interesting sometimes," she said. Thoughts of *Daett* and Lois flashed in her mind. What would Joe think if he knew all that went on? Well, he didn't yet, and maybe she could make a favorable impression on him before he found out.

"Every family has their ways." Joe took a

large bite of pie. He savored it before swallowing.

He likes the pie! Verna thought. That was another danger when one served a community staple. Every woman had her own touch to pie making. Apparently Joe liked *Mamm*'s recipe. This evening was such a *wunderbah* night. And it would only get better, she was sure. Verna glanced at Joe. "So what have you been doing this week other than farming?"

He didn't answer right away. He chewed slowly. "Not much. *Daett* and I went to the Belleville auction on Wednesday, but everything was going too high. We didn't bring anything home."

Why was Joe's face suddenly turning red? Verna wondered. Had she said something wrong? Or did Joe not like his pie after all?

Verna took a deep breath. "Did I say something wrong, Joe? Something seems to be bothering you."

Joe looked at her steadily and then spoke after a long pause. "I suppose I'd better tell you this. You'll probably find out anyway. See, I drove a pickup truck around the lot at the auction barn. One of the *Englisha* boys wanted help. I knew I shouldn't, but something overcame me for a moment."

Verna smiled slightly. "I thought it might

be something I had done."

Joe appeared puzzled. "I don't think you could do wrong, Verna. That doesn't go for me, of course. But I don't plan to give in to temptation again. When our people drive *Englisha* vehicles for any reason it can't look *gut*. Even if I was just trying to help. I'm sure some of the younger boys saw me too. That's not *gut*."

That was surely the reason he confessed so easily, Verna thought. As the bishop's daughter, he figured she'd find out eventually. *Daett* would find out and might bring it up before long.

Verna heard a tremble in her voice as she spoke. "It's okay, Joe. None of us are perfect."

He looked relieved and took another bite of pie.

"I'm glad you understand." Joe took a long sip of his milk. "This is *gut* stuff."

Verna allowed her pleasure to show. "So tell me, Joe, what else went on at your farm this week? Any exciting stuff?"

Joe laughed. "I'm afraid nothing too exciting. The pigs are growing . . ."

Verna listened and encouraged his chatter about common farm news. She soaked in each inflection and subtle change on his face.

Midnight arrived soon enough, and Joe rose to his feet. Verna stood up and walked him to the door.

"I've enjoyed this evening, Verna," Joe said as he reached for his hat. "Any chance I can come back next Sunday night?"

She wanted to jump up and down with glee like Lois did sometimes, but she lowered her gaze instead. "You're more than welcome, Joe."

"Thank you, Verna!" he said and slipped out into the night.

She shut the door and then waited by the front window until his buggy lights had gone out the lane.

"We're going to make it!" Verna said into the night. "Joe is a *gut* man, a very *gut* man."

SEVEN

On Tuesday afternoon Debbie slipped into her car a little before three and left Destiny Relocation Service's parking lot. This had been her first day at her new job, and it had consisted mostly of orientation. Things had gone well, and she was off early. Tomorrow work would begin in earnest. Now she had to deal with the beginning of rush-hour traffic. This she wasn't going to enjoy. As she suspected, she no sooner pulled into an open lane when every vehicle in front of her slowed down. She might get home faster if she took Route 522, so she turned at the next side road.

Tomorrow she wouldn't have to rush as much, but tonight she had to arrive at the Beilers' residence before their suppertime. After she'd practically invited herself to lunch last week, she couldn't do the same tonight — or even give that appearance. Not with what she wished to ask of the Beilers.

Tonight she planned to make her big play, her start into a new life. She was going to ask Bishop Beiler and Saloma if they would consider taking her on as a boarder. No doubt the bishop would find such a request from an *Englisha* girl unusual. When such a thing happened, it was usually between two Amish parties or between *Englisha* people. One didn't mix things up. That was the problem. But perhaps if she dropped hints of things beyond that . . . like the fact she wanted to eventually join the Amish faith . . . the bishop might at least consider her request. But would all that said in one evening be too much? The Beilers were cautious people, not given to sudden moves even though they knew her well. Still, this idea just might work.

Debbie drove several roads to the north. Finally she turned east on Route 522. Thankfully the traffic didn't pile up beyond the normal slowdowns caused by Amish buggies. Her thoughts of the evening ahead continued. What many a tourist only dreamed of might turn into reality for her. She already had access to an Amish home — and a bishop's at that. If things went well, she might even become Amish someday. Now wasn't that some goal to set? Certainly better than climbing the corporate ladder at

Destiny Relocation Services — her mom's latest wish for her. But here she went again with the wild thoughts that could hardly come true. Joining the Amish faith couldn't be easy.

Despite the negative thoughts, Debbie felt her pulse quicken. What if this all worked out? Then she could attend Amish church services. Would Alvin Knepp notice her there? And if he did, how did dating work in the Amish world? There were no cell phone calls between an Amish dating couple, for one thing. And Amish girls didn't make the first move toward eligible boys. That much she knew. But dating Alvin was too much of a fantasy and too much to hope for. She really shouldn't even think about it. Besides, Alvin wasn't the reason for wanting to board at the Beilers' home.

Debbie grimaced. If Bishop Beiler caught a whiff of her feelings toward Alvin, the bishop might never give his consent. And she couldn't blame him. Bishop Beiler would think her motives polluted. But they weren't. She would join the Amish faith for her own reasons — if she joined at all. Beyond that, finding love would be an added benefit. But love wasn't what she dared hope for right up front.

Debbie took the next turn, and moments

later pulled into the Beiler driveway, coming to a stop beside the familiar buggies lined up beside the barn. She parked and climbed out, taking a deep breath while closing the car door with a soft click. In the distance a team of horses pulled some farm apparatus in a field. They appeared tiny across the vastness of the open acres. Debbie waved and a hand came up in response. From here she couldn't tell whether it was Bishop Beiler or Emery. She didn't wish to meet either of them at the moment. She'd decided it would be better to talk to Saloma or maybe Verna first. It would be better that way.

Turning toward the house, Debbie watched the front door burst open. Lois raced out, bounced to a stop in front of her, and gave her a big hug. "What brings you back today? Have you found another reason to celebrate with us?"

"Not really," Debbie said. Now that she was here, how was she to begin? Obviously not with Lois.

"You look somber, Debbie. Has something happened?" Lois asked.

"No." Debbie smiled a little. "I just need to speak with your mom or Verna. Are they at home?"

"Of course!" Lois's face had brightened

87

considerably. "Verna and Ida are almost ready to begin with the chores, and I've started supper."

"Then I'll try not to be long," Debbie said.

"You can stay as long as you wish." Lois's face glowed again. "You always bring a fresh breath of air to this stale family."

"Now, Lois, that's not nice." Debbie frowned.

Lois pouted. "Well, it's true. Although Verna did finally bring home a man last Sunday night. Can you believe that? The first male company we've had on a Sunday night in, like, forever!"

"She did? That's wonderful!" Debbie exclaimed.

Lois wrinkled her nose. "It was only boring old Joe Weaver, so I wouldn't call that very exciting. His old girlfriend, Rosy, dumped him not that long ago. That tells you how interesting he is."

"Verna must think he's interesting, and she's a good judge of people," Debbie protested.

Lois grimaced. "Joe's okay if you plan to stay boring Amish — which I don't."

"Lois!" Debbie gasped. "Don't speak like that."

"Who would've thought you'd be on my family's side?" Lois said sourly. "You're *En-*

glisha and all. You should be for them, not for the Amish."

Wait until you hear what I'm here for! Debbie wanted to say, but that wouldn't be wise.

Lois led the way to the house. Verna was waiting at the front door, beaming a happy smile.

"Good afternoon!" Debbie greeted.

"And a *gut* afternoon to you," Verna replied. "What brings you out today?"

"She wants to speak with you or *Mamm*," Lois said.

"Have you got a moment?" Debbie asked as a questioning look crept over Verna's face.

Verna glanced down at her chore dress. "Sure. We don't have to go out for another ten minutes or so. Come in. Did you notice if the men have brought in the horses?"

"No, they were still working in the field," Debbie said as she stepped inside. Verna didn't know how great a compliment she had just paid her by expecting her to notice things around the farm — enough at least to comment on them. The evening was off to a good start!

"Mamm!" Verna called over her shoulder. "Will you please come in here? Debbie would like to talk with us."

"Yah!" Saloma answered. She appeared moments later.

"Thank you for giving me a few minutes," Debbie said. "I won't take long."

"*Ach,* please sit," Saloma said, gesturing toward the couch. "We have the rest of the day, do we not?"

Debbie sat on the couch. They obviously didn't have the rest of the day, but the words had a nice welcoming feel. "Well, I . . . I . . . Um, this may come as a surprise, but I . . . I . . . I need to move out of Mom and Dad's place. I'm looking for a place to board."

"Oh my!" Saloma exclaimed. She waited for more information.

Debbie plunged on. "Would you and the bishop consider taking me on as a boarder? A *paying* boarder? I don't wish to move into town, and I appreciate your lifestyle and all. It would be just so — so, well, it just seems right to me. If you'll consider it, and if it can work out for your family too, of course."

"Your parents are asking you to leave?" Saloma obviously hadn't absorbed that point.

Debbie didn't hesitate. "No, not in the way it sounds. Mom thinks it's time I moved on. Grew up, you could say, and left the nest. It bothers her to see her grown daughter still in the house and not advancing in the world."

"And they know you are asking us this?"

Saloma asked, still puzzled.

Debbie rushed, "I haven't told Mom where I'm going. But, please, it will be all the same to them. In fact, they'd probably rather see me come here than go someplace unfamiliar."

Saloma just stared at her.

Debbie tried again. "Maybe that's not quite true. They may think I'm a little weird wanting to live the Amish way, but I'm not, Saloma. I grew up around your farm, and I love how you live. You see, I don't really fit in out there in the world. It's almost as if I should have been born someplace else — like maybe into an Amish family."

"I see," Saloma said as she studied her.

This wasn't going well, Debbie decided. She'd better spill the whole thing after all. "It's that . . . well . . . I-I think I may want to go Amish eventually — if such a thing is possible. I think it is from what I know of your community."

"*Ach,* then that's different." Saloma smiled for the first time. "Do you really have such a thought in your head?"

"Yes, I do," Debbie assured her. "I've had these thoughts for a long time. I just haven't let them come out until now."

"You know this will be hard, Debbie?" Verna spoke up for the first time.

"That's why she's taking this slowly," Saloma said. "I needed to know what the end goal was before we considered this."

"You're not really thinking of going Amish, are you?" Lois choked out from where she stood in the kitchen doorway.

"Does that disappoint you?" Debbie asked, glancing in her direction. Lois's disapproval was one thing she'd expected. Would Lois oppose her? That might make this situation untenable or, at the least, uncomfortable.

Lois managed to smile. "I said last week I'd love to have you here, but joining the Amish is a little crazy, if you ask me. I want to join the *Englisha,* and you want to join the Amish. I guess it's your right." Lois's face lit up. "Say! Why don't we switch places?"

Verna gasped.

Debbie shook her head. "That wouldn't be a good idea, Lois."

"Maybe in your opinion, but not in mine," Lois retorted.

"Then we have differing opinions, I suppose," Debbie replied.

Lois shook her head. "I think you're out of your mind."

"Let's not talk about that right now," Saloma interrupted. "We will take the matter up with *Daett* and let you know, Debbie. Maybe by the end of this week. Will that work or are you in a rush for an answer?"

"I am," Debbie admitted. "But that's okay. This will give me time to talk to Mom and Dad and let them know what I've asked and that you're considering it. I don't want it to come as a total surprise."

"That would be *gut,*" Saloma agreed.

Debbie rose. "I think I've kept you long enough. Thank you so much for considering my request. I know it's strange. I suppose it's not every day that an *Englisha* girl arrives and asks to live with an Amish family and maybe join the Amish faith."

"You can say that again!" Lois said.

"I hope this works out." Verna gave Debbie a quick hug. "For more reasons than you realize."

Debbie almost asked what those were, but she changed her mind. Verna was allowed her personal reasons for why she supported Debbie joining the Amish. It warmed Debbie's heart that Verna cared.

Lois followed Debbie out the door and across the front lawn. Debbie turned to wave goodbye to Verna and Saloma, who were standing on the porch. Once they were near her car, Lois launched in.

"I didn't want to say too much in front of

Mamm, Debbie. Originally I suggested this, I know, but I wasn't serious. This is insane. Do you know what you're getting yourself into? *Daett* won't even let us date Amish boys unless they're saints. How many of those do you think exist? To say nothing of how restricted our *rumspringa* time has been. In fact, Verna and Ida ended up taking very little of it at all!"

"I'm just looking into it for now," Debbie hedged. "I won't be that involved . . . not in your family. I don't want to be in the way."

Lois made a face. "Oh, *yah,* you will be involved. *Daett* won't tolerate someone in the house who isn't considered part of the family. He'll want to treat you like one of his daughters."

Now the warm feelings rushed all the way through Debbie. Lois hadn't meant her words as a comfort, but they were the sweetest Debbie had heard in a long time. Could she really become part of this wonderful family?

Lois struggled to express herself. "I like you, of course, so maybe it wouldn't be such a bad idea. You've always been such a *wunderbah* person to have around."

"Thank you, Lois!" Debbie whispered. "Thank you for at least trying to understand. I know it's especially hard for you.

Even though I'm considering the Amish way, I really don't believe you belong in my world."

"It's okay if you think that," Lois said and shrugged as Debbie climbed into her car. "I don't think you belong in mine either."

They waved to each other, and Debbie was soon pulling into her own driveway. *Now for the hard part,* she thought as she got out of the car. Telling Mom and Dad. Perhaps things would go more smoothly than she thought. A rueful look crossed her face. No, she might as well prepare for battle. And what better strategy could she use than to prepare a real Amish meal for supper. A meal made especially for her parents. Well, perhaps a small dish since she couldn't cook that well.

A shadow crossed Debbie's face. Her mom might purchase supper in town at one of the fast-food places. She could call and tell her not to, but how would that conversation go? "Mom, I'm cooking tonight." If she said that, Mom would buy fast food for sure. She would just cook something and surprise them. She would need help . . . need a recipe or something. She smiled as the thought came to her. She would ask Lois for a simple recipe. That wouldn't be too much bother. She'd run back to the

Beiler farm right now and then zip home again. The Beilers would be on her side. Didn't the Amish believe a man's heart lay through his stomach? They would understand if she explained that if she could get her dad won over, she had a chance with her mom.

Debbie quickly changed out of her work clothes and grabbed a recipe book from the cupboard. She blew off the dust and paged through it. Nothing looked right, but of course nothing would. It wasn't an Amish cookbook. This is where Lois would come in.

Debbie raced out of the house with her keys dangling on her fingers. She got back into the car and was at the Beilers' door seconds later. Lois answered the knock, her hands damp and covered in potato peelings.

Debbie held out the cookbook. "May I borrow your wisdom for a moment? I need a dish I can cook quickly for supper tonight. Will you pick one and help me? It's important. I need to impress Dad tonight."

Lois raised her eyebrows. "So you can break the news to your parents?"

Debbie nodded.

Lois's eyebrows went higher. "You're serious about this Amish stuff, aren't you?"

"I told you I am. Please, Lois. You're a

wizard at cooking. Just close your eyes and point. It'll be the perfect one."

Lois stared at her. "You don't know anything about cooking, Debbie. Good food is not in a recipe, it's in the heart."

Desperation crossed Debbie's face. "Surely there's an easy one somewhere?"

Saloma appeared behind them. "Hi, Debbie. I thought I heard voices. Do you need something?"

"Debbie wants a recipe she can cook at home to impress her dad," Lois said.

"Ach, that's *wunderbah!"* Saloma enthused.

"Actually, it's not," Debbie protested.

Lois regarded Debbie again. "She doesn't know how to cook, *Mamm."*

"I wanted to make something special tonight," Debbie said. "I wanted Lois's opinion. But that's okay. I've bothered you folks enough. Thanks. I really should go."

Saloma stopped Debbie with a raised hand and gave Lois an encouraging look at the same time. "I think you can help, Lois. Why not go over there?"

Lois wrinkled her nose in thought. "I suppose our supper is almost ready. Can you handle things from here, *Mamm*?"

"I'm not that old!" Saloma protested. "I was feeding my family before you were born!"

"Then it's decided!" Lois wiped off her hands. "I'm going with you, Debbie."

Debbie stared. "You're coming with me . . . as in cooking at my house?"

"That's it!" Lois stepped out on the front porch. "It's not like you know how. You spend most of your time in the barn with Verna and Ida. Come, we don't have much time."

"Go on, girls. I can handle things here." Saloma waved her hand at Debbie as she stood rooted to the floor with her mouth open.

"But . . . but . . . I didn't want to interrupt . . . to take Lois away from her work."

Lois tugged on her sleeve, and Debbie turned while Saloma was already closing the front door.

"I can't do this, Lois! I can't," Debbie sputtered on the way back to her car.

But Lois didn't listen. She was muttering, "Mashed potatoes and gravy. Some kind of meat, perhaps, but maybe we won't have time for that. At least I should try . . ."

EIGHT

Some two hours later the table had been set with the best silverware. Lois was pouring gravy into a bowl when Debbie's mom pulled into the driveway.

"Shall I leave now?" Lois asked. "I can dash across the field without her seeing me."

In her mind's eye Debbie imagined Lois running, her dress flying around her. "No," she said, "it's better if you stay. Besides, Mom knows I could never make all this food. If she sees the cook with her own eyes she won't think she's being poisoned."

Lois laughed. "I want you to get the credit, you know. It was your idea."

"Like I could do anything like this," Debbie said, taking in the spread of food with a quick sweep of her eyes. "I can never thank you enough, Lois."

"Don't think twice about it," Lois said over the sound of the garage door opening.

Moments later Callie walked in. She

stopped short. "What's going on here?"

"Lois made supper for us!" Debbie chirped.

Callie was impressed. "That's so much work!" Comprehension slowly dawned. "Okay, something's up. You've never done anything like this before, Debbie. Call me suspicious, but . . ."

"Well, there *is* something I want to talk about," Debbie said. "But let's wait until Dad gets home."

"I know you said Lois is considering breaking away from the Amish life. Is this about you moving in with us for a while, Lois?"

"No, Mom!" Debbie said, shocked. "It's almost the opposite, in fact. But let's wait for Dad . . . please?"

Lois cleared her throat. "I really should be going, Debbie. I hope you all enjoy the supper."

Callie looked from one girl to the other. "What is going on here? What do you mean just the opposite?"

"I'll explain when I come back, Mom," Debbie said. "I need to take Lois home." She took Lois's arm and ushered her outside.

"You should have told your *mamm,*" Lois protested as they climbed into the car.

"I will at the right time. She's not going to take this well."

"I didn't think *Englisha* people would object to such a thing."

Debbie whipped the car out of the driveway. "Well now you know."

"I hope your mom isn't going to be too upset." Lois was all sympathy.

Debbie pulled into the Beiler driveway. "I'll smooth things over. It'll be okay."

Lois paused before she got out of the car. "You're still not 'in' you know. Don't expect *Daett* to make up his mind for a while. It'll take him a week or more to consider this, if I don't miss my guess. And I'm not sure what he'll decide."

Debbie nodded.

Lois opened the door and climbed out. She waved before heading into the house.

At least Lois hadn't said anything tonight about switching places! Debbie drove home and parked in the driveway. She entered the house to find her mom seated at the table.

"I don't object to food I don't have to fix, you know, Debbie. But this fairly shouts to me that something serious is up. So what is it? What have you got up your sleeve?"

Debbie sighed. She should have known better. Supper was growing colder by the minute, her mom wanted answers, and her dad wasn't even home yet. The meal would be ice-cold long before it could accomplish its intended purpose.

"I'm waiting for an answer," Callie said. "You're not in trouble, are you?"

Debbie glanced out the window, hearing crunching sounds in the driveway. "It's Dad. I'll explain everything when he gets in."

The front door opened, and her dad stepped in. He surveyed the spread on the table and smiled. "My, my! Have the fairies been here?"

"Sit down, dear," Callie said. "Debbie's got something to tell us."

Herbert walked closer. He stared at the food-laden table.

"You'll get to eat afterward, I promise," Callie said.

"But it's getting cold!" he protested.

Debbie almost laughed, but she turned her face away instead. Her ploy had worked! Her Dad would be easily won over, she was sure.

Debbie's mom glanced in her direction. "Shoot, girl! I'm still waiting."

The time had come. Debbie took a deep breath. "Well, Dad and Mom, the truth is that I've asked the Beilers if I can board with them for a while."

"I see," Callie said. "And they have agreed to this?"

"Well, no. Not yet. But I'm hoping they say yes."

Callie spoke slowly. "Herbert, did you hear that?"

Her dad grunted as he looked longingly at the food in front of him.

"I might as well go on and tell you the rest," Debbie said. "You both know how I've admired the Beilers all these years, especially their way of life. And . . . well . . . I-I-I think I might like to eventually join the Amish community." There! It was out in the open! Debbie let out another breath.

Her mom wasn't pleased. "So that's what they're after? Converts?"

Debbie sighed. "No, it's not that at all. *I* approached *them*. It'll be a miracle if they even let me rent a room."

"But you've just graduated from college! Life is just beginning for you, Debbie. How can you throw it all away for . . . for a life of, well, *blandness*?" her mom asked.

"I thought you were happy here," Debbie's dad said.

"I'm sorry," Debbie said, dropping her chin to her chest. "I don't want to hurt you. Really, I don't. This isn't about you and what you've provided. It's about me. You're both great parents. I just want something different. Is that so bad?"

Her mom thought about that. "I guess worse things happen to people than having a daughter join a monastery. I never could understand your fascination with those Beilers. It seems to me to be a very staid life. But I won't stand in your way. Maybe a few weeks with the Beilers will open your eyes to a few things about life. I suspect you'll come running home before summer's out."

"Well, maybe I will," Debbie acknowledged. "But I hope not . . . and I don't think I will. And I'll be right next door. It's not like I'm moving to China or something."

"I suppose you'll be putting your hair up soon? Growing it long like they do?" her mom chided.

"I think that's rushing things a bit," Debbie said. "I've just asked them to let me board there for now. You did say it was time I got out of the nest. Tried out my wings and all that."

"Going Amish is not what I meant, Debbie," her mom said. "I wanted you to *grow* as a young woman. I'm afraid with the Amish you'll just wither. You won't grow at all."

"You both are partially right," Herbert said, finally getting a word in edgewise. "But in the meantime all this wonderful food is growing cold. I'm going to eat even if no one else is."

"Men and food," Callie muttered good-naturedly.

Herbert ignored the remark and said, "Shall we pray?"

Callie huffed but bowed her head as Herbert said a short prayer.

"Amen!" he said as he reached for the potatoes in front of him.

"Take it easy, Herbert," Callie told him. "The Amish aren't quite known for their heart-healthy diet. There's probably more cholesterol on this table than you've had in a month. I had a tossed salad planned for tonight."

"My mom used to cook meals like this when I grew up in Michigan. My dad lived to a ripe old age," Herbert countered.

"And you waded through ten feet of snow in stocking feet," Callie snapped.

Her dad didn't respond. Instead, he turned to Debbie. "So tell me the details about your Amish venture."

"Don't be encouraging the girl," Callie said. "Remember what she's throwing away — including all that college money we spent on her."

"I think Debbie ought to make up her

own mind," Herbert protested.

Callie helped herself to the food and didn't answer.

Herbert shrugged. "So, Debbie, what were you going to say about this venture of yours?"

Debbie felt joy rise in her heart. "I guess I've always admired their lifestyle, Dad. Like the peace they seem to radiate. In fact, I think I like most everything about them. I always have. I guess completing college and beginning the new job brought things to a head. I think it's time I pursued my dream to see if it's what I really want."

"Are you quitting your job?" her dad asked, frowning. "After I pulled strings to help you get it?"

Debbie winced. "No, I can't do that. I need money to pay for my room and board. I don't want to sponge off the Beilers or you."

"Thank goodness the girl has that much sense," Callie commented.

"She's your daughter," Herbert said. "Of course she has sense."

Callie didn't appear mollified. "Then why isn't she acting like it?"

"Because everyone is different." Herbert seemed to ponder his own statement. "I think we should wish Debbie nothing but the best."

"Thank you," Debbie said. "I appreciate that, Dad."

"What about Doug?" Callie asked.

"I saw him Saturday night, and I told him my plans," Debbie said.

Her mom thought for a moment. "I'm sure he was thrilled at that news. Or is he considering donning a black hat and suspenders himself?"

Debbie laughed as she imagined Doug in suspenders. "No, Mom."

"I didn't think so. At least your taste in lifestyle isn't contagious."

"You're sure right there," Debbie assured her. "I imagine very few people wish to join the Amish, and even fewer succeed."

"And may you be one who doesn't succeed," her mother said quietly.

"Mom, I'm sorry you don't approve. But if I don't do this now, I'll always wonder what might have been. I wish you could see how important this is to me." Debbie thought she might break into tears if her mom didn't ease up.

Callie noticed her daughter's frustration and changed the subject. "Amish food is good at least."

"Thanks. I didn't have much of a hand in making it," Debbie admitted. Perhaps the tide of this argument had turned, she thought, and they could converse on more pleasant subjects.

Her dad, though, wasn't finished with his questions. "Will you be staying single all your life?"

Debbie gave him a sweet smile. "Dad, don't worry about me. I can take care of myself."

"That's what you think!" Callie said. "I do want grandchildren someday."

Debbie noticed a sudden softness around her mom's eyes. "Mom, there are single men in the Amish community, you know!"

Her dad burst out with a laugh. "That's the funniest thing I've heard in a long time. I would say from the size of their families there must certainly be a few."

"Herbert, be decent!" Callie protested.

"Just sayin'." He reached for another slice of meat, a grin still on his face. "Who knows? We might end up with a dozen grandchildren!"

"Dad!" Debbie said, her face turning red.

Callie, on the other hand, turned serious. "Debbie, is this about a specific Amish man? Have you met someone? Is that what's behind all this Amish talk? Perhaps someone who hangs around the Beiler place?"

Debbie choked. "Mom, the Amish don't

'hang around' anywhere. They work all day during the week, but I've never been to one of their Sunday meetings. How could I have met someone?"

Her mom murmured, "Remember, I said *grandchildren,* Debbie. But not a dozen, okay?"

"Mom! I don't even know the man." As soon as she said it, Debbie wanted to bite her tongue.

"*Aha!* So there *is* a specific man!"

"Not like you mean. There is a man I've admired. Can we talk about something else? This is embarrassing."

"Look at her, Herbert!" Callie said. "She's blushing redder than a rose in summertime. Our girl's in love with an Amish man."

"Well, you said you wanted grand-children," her dad responded with a smile.

"Mom! Dad!" Debbie almost hollered. "Please! This is not funny!"

"Okay, honey," her dad said. "Callie, I think we should leave Debbie to her own decisions and choose to be happy with the results. Agreed?"

Her mom thought for a moment before she nodded.

Debbie was thankful Lois hadn't stayed. If she'd heard this conversation and shared

it with her parents, what would they think
of her?

Nine

The following Saturday afternoon Bishop Beiler stood by his barn door and peered down the lane. The first warm, summer breeze blew across his face. He pushed back his hat. The sound of a buggy coming traveled toward him in the still air. It soon came into view, and the bishop sighed. That would be Deacon David Mast's buggy from the looks of it. This could only mean one thing on a Saturday. There was church trouble afoot. Adam sighed. Likely one of the deacon's regular visits with a family had turned out badly, and he needed a consultation before presenting whatever the matter was to the rest of the ministers tomorrow morning at the church service. Or, worse, perhaps something completely new had come up that needed urgent attention.

The bishop sighed again. He was already weary from his thoughts all week. His head ached with the trouble Lois had caused with her desire to plunge into the *Englisha* world. And then Debbie from next door had come over with her wish to board at their place. Saloma had claimed Debbie was considering joining the faith, which was hard to imagine. An *Englisha* hadn't become part of their Amish community in a long time.

He should give Debbie an answer soon, and so far nothing definite had presented itself. If he said *nee,* he risked offense to a potential convert. If he said *yah,* trouble might also lie ahead. A convert always ran into rough waters when he or she attempted to live out the faith. It was hard enough to live by the *Ordnung* when one was born into the faith.

And was he willing to accept the responsibility of having the young woman live in his own home? That would magnify any issues that might arise a hundredfold. But perhaps he shouldn't be thinking about the end of the road before Debbie even began the journey. She had only asked to board at their place. She had always been very respectful of their ways and beliefs. Debbie might be the answer to his problem with Lois. He had to consider that possibility too.

He walked toward the hitching post as the horse and buggy turned in the driveway. He met Deacon Mast as he climbed out of the buggy. "*Gut* afternoon."

"*Yah,* I suppose so," the deacon grunted.

A smile flitted across Bishop Beiler's face. This wasn't funny, and he'd sighed himself not moments ago. But he couldn't help but smile at the look on the deacon's face. Perhaps shared misery indeed reduced sorrow. "Is it that bad?" he asked.

"Enough that I thought you should know about it. You might even wish to make a visit yourself this afternoon."

Another sigh was ready to escape his lips, but Bishop Beiler thought better of letting it out. Church work must go on, and he must bear it with fortitude. Especially in front of a deacon who appeared weary himself. Sometimes church work was too much for any man to carry with joy.

The deacon glanced down before looking at the bishop. "It's Henry Yoder again. He bought himself a brand-new hay cutter. And he was seen running it in his field last week using his *Englisha* neighbor's tractor."

"Not again!" Bishop Beiler groaned.

"*Yah,* I'm afraid so. And he had the same story as before. Claims he borrowed it only for a few rounds. When I mentioned that he'd used the tractor almost half a day, he didn't deny it. Seems every time he buys a new piece of machinery this comes up."

113

"There's no rule against new machinery," Bishop Beiler mused. "But maybe there ought to be in Henry's case."

"*Yah,* I have thought of that." The deacon nodded his head with vigor. "But how would such a thing be handled?"

"That can't be done, of course," Bishop Beiler said. "We can't make a special rule for one man. And Henry knows that."

Deacon Mast looked away. "There's more to it, Bishop. Henry refuses to repent this time. He wants our understanding for this habit of his. He wants an exemption."

"We can do no such thing! If we did soon the entire community would want exemptions from the *Ordnung*!"

"That's what I told him, but Henry's not budging. Said he wants to speak with you himself. He claims your family isn't living right either."

"This cannot be!" Surprise covered Bishop Beiler's face. "I do not play favorites, David. If my family is in sin, then I wish to be told."

"I told him that," Deacon Mast said at once. "But don't let him get to you, Adam. Henry's trying to stir the hornet's nest. Get a few loose bees flying around so we leave him alone."

Bishop Beiler stared across the open

fields. "Everyone knows the problem I have with Lois. I'm not hiding a thing there. And with the other children, I believe they're innocent of any wrongdoing."

The deacon regarded him for a moment. "Have you forgotten about Joe Weaver, Adam? He's dating your Verna, isn't he?"

Bishop Beiler ran his hand across his face. "*Yah*. But Rosy dumped Joe. I don't like Joe coming around, but that's not an *Ordnung* matter the last time I checked."

Deacon Mast chuckled but said nothing.

"So what is Henry accusing my family of?"

"He wouldn't say, Adam. That's why I think you should go speak with him."

Adam pulled back a step. "You think I'm hiding something?"

Deacon Mast shook his head. "*Nee,* but someone else might be. And there's no way to find out but by hearing the man out. Better done on a Saturday afternoon, I think, then have him announce the supposed transgression at a members' meeting some Sunday morning."

"*Yah,* you're right there," the bishop allowed. This was all he needed — some violation by one of his children of which he was unaware. There were few ways a leader could lose the people's confidence faster — a bishop who couldn't see the sins of his own children.

"Perhaps it's a small thing," Deacon Mast ventured. "Something unworthy of mention once it sees the light of day."

Bishop Beiler shook his head. "Henry knows better than to make a fuss over nothing."

"Then you will see to it? Before tomorrow morning, I would hope?"

Bishop Beiler sighed again. "It's not like I had plenty of idle time this afternoon."

"*Da Hah*'s vineyard sure grows weeds quickly, does it not?" Deacon Mast said as he climbed back into his buggy. He didn't wait for an answer, but jiggled the reins. His horse moved forward and plodded out the lane.

Truer words couldn't be spoken, Bishop Beiler thought, as he watched the buggy drive down the road. Now he had something else he needed to look into on top of all the other decisions already on his mind. Well, he shouldn't complain, he supposed. *Da Hah* always gave grace for every trial. Somewhere, sometime the light of God would shine on this one.

Bishop Beiler headed for the house, and entered the washroom. After washing up, he found Saloma hard at work in the kitchen.

She glanced up at him. "That was Deacon

Mast," she commented as she searched his face. "Was it very troubling . . . the news the deacon brought?"

He didn't answer her. Instead, he asked, "Are any of our children misbehaving? Besides Lois's focus on the *Englisha,* I mean."

"Not that I know of, Adam. You know they try hard to follow the *Ordnung* and honor your position as bishop."

"What could it be then?" he asked as he stroked his beard.

She touched his arm. "What news did Deacon Mast bring you?"

"That there has been mention of something amiss in our family. I wish I knew what it was specifically, Saloma. That's what I must find out." He thought for a moment. "It must be Verna's dating that Joe Weaver. *Yah,* I knew I never should have allowed that."

"You're not talking sense, Adam," she said. "What's going on?"

He didn't answer as he turned, looking back long enough to say, "I'll be back before long."

"What about Debbie?" she called from the washroom door. "You must make up your mind and soon."

He paused to call back, "I'll think about it

some more when I come back."

That seemed to satisfy her because she closed the washroom door. Bishop Beiler found his horse, Milo, in the barnyard. He snapped a tie rope onto the halter and led him inside. There the bishop threw on the harness, and minutes later he was ready to hitch Milo to the buggy. Just as he led Milo out, a buggy turned in the driveway.

The bishop paused with a sigh on his lips. Now who had come to cause more trouble? As if in answer, the buggy stopped near him and Alvin Knepp jumped down. "*Gut* afternoon, Bishop."

"*Gut* afternoon to you, Alvin. Do you need something?"

A slight grin played on Alvin's face. "I'm not going to cause church problems, if that's what you're thinking. I was wondering if I could borrow your singletree for the week. I broke mine, and it's in the repair shop."

Bishop Beiler felt his face relax into a smile. "I have an extra one in the barn. You're welcome to it. If you'll hold Milo, I'll go get it for you."

"I can find it, I'm sure. Don't let me hold you up. I see you're going somewhere."

The bishop accepted the offer with a nod of his head. He climbed into the buggy and took off. He glanced back to see Alvin tie his horse at the hitching rack. The bishop turned his thoughts to Henry Yoder and his church-related trouble. Surely there was some simple answer to this problem. But with Henry nothing was ever easy. The bishop settled in the buggy seat for the twenty-minute drive. Each second dragged along like a plow in heavy soil. He thought the matter over in thorough detail and was more convinced than ever. Whatever Henry had to say about his family surely involved Joe Weaver. There could be no other explanation. None of the children other than Lois had been misbehaving. He watched them too closely not to know.

Emery and Lois were still in their *rumspringa* time, so if either of them had done something he didn't know of, it wouldn't be a matter of grave concern. But even Emery was having a quiet *rumspringa* time by most standards. And Verna and Ida always kept themselves under strict control. Neither girl had really taken advantage of their *rumspringa* time before they joined the church, for which he was grateful. In Emery, he had full confidence. This fall when the next baptismal class began, Emery might even join the church.

The bishop pulled back on the reins and slowed Milo for the turn into Henry Yoder's driveway. He stopped beside the barn, jumped out, and tied Milo to the hitching post. He rapped on the barn door and pushed on in when he received no answer. Barns were different from houses. You were expected to enter and check. The owner might well be at work somewhere inside and not hear the knock.

"Howdy there!" Bishop Beiler hollered out. He stood still as he waited for an answer.

A faint shout came from the direction of the haymow. Moments later a man's legs appeared, and the rest of Henry soon followed. He slapped at the straw on his pants and took his hat off to shake it. Henry grinned. "Haymow's about empty. I'll sure be glad to see the first hay cutting put up."

"Yah," Bishop Beiler agreed. "It shouldn't be long now. Maybe in a week or so."

Henry leaned against the wooden ladder. "Thought I might try a little practice cutting myself last week. Had to pick up a new machine. You know how that goes."

Enough of this skirting of the issues, Bishop Beiler decided. He glanced down at the barn floor before he spoke. "Deacon Mast came by to say you had something against me, and that I'd better look into it."

Henry didn't appear pleased. "That's putting it a little harshly. You know how things get mangled up between mouths. I thought it was you who had something against me."

Bishop Beiler didn't hesitate. "We have to uphold the *Ordnung,* Henry. There's nothing new about that."

Henry dropped his head. "Each man has his weakness. Mine is that I can't keep away from the neighbor's tractor."

"And for three or four hours it sounds like."

Henry winced. "Remember how things get mangled up, Bishop."

Bishop Beiler met his gaze. "It's time you became a better example for your family and the community, Henry. Your children are growing up and looking to you for lessons on how they should behave. We can't have this kind of thing going on all the time. Maybe it's time for a knee confession. Perhaps it would stick then."

Henry frowned. "Why would you say such things with what's going on in your family?"

Bishop Beiler stepped closer. "Deacon Mast told me you had something against me. Maybe you'd better tell me what it is, Henry."

"I'm sure the church would also wish to hear about it, Bishop. So maybe I should tell them first?"

Bishop Beiler sighed. "That's not going to work, Henry. I'll tell the congregation I offered to make things right, but you held out so you could embarrass me in front of everyone."

Henry swallowed hard. "Okay, I'll tell you. Your eldest daughter's boyfriend, Joe Weaver, also seems to have a liking for *Englisha* vehicles. He's been driving them around at the auction barn in Belleville for quite some time now. How's that for being a bad example to our young people? At least I keep my things hidden behind the barn for the most part."

Bishop Beiler gathered his thoughts. "And you know this for sure, Henry?"

Henry glared. "I saw him myself, Bishop. Quite a few times."

Bishop Beiler squared his shoulders. "Then it will be taken care of. And you can give your regular confession the same Sunday he does. But the next time I will call for a knee confession. I'm warning you, Henry, so take this seriously."

Henry didn't say anything, so Bishop Beiler headed back to his buggy. So this did involve Joe Weaver. *Well, confound it!* he thought as he untied Milo and climbed into the buggy. Joe would confess in front of the church or he'd never bring Verna home from a Sunday-night hymn singing again. He drove Milo down the road. Now he knew the answer to the question of the *Englisha* girl. Debbie could move into their place. If Henry was determined to make trouble for his family, then he'd better take all the steps to help himself he could. And having Debbie live with them might keep Lois at home. Who knew but that *Da Hah* had supplied this very answer for his problem and he'd been too blind to see it. What better help could there be for Lois than someone living in the house who knew the *Englisha* world so well and could warn against its dangers?

Bishop Beiler pondered the matter some more and felt a weight lift from his shoulders. This was indeed from *Da Hah.* The bishop hummed the Praise Song then allowed his voice to rise above the beat of Milo's hooves. Even when another buggy passed him, he waved and lowered the volume only a little. The day had turned out pretty well after all. There was still the administration of church discipline that lay ahead, and what Verna likely would have to say when she heard about Joe's transgressions, but he could handle it. Verna would have to learn that he knew what he spoke of when it came to men. Maybe she would think twice about allowing Joe to bring her home again.

TEN

Later that evening Verna walked into the living room. *Mamm* was sitting on the couch with her hands clasped in front of her, a strained look on her face. *Daett* was in his rocker not smiling. Had she done something wrong? But what? "You called for me, *Daett*?" Verna asked.

Daett cleared his throat. "A matter has come up that concerns you, and . . ."

"Me?" Verna sat on the couch. "I haven't done anything wrong."

Her *daett* watched her intently and said, "If you'll let me finish, I'll tell you."

Verna fell silent. *Daett* was about to tell her she couldn't see Joe Weaver again. But why? She felt the words to come would be like an ax falling toward a fallen tree limb, prepared to split it wide open. And she would split, Verna told herself. Her heart would tear at the seams. How could *Daett* do this to her? And for no reason at all! The date with Joe had gone so well.

Verna's thoughts hung in the air as her *daett* spoke again. "It has come to my attention that Joe Weaver is driving *Englisha* vehicles at the auction barn in Belleville. The ministry will be asking him to make a church confession on the matter. Normally you wouldn't be told about these church matters, Verna, but since you're seeing the boy, I thought you should know."

"But, *Daett,* Joe already told me".

Bishop Beiler raised his eyebrows. "You knew of this?"

Verna clutched the side of the couch until her fingers hurt. "Joe told me in confidence as a confession, and it was intended to go no further."

Bishop Beiler sighed. "I told you to stay away from the boy, Verna. Nothing *gut* is coming out of any of this. Perhaps you see now why Rosy dropped him. She probably found this out herself and had the *gut* sense to get out of the relationship. I wish I could say the same thing for you." Bishop Beiler looked at Verna for a moment. "Or have you cut off the relationship and haven't told us?"

Verna struggled to find her voice. "No, I haven't . . . and I'm not going to. Something is going on here that's not right. Driving an *Englisha* vehicle isn't such a serious transgression of the *Ordnung.*"

"It's serious enough, Verna," *Mamm* interrupted. "Were you not concerned when Joe told you?"

Verna winced. "Of course I was. But he's sorry, *Daett.* And he confessed on his own. Doesn't that mean anything?"

"Then he can say he's sorry to everyone," Bishop Beiler told her. "Now I've said enough on the matter. Tomorrow when you see Joe, you can tell him what's coming. If he's really sorry, he can make his way over to Deacon Mast and save the poor man a trip on Saturday. *Da Hah* knows this church work wears us all down to the bone."

Verna got to her feet and steadied herself with one hand on the couch. Her *daett* didn't seem to notice her discomfort.

"One thing more, Verna. There is a bit of *gut* news to come out of the day, I suppose. Debbie, your friend who wishes to board here and perhaps join the community later — I've decided to allow it. You can tell her whenever you wish. My house and heart are open to her request."

You're trying to throw my boyfriend out of the house, but you're welcoming in an Englisha girl? Verna wanted to say. Instead, she whispered, "That is *gut* news indeed, *Daett.*"

127

"*Yah,* it is." Bishop Beiler settled back into his rocker. "You know I work hard to keep my own family in *Da Hah*'s will. But with Lois I seem to have failed completely. Perhaps we can do some *gut* to someone who sees value in our faith and, at the same time, maybe Debbie can help us with Lois."

Right after noticing *Mamm*'s sympathetic glance, Verna fled toward the stairs. At least someone was concerned about how she felt about Joe! And *Daett* hadn't demanded she cut off her friendship with Joe and send him down the road like Rosy had. So was *Daett* trying to understand? And she must likewise try to understand where he was coming from. In the church world certain things must be done, and her *daett* was only doing his duty.

Why hadn't she been born the daughter of an ordinary man? To some *daett* who sat on the church benches each Sunday, farmed during the week, and gave no thought to how people watched and criticized every move he made. How peaceful that life would be. But it was sinful to wish one were in a different place from what *Da Hah* had willed. That much she knew. "Please forgive me, dear *Hah,*" Verna whispered as she rushed into her room. "I'm trying to be content, but it's so hard. What if I lose Joe through this? It can't happen! It just can't!" She threw herself on the bed and buried her face in her pillow. She had to gain control of her emotions, but how? This was her first serious chance at love, and her heart would surely break if she had to stop seeing Joe. Should she tell Joe on Sunday night about the problem? Maybe that was the way out of this situation. She could act innocent and allow Deacon Mast to arrive the following Saturday afternoon and tell Joe himself. That way she could enjoy Sunday night with Joe, and they wouldn't have to speak about this church problem. On second thought, how could she be so devious? It would involve a front of cheerfulness all Sunday evening while her heart would be in an agony of suspense. And what if Joe found out later that she knew and hadn't told him? Hadn't he taken her into his confidence about the incident to begin with? He would expect her to watch out for him.

Nee, if their relationship had any chance of survival, she would have to tell him. It was the only honest thing to do. Surely Joe would understand. She'd explain what she'd been told, which wasn't that much. *Yah,* she would tell him, Verna decided, as she sat up on the bed. It was high time she acted her age. There were more profitable things to fill the evening with than tears. The first was the matter of *Daett*'s decision on Debbie. She must be told, or rather her sisters should hear it first — Lois especially. Perhaps afterward they could all walk down and tell Debbie the *gut* news.

A faint smile spread over Verna face. *Yah,* that would be *gut.* They were sisters, and like sisters they should go together. Verna walked across the hallway to Ida's room and rapped on the door.

"Come in!" Ida called out.

Verna opened the door to find Ida on her bed, her nose in a book.

"Reading, huh?"

Ida looked up, her gaze searching Verna's face. "What have you been crying about?"

Vern looked away. "Nothing much."

Ida didn't appear convinced. "I heard *Daett*'s voice downstairs. Was that it?"

"*Yah,* but it doesn't matter now. What I wanted to ask . . . will you go with me down to Debbie's place to tell her *Daett* says she can move in whenever she wishes? I thought it would be nice if all three of us went — you, Lois, and me. Sort of like sisters inviting another sister into the family."

Ida's face brightened. "That would be *gut*! I'm glad it's happening." She got up and laid her book on the bed. "Let's go. I'll finish when I get back."

"What are you reading?" Verna glanced at the cover.

"One of Christmas Carol Kaufman's books — *Light from Heaven.* It's *gut* reading."

Verna grimaced. "Sorry, but the main character joins a more liberal church, so you'd better keep the book out of sight right now. *Daett*'s on the warpath."

Ida's hand reached out for Verna's. "Did *Daett* make you cut off your relationship with Joe? Is that it?"

Verna shook her head as they went out into the hall and headed toward Lois's room. Verna didn't knock before she stuck her head in. "Ready for a little jaunt, sister?"

"Where to?" Lois asked.

"Down to Debbie's. *Daett* just told me she can move in if she still wants to."

"Of course I'll come!" Lois's feet hit the floor, and she quickly appeared in the doorway.

"Which room will be hers?" Ida asked.

"I think she should have my room," Lois offered. "I'll take the guest room across from Emery."

"You just want a new room!" Verna said as she snickered.

131

"I do not!" Lois protested. "It's for practical reasons. Debbie would feel more at home closer to the two of you."

"I thought she was also your friend," Ida said as they went down the stairs and stepped into the living room.

"She is, but . . ." Lois stopped as her *daett* looked up and saw them.

"Off to somewhere?" he asked.

"A sisterly stroll down to Debbie's," Verna said.

He looked pleased as they went out the front door.

Lois ran on ahead once they reached the driveway. She did a little dance on the blacktop road. An *Englisha* car came from the west and slowed down. The passengers waved with broad smiles on their faces.

"I think I'm blushing bright red and pink," Verna told Ida. "That was probably a sight no tourist ever saw before. An Amish girl doing a jig for them."

"At least there were no cameras snapping pictures," Ida pointed out.

Verna laughed. "They probably dropped them from their astonishment."

"*Yah,* and broke the lenses to pieces." Ida glanced at Verna, who broke into giggles.

"What are you two laughing at?" Lois hollered over her shoulder as she did another twirl on the road.

"*You,* of course! Stop it now," Verna told her. "Debbie's parents will think we've all lost our minds."

Lois held still and waited for the two to catch up. Then she deadpanned, "I think I'm leaving now that Debbie's moving in. That's the real reason I want the guest room. I won't be around much longer."

Ida and Verna looked at each other.

"Don't look so shocked," Lois told them. "You knew this was coming."

"But you're not serious," Verna chided. "You've said things like this before."

"I mean it this time," Lois said.

"Then you'd better tell *Daett* and not us," Verna said. "I won't believe you until that happens."

"Oh, I'll tell him . . . eventually," Lois said, a bit more subdued.

"Uh huh," Verna said. "Well, I won't be holding my breath."

When they reached the Watson house, Debbie greeted them at the door. "What a surprise! I wasn't expecting you, and certainly not all three sisters. How delightful!"

"We came down right after we found out," Verna said. "*Daett* said you're welcome to move in whenever you want to."

"This is great news!" Debbie said, her face

glowing. "What an answer to prayer for me. I was hoping your dad would let me know before too long."

"When are you coming?" Lois asked.

Debbie thought for a moment. "I guess that depends on you. I don't want to barge in. You might need time to adjust."

"We'll clean my room at once, from top to bottom!" Lois declared. "And then I'm moving into the guest bedroom. You'll have my room — the best bedroom in the whole house."

"I wouldn't think of that!" Debbie objected. "I'm pushing no one out of her room."

"But you're not pushing me out," Lois said. "Of course, if you prefer, you could move in with me. My bedroom is large enough for two. Wouldn't that be even more *wunderbah*?"

"You would do that for me . . . really?" Debbie appeared thrilled.

"Of course! We'll be like real sisters. Almost like we grew up together."

Verna snuck a glance at Ida's face as Debbie and Lois hugged each other. Ida appeared pleased. Debbie was clearly an answer to all of their prayers. She would be a stabilizing influence in their lives, especially for Lois. Truly *Daett* had made a wise choice.

Debbie waved them inside. "I declare! All of you must come in and celebrate with a glass of orange juice."

"Are your parents at home?" Verna spoke up. "We might disturb them."

"They're eating out tonight," Debbie said. "I have the house to myself. This is such a night to remember!"

Lois led the way inside and seated herself at the kitchen table. Verna and Ida followed. Verna smiled as Debbie poured glasses of orange juice from a paper carton. It was sweet to the taste and almost like what they pressed from ripe oranges at home.

Debbie seemed to read her mind. "Just think, Verna, soon I won't be using paper cartons. I'll have the *real* thing."

Verna beamed. "*Yah,* and we are very glad to have you."

Eleven

On Sunday night after the hymn singing, Verna stood in the soft glow of the buggy lights as Joe tied his horse to the hitching post at the Beiler house. All the way home she'd struggled to hold a cheerful thread of conversation. The dread of what she had to tell Joe was heavy to carry. Their conversation had been pleasant enough — all about the nice week of weather and the spring crops growing in the fields. Joe had been pleased with the size of the first cutting of hay. "It'll be our best in a long time," he said. "*Daett* thinks we'll save plenty on feed costs come winter."

Apparently she'd done well with her responses . . . or perhaps Joe didn't know her that well. Either of her sisters would have asked long ago what was bothering her.

"Ready to go inside?" Joe asked, causing Verna to flinch. Joe laughed. "Sorry, I didn't mean to startle you."

"I'm a little jumpy tonight," Verna said.

Joe didn't say anything to this, but he looked toward the barn as they walked to the house. Finally he said, "Your *daett* and Emery really keep things up well around here."

"*Yah,* I suppose so." Verna held open the front door.

"With him being a bishop and all," Joe continued, "seems like that would take up plenty of time in itself." He walked into the house and hung his hat on a wall hook by the door.

"It does." Verna closed the door behind them. Right now she didn't want to think about *Daett*'s bishop duties or about what she had to tell Joe. But she couldn't avoid it forever. She motioned with her hand toward the couch. "Have a seat. I'll be right back."

His smile never dimmed as she left him. Joe expected shoofly pie again, she was sure. And a full pie sat on the kitchen table. But she wouldn't be able to get a bite down herself, nor did she think she could sit on the couch and smile while Joe ate. She couldn't feed a man and stab him afterward. Better the truth first. They could make up afterward because she was sure this wouldn't go well. The throb of her heart was all the proof she needed of that.

Verna gathered herself together and slipped back into the living room.

Joe looked up. The surprised expression on his face grew as he took in her empty hands.

"I'm sorry, Joe," she whispered. "I have something that needs saying first, and then I have shoofly pie in the kitchen . . . and ice cream also, if you want it."

His surprise changed to alarm. "Verna, what is it?" He moved closer.

She kept her gaze on the floor. "*Daett* found out about your driving of the *Englisha* vehicles at the auction in Belleville. Deacon Mast will be over next Saturday to ask for your confession at church. *Daett* suggested you make the trip over to Deacon Mast's place first."

She took a quick glance at his face. It was dark and troubled.

His voice trembled as he accused her. "You told your *Daett* what I told you, Verna? That was said to you in confidence!"

She tried to take in a deep breath. "*Nee,* Joe. *Daett* found out from someone else."

"But who would say such a thing?"

"I don't know. Really, I don't. *Daett* doesn't tell us much about such church matters."

"Your *daett* must be better at keeping

138

things to himself than his daughter is then."

Verna flinched at the bite in his voice. "Surely you don't think that I . . ."

"What else am I to think?" Joe cut in, his face reflecting hurt and anger. "It's hard to imagine anything else, Verna. Perhaps you let it slip somehow. Or you asked your *daett* his opinion of a man who would do such a thing. Are you worried about my character, Verna? Is that what it is?"

Joe had risen, and Verna rose to. She almost grabbed his hands, but remembered she had no such privileges. This was only her second time home with him. Oh, why had she even opened her mouth? Perhaps there was an easier way to handle this. Her voice sounded shrill in her ears. "Joe, please! It's not like that at all. *Daett* found out from someone else, and I don't know who it was."

He clearly wasn't convinced. He took a step toward the front door.

Verna followed. "Don't doubt me, Joe! I hated to tell you. But I thought it would be much worse if you found out later that I knew about this and didn't tell you."

He stared at her and then grabbed his hat from the hook. "I had hoped for better things between us, Verna. I'm sorry, but I trusted you and you betrayed that trust. No one else knew about my driving at the auction. I've told no one but you." Joe let the words hang as he walked out the door.

Verna rushed outside on the porch and followed his dark form with her gaze. He crossed the lawn and untied his horse. What had gone wrong? What had she said to make things this bad? Not in her worst imagination had Joe left without a chance to talk things out.

Joe's buggy lights came on as he swung it around in a tight turn in the driveway. Verna heard him say "Get up!" and Isaiah took off. She didn't move until they were out of sight. Her feet seemed frozen to the porch floor. The slight spring breeze that blew across her face felt like a winter blast in January.

This couldn't be her fault. It simply couldn't. What had Joe said? Something about expecting better things between them. Had this been the quarrel with Rosy? Had Rosy spilled confidences about him? It must be that. Nothing else made the least bit of sense. And now Joe was gone. She wanted to cry and run into the night after him. She wanted to find him, hold on to the buggy lines, and beg him to return. But none of that was possible. Joe had left, and she was a twenty-four-year-old without prospects again. Now no man would come within a mile of the house on a Sunday night. Not after this news leaked into the community . . . this tale of a bishop's daughter who tattled on her boyfriend to keep him in line. What man would desire such a woman for his *frau*? No man would desire a bishop for a father-in-law who would haunt every waking minute of his life.

Verna moved off the porch and took small steps across the yard. Where she was going, she had no idea. Away from the house for a while . . . and away from people. Away from the pain wracking her chest. But there could be no escape from that no matter where she walked. She passed the barn, its silhouette stark against the star-filled sky. She glanced over her shoulder and paused at the sight of the full moon on the horizon. Its glow flooded the sky and would soon fill the dark fields with soft light. She kept walking. Open fields stretched out in front of her for miles, dotted with the occasional shadows of homesteads. Debbie's place had a single light on in an upstairs window. Its electric haze flooded onto the lawn. A sob caught in Verna's throat, and she headed in the other direction. Soon she found her way along the path that led to the back pastures. "Dear *Hah*," she prayed out loud as her eyes swept the starry heavens, "somehow You have to

141

help me. All of us really. *Daett* is so burdened with his church work it's almost like he's forgotten how to trust people. Yet what do I know about anything? I'm still young, but I feel so old. What am I going to do if this misunderstanding with Joe can't be solved? And what hope is there of clearing it up? Joe wouldn't listen to me. I don't how to speak with a man, so what use would it be for me to try again?"

With slow steps she moved further away from the buildings. She allowed the pain inside to overwhelm her. Better to have a breakdown out here where no one could hear her than inside the house. Verna jumped when the sound of flapping wings burst from the fencerow, and a dark shadow flew across the fields. A nighthawk — perfectly harmless — but still she walked away from the fence. In the distance the forms of the horses came into focus as the first of the moon's rays crept across the field.

Verna watched until the moon had risen high enough that the shadows of the horses moved when they did as they grazed. Joe would be leaving about now if things had gone as they should have. She should turn back. Perhaps a good night's sleep would help — if she could sleep at all. Tomorrow morning would be here before long, whether she wished for it or not. Life would go on. *Mamm* would be up before dawn to begin the Monday wash, and she would expect all of them to perform their regular chores. Only the most severe of sorrows interrupted that flow, and Verna knew this was not one of those.

In fact, she should be ashamed of herself. Many a girl had her boyfriend walk out on her. Some of them with longer relationships than she had with Joe. Hadn't Joe experienced rejection by Rosy after they'd dated for two years? She should take that into consideration. Perhaps his heart hadn't yet fully healed. Was he distrustful of women now because of Rosy?

Verna walked back toward the house with the moonlight in her face. Her steps quickened the closer she came. She opened the washroom door and slipped in. She tried to cross the kitchen floor without noise. Still *Mamm*'s bedroom door squeaked open as Verna blew out the kerosene lamp in the living room. Her *mamm*'s form appeared.

"Verna, is that you?"

"*Yah, Mamm.* I'm going upstairs."

"It's past twelve o'clock, and you have no light."

"I just blew it out, *Mamm.*"

"Did Joe just leave?"

"He left a long time ago, *Mamm.* I was outside walking by myself in the moonlight." She couldn't hide her pain from *Mamm.* Besides, mothers eventually found out the whole story anyway.

"You had best relight the lantern and tell me what happened," *Mamm* said as she settled on the couch. "I want to see you while we talk."

Verna lit the lamp but kept her back turned toward *Mamm.* She needed to get herself together first. Finally setting the lamp on the table, Verna sat down and told the whole story, right up to Joe's sudden departure.

"*Daett* will have to deal with this," *Mamm* said once Verna finished.

"But what can he do? I messed this up myself."

"There's a lot your *daett* can do. He can tell Joe where he got the information, and that ought to clear the matter."

"*Mamm,* I don't know. It's all gone wrong now. Joe doesn't trust me. You don't have to bother *Daett* about this. It won't do any good."

Mamm smiled. "*Daett*'s not going to eat me alive, Verna. I've lived with him for many years. Church matters have always weighed heavy on his heart, and he believes in confidentiality. I may not be able to convince him to talk to Joe, but I will try."

Verna sobbed gently. "It's no use, *Mamm*. It must be *Da Hah*'s will for me to never have a husband . . . never have a family."

"Now, now, you mustn't say that, Verna. Things are changing around here." *Mamm* touched Verna's arm. "Your *daett* will understand. It's hard enough to get a *gut* man without chasing one away unnecessarily."

"Then you think Joe is a *gut* man even if *Daett* doesn't?"

When *Mamm* nodded, Verna reached over and gave her a long hug.

"*Yah,* Joe Weaver's a *gut* man," *Mamm* whispered. "Now get to bed. We have a full day tomorrow."

"*Yah, Mamm,*" Verna said through her tears. She found her way upstairs as *Mamm* blew out the kerosene lamp. When Verna got to her room, she stood by the window for a few moments, letting the moonlight wash over her again. Her heart had been comforted with *Mamm*'s words. *Da Hah* had heard her prayer out in the pasture, and perhaps He would soon answer. "Please let it be so," she whispered toward the star-filled sky. "I don't want to lose Joe."

TWELVE

The following Saturday found Debbie unloading suitcases from the back of her car onto the graveled driveway at the Beilers' house.

When the last suitcase was on the ground, the front door burst open and Lois bounced out. "You're early! We just finished eating breakfast. I thought you'd be sleeping in!"

Debbie straightened her back. "I couldn't sleep. I'm too excited!"

"So am I!" Lois raced up to give Debbie a hug. "I'll help you carry these in. They're all going in my room, remember?"

"Do you think this is wise, Lois?" Debbie said as she hesitated. "An *Englisha* girl has lots of clothing. And there's only one closet."

"My clothes only take up one tiny corner." Lois held her fingers inches apart. "And whatever won't fit can go into the cedar chest or one of the empty bedrooms."

Debbie smiled. "This is so thoughtful of you. I know I'll love this more than I can ever say." Debbie knew she'd eventually need to pare down her wardrobe. That would be part of the adjustment toward the life she really wanted. It was a joy — even the thought of it. *Downsizing!* At home she was required to constantly purchase new outfits. Here the women wore the same dresses until they wouldn't hold together any longer.

Lois dismissed the praise with a wave of her hand. "It's nothing, Debbie. So which suitcase goes first?"

"It doesn't matter," Debbie said. They all looked huge right now. Way too much stuff. She felt like she should grab half of them and race right down to the Goodwill Store and toss them into the donation dumpster. But Lois was already dragging one of the suitcases toward the house. Besides, the Amish made changes after long thought and contemplation. Debbie would begin by learning from them this most simple of lessons. Tonight after she had plenty of time to think, she would sort through her clothing. She pulled the last suitcase from the trunk as Verna and Ida came out of the house. They greeted her with cries of "*Gut* morning!" from the front porch.

"You are such dear friends to share your home with me," Debbie said as she ran forward to give them both long hugs. She took a step back. "Well, here I am! Tons of luggage and all."

Verna and Ida beamed. They followed her back to the car to grab a suitcase apiece. Debbie paused to close the trunk and shut the doors. She caught up with the two in a short sprint while carrying the final suitcase.

Saloma met them at the door. "So you made it! Everything okay, Debbie?"

Of course I did! Debbie wanted to say. *I'm determined.* She gave Saloma a quick hug instead. The three Beiler girls disappeared up the stairs.

"It's so *gut* to have you in our home," Saloma said.

Debbie smiled and then turned her head as a buggy came into the driveway. She stiffened when she caught a glimpse of the man's face, especially when she caught his eye.

"That's Alvin Knepp. Do you know him?" Saloma asked.

"No . . . ah . . . yes . . . that is, I know who he is. That's all." How was she supposed to explain? Why was Alvin Knepp at the Beilers' place on a Saturday morning? Had destiny already crossed their paths . . .

or *Da Hah,* as the Amish would say? A warm flush spread over her face as she stepped into the house. Saloma looked puzzled, which was understandable. What *Englisha* girl turned red upon seeing an Amish man, even if he was good looking? Hopefully Saloma wouldn't ask any questions.

Bishop Beiler greeted Debbie from his rocker. "*Gut* morning!"

Debbie returned the greeting, adding, "I'm so happy to be here. Thank you again for allowing this."

The bishop nodded.

"Alvin Knepp just drove in," Saloma announced.

"*Ach, yah.*" Bishop Beiler rose. "He's probably bringing back the singletree he borrowed while his was being repaired. I hope he hasn't broken it."

"The Knepps are such a poor family," Saloma said, turning toward Debbie as if she needed an explanation. "They started borrowing from us a while back. I guess they figured out we're the only ones who will loan things without giving sermons." A pleased look spread over Saloma's face. "The rest of the community thinks there's still hope the Knepp family might improve their ways. Adam, on the other hand, is glad someone doesn't make problems regarding obeying the *Ordnung* . . . even if they can't seem to get their hay in without it getting wet."

Just great, Debbie thought. So Lois was correct about the Knepps' status. And I'm infatuated with an inept Amish farmer. No wonder Mom has no confidence in my judgment.

"Do the Knepps keep the *Ordnung* well?" Debbie ventured as Saloma led the way upstairs.

Saloma gave a short chuckle. "They cling to it like it's their last hope in this world. Adam says he wishes he had a whole community of people like them."

At least she recognized dedication when she saw it, Debbie told herself. And wasn't that what she wanted? Purpose in life? And what did money matter? She'd seen enough of what money purchased. Happiness and contentment weren't even near the top of the list. But she had to stop these romantic thoughts about an Amish man she didn't even know. What were the chances Alvin would pay her more than a sideways glance. None! When it came right down to it, she wasn't even Amish, and now that she knew the Knepps stuck to the *Ordnung* she'd better forget about Alvin. But why had Alvin looked her way in such a forthright manner

150

this morning? Debbie wondered. She was sure he'd had intensity in his gaze when he recognized her. Or was that just wishful thinking?

At the top of the landing, Saloma said, "Lois said you two were going to share her room." She led the way into Lois's bedroom where happy chatter was pouring forth.

"Okay, girls, quiet down," Saloma ordered gently.

Debbie walked in with her suitcase in front of her. Lois bounced up from one of the twin beds set against the wall. Verna and Ida waited beside the suitcases they'd carried up. Debbie slipped hers under the other twin bed. It contained her makeup kit — her *large* makeup kit. The thought hadn't occurred to her before, but she was sure makeup wasn't appropriate in an Amish household. She didn't wish to tempt any of the Beiler daughters, especially Lois. And if the bishop found out, perhaps he wouldn't tolerate such a worldly thing in his house. But her quick movement with the suitcase hadn't escaped Lois's eye, Debbie noticed. She would have to deal with Lois later.

"I think I'll unpack these suitcases right now. I'll put the things that don't fit in the closet out here on the bed. Maybe you can help me figure out where to put them, Lois.

Or I can give them away." But Lois's attention had been drawn away from Debbie.

"Who's visiting, *Mamm*?" Lois asked as she peered out the bedroom window.

"Alvin Knepp," Saloma said from the doorway. "He came to bring back what he borrowed last Saturday,"

"Oh, that man." Lois turned up her nose. "I'm surprised his buggy holds together enough to drive over here."

Saloma responded at once. "That's not a Christian attitude, Lois. The Knepp family has many *gut* characteristics. For one thing, they're faithful church members who appreciate our ways and don't envy the *Englisha.*" Saloma gazed at Lois, and then she left the room, going back downstairs.

Clearly Lois got the message directed to her. She stepped away from the window with a hurt look on her face. The words must have stung more than she wished anyone to know.

Debbie slipped over to Lois's side and gave her a quick hug. "Your mother didn't mean it quite like that, I don't think."

"Mean what?" Ida asked, already busily hanging Debbie's dresses in the closet.

"*Mamm* just preferred Alvin Knepp's actions to her own daughter's," Verna offered. "And Lois had her feelings hurt."

"Oh." Ida went back to work on Debbie's dresses.

Verna glanced toward Lois. "*Mamm* has her reasons, you know. And you could do something about that."

"I can't help it that I love the *Englisha* world," Lois said.

Verna studied her sister's face. "I hope you take care of that problem of yours before it gets you in plenty of hot water with *Daett.*"

Lois ignored Verna. "You know what?" Lois said, her face brightening. "I'm going to be happy. I have Debbie now. She'll bring a refreshing wave of brightness and color to this house. Look at those dresses you're hanging up, for example. We've never had anything like these in the house before. And Debbie has her makeup kit along, I'm sure. I can try some on tonight — just for fun, of course. I'll have it all washed off before church tomorrow morning."

Looks of horror crossed Verna and Ida's faces.

Debbie's words rushed out. "No, Lois! You will do no such thing. That's not right. In fact, I'm no longer going to use makeup myself."

Lois's joy faded, and Debbie's mind whirled. Should she have made such a commitment . . . and so soon? What about her appearance at her job? What would Mr. Fulton think? If she didn't back down right now, there was no way she'd sneak around later and put on makeup in secret. Still, she couldn't change her mind now — not in front of Lois.

Lois struggled to hide her disappointment. "At least you have these *wunderbah* dresses. May I try one on tonight?"

Debbie didn't want to say no to Lois twice in a row. And she wore the dresses herself, and Bishop Beiler knew that. Debbie glanced at Verna and Ida for guidance. They both shrugged. "Okay then," Debbie allowed.

Lois was all smiles again. "Tonight then! After everyone has gone to bed, I'll slip one on. I'll look like a princess ready for a ball."

"You don't have to be so dramatic," Verna said with a glance toward Debbie. "Well, welcome to the Beiler family, Debbie. I hope we aren't scaring you off already."

Debbie allowed her pleasure to show. "Not at all! And your secrets are safe with me."

"Verna lost her boyfriend last Sunday night," Lois offered.

Debbie looked up, startled. "She did? I'm so sorry to hear that, Verna. How did it happen?"

"There was a misunderstanding," Verna said.

"*Daett*'s supposed to straighten it out this morning," Ida offered. "That may be his buggy going out of the driveway right now."

Lois took another peek past the drapes. "It is. But I don't think he can change Joe Weaver's mind. That whole family's awfully stubborn and high-minded."

"You can keep your opinions to yourself," Verna snapped. "I like Joe just fine, and he'd make a decent husband. You'd do well to find someone like him yourself."

Ida spoke up. "Maybe we all can if Verna gets this straightened out. Otherwise I'm afraid we're all staying old maids."

"Not me!" Lois piped up. "I'm joining the *Englisha*."

"You keep saying that, but you don't mean it, Lois," Verna lectured. "So stop terrorizing *Daett* and *Mamm* about it."

Debbie smiled. "I'm already learning that Amish families sometimes bicker just like we *Englisha* do. You really are normal human beings, after all!"

With that, all the girls laughed and busied themselves emptying Debbie's luggage and putting stuff away.

THIRTEEN

Hours later Debbie stood in the middle of the Beiler kitchen laughing so hard she was clutching her sides. The bowl of flour in her hands had leaped free and landed on the floor, where it unceremoniously skidded across the linoleum and clattered to a stop against the stove leg. It tipped over and spilled its contents all over.

Lois, in the midst of a fit of giggles, was seated on a kitchen chair. They made quite a sight amid the white powder mess. There were even puffs of flour that had drifted up one wall. This whole episode had begun with Lois's determination that a proper first step into Amish life would be to learn how to cook.

"I can teach anyone how to cook!" Lois had bravely declared. But even she hadn't envisioned this route to success.

"You're doing *gut*!" Lois choked out as she tried to get hold of herself. "That was almost a perfect arc as the bowl flew across the floor."

"Not quite what I would call cooking," Debbie declared. "Now where is the broom? I'm afraid I'll burn your mother's house down if I keep going like this."

"There's no danger of that." Lois still appeared quite confident. "I'm here, and it's a Saturday afternoon. We can clean up a dozen messes and disturb no one's schedule."

"Trying to be positive, are we?" Debbie asked as she opened a closet door and pulled out the hand broom and dustpan.

"Be careful!" Lois said too late as puffs of flour rose in the air with the slightest push of the broom.

Debbie glanced toward Lois. "Should we wet it down?"

Lois's eyes grew large. "You don't know *anything* about cooking, do you?"

Debbie grimaced. "You already know that. What happens with wet flour?"

"You mean what happens with glue. That's the result when you mix water and flour. Turns everything into a paste that sticks fast."

Debbie made a face. "Maybe I should move into the haymow. It might be safer."

Lois giggled. "I'm going to make a cook

157

out of you yet. We'll have lessons every day if necessary."

"You'd better stick with Saturdays." Debbie completed a dry sweep of the flour the best she could. Lois filled a plastic bowl with hot water and soap, ready to get down on her knees for the finishing cleanup.

Debbie held up her hand. "That's my job. You're not cleaning up my mess."

"*Yah,* I am!" Lois got on her knees undeterred. "And I'm directing from down here. Get going again with measuring the flour. We're going to have a cake made before you know it."

Debbie didn't move. "I think I've changed my mind. I'll run into town for a cake mix."

Lois made a stern face. "Debbie! You want to be Amish, don't you? Every Amish woman knows how to cook . . . from *scratch.*"

This morning's glimpse of Alvin flashed through Debbie's mind. Yes, she most certainly did wish to cook — and with competence. Even if her dreams of Alvin were nothing more than that, the cooking skills she acquired from Lois would serve her well.

Lois nodded as if she'd interpreted the look on Debbie's face. "You begin with measuring the flour, like we just did. After that you add brown sugar and the rest of the things listed in the recipe."

Debbie glanced over the list of ingredients as Lois scrubbed the floor. It wasn't right that she was up here in the midst of carrot cake preparations while Lois was down on her hands and knees like a common servant. Yet that was how the Amish women conducted themselves, and she wouldn't change that by a simple protest. Rather, it would be better if she took lessons and imitated them. Such ability surely came because of one's humility, not because one was worried how things might appear to others.

"When all the dry items are in," Lois said from down on the floor, "I believe the eggs and oil come next. Be sure to mix those in thoroughly. I'll come help with the grated carrots in a minute."

"Hold fast to the bowl!" Debbie muttered to herself, which elicited giggles from Lois. "What's going to happen when I stir? I was only moving it around the last time — and look what happened!"

Lois laughed harder. "I think you tripped, if I remember right."

Debbie laughed. "Miss Graceful, I know. I say keep me out of the kitchen!"

"We'll soon have you tripping along as light as a feather in the wind," Lois quipped.

Debbie grimaced again. "I'm glad someone sees hope in this situation."

Lois paused and looked up at the sound of buggy wheels in the driveway. "That would be *Daett* coming home, I'd guess."

Debbie took a quick look out the window. "It is."

Behind them quick steps came down the stairs and the front door slammed.

"That would be Verna going out to see if *Daett* has news for her." Lois got to her feet. "Poor Verna! I feel sorry for her. Actually I feel sorry for all of us girls. *Daett* will never allow any of us to date, let alone marry. But why should I worry? I'm not staying Amish and following his rules forever."

"That's your dark side speaking," Debbie said as she stirred the ingredients, hanging on to the bowl tightly with one hand. "I think your dad's concerned, that's all."

"I personally place more hope for love in the *Englisha* world," Lois declared, her eyes shining for a moment.

Debbie looked at Lois's beaming face. Did Lois have a boy she admired out in the world? It would explain her fascination better than anything else. And it was something she could understand. Wasn't the same thing in her heart? Except an admiration of an Amish man? Only her desire went deeper

160

than finding love. But perhaps Lois's did also. Debbie started to ask about it but stopped. Now was not the time.

Lois rose, dumped the soapy water into the sink, and rinsed the rag. Then she washed her hands and moved over to work at the counter and grate carrots. The front door slammed again. Verna, her face grim, walked past the kitchen doorway without a glance.

"*Yah,* just what I feared," Lois said quietly. "It didn't work."

"Maybe you should comfort her," Debbie suggested.

Lois shrugged. "I would if I could. But there's not much to comfort oneself with around here. 'Wait for the man until he comes around,' *Daett* probably told her. Or maybe Joe's not decent enough. Or maybe he's not obeying the *Ordnung* in other matters too. With the men *Daett*'s chased away already, poor Verna's been through too much. Now she's finally set her heart on one badly enough to fight for him. *Daett* should be careful, if you ask me."

Obviously no one would ask Lois, Debbie thought as she stirred the cake ingredients until she could discern no visible lumps. She jumped when the bishop opened the washroom door. She'd been too lost in her

161

thoughts to hear his footsteps.

His face broke into a bright smile. "I see we have an *Englisha* girl busy cooking in our kitchen. What do you know! We'll make a decent Amish woman out of her yet."

"Daett!" Lois protested. "You'll make Debbie feel bad, like she's not decent already."

Bishop Beiler's face glowed. "On the contrary, daughter of mine, I mean my words as a great compliment. Being willing to mend the weaknesses in our lives deserves praise. Debbie's obviously willing to do that."

"Thank you," Debbie managed to get out. This discussion of her while she was present disconcerted her, but she would learn fast. And it helped that she already knew enough of Amish ways not to be offended by the things they said that might not ever be said in *Englisha* homes.

Bishop Beiler pulled out a chair and settled in. Debbie stole a glance at him. "The cake's not done yet, and once it is, its edible quality may be in question."

The bishop laughed. "You have a way with words there, Debbie. We should take lessons from you. I'm just a simple Amish man, as *Da Hah* knows. I tried to read Shakespeare once in my younger days, but I didn't get far."

"We studied him in English class," Debbie said. "I probably didn't get much further than you did."

The bishop sobered. "Education is *gut* if you also reach the heart. But, sadly, so much of the world's education fails in that area."

Debbie nodded.

Lois snapped, "Don't you think you should be listening to Verna's sorrow right now, *Daett,* instead of talking about the bad side of *Englisha* education?"

Bishop Beiler remained silent for a moment. "You do speak the truth, Lois. And I don't fault you for it. My heart is indeed in great pain because of Verna. I did this morning what I could do, and now it's up to *Da Hah.*"

"That's what you always say." Lois didn't appear mollified. "Don't you see that Verna has her heart set on this boy? For once you ought to help her instead of work against her. Before you know it, you'll have a houseful of old maids no men want."

Debbie glanced at Bishop Beiler. She expected a look of anger in his face, but he appeared quite serious. His words were measured. "We must all have patience, Lois. I know I've said that before, but it's still true. Things will work out as they are intended. You speak of old maids in the house, but I also don't want a bunch of sons-in-law who can't keep my daughters happy and their feet inside the fence of faith. I don't need family members who are always looking for greener grass on the other side. That I will not have. And just for your information, Joe seemed quite understanding of what I told him."

Debbie held her breath for a moment. Should she leave the room? This sounded like a private conversation. She glanced at the bishop and Lois. Neither seemed the least bit troubled by her presence.

Bishop Beiler continued. "I disclosed my source of information to Joe, which is not something I'd normally do. I bent the rules for Verna's sake. I assured Joe she had nothing to do with informing me of his error. I think the boy will come around. If you ask me, his heart is still wounded from the way Rosy dealt with him. Those things take time to heal. If Verna had followed my advice and waited a few months, Joe might not have reacted like he did."

Lois still didn't appear convinced, but she kept her mouth closed.

The bishop nodded in Debbie's direction. "Sorry to bother you with family problems, but you're in the household now and we keep no secrets. A little family matter, and you're now here to hear it all."

"A *little* matter?" Lois murmured loud enough for her father to hear.

Her *daett*'s head turned in her direction. "*Yah,* I will admit it's a big matter, Lois. And I should watch my words better than I do. I am sorry."

Lois lowered her head. "I'm sorry for snapping at you."

The two looked at each other, and Debbie couldn't help but notice how their faces softened. How beautiful this was. They mended fences before any hard feelings could fester. And yet they had freely been allowed to say what was on their hearts.

Bishop Beiler got to his feet. He leaned toward the bowl Debbie was holding. "What have we there? Did you say a cake of some sort?"

"It's supposed to be carrot cake." Debbie made a face. "But with me making it, who knows? We might have burnt upside down carrot cake."

Amusement crossed the bishop's face. "I'm sure Lois will keep you on the straight and narrow. She's the best cook in our family — and that's saying a lot."

Lois's face glowed with the praise as the

bishop left, going back outside through the washroom door.

Debbie took it as another lesson to learn. Always share a word of compliment, especially when it's deserved.

A few minutes later Verna appeared from the stairway. Her face was tear-stained.

Lois rushed over and gave Verna a long hug. "Was the news that bad?"

Verna choked back a sob. "Not according to *Daett,* but my heart doesn't feel much better. Joe still has to give a confession in front of the church. And all for just driving an *Englisha* vehicle to help someone out. I suppose he's not going to come anywhere close to me until long after that embarrassment has died down."

"Just stay strong," Lois comforted.

Debbie sent Verna a warm smile when she glanced toward her. There didn't seem much else Debbie could do at the moment with her hands covered in cake ingredients.

FOURTEEN

That Saturday night at the supper table, as the evening light faded outside, everyone bowed their heads for prayer. Debbie had been here before at mealtimes, but the sound of Bishop Beiler's words stirred her spirit. Now she would be here every night, involved in this ritual, the ebb and flow of Amish life like the very sands of time itself.

The bishop's voice rose and fell, and even the kitchen seemed to listen. "Now, unto You, O God, the most high God, we give glory and honor and praise. Look upon us, Your humble servants, at this evening hour. Have mercy and compassion upon our weaknesses. Remember that we are made of dust and prone to error. Forgive us, as we also forgive those who offend us. Bless now this food which has been prepared. Bless especially Debbie, who is with us tonight. Let her feel a part of the family, and bless her parents who have raised such a godly daughter. Amen."

Debbie's face turned red at Bishop Beiler's words of praise. She glanced around at the others, but no one seemed bothered in the least. Lois even sent a sweet look her way. After the "amen," Emery dished out some mashed potatoes while he stared at the carrot cake that sat in the middle of the table. The cake was right where Lois had insisted it go. If the choice had been Debbie's, it would have been hidden in the pantry, or better yet, the basement. The effort was sure to be a total disaster. She just knew it. She tried not to panic. If she only knew for certain how it had come out. But Lois had watched her spread on the sticky frosting. "You're not going to taste it beforehand — not one tiny piece!" she stated.

"What difference does it make if one little corner is gone?" Debbie had begged. Hot and cold flashes had run up and down her back. Somehow she had to relieve her mind of this agony of suspense. She *had* to taste the cake before it was served. "What if it's simply awful? What if it makes people sick?" she had worried.

"You're not a *gut* judge anyway," Lois had said. "You're too tense. And we don't cut pieces out of the pan before we serve."

Debbie had groaned but given in. Now all

168

her tension had returned as she watched Emery stare at the cake. She finally dared whisper in his direction, "Is there something wrong with it?"

He studied the pan some more. "I thought there was something different looking about it. So you made it?"

"Yes," she said. At least he didn't frown at the revelation. "What's different?" Debbie croaked.

Emery shrugged. "There are smear marks up the side of the pan. Lois would never do that. But that shouldn't change how the cake tastes. That is — if you didn't miss a cup of flour or something."

"Emery!" Lois snapped. "Behave yourself. Debbie made a perfectly *gut* carrot cake."

Debbie stared at the cake pan. Indeed, there were smudges up the side of the pan and now baked on in dark brown. She would have to remember that the next time she emptied batter into a cake pan. Mercy sakes, there were more things to cooking than she'd imagined. No wonder she didn't like it.

"She's never cooked around here before," Emery said, which jerked Debbie out of her thoughts. "Has she cooked at home?"

Debbie cast around for something to say, but Lois beat her to it.

"That's a nasty question to ask, Emery. Maligning a woman's character like that. I personally oversaw the making of this cake, and Debbie did just fine. So there!"

Emery obviously didn't buy a word of this. He wrinkled up his nose and poured gravy onto his mashed potatoes.

Debbie glanced at Lois, and they both smiled. If he'd seen the flour bowl fly across the room earlier in the day, he wouldn't dare touch the cake!

"I'm sure Debbie did just fine," Bishop Beiler said. "I was here while she stirred the batter. In fact, I'll be the first one to taste it when we're ready. We'll see what kind of cake we have."

"Oh! Please, don't do it!" Debbie begged. "You don't have to do that, Bishop Beiler. The cake might be awful."

"It might *kill* you," Emery teased.

"Emery!" Bishop Beiler had reproof in his voice. "Debbie's expressing a proper humble attitude for a young woman to have. I like that. And I'm sure the cake will be fine. In fact, let's settle this matter right now. Slide the cake over here, *Mamm.*"

"I'll get the clean plates then." Saloma leaped to her feet. She went to the counter and grabbed a stack. "Here they are." She placed the plates within the bishop's reach,

170

along with a sharp knife.

The bishop cut a large piece, transferring it to a smaller plate. He sectioned off a portion with his fork and took a bite. A thoughtful look came across his face as he chewed.

Oh, she was going to die if this turned out horribly! Debbie thought.

The bishop appeared pleased. "Perfect!" he pronounced. "The best I've tasted in a long time."

"You're just saying so," Emery protested. "Let me check it out."

"But it's not time for dessert," Saloma said, apparently pushed beyond her level of tolerance by this break in routine.

"Let him try it," Bishop Beiler overruled. "Let the boy see what kind of cake our *Englisha* girl has stirred up."

Emery cut a small piece and popped the portion into his mouth.

"There! Now we'll see who was right!" Lois launched into Emery before he even swallowed, "Isn't the cake just a marvel?"

"Not too bad," Emery allowed once he could speak.

A satisfied expression settled over the bishop's face.

Saloma didn't wait long before she proclaimed, "Okay! Now that is settled! We can get back to our meal. Pass the corn, Verna.

It's already getting cold."

"You did okay!" Ida whispered in Debbie's ear.

The hot and cold flashes ran up and down Debbie's back again, but this time from pleasure. She'd never thought praise for a simple thing like a baked cake could mean so much. She filled her own plate as the good dishes were passed around and listened to the chatter of conversation. Her cake was soon forgotten as subjects ranged from the plans for tomorrow's church service, which would be held at Deacon Mast's place, to how they would drive home from the Sunday-night hymn singing.

Verna's face had fallen at the mention of the hymn singing, but she hid it with a drop of her gaze until she gathered her composure. Debbie noticed Ida had reached under the table to squeeze her sister's hand. The two gave each other quick smiles and soon joined in the conversation.

After supper they all followed Bishop Beiler into the living room, leaving the dishes on the table. The bishop sat in his rocker, opened his Bible, and read a portion of scripture from the book of Ephesians, starting with, "Be ye therefore followers of God, as dear children; and walk in love . . ."

Debbie settled on the couch and allowed

the feelings from earlier to overtake her again. How wonderful that she was really living in the Beiler home . . . an Amish home. This was exactly what she'd longed for all these years.

Bishop Beiler finished reading the scripture passage, and they all knelt in prayer. Afterward, Debbie followed the three girls and Saloma back into the kitchen. Emery headed upstairs in a rush over something.

"He's leaving before long," Lois whispered in Debbie's ear. "Emery's spending the night out somewhere. He sometimes doesn't come back until early morning."

Debbie nodded as she remembered Emery was on his *rumspringa* time. "That's nice to know. If he comes creeping up the stairs tonight I won't be scared," Debbie whispered back.

Lois giggled. "Sometimes I go with him, but Emery's not a lot of fun. He doesn't do *Englisha* stuff."

Debbie picked up several plates and carried them to the counter. Saloma stopped her when she came back for more. "The two girls and I will take care of the supper dishes, Debbie. Maybe you and Lois want to walk down to your parents' place. Let them know how you're doing on this first night of your stay here."

"That's a great idea," Lois said at once. "Let's do it."

"I guess," Debbie said. "But Mom knows where I'm at." She hadn't thought about a visit home this soon.

"It would still be *gut* to touch base with your mother," Saloma insisted.

"Come on." Lois pulled on her arm.

Debbie followed but sent a protest over her shoulder. "I should help with the dishes."

"You'll have plenty of time for dishes another time," Saloma called after them.

Once they were outside, Debbie headed toward her car, while Lois took a few steps in the other direction. She stopped and looked at Debbie. "*Mamm* said to walk."

Debbie shook her head. "I'd be more comfortable driving."

Lois stayed where she was, and Debbie climbed into her car. She found her keys in the glove compartment. She couldn't explain why she felt taking the car was necessary. Maybe her mother would feel better if she drove in instead of arriving on foot. The Amish culture shock might be less severe. There would be plenty of time to walk to her parents' place later.

Lois finally shrugged and climbed in when Debbie drove the car over and stopped

174

beside her. She probably figured this was *Englisha* laziness, Debbie decided, but she didn't really wish to explain. Lois didn't protest during the short ride, but she spent the time brushing imaginary crumbs off her dress.

Debbie laughed. "Mom knows we've both been working. And your dress is clean anyway."

"Just making sure." Lois gave her dress another couple of swipes as they climbed out of the car.

No one answered her knock, so Debbie walked on in. Both her parents were sitting on the couch with the TV on. Her dad hit the remote when she appeared with Lois close behind.

"Well, who comes in here?" Joy spread over her dad's face. "Are you settled in at your new abode?"

"I think so." Debbie bent over to give him a hug. "I thought I'd come down and let you know that all is going well. Actually, Saloma suggested I come."

"Do sit down." Her dad motioned toward the other couch. "And hello, Lois. How are you doing?"

"I'm fine," Lois chirped. She looked around as usual, but mostly she stared at the picture on the TV.

"Just watching another episode of *Mad Men*," Debbie's dad said. "What a series! Absolutely amazing how they've recreated the sixties."

"Dastardly series if you ask me," Debbie's mother complained. "Men treated women horribly back then."

Lois followed the conversation wide-eyed until Debbie interrupted. "I guess we'd better head back. I still have to see about what to wear tomorrow. Are either of you going to church?"

"I think I'm going," her mother said. "I don't know about Herbert. Depends on how late he stays up watching TV."

Her dad laughed. "Debbie, why don't you come by at the regular time, and you can ride with us? If you're still attending our church, that is."

"Yes, that's fine," Debbie agreed. "I'm not quite up to attending an Amish church service just yet. She pulled on Lois's arm. If she didn't get the girl out of the house soon, Lois was going to plop down on the couch and join her dad in watching *Mad Men*. Debbie figured she'd never get Lois home then. And she certainly didn't want to explain it to the bishop.

Lois was still looking over her shoulder as they reached the front door. When they went outside and climbed into the car, Lois asked, "What was that *wunderbah* show about, Debbie?"

"It's not something you want to see," Debbie assured her. "It's from a totally different world."

"That's what I liked about it." Lois was entranced as Debbie drove out of the driveway. "I like worlds different from mine. That's why I like you, Debbie."

Debbie nodded. "Thanks, Lois. You're a wonderful friend, but my world isn't what you think it is." Lois didn't look convinced, but Debbie decided she'd keep saying it until the truth sank in. Bishop Beiler might have allowed her to stay in his house for this very reason. Her moderating influence on Lois might be something the bishop was counting on.

When they arrived back at the Beilers', Debbie parked the car beside the buggies. They climbed out, and Lois led the way inside. In the kitchen Ida was stacking the last of the dishes in the cupboards. Debbie offered to help, but Saloma waved them on upstairs. "You've done enough today, both of you. Go and finish unpacking and get your jabbering out of you. I don't want noises coming from your bedroom late into the night."

"Thank you for everything," Debbie told Saloma before she followed Lois up the stairs.

In their room, Lois held one of Debbie's best summer dresses — a bright-yellow polka dot — high in the air in front of her. "May I try this one on?" she begged. "Please? I'm going to weep all night if I can't. Especially now that I've seen it. Just thinking about how it will look sends shivers up and down my back."

Debbie closed the door behind her. She looked for a lock, but there was none. "What if someone sees you, Lois? Your dad will think I'm corrupting you."

"You promised!" Lois clutched the dress closer.

"Well, okay," Debbie conceded.

Lois's face glowed as Debbie helped her drop the dress over her head and settle it on her shoulders. The Amish girl seemed quite adept as she fastened the buttons, which Amish dresses didn't have. She turned around and asked for Debbie's help with the zipper. When they were finished, Lois pulled the hand mirror from a dresser drawer and spent long minutes looking at herself, repeatedly moving the mirror up and down to see the full dress.

"Like it?" Debbie asked. Lois *was* beautiful, she thought. And if she were honest, Lois had natural grace. But Debbie wasn't about to admit that fact out loud. Lois needed no encouragement in this area.

"It's absolutely divine!" Lois exclaimed. "I feel like I'm going to float away on the clouds and never come back."

Debbie laughed. "I don't think it's quite that good. Now, help me into one of *your* dresses."

Lois came out of her trance. "You want to try on one of *my* dresses?"

"Yes, if you don't mind."

"I guess, but they're *ugly,* Debbie. Are you sure?"

"I don't think they are ugly."

Lois took in a long breath and went to her closet. She brought out a dark-blue dress. Skepticism was written all over her face.

Debbie held out her arms, and Lois helped her slide the dress on.

What followed was a long pinning of dress pieces and a few yelps from Debbie when she tried to do some of the pins herself.

Lois giggled. "It takes practice, believe me. You push the pin in, holding your finger underneath for protection. Then you push it out again, so you don't get stuck with the point during the day."

Debbie tried the next pin with better success, and soon the task was completed.

Lois handed her the mirror, and Debbie repeated Lois's process from earlier.

"It does look a little better on you than on me," Lois allowed.

"It's *divine*!" Debbie said. Both girls dissolved into a fit of giggles and fell on the bed thinking how odd this was. An *Englisha* girl in an Amish dress, and an Amish girl in a bright-yellow polka dot outfit.

Debbie's life with the Amish had surely begun, and someday, hopefully, she would take it all the way. Before long she would attend an Amish church service — if Bishop Beiler would allow it. Not this Sunday, but soon. Debbie could feel it in her bones. But right now there was work to do. She had to separate the clothing she didn't absolutely need so she could drop them off at the thrift store next week. And she needed to keep Lois away from the makeup kit until she figured out what to do with it.

FIFTEEN

When the time came for Joe's church confession, Verna kept her head down. This horrible day had started hours ago when church began. As usual, she was seated in the older girls section for the three-hour church service. Now the last note of the last song rang in the air. Her *daett* stood. Verna knew most everyone expected dinner in a few minutes, but she knew what was coming. Today's church confessions lay ahead of them. Joe, and likely Henry Yoder, who was the culprit in all of this, were going to experience the public humiliation that fell on transgressors of the *Ordnung.*

Everyone waited in silence as Bishop Beiler's voice swept through the house. "Now that *Da Hah* has blessed us with another day of worship, will the members please stay seated while the others are dismissed?"

There were no groans as might be expected in an *Englisha* environment. The

Amish were too reverent for such things. There were a few startled looks as the nonmembers rose and poured out of the house.

Verna glanced over at Joe. He'd refused to look her way even once during the long church service, even though he sat in plain sight in the unmarried boys section. Thankfully she noticed he wasn't making eye contact with any other girls either. Perhaps there was still hope their broken relationship could be mended. If Joe would so much as glance in her direction, she'd send him the sweetest smile she could manage. It didn't matter who else might see it at this point. She would let them think what they wished.

The slam of the front door rang through the house and jerked Verna out of her thoughts. She glanced around to see a few of the younger girls peeking out of the kitchen doorway. Bishop Beiler gave them a brief stare, and they vanished. He turned to the people sitting on the benches.

"As we all know, *Da Hah*'s vineyard needs work done to it from time to time. None of us ministers would object if He were here Himself to care for His people, but *Da Hah* is not. He has left us in charge. So we wish to proceed today with humility and broken-heartedness. It gives none of us joy to exercise church discipline, but it must be done." Bishop Beiler paused and nodded at the row of ministers who sat with bowed heads. "It has come to our attention that two of our brethren have been found in transgression. It is always a serious matter when the *Ordnung* is broken. These are rules we have all agreed to live by as part of our community. It troubles all our hearts when trust among the people of *Da Hah* is breached. I ask that our brothers Henry Yoder and Joe Weaver please leave the room. We will call them back inside when we are finished."

Verna held her hand over her heart as Henry stood, followed by Joe. They both walked down the benches to the aisle. *Joe looks so troubled,* Verna thought. *But he's doing what is required of him. Isn't that a gut sign?* Oh, if only some hope could rise in her heart. If Joe only knew how she ached for him. Perhaps then he'd give her at least a small sign. Perhaps even a hint of a kind look. She watched as the two brethren walked toward the door. Joe's gaze didn't stray from the floor. Didn't he understand that she had no part in this matter? Hadn't *Daett* explained who had told the ministers about his transgression?

When the men had exited and the door closed behind them, Bishop Beiler lifted his head. He spoke with a steady voice. "Both of our brethren have agreed to this confession, for which we are grateful. And now I will present what happened to see if the church is willing to accept their confessions. Some of our youngest members may ask why we cannot accept confessions without the voice of the church, so I will take some time this morning to explain that."

A few of the men settled lower on the benches. This would take some time, but Verna really didn't care. The end would come with Joe seated on the front row, where he would speak his confession of failure. Verna forced her mind back to what her *daett* was saying.

"The early church had such a standard. They believed that all members should be involved in deciding if a transgressor had truly repented and if his punishment was suitable to the sin. With that in mind, we will now proceed."

Bishop Beiler paused for a moment. "Henry Yoder has in the past confessed to the problem of using his *Englisha* neighbor's tractor to pull around the new equipment he buys. Henry understands this is against the *Ordnung,* and yet he continues to fail in his attempts to resist this temptation. So the ministry recommends that another confession be taken at this time. Deacon Mast has also visited the *Englisha* neighbor, asking him to respect our ways. Perhaps he can be an aid to Henry by refusing to loan his tractor. We have no hold on the *Englisha* neighbor, but he has, in his kindness, told us that he will consider our problem and our solution. For this, Deacon Mast has heartedly thanked him. If these solutions don't stop Henry from further transgressions, we expect other disciplines will need consideration."

Bishop Beiler shifted on his feet and clasped his hands in front of him. "Our other brother, Joe Weaver, has admitted to driving *Englisha* vehicles at the auction barn in Belleville. Not out in front where his actions would be widely noticed, but behind the scenes. He claims his intentions were to help out when the auction people were short-handed. Joe understands he was in the wrong and has agreed to make his confession. We expect no further problems on the matter."

Bishop Beiler's gaze swept over the ministers' bench. "If the ordained brethren will now take the voice of the church, we can proceed with this matter."

Both ministers and Deacon Mast got up at once and began moving among the benches to ask each member if they agreed to the actions being taken. Men leaned toward the ministers and deacon and whispered in their ears. The women did likewise. Most didn't take long, although a few of the men did. They were the ones who were usually longwinded in any response. It was their chance to exercise church authority, and they made the most of it.

Some men were like that, Verna knew, but she couldn't imagine Joe would act in such a manner. He was much too kind and tenderhearted. In front of her, Deacon Mast moved down the unmarried girls' bench. His head went up and down like Emery's fishing bobber on late-summer afternoons down by the creek. As he drew closer, each girl whispered her line at lightning speed. Deacon Mast looked mighty uncomfortable surrounded by all these females even though he had four daughters of his own.

Verna managed to mutter her line once Deacon Mast arrived in front of her. "I have no objections with the solution the ministry has presented," she said. The deacon was gone a second later, and he finished within minutes. Deacon Mast circled back, and joined the other two ministers on the front bench. Verna took a deep breath. The vote hadn't taken that long, and now the moment she dreaded was here.

Bishop Beiler leaned over and motioned for Deacon Mast's report. The deacon cleared his throat. "I found no objections to our proposal from any of the sisters or from the men I questioned."

Bishop Beiler nodded. Minister Kanagy was next. He was a short, thin, nervous young man. "I found few objections. Most of the members were in full agreement with the counsel of the ministry. One brother did wish that things concerning Henry Yoder could be handled a little more discreetly. It seemed inappropriate to him that an *Englisha* should have learned about a church problem. But the brother said he would agree with the action we took."

The bishop looked irritated by the rebuke, but he motioned for the next minister to report.

Verna realized her *daett* knew he was pushing a church boundary when he involved the *Englisha,* but she knew he must have done so for a very good reason. What that was, Verna couldn't imagine. Did it have anything to do with Henry's view of Joe? Was *Daett* concerned enough about her relationship with Joe to take a risk? If Henry had thrown a fit and refused to make the confession, his complaint against Joe might have been more difficult to clear up. The involvement of the *Englisha* neighbor might have shamed Henry into cooperation.

Verna turned her attention back to the ministers. Minister Graber, a thick, heavy-set man with a high-pitched voice, was in the middle of his report. Verna's thoughts wandered back to her *daett* and Henry Yoder's *Englisha* neighbor. Could *Daett* really have taken that risk for her? Did he care that she was growing older and had few marriage prospects? How *wunderbah* that would be to have his support. And why couldn't it be true? *Daett* was kindhearted enough even under the weight of his church duties. Maybe *Mamm*'s talks with him in private had been effective. Either way, this might be the most comforting thing to happen today, and Verna needed something to soothe her soul. With *Daett* on her side, she had so much more hope for the future.

Minster Graber concluded his remarks, and Verna realized she had no idea what he'd said. Had everyone agreed to the ministry's course of action?

Daett was on his feet. "We thank all of you for participating in this important church activity. As for the several concerns that were brought up about the *Englisha* neighbor's involvement, I can assure you we will not be doing this as a normal practice. We proceeded on that issue with Henry's knowledge and with the hope that it would help him. That is all I have to say on the matter. Deacon Mast, you may now call in the two men."

Deacon Mast stood up, walked down the aisle, and disappeared outside. He returned within minutes with Henry and Joe in tow. The deacon sat on the bench by the ministers, and the two men sat down on a bench in front of them, facing the people.

Bishop Beiler approached the two men. "The vote of the church has been taken. We are in agreement with the measures we have spoken to you about. You may make your confessions now."

Henry went first and spoke rapidly. "I confess before *Da Hah* and His church that I have failed. I beg their forgiveness and commit myself to walk in repentance and humility free from further transgressions on this matter."

"It is granted," Bishop Beiler said. His gaze moved to Joe.

Joe spoke slower and kept his head bowed.

Verna pinched herself to keep her sobs inside.

When Joe was done and the bishop had accepted his confession, the church members were dismissed.

Verna waited for a moment to calm herself and then headed toward the kitchen. She stole a glance at the bench in front where Joe had been seated, but he was gone. In spite of her surge of hope earlier, it was likely that Joe was gone from her life. But she mustn't think such negative thoughts. *Daett* had been kind to her. He had possibly taken great risks for her benefit, so she must not despair. There must be something she could do to reach Joe. If he wouldn't come to her, then perhaps she should make the first move. But what could that be? She'd already tried everything usually allowed Amish women.

Deacon Mast's *frau,* Susie, appeared in front of her. Verna jumped.

"Sorry," Susie said and smiled. "I didn't mean to scare you, but we need help with the tables."

"That's okay," Verna replied as an idea flashed through her mind. "I'll help with the unmarried boys' table."

Susie nodded with appreciation. Not many girls volunteered for the task of waiting on the boys' tables — not with the teases they usually had to endure.

Susie pointed toward the stair door. "Head right that way."

Verna didn't waste any time. She went into the kitchen, grabbed several bowls of peanut butter, and with weak knees went down the basement steps. Her *daett*'s voice rang out, calling for the first prayer. She waited at the bottom of the stairs until he finished.

"Well, well, service already!" Paul Wagler, the greatest tease of the unmarrieds, announced her presence. "Aren't we all special today? Usually we have to holler our heads off to get any attention down here."

"Consider yourself spoiled rotten today!" Verna shot back with a good-natured smile.

Everyone joined Paul in raucous laughter except Joe, who was seated at the other end. He didn't even look up. Verna sidled that way, placing peanut butter bowls down the table. The boys in her wake got busy smearing peanut butter on their bread. Perhaps if she hung around Joe would eventually look up. She didn't dare go up to him and speak.

"And what does the charming young Beiler girl have on her list for tonight?" Paul hollered in her direction.

"I'm certainly not going home with you!" she snapped.

Paul bent over with laughter, obviously

enjoying the moment.

He was such a flirt, Verna thought, but *gut* looking at that. Why he didn't settle down with some girl was anyone's guess. He'd dated a few once or twice, but he always cut off the relationship. Not that she'd ever felt any interest in being asked home by Paul. He would make someone a *gut* catch though.

"Listen to the girl's brave words," Paul said now that he could breathe again. "That's spoken like a true bishop's daughter. Why is the young maiden still single, boys? Ask yourself that question."

Before Verna could think of what to say, another man spoke up. "Why don't *you* answer that question, Paul?"

"Well, she might already be spoken for, if the truth were told," Paul retorted before joining in the laughter again.

Verna studied Paul's handsome face as she tried to think of what to say. Out of the corner of her eye, she saw Joe finally look her way. He didn't look displeased. Maybe Paul had done them both a favor with this public tease. And if Paul didn't think they'd broken up permanently, that must mean Joe hadn't told him they had. Paul was, after all, Joe's *gut* friend.

Verna sent Joe a quick smile. He dropped

his eyes but hope rose higher in her heart. For the rest of the meal, Verna raced up and down the steps and served the table. She stood still when her *daett* called for prayer again and watched afterward as the unmarried boys filed up the basement steps. Not once did Joe glance at her again. Still, she'd hang on to what hope she had. There was nothing else to do.

SIXTEEN

On the first Sunday in June, the morning sun hung just above the horizon. Debbie rode in the single buggy with Verna seated on the other side. Lois sat in the middle with Buttercup's lines in her hands. Debbie could hardly believe she was finally going to attend her first Amish church service. For a moment she listened to the beats of horses' hooves all around her and her excitement grew. The great moment of adventure had arrived, and now it seemed like the whole community had come alive in the stillness of the early dawn.

Debbie took deep breaths of fresh air and pulled her shawl tighter over her shoulders. Lois and Verna didn't seem to mind the chill, but they were used to riding in a buggy. There was so much of the Amish life Debbie hadn't yet experienced even though she'd grown up so close to the Beilers. Attending a church service had been the most unlikely possibility. That was a line one didn't cross easily. It was a wonder now that Bishop Beiler was allowing her to attend. She'd asked him last night, and when he'd said *yah* Debbie's heart had raced in anticipation. For Bishop Beiler to allow her to visit surely meant he thought well of her. She'd tried so hard these past three weeks to fit in, and apparently her efforts were succeeding. After the decision last night, there had been a mad rush upstairs with Lois to pick out a dress. She had tried on a few, accompanied this time by a few less giggles than the first attempt.

This morning Saloma had given her an approving look when she came downstairs. Debbie decided she'd still wear her regular dresses for work at Destiny, but from here on out on the weekends and evenings at the Beilers' she'd wear Amish clothes.

Her makeup kit had sat unopened these past weeks. Debbie's lack of adornment had provoked a few stares from Rhonda and Sally at work, but they soon got used to it. Debbie even wondered if she should drive to work in a buggy to fit her new lifestyle. She'd do it too if it weren't so far and impractical. If she arrived by buggy she'd at least have rosy cheeks. That glow would be better than any touch of makeup. She was sure of that.

Verna leaned back and spoke around Lois's back. "Are you cold, Debbie? There's extra blanket on my end. Just pull on it."

"A little," Debbie said as she drew the blanket tighter around her knees. "But it's okay. I'm enjoying the ride."

Verna looked forward again. They heard the sound of a buggy coming up fast behind them, and soon it whirled past. The man inside leaned out with glee written on his face. He waved.

"He's got nerve, that man!" Lois snapped. "It's not even decent the way he acts."

"Paul's his own character," Verna muttered. "He means no harm."

"Surely you're not after him now that Joe's no longer coming around?" There was alarm in Lois's voice. "Even *I* know enough to stay away from a boy like that."

Verna sighed. "He was teasing me at church the other Sunday, and I can't say I didn't enjoy it. But I know better, Lois. He'd be a catch, but he gets over girls quickly. Believe me, I'm still waiting on Joe."

"You poor girl!" Lois was all sympathy. "Well, be assured that I think highly of Joe — as far as Amish men go. Better than Paul Wagler at least."

"Be decent, Lois, please." Verna turned

around to peer down the road as another buggy approached.

What did they mean about Paul Wagler? Debbie wondered. *Who was he?* She didn't dare ask. He seemed quite handsome and dashing in the brief glimpse she'd gotten. Wouldn't any Amish girl be honored to have him pursue her? But that apparently wasn't the case with Lois. Was he a flirt? Or too full of himself? The Amish made big issues out of such things. Now the sound of the buggy behind them was getting louder, pulling Debbie from her thoughts. But the driver didn't attempt to pass them. Lois had let out the reins, and Buttercup was now clipping along at a faster pace. Lois must not want another buggy to whirl past them.

"Do you think Joe will get over his hurt before long?" Lois asked, giving Verna a quick sideways glance.

Debbie watched for Verna's response. Lois wasn't normally this sympathetic to her elder sister's troubles, but this one had the whole family concerned. Debbie had heard their whispers at odd moments during the evening hours. She also saw it in their glances at each other whenever Verna's face clouded over — which was often, it seemed. The problem of Joe wore heavily on all of them. Even the bishop had concern written on his face when a conversation near him broached the subject.

"I wish I knew."

Debbie thought Verna's voice sounded weary.

"But let's talk of something a little more cheerful, shall we?" Verna continued. "Debbie's coming to church for the first time. That will be quite a happy experience, I hope."

"I went over everything with her last night," Lois said, acting as if Debbie weren't sitting beside her in the buggy. "She's ready for all eventualities."

Verna appeared amused. "Did Debbie teach you that big word?"

Lois sputtered, "I learned that word listening to the *Englisha* talk at the health-food store, mind you. And there's nothing wrong with that. They talk so much more educated than we do."

"Don't start on that this morning," Verna begged. "At least appreciate what you have. Take some examples from Debbie and how she acts."

"Oh, she understands me." Lois tossed her head so her bonnet shifted sideways. With one hand, she straightened it.

"I'm used to Lois's feelings, Verna," Debbie said, interrupting their conversation. "And I do understand, I guess. I come from that world, and there are exciting things out there. But I like this simple life much better."

"See!" Verna sounded triumphant. "Debbie has much to say that you could learn."

Lois didn't answer. She stared straight ahead.

"She's not angry," Verna assured Debbie when Debbie glanced her way. "Lois doesn't like being reminded of the decent heritage she has."

Debbie settled back into the buggy seat. The last thing she wished this morning was to make an issue out of her *Englisha* ways. Lois was peeved regardless of what Verna thought. Maybe if Debbie maintained her cheerfulness, Lois would get over her hurt feelings. "All I can say is that I'm happy to be here," Debbie stated. "And I'm sure Lois finds much to appreciate with this wonderful life, don't you, Lois?"

"I like that you're here."

Lois didn't sound too mollified.

Debbie noticed a smile flit across Verna's face as they drove on. Lois said nothing more, but her fascination with the *Englisha* world was tempered for the moment. At least Lois hadn't followed through on her threat to attend college this fall. And perhaps Debbie had played a small part in this change of mind. If she had, she was thankful. She was sure Lois wouldn't find the *Englisha* world as fascinating as she thought she would.

Debbie pulled the buggy blanket tighter and lowered her head. Her face was turning colder by the minute. Her heart, though, was pounding faster the closer they came to the meeting place. She was going to see Alvin Knepp today, and he would see her in an Amish dress. What would he think of her? Would he think of her at all? Yes, he surely would! Hopefully, he was developing an interest in her. Even Bishop Beiler's eyebrows had been raised yesterday when Alvin drove in their lane again . . . to borrow a bag of oats, he said.

"It's becoming quite a habit of the boy to stop by here on Saturday mornings," Saloma had commented when the bishop had come in after Alvin left.

Bishop Beiler had nodded. "*Yah,* it does seem a bit strange." He'd stroked his beard and puzzled over the matter. "There's no reason for them to run out of oats this early in the spring."

"Maybe he wishes to take the place of Deacon Mast," Lois teased.

Everyone laughed except Debbie. She

wasn't quite sure what the joke meant. Apparently Deacon Mast's duties weren't considered the pleasant sort.

A twinge of guilt plucked at her heart, but Debbie pushed it away. She'd not been dishonest by keeping her silence. If it had occurred to one of the Beilers to ask her about Alvin, she would have admitted that he fascinated her. But Alvin wasn't her motivation to attend church, Debbie reminded herself. She'd wanted to attend the Amish church the first chance she had, so she'd asked. From there — once she had Bishop Beiler's approval — all it had taken was a quick trip down to her parents' place to let them know she wouldn't be attending church with them in the morning.

Her mom had appeared resigned before the words were out of her daughter's mouth. It was as if her mother had expected such news. Her dad, on the other hand, had seemed pleased. "I wish you the best, Debbie, whatever this adventure of yours is all about. I don't understand it, and neither does your mother. But we've always believed in supporting you when you've really wanted something. And this you seem to want."

"Thank you, Dad," Debbie had responded.

The blessing of Dad's approval was wonderful, Debbie thought as she watched the road ahead of her. The well-kept, white farmhouse of Henry Yoder came into view. Lois had told her last night that this was where church would be held today. Debbie had gone silent for a moment before saying, "But isn't that the man you told me about? The one who made a church confession the other Sunday, along with Joe Weaver?"

"*Yah,* the very one," Lois had said.

"But isn't he still angry?" Debbie had wondered.

"He's supposed to be humbled," Lois had told her. "But I doubt it. Still, there's no reason we can't have church at his place. Anyway, these things are scheduled a year or so ahead. They can be changed only under the direst of situations."

All of this intrigue fascinated Debbie. She'd grown up around the Amish, and yet she knew so little about them and their traditions. Only after Bishop Beiler had opened his home to her had she been allowed to see the inside workings of the community. What a blessing that was! And she was most thankful. What if Bishop Beiler hadn't allowed her to stay? Debbie winced at the thought. She wouldn't be on her way to the services this morning with Verna and

Lois, for one thing. "Thank you, Lord, for watching over me," Debbie prayed silently as Lois guided Buttercup down the Yoder driveway. Their buggy bounced toward the line of several other buggies that had stopped at the end of the sidewalk where shawl-draped women climbed out, taking their time as they extracted smaller children from the backseats.

Verna gave a little wave as they went past and whispered to Lois, "Slow down. You don't have to make such a grand entrance."

"I'm showing off my visitor!" Lois pulled Buttercup to a stop beside a line of parked buggies.

She was doing nothing of the kind, Debbie thought as she watched the line of men standing near the barn who were now looking their way. Lois wanted attention for herself, even if she had no plans to stay Amish.

"Now you have Paul coming toward us," Verna hissed as they climbed out of the buggy.

Lois made a face. "I do declare he's got his eye on you, Verna."

"He does not!" Verna retorted.

"Then who else is he looking for?" Lois shot back.

Verna colored slightly but had recovered

by the time Paul arrived.

Lois cooed, "If it isn't Mr. Charming himself. I didn't think you stooped to helping poor girls unhitch."

Paul laughed. "I do declare it's the bishop's daughters themselves. And who is this charming visitor who graces your buggy this morning?"

Debbie turned to face the full force of this man's charm, of which he had plenty, she had to admit. "I would be Debbie Watson, an outside girl," she told him, giving a quick nod of her head. "And I'm staying at the Beilers."

"*Yah,* we've all heard about the pretty *Englisha* girl living at the Beilers," he said, his grin broadening. "But why are you in . . . well . . . Amish clothing?" As he talked, he was undoing the tugs on their buggy.

"Leave her alone!" Lois snapped. "She's not for you."

"Mind your own business." Paul dismissed Lois with a wave of his hand.

Debbie glared at him. It was time she changed her tactic. "Maybe I misspoke. I really meant to say that I'm a visiting *Amish* girl."

Paul laughed. "You can't fool me. I suppose you speak Dutch then?"

"Okay, so I'm *Englisha*," Debbie pronounced the German word with care. "Now are you happy?"

"*Yah,* I am. And I hope you feel welcome," Paul said, still grinning. "At least I'm doing my part to welcome you by coming out to help unhitch."

"Glad to hear you're *gut* for something," Lois said, sinking in her barb as she handed him the tie rope.

Paul ignored Lois as he clipped on the tie rope and led Buttercup toward the barn.

"I think you blew our young charmer off his feet," Verna whispered to Debbie as the three girls headed toward the house.

"I didn't intend to," Debbie whispered back.

Lois said out of the corner of her mouth, "I think our Paul's taken quite a shine to you."

SEVENTEEN

Some fifty minutes later Debbie sat on a hard, backless bench inside Henry Yoder's house trying to hold still. The service had begun less than an hour ago, but already it felt longer. It wasn't like she hadn't been warned last night about the discomforts of an Amish church service. Lois had made that clear in her description of the three-hour service that went from nine to twelve.

"And doesn't get out one minute before that," Lois had told her with a grim look. And then Lois had asked, "How long do your church services last?"

"It varies," Debbie had mumbled, but Lois hadn't looked convinced. Clearly Lois thought *Englisha* church services lasted a matter of minutes. Which wasn't true, but at least they did sit on padded pews.

Debbie shifted in her seat between Lois and Verna. Ida sat a few girls down and gave her a smile when she glanced that way.

Debbie smiled back but jumped when another song number was hollered out from the other side of the room. That was one thing Lois had failed to mention, but she probably hadn't considered the loud announcement of each song number a thing worthy of report. It was amazing what one became used to — if one were raised with it.

There were also other things she would have to get used to, like the unmarried boys with their smooth chins who sat across the room in long rows. Behind them sat the married men with bearded faces, most of whom made only brief eye contact with her. She was obviously the new girl this morning, and both the married and unmarried males were curious. Most, though, lost interest after the first minutes — except Paul Wagler.

For someone with a reputation as a tease, Paul appeared serious enough. He'd gaze at her intently for long moments, obviously mesmerized with her every move. This she wasn't used to. And it was something Lois hadn't mentioned. How could she? Clearly no one had anticipated that Paul would be so smitten with her. Thankfully, Verna claimed Paul got over girls quickly, so surely she wouldn't have to endure this for more than a few Sundays. As her new person allure wore off, everyone — Paul included — would leave her in peace.

They'd have to, Debbie told herself, because she did want to continue her Amish church attendance. If there had been any doubt in her mind, it had been dispensed with already. The singing had done that. It was magnificent. The sound rose and fell like she imagined the chants of medieval monks did. She'd never heard anything quite like this before. Here a whole group of people — male and female — sang in unison without accompaniment.

Debbie lowered her head and drank in each drawn-out note. The sound seemed to feed her soul, even though the words were in German, and she understood only a few of them. Once she learned the language better, which she would now make a concerted effort to accomplish, the effect would be even more profound. Debbie looked up to see Paul's gaze fixed on her again. He glanced down at his songbook at once. Despite his present interest, Debbie knew his attraction to her would never grow into a deeper relationship even if he wanted it to. She'd been through this before. In his own way, Paul reminded her of Doug though, of course, Paul didn't make phone

208

calls and hadn't begged for dates yet. Paul would get over her soon enough. What she wanted was a relationship that would reach her heart. Someone like Alvin Knepp, who was seated clear over on the other side of the room, might be able to do that. She'd looked forward to seeing him today. Soon after they had walked in this morning, Alvin had glanced at them . . . at Debbie . . . for a moment. A rush of color had run up his neck. He'd looked down at once. He was obviously shy, but he had at least recognized her, Amish dress and all.

The thought sent warm circles around her heart. How wrong of her to have designs on an Amish man she hardly knew, but she couldn't help herself. Bishop Beiler's opinion of her would doubtless falter if he found out. But perhaps it wouldn't. The Amish were quite open about such things, and she did wish to join the faith, didn't she?

Debbie glanced toward Alvin again but couldn't catch his eye. Which was just as good. Being too forward wasn't wise. She would have to remember that. And now that she noticed, the eligible girls around her kept their eyes on their songbooks most of the time. She promptly did the same, but moments later she caught movement in her side vision. Debbie looked up to see a line of men coming down the stairs. As others also noticed, the singing stopped. The ministers were coming back from their morning meeting upstairs, according to what Lois had told her last night. And now the preaching would begin after the men were seated. Lois had said there would first be a short sermon, followed by a scripture reading, and then a much longer sermon.

"No one in the congregation knows which minister will preach before he stands up," Lois had told her. "In fact I don't think the ministers know until they have their little meeting upstairs. It keeps us from depending and leaning too heavily on one man." Lois had pondered that for a moment before she asked, "I suppose your church doesn't do that?" Lois hadn't waited for an answer before she'd gone on to another subject.

The answer would have been a simple one, though, Debbie thought. With only one pastor, there wasn't much question who would preach the Sunday-morning sermon unless a visiting pastor was brought in. And that was usually announced beforehand.

Debbie brought her attention back to the present. The first minister had risen to his feet. Everyone watched his bowed head as he waited for a few seconds before he said anything. Lois had said that unless there were visiting ministers, the responsibilities to preach fell between their two ministers — Ministers Kanagy and Graber — and her *daett*. From Lois's description of the two ministers, this was Minister Graber. He was a well-rounded man of medium height with a high-pitched voice.

Moments later Minister Graber's voice filled the room. Debbie refocused and listened to his lilting tones for over thirty minutes. She could learn to like him, she decided, once she understood German. He sounded serious enough, like there were worthy weighty matters beneath that high-pitched voice of his.

After Minister Graber sat down, Deacon Mast stood up and had the whole congregation stand while he read the scripture. Then a few of the men and a whole line of young boys filed outside.

"The bathroom break," Lois had told her last night.

This had been more information than Debbie had wished for, but Lois hadn't seemed to notice. Everyone talked about such things with great frankness, but Debbie hadn't quite gotten used to it.

Lois had continued. "*Daett* tells the men at the members' meetings to find a way to change their ways if they're going out too often during the scripture reading. At least that's what I've been told."

Debbie had turned red, and Lois had laughed and then said, "Sorry, I didn't mean to embarrass you."

"Just tell me about the rest of the service," Debbie had told her.

Debbie stole another glance across the room toward Alvin. He stood there with his head bowed. He obviously had no plans to leave. Debbie looked away at once. She wouldn't think about such things anymore. Her neck had probably turned red already. Why did Lois have to bring up such subjects anyway? Now she'd think about which of the men left and which didn't every time the scripture reading came.

Deacon Mast finished his reading and closed his Bible. Debbie sat down with everyone else. She caught Paul's gaze on her again and snuck her hand up to rub her neck. As full of himself as Paul was, he would think she was blushing over his look. Sure enough, a pleased look crept across his face. Now she would never hear the end of him. Not if he thought she was smitten with him. Early impressions were difficult to overcome.

Bishop Beiler spoke next, and Debbie

turned her attention toward him. He even had a better voice than he used at home for the scripture readings. He was obviously used to his role and comfortable with public speaking. In her world, Bishop Beiler would have been considered a grand preacher. He might even be in charge of a large church by this point in his career. In the Amish world, Bishop Beiler carried out his duties, and he performed them to the best of his ability with no thought of advancement.

This was a holy calling in every sense of the word, and Debbie liked it that way. It was much better that a man should preach from his heart with all worldly motives removed. As Debbie listened, peace settled on her heart. She could understand Bishop Beiler a little better than the other preachers since she'd been around him for so many years. But there were still many words that made no sense at all. She had much to learn, that was for sure. But she had planned on this, and now it was apparent she'd need to move learning German to a higher priority on her list. The day she could fully understand Bishop Beiler's preaching would be among the happiest days of her life, she was sure. That and when she gained the attention of Alvin.

Debbie kept her eyes on Bishop Beiler

until he brought his sermon to a close almost an hour later. After that there were "testimonies" or "words of agreement" given by several of the men. And the minister who hadn't preached also said a few words. This Lois had all described.

Finally, Bishop Beiler rose to his feet and added his final remarks. Then he sat down and a song was sung. This seemed to take a long time, and then the final dismissal came, along with the rush of the younger children as they dashed outside. Debbie turned completely around for a look at the clock on the living room wall. Lois had been right. It was ten minutes after twelve.

"Are you stiff?" Verna whispered.

"Not really." The truth was that once the preaching had started, she'd been pulled in and there hadn't been time to notice much else.

"Come with me," Verna told her. "I'll have you help me with the tables. Would you like that?"

Debbie beamed. "Yes, of course! I don't know much about cooking though."

Verna laughed. "You don't have to for this. The cooks have the food ready, and all we do is pass it out. Peanut butter bowls, red beets, cheese, coffee, and bread plates. How difficult is that?"

Verna made it sound so simple. There had to be more difficulties involved, but she was still game. What better way to learn to be Amish than to help out where she could?

"We'll stay away from the unmarried boys' table." Verna leaned toward her to whisper, "I don't think you want to face their teasing today."

"I think that would be wise," Debbie whispered back. She did want to see more of Alvin, but now was not the time. He seemed unsure of himself, and with Paul around those feelings wouldn't be helped. She didn't have much experience with insecure men, but she could figure that out. From her point of view Alvin had no reason for his insecurity. Bishop Beiler was his friend, and the community accepted him even with his father's reported poor farming methods. She would have to see what she could do to encourage Alvin.

When they arrived in the kitchen, the younger girls had smaller bowls of peanut butter filled from a larger bowl. They set them on the counter as they finished. In one corner of the kitchen, dishes of red beets, cheese, and jam were also lined up.

"Fill your hands with bowls of food," Verna said as she made her own selections.

Debbie followed her example. With their

hands full, they moved back into the living room where the rows of benches had been turned into tables. This was a simple enough maneuver and ingenious at that. Wooden legs with slots along the top held two benches apiece, which raised them to table height. The women sat at one table and the men across the room at another. Through the bedroom doorway, Debbie noticed smaller versions of similar setups. This was simplicity itself, Debbie thought. She could serve these tables even with her meager cooking skills. Verna hadn't exaggerated in the least.

EIGHTEEN

A little before six o'clock that evening, Debbie stood in a long line of older girls as they moved out of Henry Yoder's living room. The older boys had their own line a few feet away. Everyone chatted with each other as they waited their turn to file past the food laid out on the kitchen counter. Henry Yoder stood in the kitchen doorway. He directed the flow of young people with quick waves of his hand. He appeared pleased as he had all day. It occurred to Debbie that a church event hosted at your house was an enjoyable occasion in Amish life.

"Come on, come on!" Henry said. "The singing starts at seven thirty, and the women still have to clean the dishes."

"Maybe you can help!" one of the boys wisecracked. "Give them dainty hands of yours the treatment they deserve."

In the midst of the laughter, Henry lifted

his hands to peer at them. A look of horror crossed his face. "I do declare, they've been well kept."

Debbie laughed along with the rest. It was obvious Henry's hands were callused, which was the real reason he had lifted them up so high — to display what he had.

"He's a real show-off," Verna whispered to Debbie as the two lines inched forward.

"That's what I thought," Debbie whispered back.

"He's also the one who got Joe in trouble." Verna's face darkened.

Debbie leaned toward Verna. "Joe will get over it soon. Don't worry."

Verna face brightened. "Have you heard something?"

Debbie shook her head. "I just know you're decent, Verna. Of course Joe will be back!"

"Oh . . ." Verna didn't appear convinced.

Debbie wasn't all that confident herself. But Verna was nice and decent, so why shouldn't Joe come back? It seemed a safe guess. Plus Verna needed encouragement, even if the matter went south later. If Verna's confidence was kept high, she'd be more attractive to the next boy who paid her attention.

"Howdy there!" A familiar voice interrupted Debbie's thoughts. She hadn't noticed that the girls line moved slower than the boys'. Paul must have crept up on her while she looked elsewhere.

"Good evening," Debbie returned, giving Paul only the briefest of glances.

He grinned broadly. "What's wrong? Have a rough afternoon?"

"No!" Debbie glared at him now, which produced chuckles from the boys around him. Obviously they were used to Paul's teasing the marriageable girls and felt no shame when they enjoyed the humor along with him.

"I thought you might have missed your beauty sleep worrying about me." Paul smiled.

He'd obviously just warmed up on the first round, Debbie realized. She wanted to shoot something smart back at him, like *I'd forgotten you existed* or *What did you say your name was?* but that would only make things worse. She smiled sweetly instead and said, "Are you saying I need more beauty sleep?"

"Oh, now that was *gut!*" came from several of the young men in line. One of them added, "That's giving it back."

They all looked pleased at Debbie's retort. Apparently not many Amish girls dared give

219

Paul back what he dished out.

Debbie decided she'd need to remember that in the future.

Paul just grinned as the others chuckled around him. They all knew she'd bested him at his own game.

She had to admit Paul recovered himself well.

Before either of them could interact more, the food line moved forward. Debbie filled her plate from one side of the table, and Paul stood across from her and piled food on his plate. He paused and asked conversationally, "How's life at the Beilers' place going?"

Debbie stole a glance at his face. He appeared serious enough, and the teasing look was gone. Maybe Paul did know how to carry on a decent conversation. "I love it," she said. "They're the most wonderful people."

Paul caught sight of Verna standing behind Debbie. He quipped, "I heard the bishop's daughters are all top of the line. So you're in *gut* company, I'd say."

"You don't have to waste your words on me," Verna shot back.

Paul laughed and slapped his free hand on his chest. "She wounds my soul. There's nothing like the barb of a bishop's daughter to tear the heart to pieces."

Verna joined in the laughter with everyone around her, but Debbie sensed a sadness about her eyes. Her state as a bishop's daughter wasn't exactly an accomplishment in Verna's estimation. Not with what she'd gone through already.

Debbie turned to give Verna a sympathetic look as they left the food table. *Dear God,* Debbie prayed silently, *help Verna's heart heal from her hurt. Allow Joe to see what a wonderful person she really is.* She turned and headed toward the kitchen doorway but stopped short at the sight of Alvin still in the line. Her abrupt halt sent a splash of gravy on her plate into the air. It landed with a soft splat on the hardwood floor. Behind her, Verna gasped. Debbie groaned. What a clumsy move — and at her first Amish Sunday-evening supper and hymn singing! First impressions were hard to overcome. Now she'd always be the "gravy spiller" in the eyes of the people here . . . or perhaps even worse. The gravy had landed not a foot from Alvin's black shoes.

Alvin had rushed forward and was on his knees wiping up the dark liquid with a towel someone had handed him. Amish people were the model of efficiency, Debbie thought as she set her plate aside. She protested, "Here, Alvin, give me the towel and let me clean that up."

He glanced up with a shy look. "I've just about got it."

"I can finish. Please, it was my fault."

He surrendered the towel, and stood up. Debbie dropped down and wiped up the remainder of the gravy before she glanced up at him. "I'm so sorry. I'm not usually this clumsy."

"It happens to everyone," he said and moved on with the food line.

Surely Alvin didn't despise her? His smile had been weak but genuine enough. And he didn't seem like a person who faked things. Not like Paul. And he had helped her.

"Here, I'll take the towel." Verna's voice interrupted Debbie's thoughts. "And get up off the floor. We're holding up traffic."

Debbie handed Verna the towel and scrambled to one side before she stood. That wasn't the smartest action either. She shouldn't scoot sideways like a crab. The older girls who were going past gave her kind looks. One of them even asked, "Are you okay?"

"Yes, thank you," Debbie whispered as she retrieved her plate. She waited a second for Verna to return from where she'd dropped off the towel. One thing she could be thankful for — Henry Yoder hadn't been around to witness this debacle. Where he'd gone, she hadn't noticed, but he would have waved his arms around, no doubt, and added to her discomfort.

She glanced back and saw Alvin staring at Paul, who was deep in laughter at some joke. The thought raced through Debbie's mind that Alvin must have seen the exchange between Paul and her earlier. Their words and laughter had been perfectly harmless, but they might not appear so to Alvin. He didn't come from her world where young men and young women freely conversed without significance attached. And Alvin knew of Paul's reputation. No doubt it looked as if she were the latest in a long list of Paul's conquests.

But none of that was true. Debbie had simply been herself when confronted by a man of Paul's nature. She wanted to rush after Alvin and explain. She wanted to tell him that he had no need for worry, that she found him a whole lot more attractive than Paul. But with Amish people, that would likely be the wrong approach. Women didn't assert themselves in such a fashion. No, she would have to exercise traits she hadn't known much of in her life — patience, prayer, and submission to the will of God.

Here these were needed in strong doses.

"Are you all right?" Verna asked, as she appeared in front of Debbie.

Debbie sighed. "I guess so."

Verna appeared amused. "It wasn't that bad, Debbie. Don't look like you've lost your best friend over a little accident. It could have happened to anyone."

It's Alvin, not the gravy, she wanted to say, but she didn't. Some things were best left unsaid. She followed Verna to the table for the older, unmarried girls. After they sat down, Debbie took a few bites and glanced around. Another thought occurred to her. She hadn't seen Joe all evening.

Debbie leaned toward Verna. "Where's Joe?"

Quickly tears sprang to Verna's eyes, but she brushed them away. "He's coming later . . . I hope."

"Oh, Verna!" Debbie said, watching as Verna struggled to keep her emotions in check. What could this mean? Why wasn't Joe here? It had to be pretty serious from the little Debbie knew about church attendance. But maybe Verna was right, and Joe would come later. She reached under the table to give Verna's hand a quick squeeze, and her friend rewarded her with a grateful smile.

Ida and Lois, who were with another group of girls across the room, came over when they were finished eating. They pulled chairs up behind Verna and Debbie.

"That was so hilarious!" Lois teased. "Your spilling gravy across the floor, I mean. I thought I'd never stop laughing."

Debbie glared at her. "Embarrassing, that's what it was. And you can stop laughing."

"I saw Alvin rush to your rescue," Ida said. "Is there something you want to tell us?"

Debbie tried to keep the heat from her face. "That's only because I almost covered his pant legs and shoes with slimy gravy."

"That's right!" Lois tried to control her giggles. "And Alvin rushed right out of line . . ."

"Girls, come on!" Verna spoke up. "You're making a big deal out of nothing."

Ida gave Debbie a quick glance. "I'm sorry. I didn't mean to imply anything."

Maybe it was dishonest of her, but Debbie couldn't admit her attraction to Alvin right here in front of everyone. Yet if she left Ida under the wrong impression, that wasn't an option either. Good old Amish honesty had apparently taken hold of her conscience.

Neither Verna nor Lois appeared to have

noticed her silence. They talked on about Joe's absence and Verna's hope that he would soon arrive. Ida, though, had noticed Debbie's hesitation. She waited with an expectant look.

"There *is* something to it," Debbie finally whispered in Ida's ear. "I . . ."

Ida squeezed her hand. "You don't have to say anything more, Debbie. I understand. Your secret is safe with me."

"Thank you," Debbie croaked out.

Lois glanced at them. "What are you two whispering about?"

"Secrets." Ida smiled sweetly.

"Then you have to tell me!" Lois demanded.

Ida settled into a painful silence. It was up to Debbie to throw Lois off the scent. She leaned toward Lois and whispered, "I think Alvin Knepp is cute."

Lois giggled. "Then you ought to swoon with all the attention Paul shows you."

"Don't worry, I'll leave him for you," Debbie teased.

Lois laughed and appeared satisfied.

Ida sent Debbie a grateful look as Henry Yoder made his appearance, once again his arms waving. "Okay! It's time to get busy. If the girls will get started on the dishes, the boys can help me set up benches in here."

226

Loud hollers of "We're already busy" came from the boys' side of the table, followed by some smart aleck who produced even louder laughter with his remark, "I think the boys should manage the kitchen."

One of the girls retorted, "You wouldn't know how to wash a plate, let alone show someone else how."

Debbie joined in the laughter as everyone got to their feet. She followed the Beiler girls out to the kitchen. With the large number of girls present, they could hardly fit into the room, let alone all find work. Debbie managed to grab one plate and dry it with the tail end of a towel Lois had in her hand. They leaned against each other and gave in to the giggles. No one noticed in the press of the crowd. The stress of her first full day of Amish church services had gotten to her, Debbie told herself.

The work was almost completed when Henry appeared again. "Time to get going, girls! Almost seven-thirty."

The crowd began to move, and Debbie stayed close to Lois as they filed into the reordered living room. The benches had been set up again in close imitation of the morning's church service positions, this time with one aisle down the middle. On one side the unmarried boys were already seated, facing the unmarried girls. Debbie rushed toward the back and found a seat still empty in the third row. If she'd sat on the front bench where Paul could watch her unhindered, that would have been a little much, though most of the other girls didn't seem to mind the seats further up. She would get used to this eventually, she told herself. One couldn't hide out in the third row forever.

Debbie snuck a glance between the shoulders of the girls in front of her. Sure enough, Paul was looking her way. She gave him a sweet smile. That probably wasn't very wise, she thought, but she figured he deserved the same medicine he dished out. It might confuse him or make him grow up. Debbie glanced further down the rows of unmarried men, but there was no sign of Joe. Poor Verna! Her heart would bleed tonight. She must remember to give her friend an extra-tight hug once they arrived home.

Debbie's attention was brought back to the hymn singing when someone hollered out a number from the front row of the boys' section. The singing began at once. These were faster tunes, she noticed, and she joined in as much as she could. She would enjoy every moment of the evening with such beautiful melodies. Indeed, this day had been a blessed one. It wouldn't be long now until she found her place fully among these wonderful people.

NINETEEN

Almost three weeks later, on a Saturday morning, the first day of summer heat had moved in. Bishop Beiler stood in the barn and threw the harness on Milo. His face was drawn in grim lines. The report he'd heard last Sunday from Deacon Mast hadn't been good, and he'd dreaded this trip all week. He should have gone to visit Henry Yoder on Monday night, but he had put it off until the last minute. Perhaps some vain hope still floated around in his heart that Deacon Mast's buggy would appear at any moment with news that this trip wouldn't be necessary.

But that hadn't happened. The matter with Henry was beyond Deacon Mast's duties anyway. The deacon usually spoke with erring members who had committed first transgressions and perhaps a second. When the problem persisted, as it did in Henry's case, this added great gravity to the matter so the bishop must get involved.

Bishop Beiler groaned at the thought. Why was the man so stubborn? After the stern warning given at Henry's last confession, surely he would have learned. But that apparently wasn't the case. At least not with the account Deacon Mast had given at the last Sunday-morning minister's meeting. Henry Yoder had moved well beyond using his neighbor's tractor for field work. It was said that he'd purchased a tractor for himself — a tractor with rubber tires still mounted on it.

Deacon Mast claimed a solid report had come in on the matter from a very reliable source. After he'd heard who had given the report, Bishop Beiler agreed. Amos Shirk's wife, Rhonda, rarely got things wrong. The woman had the sharpest eyes in the community when it came to *Ordnung* transgressors. She also had the close ear of Deacon Mast since she was his aunt. Coupled with the stable constitution of her husband, Amos, who made sure Rhonda kept a level head on herself, any report coming from the Shirk household rarely proved false. And Rhonda said she'd come home late one night from town and saw Henry cutting his hay with his new rubber-tired tractor.

Bishop Beiler sighed. And here he'd

thought things were going so well these past few weeks. The *Englisha* girl, Debbie, had settled in and was now attending the services on Sundays — and wearing Amish dress at that. The rest of the time Debbie wore *Englisha* clothing and her car still sat behind the barn at night. Those weren't *gut* things, but Debbie had brought a great peace to the household by the influence she had on Lois. There could be no other explanation for Lois's change of attitude. It had been more than two weeks now since she'd said anything about her desire to jump the fence into the awful world that lay out there.

One could almost call the past few weeks peaceful, Bishop Beiler thought as he pushed open the barn door. A bishop's life was never quite at that state; there was always some wrong that stirred or was about to. Though he might have become a little jumpy in his years as bishop, Adam was reminded by his *frau* often that "*Da Hah* will take care of things." Saloma would say, "Isn't that what you preach Sundays in your sermons?"

Yah, he admitted to himself. It was so. But the practice of a thing was always harder than it was to preach it, and right now everything appeared a burden. Perhaps if he got this Yoder matter off his mind, the next Sunday services would be a joy instead of further dread. But what if all that was said about Henry were true? Or even worse, what if it were true and Henry refused to repent? The bishop would only have a bad report to give at the next ministers' meeting, which would mean more talk, a late start to the church service, and things would get worse from there. Bishop Beiler jerked on the halter, signaling Milo to move forward through the barn door. Why couldn't people stay inside the fence established by the *Ordnung*? Instead they saw supposedly greener blades of grass on the other side. This grass always proved to be the same old grass that grew inside the fence. The bishop had preached and preached this truth, and everyone agreed in theory. But then it happened again. He supposed if it hadn't been Henry this time, someone else would have taken it on him- or herself to cause trouble.

Bishop Beiler hitched Milo to the buggy and drove out of the driveway. Saloma appeared for a brief moment in the doorway and gave him a little wave. He waved back. She was a *gut frau,* there was no doubt about that. He couldn't carry this load without her. But then *Da Hah* never gave a burden without the means to bear it. He would have to keep this in mind when it came to Henry Yoder.

Milo's hooves set up a steady clip on the road, and a dark cloud settled over Bishop Beiler's mind as he drove along. He'd known it was there for some time, but it was the drive over to the Yoders' place that made it seem worse. And then there was Verna's continued trouble with Joe Weaver. His daughter still mourned the boy's leaving. Her fear that Joe would never come back was unfounded, he told himself. He'd made it clear that Verna had no hand in the disclosure of the driving transgression. Surely Joe was just taking his time about the matter. And that showed depth of character in the bishop's opinion.

This wasn't Verna's opinion, though. He did declare, that girl moped around the house on Sundays in an almost indecent manner. Before long he would have to speak with her again about it, but so far his heart wasn't in the rebuke. He'd been partly to blame about this trouble. Well, Henry Yoder and himself.

Maybe the entire situation had only shown Joe what it would be like to marry into a bishop's family. He might have second thoughts about marriage into a family that had to place church work above other considerations.

Bishop Beiler gently slapped the reins against Milo's back, encouraging him on. Joe Weaver wasn't that great a loss, but that wasn't something a father told his daughter when she was still grieving over the situation. Joe wasn't that bad a choice as a son-in-law either. His former girlfriend, Rosy, obviously had some complaint against him, but the bishop had never been able to find out exactly what. Maybe the girl simply found a better option in someone else. And that was what he wished Verna would do. But she clearly had no plans other than Joe, so he'd better work with the girl if he could. And it was true what Verna had said. She was over twenty-four now, and every month her chances of marriage to a decent man in their community dwindled. And Ida was in much the same shape, but she didn't seem as worried.

On the other hand, either girl might succeed with one of the community's widowers in the years ahead. That wasn't a bad option. He would actually prefer it over a greenhorn who had never been married. But most young women didn't look at things that way. They wanted a man's heart first, rather than get one secondhand. And he couldn't blame them for the sentiment.

Saloma likely had been of the same mind.

The bishop neared Henry's place, and Milo neighed to several of his horses grazing in the field. The sound brought the bishop out of his thoughts. He tightened the reins and steered the buggy into the driveway. Henry's smiling face appeared in the barn doorway before Milo came to a stop.

"The bishop himself!" Henry said. "Don't you have a deacon anymore?"

"Seems you know you're needing one," Bishop Beiler replied as he climbed down to tie Milo to the hitching post.

Henry's pleased look never dimmed. "I've been behaving myself tolerable, I think."

"I guess we'll see about that." Bishop Beiler pasted a pleasant expression on his face. "Have you time for a little talking? Perhaps in the barn where we can sit on a hay bale?"

"This looks like a right smart spot to me." Henry leaned against the buggy wheel. "I can't imagine what there is to say unless Joe Weaver's been driving *Englisha* vehicles again."

The man has his gall, Bishop Beiler thought. He swallowed. "Joe's been behaving himself — at least from what I know. That isn't the report I've been hearing about you though."

"Ach." Henry twirled his straw hat in his hands. "You know how people talk. It's mostly hot air, I suppose . . . whatever it is you've been hearing."

"Seems like you can't stay off rubber-tired tractors, I'm told. Done bought your own — with rubber still on it."

"Now that's a nasty thing to be saying around." Henry didn't appear happy in the least. "I wish people would mind their own business like *Da Hah* tells them to. Isn't that in the scriptures somewhere? I think Deacon Mast just read it in church last Sunday."

The bishop hid a smile. "It may be, Henry. But that's not the point we're discussing. We're talking about you now. About how you're behaving yourself."

"Okay . . ." Henry seemed to ponder the point for a moment. "I will confess I did buy a new tractor, but there's nothing indecent about that. Come see for yourself." Henry waved his hand to the side and led the way to the barn door.

Owning a new tractor was within the rules of the *Ordnung,* Bishop Beiler thought, so why had Henry wanted to speak outside all this time? He was hiding something.

Henry pushed open the barn door and said with a flourish, "See! Brand-new but perfectly within the *Ordnung.*"

Bishop Beiler walked up and ran his hand over the steel-rimmed tires on the back of the tractor. "It does look like it, and, *yah,* it is brand-new. And you sure couldn't be working in the fields with these magnificent steel wheels."

Where Henry had gotten the steel rims was hard to tell. These had to be custom made for such a new tractor model. Most of the Amish purchased the oldest tractors they could find for that very reason.

Henry didn't appear pleased at the bishop's detailed inspection. "I got a lot of money in the thing, but it's what I wanted."

Bishop Beiler met his gaze. "I'm sure it came with rubber tires when you bought it. Did those stay at the dealer?"

Henry didn't say anything, which didn't surprise the Bishop at all. He sighed inwardly. He was too old for this kind of work. That was the reason deacons were assigned to tasks like this. They could best ferret out this kind of maneuvering. The bishop was sure Henry had used the rubber tires and now had them hidden somewhere with plans to get more use out of them later. That was the only scenario that made sense. The bishop looked around and then walked over to a dark corner of the barn. He poked around a pile of gunny bags with his foot. A huge rubber tire appeared, followed by another one. He turned and faced Henry. "Would these be the ones you were seen using the other day?"

"I'm taking them back to the dealer," Henry said at once. "I had to bring the tractor home. I switched the tires for the steel rims when I got it home last week."

"Which means you got a little use in while you had the chance. And the tires are still here. I'm disappointed in you, Henry. You know better than this."

Henry sputtered. "Okay! I took it for a few rounds in the field with the regular tires, that's all. But that shouldn't be a huge matter of concern."

Bishop Beiler sighed aloud this time. "You will take the tractor and the tires back to the dealer. This temptation is too much for you, Henry. Do that and we'll settle for another church confession — but on your knees this time."

"Surely not, Bishop Beiler!" Henry appeared shaken. "I can't do that . . . really!"

"I will consult with the other ministers before making a final decision, of course," Bishop Beiler said. He saw a look of hope flash on Henry's face. "Henry, they'll probably think I'm going too easy on you even with those two conditions."

Henry scowled. "I find neither of those terms acceptable, Bishop. A man should not be blamed when he drives his new tractor around the field a few times before he changes the tires."

It was more than a few times, based on Rhonda's report, but the bishop didn't want to say anything that might reveal his source of information. He shook his head. "Think about it, Henry. I'll consult the others, but you'd better plan on taking that tractor back."

Henry said nothing but looked quite glum as Bishop Beiler turned and went outside.

He hoped Henry would see the sense in his punishment. One thing was certain — the ministry couldn't allow a brand-new tractor that could use rubber tires to be in the hands of someone with the problem Henry had. It would turn into a merry chase trying to keep the *verboten* tires out of Henry's reach. And who needed those kinds of games? His bishopric would turn into the laughingstock of the Amish world.

He reached the hitching post, untied Milo, and climbed into the buggy. Swinging Milo around in the lane with a smart slap with the lines, Bishop Beiler sighed again. His Saturday church work should be done now, but it wasn't. That much was clear. Henry hadn't taken the rebuke well. So now the bishop wouldn't be returning home to think peaceful thoughts for the rest of the evening. Rather he'd be remembering Henry's scowl and probably lie awake half the night concerned about what was going to happen.

Surely Henry had no plans to flaunt the *Ordnung* outright, did he? There was not a member in the community who would vote to overlook such action. They knew everyone had to obey the rules or no one would. What course did Henry have but to obey? None that were acceptable, the bishop thought. He'd bring the matter up in the next ministers' meeting. They would agree to an action, inform Henry, and then wait. Maybe a little time would soften Henry's resolve so he could accept the correction. It often worked that way with members who transgressed. If they were pushed too hard, nasty things could happen. Things no bishop wanted to consider for his people. All around them were liberal churches just waiting to snatch up any dissatisfied members of his flock. They wouldn't get a chance with Henry if the bishop could prevent it. And yet some kind of repentance on Henry's part was necessary. He'd have to bend the knee this time. In his heart first, followed by a confession in front of the church. There was no other way to maintain discipline and help Henry.

Bishop Beiler urged Milo on. Now that he'd made up his mind, a level of peace flooded his heart. He would take the rest of the day off once he arrived home. He'd read scripture for the possible preaching of the Word at the next Sunday service. Saloma or one of the girls might even bring him a glass of apple cider from the stock they had stashed in the basement. *Da Hah* had blessed them with great bounty last year.

"Get up, Milo!" he hollered out the windshield before he settled comfortably into the buggy seat for the ride home.

TWENTY

The following morning Bishop Beiler sat in his rocker as the early sunlight flooded into the living room. The words in his open Bible ran together as his thoughts wandered. It wasn't a pleasant task that lay before him. Even after much thought, something about Henry's attitude was still troublesome. This situation seemed like more than the normal rebellious streak that often seized an erring member and lasted for a short season. This might turn into more of a difficult case than what it already was. Perhaps he should back down from his threat of a knee confession. Such extreme humiliation on the part of a member in front of the whole church was always an unfortunate occasion and disliked by everyone. Henry considered himself a man of moderate esteem in the community, and such an action would affect him deeply.

That was the problem with men who thought themselves better than others,

Bishop Beiler told himself. He rocked while he considered the matter. *Nee,* Henry had been warned. And the bishop had already taken a risk when he'd suggested and the ministers had agreed to involve the *Englisha* neighbor the last time they'd dealt with this. Henry had been given his chance, and he'd chosen to go around the barriers set up for his own protection. There was no option but to proceed as planned. The bishop focused on the page in front of him, but he glanced up when Verna tiptoed in.

"Do you have a moment, *Daett*?"

He closed his Bible at once. "Why, of course, Verna. For my eldest daughter, I will always take the time."

Verna shifted nervously on her feet, and he motioned for her to sit. He figured he already knew what the problem was. Verna's dark countenance had hung over the house all morning again, even with her best efforts to hide it. She likely knew by now the reason for his trip to Henry's place yesterday. Her worry that Joe Weaver would never come back had increased, he was sure.

Verna made no attempt to hide her concern. "Will Henry Yoder be under discipline again?"

Bishop Beiler cleared his throat. "I went to visit him yesterday, but beyond that it might be best if church matters were not discussed at home. Let me assure you, though, that Joe's name was not mentioned."

"So this time it has nothing to do with him?" Verna's face brightened considerably.

Bishop Beiler nodded. "This time Joe is out of it."

"And you are sure?" she asked, her eyebrows raised.

Bishop Beiler was silent. The way she asked the question made him hesitate. Did he know everything? Maybe Henry had more tricks up his sleeve and hadn't revealed them ahead of time.

"I believe so, Verna," he finally said.

She struggled to keep the look of despair off her face. "I hope so because I do so miss him, *Daett.*"

You haven't even dated him that long, he wanted to say . . . but he didn't. His daughter's heart had obviously settled on the boy. It would be best if he refrained from negative comments. She could do much worse, he supposed. "Perhaps Joe will come back soon," he said. He touched her hand and spoke with great tenderness. "*Da Hah*'s work must be done, Verna. Let us pray that Joe will not see things in the wrong way, shall we?"

Verna nodded and bowed her head as her *daett* prayed. A moment after his "Amen," she was gone.

Bishop Beiler sighed. This was too much for one man. He shouldn't have to lead the church and raise a family at the same time. The lot of bishop should only fall on old men whose children were solidly in the faith and safely married. Was that not the scriptural recommendation on the matter? And yet these were wishful thoughts. Since the days of bitter persecution endured in Switzerland, the members of the faith had decided that a martyred minister must be replaced immediately. And most of the movement's adherents in those days were young. There had been no other option, and now tradition had settled in. *Da Hah* chose whom He willed, and He gave the man the grace to carry the load. Somewhere there was aid for him, he decided — if he would only believe.

He tried to focus again. He stared at his Bible as the bustle of the house continued around him. All he could see, though, was the smiling face of Henry Yoder as he stood outside his barn yesterday. Against that backdrop lay the upcoming ministers' meeting at Cousin Benny's place.

"Isn't it time you get ready for the ser-vices?"

Saloma's voice made him jump. "*Yah,* it is." He laid his Bible aside. "The time was getting away from me."

"The girls have already gone," she told him. "We must not be late."

The house had grown quiet but he hadn't noticed. He rushed to change into his Sunday clothing. He'd harnessed Milo when he did morning chores, so the horse was ready and waiting inside his stall. They wouldn't be late.

"I'll have the horse up in a minute," he muttered after he came out of the bedroom. He grabbed his black felt hat and sprinted out the door.

Saloma was waiting for him beside the buggy when he came out of the barn with Milo. She held up the shafts, and they had Milo's harness attached in minutes. Saloma climbed into the buggy. He threw his wife the lines and climbed in himself. The bishop took the reins and hollered, "Get up!" Milo twitched his ears and took off with a leap. Soon he settled into a steady trot. Around them, others joined in, making a procession all headed to the same place.

"Debbie's sure a blessing at the house," Saloma ventured. "She's so taken with our way of life. She loves the place, and her words to Lois are like those of *Da Hah* speaking right through her."

The bishop listened as he drove. Saloma probably thought he needed encouragement this morning, what with his spirits so low over Henry Yoder's case.

"She baked her first loaf of bread Saturday," Saloma continued. "With Lois helping her, of course."

"That's *gut.*"

"She's touching Lois's heart deeply. I don't know what we'd do without her."

"*Yah.* I was thinking on that the other morning. I keep forgetting the *gut* things we do have — what with Verna's sorrow hanging over us. Did you hear her speak with me this morning? I'm afraid I had nothing wise to share with her."

"We can only pray." Saloma's hand found his and squeezed. She didn't do that often anymore, but they were not too old for love. That he also forgot sometimes. Now that he thought of it, he hadn't kissed her in a long time.

"What are you thinking, Adam?" she asked teasingly.

He noticed her eyes were twinkling when he glanced at her. Saloma knew *gut* and well what he was thinking. And she was pleased to have distracted him from his worries. But it would not do to pull into the meeting place while he was thinking of kisses — even if they were with his own *frau.*

"You're sweet!" he told her. "And you know what I'm thinking."

She squeezed his arm as they turned into Benny Beiler's lane. He pulled to a stop at the end of the walk.

"You look handsome this morning," she said as she climbed out of the buggy. She paused to send an adoring look up at him.

Pretty soon he would blush like a young bridegroom, he thought. But she did know what needed saying to lighten his load. He sobered as he pulled forward and came to a stop beside the line of buggies. Several of the younger boys ran up to help him un- hitch.

"*Gut* morning, Bishop," they sang out, their cheeks rosy.

"Have you been playing in the barn and falling down the haymow?" he teased.

"Oh, *nee*!" Their faces were horror stricken. "*Daett* won't let us play anywhere on Sunday mornings except behind the buggies. We might tear our clothing."

"I think that's a *gut* idea," Bishop Beiler told them as he led Milo forward while two boys held the buggy shafts. They lowered them to the ground with a flourish. *They are the hope of the church,* the bishop thought as he led Milo away. This was the young blood that grew up right under the adults' noses. And often the boys didn't receive the notice and thanks they deserved. He was glad they felt comfortable enough to help him unhitch. And they had even called him bishop! Perhaps he wasn't doing everything wrong as he clutched at the helm of the church. He led Milo into the barn.

After tying the horse among the other ones, the bishop went outside and greeted the line of men gathered beside the barn. He shook their hands and said, "*Gut* morning." He made sure Henry Yoder got an extra hearty handshake. At the end of the line he took his place and pulled his pocket watch out. There were still a few minutes before it was time for the morning's trek inside. Saloma had been correct when she hurried him along though. A bishop who arrived late for the service was not setting a *gut* example.

Beside him Minister Graber asked in his high-pitched voice, "How's your first cutting of hay coming along?"

"Didn't dare try it last week." Bishop Beiler chuckled. " 'Rain's threatening,' I thought, and Emery agreed. Don't tell me

250

yours is in."

Minister Graber tucked his overflowing stomach inside his britches. "I'm afraid so. Though it did catch a shower right after the cutting, but we should be okay."

Minister Kanagy leaned forward with a grin. "Next time check the barometer before you cut hay. She was a-goin' down last week."

They all laughed. Minister Graber's aversion to the commonly used barometers was well known. He declared his nose a better indicator of weather than that *Englisha* invention.

Bishop Beiler pulled out his watch again. "Well, we'd best be going on in."

The others nodded and followed him at a slow walk toward the house. Behind him the men fell in line by age. They jostled playfully when things got mixed up. The mood was *gut* this morning, Bishop Beiler thought. Henry Yoder must not have run his mouth yet. Maybe he hoped if he kept a low profile the matter would blow over.

He forced his thoughts back to the present and took a detour through the kitchen. There he shook a few of the women's hands. The other ministers followed his example, but the other men and the boys had split off and gone into the living room. By the time the bishop took his place up front, the benches on the male side were full.

The women soon filed in, followed by the unmarried girls, and then the younger girls. When everyone was seated, the first song number was hollered out. Bishop Beiler stood at the first note and led the ministers upstairs. Now that the moment had arrived, his thoughts weren't quite as dark. Perhaps *Da Hah* was already giving His grace to bear the duty of the moment.

He opened the first bedroom door he came to and found a row of chairs set up. The others sat down when he took his place. Deacon Mast closed the door with a soft click, and Bishop Beiler cleared his throat. "*Gut* morning again. *Da Hah* has given us a fresh day in which His work can be done. We must remember to always give thanks for the gifts from His hand. So why don't we pray first?"

They bowed their heads as he led out, "Now unto You, most gracious heavenly Father, we give thanks. For Your goodness, for Your grace, and for Your Son, Jesus Christ, who came to this earth as a child to die for our sins. Help us today, O Lord. Give us wisdom as we seek Your will. Enlighten our hearts with Your Holy Spirit. Amen."

Bishop Beiler glanced around the room, but no one looked at him. The men kept their eyes focused on the floor. They must know he didn't have *gut* news to share, he thought. "I was over to Henry's place yesterday, and it didn't go that well, I'm afraid. Henry has purchased a new tractor — a brand-shiny-new one."

"Surely he had the dealer change the tires?" Minister Kanagy said hopefully.

"*Yah,* Henry knows that much," Minister Graber said and nodded his head.

Bishop Beiler sighed. "No, he didn't. Rhonda spotted him working in the fields with the rubber tires still on. He did have them changed when I got there, but he had them hidden under feed bags in his barn."

"Now I've heard everything!" Deacon Mast exclaimed.

Minister Graber squeaked, "Has Henry admitted to this?"

Bishop Beiler nodded. "In so many words, *yah.*"

"I would still wish to speak with Henry myself," Minister Graber said, shifting on his chair.

"That's fine with me," Bishop Beiler told him. "I'm not planning to move too fast on this matter, but we can't leave it unattended either. If any of the others wish to make a visit over to Henry's place, by all means do so. Perhaps you can talk sense into his head. In the meantime, I told him I would settle for a knee confession and the tractor returned to the dealer. Henry doesn't need a nice new one that can use rubber tires with the problem he has." No one disagreed with him, so that was *gut.* Now it was just a matter of time, and he could wait. "We will speak more about this in a few weeks then. In the meantime, I hope Henry sees the error of his ways. But he can't continue like he is — breaking the *Ordnung* regularly."

They all nodded in full agreement. Indeed, this was something the bishop could be thankful for. Either of these ministers or the deacon could make trouble if they took Henry's part. But they didn't, and they understood what should be done.

"Let us move on then with any other issues we may have," Bishop Beiler directed.

The rise and fall of their voices continued.

TWENTY-ONE

Late that afternoon, Verna and Debbie drove Buttercup toward Cousin Benny Beiler's place, headed back for the Sunday evening hymn singing. The sound of other horses' hooves beating the pavement filled the air around them, and the peacefulness of the evening hung in the air. Verna was in a particularly lighthearted mood. This morning she'd caught a glimpse of Joe's *gut* heart, and now, for once, she could look forward to both the supper and the hymn singing. It wasn't like last Sunday when her spirits had failed her so she'd stayed home.

"He might be there this evening," Debbie commented, as if reading Verna's thoughts.

"He might!" Verna agreed as she allowed hope to rise in her heart again.

Daett had preached this morning about Noah and the flood. He'd explained how *Da Hah* had directed Noah to prepare a boat that saved his whole family. She hadn't paid much attention to her *daett*'s words as she darted quick glances at Joe. He wouldn't look back at her, and that had discouraged her. His face appeared so troubled but still strong.

It was in the last part of *Daett*'s sermon, when her heart had sunk the lowest, that she had seen things plain as day. Joe regretted their broken relationship just like she did. He wished things hadn't turned out the way they had, but because of his pain he was afraid to risk seeing her again.

This was like a light sent from *Da Hah* straight into her heart. Now she could hope again. Even if she couldn't do much else, she would stay the course. She would give Joe the attention he needed whenever possible and leave her heart open. Joe would return! Like a flower to the bee, so her love was to him. She'd almost laughed out loud in the middle of the service at this insight but pinched herself to stop just in time.

Verna had served the unmarried boys' table afterward filled with the joy of her discovery. She'd hoped Joe would at least open up enough to give her one little smile. Instead, he'd focused all his attention on his food — even when the whole room roared over one of Paul Wagler's jokes.

Joe would come around, Verna told herself. She hadn't imagined the hope that had come to her during *Daett*'s sermon. *Da Hah* had sent those thoughts to her. They had come like Noah's boat so she wouldn't sink under the waves. She wouldn't let go of this hope until Joe came around or dashed her heart against the rocks by dating another girl. But Joe would never do that! He couldn't! He loved her! Verna was certain of that.

Debbie's soft touch came on her arm. "You seem troubled, Verna."

"Oh *nee*, I'm happy!" She clucked to Buttercup to keep up the pace.

Debbie looked at her with skepticism.

Verna giggled. "I guess my nerves have been a little shot at times. That's all."

Debbie squeezed her arm. "You worry me, Verna. There are doctors who can help, you know. You don't have to be ashamed of accepting aid."

"I'm okay, Debbie." Verna gathered herself together. "This is almost over. I'm sure of it."

"Verna, please . . ." Debbie clutched her arm.

Verna shook her head. "Joe will come around soon. That's what I'm trying to say. I feel it so very strongly."

"Woman's intuition?" Debbie still looked

skeptical but less worried now.

"I guess so. I was thinking about Joe at the service this morning. He has a heart of gold. It's broken right now, but he's every bit the treasure I think he is."

"Okay . . ." Debbie settled back in the seat. "But you can talk to me if things get any worse."

Verna nodded and pulled into Cousin Benny's driveway. She drove past the house to park beside the barn. A few boys lingered in the yard and glanced their way.

"Looks like we might get some help," Verna said.

Debbie whispered from the other side of the buggy. "He's coming from the barn. Don't look."

Verna froze. Had she heard Debbie correctly? There was only one man to whom Debbie would refer in that tone. "What am I supposed to do?" she asked.

"I don't know," Debbie said, "but I'm getting out now. This is your moment, Verna."

Debbie climbed down from the buggy and smiled her brightest. "Hi, Joe."

He returned the greeting and slowed his pace as he approached the buggy.

Debbie gave a little wave to Verna and made a dash for the house.

Verna tried to calm her heart as she

caught the first glimpse of Joe as he came around the side of the buggy. She waited, unable to move as first Joe's hands appeared on the buggy door, followed by his upturned face.

"*Gut* evening," he said.

Verna forced a nervous smile. "*Gut* evening. How are you?"

"I'm fine, I suppose," he said. He paused before starting up again. "Verna, I'm sorry for the way I've been acting." He glanced at the ground, momentarily tongue-tied. His hat was shielding his face.

Verna wanted to reach out and hug him, to do anything but sit here and not move, but she didn't dare. She saw his heart again like she had this morning. Joe needed to reconcile with her at his own speed.

"Can you forgive me?"

His hat brim came up and she saw his sorrowful eyes. "Joe, of course I forgive you. I forgave you a long time ago."

He wasn't finished. "I mean for not coming back right away. For taking so long to get this . . . this thing settled inside me."

She reached out to touch his arm. "Joe, you know you're forgiven. I've forgiven you with all my heart."

"You have?" The first hint of joy crossed his face.

She drew back her hand. He must not think her forward. "I've been missing you a lot," she offered. "Wishing I could have made things plainer . . . that night . . . you know."

He hung his head again. "It was all my fault, Verna. I know that, and I knew it then. But I couldn't say the words. I guess it was easier with the hurt to just leave. But running away isn't what I want. It's not . . . right."

"Oh, Joe!" She pleaded with her eyes as she said, "You don't have to run from me or from what happens. I trust you. I really do."

A shadow crossed his face. "I can see that, Verna. And I'm sorry for not seeing it sooner."

"Sometimes a wound takes a while to heal, Joe."

A surprised look sprang to his face. "Do you know about . . . her . . . about Rosy? About us?"

"*Nee*, Joe," she said quickly. "I don't. I was just saying in general."

How was she supposed to describe her insight from this morning? And how could she tell him he had a heart of gold? That wouldn't be appropriate. They had, after all, only seen each other a few times. Even with that, it seemed like she'd known his heart all her life.

He seemed to accept her explanation. "May I see you home tonight then? Or is that too soon? I can wait. And I will understand."

She took her time to answer even though the words wanted to burst out in a great rush. *Of course I'll go home with you! I would have agreed to that weeks ago!* "Debbie and Ida can take this buggy home," she said. "Or Lois since they're both coming with Emery."

"Then it's decided." A soft smile filled his face.

He looked happier than he had in weeks. Oh, how many precious moments had been wasted already? "Maybe we'd better get this horse unhitched," she ventured.

He moved with care and took his time removing the tugs on his side while Verna climbed down and worked on the other side. She wondered if Joe was as delirious with joy as she was. She had to move slowly so she wouldn't shriek out loud.

Joe left with Buttercup and headed toward the barn. Verna waited for him.

Debbie was chatting with two men in the yard and glanced her way. Verna gave her a little wave so Debbie would know everything

261

had turned out well. She seemed to understand. Verna watched as her friend turned toward the house with the two men in tow — one of whom was Paul Wagler.

Verna felt as if a great weight had fallen from her shoulders. Her heart could beat again unhindered. This situation with Joe must never happen again. If they ever had another falling out, she feared she might never recover. She pushed the dark thought away as Joe came out of the barn. It wasn't time yet to think of marriage, but rather of the time to heal. They had both been through difficult moments. She must remember that. Tenderness was in order . . . and lots of time spent together.

"Shall we go inside?" Joe asked from a few feet away.

She laughed. "I'm sorry! Was I in a daze?"

He nodded. "You looked like it anyway."

"I'm happy, that's all. I'm so happy, Joe."

"And so am I, Verna," he said and took her hand for a moment.

"Supper's about ready, I think. We'd better go inside."

Joe didn't move. His face looked troubled again. "I need to tell you something else, Verna." He paused for a long moment. "It's . . . it's one of the reasons I didn't come back these last few weeks. I'd best say

262

it now since I'm afraid you'll find out eventually. I want you to hear it from me."

"*Yah?*" She waited nervously. Had the next shock of their relationship arrived already? Well, she would cling to what she'd realized this morning at the service. Nothing would shake her conviction that Joe was her man.

"I used to date an *Englisha* girl — back in my *rumspringa* time, Verna. For over a year. That's why Rosy broke off our relationship. She found out."

"For *that* she left you?" Astonishment was written on her face. "But, Joe, what does that matter now?"

He shrugged. "I only know it did for Rosy."

"Did you tell her?"

He hung his head. "*Nee,* someone else did."

"So why are you telling me?"

"It's better that way, Verna. If you know now, you can decide."

Torment filled his face. He really did expect her to send him away. The poor man. Verna stepped closer. "Joe, I don't care about the *Englisha* girl. We all do things we shouldn't."

He appeared puzzled. "You perhaps dated an *Englisha* fellow in your *rumspringa?*"

Verna laughed. "*Nee,* Joe. But it doesn't

263

matter to me that you dated an *Englisha*. You didn't marry her or something, did you?"

He shook his head and added, "There was nothing like that, Verna."

"Then we're okay!" she chirped.

Relief spread across his face. The wound Rosy had given Joe must indeed have cut deep. Much, much deeper than she could comprehend. Well, it was nothing that her love, along with *Da Hah*'s help, couldn't heal.

"Come, Joe!" She pulled on his hand. "It really is supper time. And I'm afraid I have no pies awaiting us at home, so you'd best eat your fill."

He appeared pleased. "Seeing you will be plenty satisfying, Verna. And I really mean that."

"That's nice of you to say." She let go of his hand and walked toward the house.

Joe hurried to catch up.

TWENTY-TWO

On Monday morning, a week later, Verna hummed a tune as she washed the dishes. Everything looked so much brighter now. The early July sunlight poured in through the kitchen window, and the field near the barn was filled with mown hay. Her outlook on life had greatly improved because Joe's heart and hers had mended with the time they'd spent together recently. It had been two Sunday nights now that they'd enjoyed each other's company after the hymn singing. Deep in conversation with each other while sitting on the couch, Verna couldn't stop looking into his strong, handsome face. She was sure no one had ever felt as happy as she did when she was with him.

She jerked her head around as quick steps sounded on the stairs behind her. Debbie rushed into the kitchen, obviously on her way to work at that *Englisha* place in Lewistown.

"Having a good morning, are we?" Debbie asked.

"I am!" Verna said, practically glowing. She couldn't help but have a *gut* day unless *Da Hah* decided to break her heart again. And He hardly seemed about to do that this morning.

"I'm so happy for you!" Debbie gave Verna a quick hug. "I do confess I kept holding my breath the past two Sunday nights, expecting another breakup between the two of you."

"It won't happen," Verna said with a grin. "We're getting along just fine."

"That's certainly what it looks like," Debbie allowed. "I was determined to awaken when you came upstairs last night. I thought I'd come over and wish you congratulations for your continued success. But I must have slept soundly."

"That's so sweet, Debbie," Verna said. "But I don't want anyone waking up for me. Not once it's past midnight."

"Well, it's so great that you had a good time," Debbie said as she dashed out the washroom door.

Verna looked out the kitchen window and watched her friend leave. Not until Debbie was in her car and had driven out the lane did the thought cross Verna's mind. Debbie was in her Amish dress. She'd worn Lois's Sunday dresses for the weekends, but she'd always worn her own *Englisha* clothing during the week. Had that changed now with Debbie's steady journey toward the Amish way of life? That was another great happiness to add to her joy this morning. What a blessing Debbie was to their family, and now Debbie dared show her intentions to the *Englisha* world! Would her boss be happy about that? *Yah,* apparently. Things must be okay at work if Debbie had enough nerve to wear Amish dresses that were unstylishly long.

Debbie didn't speak a lot about her job. Here at home her focus was on learning the Amish lifestyle. Lois gave her cooking lessons at least once every week, and sewing lessons were on the list somewhere. How Debbie managed all that plus a regular *Englisha* job was hard to imagine. Maybe that's why she was always rushing around, especially in the morning. She was a brave and determined girl, and Verna admired her a lot. It took great courage to change one's lifestyle the way Debbie planned to. And *Daett* liked and approved of Debbie too. That was its own miracle all by itself.

Verna glanced toward the basement stairs as footsteps sounded. Ida appeared with an empty hamper basket. Her cheeks were rosy from her outside work. She'd hung another load of clothing on the wash line. Verna had been out in the barn earlier with Ida while Lois made breakfast. Lois was in the sewing room now, busy with a dress pattern.

Verna glanced at Ida. "Do you need help? I'm almost done here."

"*Nee,* all I have is a load from Emery's room." Ida muttered, "Boys — what a mess they make! More dirty clothing from one boy than ten girls."

Verna smiled. Emery *was* a little spoiled, but then Ida did exaggerate.

"I'm getting a clean man — once the time comes," Ida said as she plopped down on a kitchen chair.

Verna hid her look of astonishment. Ida never sat down for a minute in the middle of her wash day. At least not until every last piece was on the line, so she must have something serious on her mind. Verna turned toward her. "Did something happen I don't know about? Were you asked home from the hymn singing for next Sunday night?"

Ida laughed. "*Nee,* of course not. But that doesn't keep one from thinking, especially since you and Joe patched things up. Do you think *Daett* would allow me to say *yah* if someone did ask?"

"Certainly, Ida. I'm sure he would." Verna made her voice sound cheerful. She wanted to hide her lack of confidence lest Ida notice and her hopes end up dashed before they ever took flight. The truth was, what their *daett* would say was far from certain. And after the trouble she'd had with Joe, *Daett* might be more wary than ever. The thought cast a dark shadow across her heart. Things with Joe must continue to go well. Especially if Ida had hopes some boy would bring her home soon.

Ida said, "I'm not so sure what he'd say."

Verna ignored Ida's gloominess. "Has someone perhaps . . . ?"

Ida laughed. "Paid me attention? Hah! Now that would be the day."

"Ida, you mustn't think like that! There's someone out there for you. I know there is!"

Ida jumped to her feet. "What in the world am I doing? My wash isn't done yet."

Verna watched Ida dash off to go upstairs. Some man *had* paid attention to Ida. She was sure of it. But who could it be? Should she inquire further? What *gut* would that do? She couldn't help Ida beyond making sure there was no further *kafuffle* with Joe.

Well, she would do exactly that, Verna decided.

Ida appeared with her hamper full of dirty pants and shirts. "Almost done!" she said as she continued her dash toward the basement stairs.

Something was definitely bothering Ida. She was acting quite strange this morning. Verna finished the last of the dishes and slipped into the living room. *Mamm* was on the couch knitting. The whirr of Lois's sewing machine rose and fell in the distance. Verna wished to speak with someone about Ida, but Lois had the door closed. She probably didn't wish to be bothered. But this was important, and *Mamm* probably wouldn't know the answer to her question.

"I have to speak with Lois," Verna announced as she motioned toward the sewing room.

Mamm raised her eyebrows but didn't offer an opinion.

Verna opened the door and quietly stepped inside and closed the door behind her.

"What?" Lois asked not looking up from her work.

Verna waited until the next line of thread was finished. "Something about Ida bothers me this morning, Lois. Has a man been pay-

270

ing her attention?"

Lois looked up. "Ida? She has been asked to be taken home?"

"*Nee,* I'm asking if you noticed anything, that's all."

"Well, don't ask me. How would I know? Don't bother me now. I'm trying to focus."

"Then focus on my question," Verna insisted. "Have you seen anything?"

Lois groaned but stopped and took a few seconds to think. "No one except Paul Wagler. But he flirts with everyone."

"*Yah,*" Verna allowed. "But I thought Paul was giving Debbie the most attention. Unless I miss my guess, Ida's got someone in mind, although who it is I can't imagine."

"You never know." Lois looked down and her sewing machine whirred again.

Lois didn't know more than she did, Verna decided. She opened the door, stepped out, and closed it behind her. She walked into the kitchen and slipped out the washroom door. Ida was outside placing clips on the line to hold the last load of clean clothes to the line. Verna grabbed a few clips and held them in her mouth as she reached down to pick up a pair of Emery's pants and pin them to the line. She turned to Ida. "You might as well tell me what's bothering you. I know something is."

Ida wrinkled her face. "I'm just worrying, I guess. Like everyone does sometimes. You know, about what life holds. Maybe after a few years this single life will get better."

"My, you're morbid!" Verna said before laughing. "It's not the end of the world, you know. Look at me — I'll be twenty-five before long."

"*Yah,* and married by this fall, if I don't miss my guess. Has Joe kissed you yet?"

Verna figured her cheeks were turning into flames of red about now. She took a deep breath. This wasn't how she wanted the conversation to go. Ida's words troubled her, and not just because she'd never talked about such things before.

"You don't have to tell me," Ida interjected, a little red-cheeked herself. "I suppose I shouldn't be thinking about such things."

"Well, he hasn't," Verna admitted. "And, *yah,* I'm hoping for a fall wedding. But it takes a willing man, you know."

"Oh, he's willing enough," Ida said.

"Do we have to have such plain talk?"

Ida laughed. "You're the one who started it, remember?"

"But there is someone you're interested in, isn't there?" Verna pushed.

Ida took a moment to answer. "*Yah,* if you

must know. But I think it's just on my part. He would never give someone like me a second glance."

"But he has given you *one*?" Verna glowed. "Tell me, Ida, who is he?"

"Calm yourself." Ida's face burned red. "It's nothing but my imagination. And that's all it will ever be."

"But you must not say so, Ida. Look what has happened between Joe and me. Even after the awful *kafuffle* we had."

Ida laughed bitterly. "You have no idea what you're talking about."

"Then speak plainly for once. I'm tired of beating around the bush."

Ida's face flamed again. "If you must know, it's Paul Wagler. Are you happy now?"

Verna gasped. "Oh, Ida, no!"

Ida hung her head. "*Yah,* I'm afraid so. My heart has gotten ideas of its own, and there's nothing I can do about it."

Verna dropped the shirt she held into the hamper. "You must get this out of your heart at once, Ida," she scolded. "There's not a bigger flirt around than Paul."

Ida groaned. "You think you're telling me anything new? If Paul would only settle down with someone maybe I could get him out of my mind. But he keeps flitting around like a bee between flowers. And my heart

273

beats faster hoping that one day I'll be one of those flowers — like maybe the *last* one."

"Has he given you any reason to hope, Ida?"

Ida shrugged. "A smile here and there while he's stealing glances at Debbie. Now there's a flower he's landed on. Clinging to it is more like it."

Verna reached up to clutch the clothesline. "Ida, please don't tell me you're jealous?"

Ida laughed. "Jealous of Paul's attention? *Yah,* but not of Debbie. She cares nothing for the man."

"And you know this?"

"*Yah.* Debbie has told me."

"Does she care for another Amish man?"

Ida wrinkled her face. "You can ask Debbie about that. I promised not to spill her secrets."

Verna sighed. "I'm not worried about Debbie. She can take care of herself. It's you I'm worried about. This is never going to happen, Ida. Not with Paul."

Ida didn't say anything more because there was nothing more to say. The two finished hanging up the clothes and walked toward the house.

"I'll be happy with what *Da Hah* has given me," Ida said at the basement door. "It just takes me a while to adjust. Seeing you and

Joe though . . . I have to admit it . . . makes things worse. I don't want to spoil your joy, Verna. Believe me! I'm very happy for you."

"I believe you." Verna gave Ida a hug.

Ida, holding the empty laundry basket, hugged her back with one hand. "We'll always be sisters," she whispered. "And when you bring your little *bobblis* home, Verna, I'll love them like my own."

Verna stared off into the distance. "You don't know yet what *Da Hah* has in store for you, Ida. He never gives anything we don't need."

"Then this may be what I'm needing — the single life." Ida tried to look happy. "I will pray *Da Hah*'s presence carries me through my life even if I never have a man to hold me in his arms."

"Oh, Ida." Verna wrapped her sister in another long hug. "You mustn't say such things. Soon you'll have both of us crying."

"I know." Ida took a deep breath, gathering herself together.

"I will pray for you," Verna whispered as they went inside.

Mamm looked up at them with a strange expression, but she didn't comment as Ida headed upstairs and Verna remained in the kitchen.

TWENTY-THREE

Three weeks later, on a late-July evening, Debbie walked toward her parents' place with a bag of freshly baked bread swinging in one hand. Supper was finished at the Beiler farm, and the evening stretched out in front of her. They'd eaten early even though Emery was still in town on an errand.

"He can eat when he comes back," Saloma had declared. "I'm not keeping *Daett* waiting."

Debbie felt a glow inside as she thought about the memory. Her time with the Beilers was going so well. Still she checked in briefly with either her mom or dad at irregular intervals. Tonight warranted a prolonged visit. Not that anything special had happened. She simply wanted to stay in touch with them. There was no reason to make them feel she'd abandoned them even though her mother had wanted her out on her own and making her way in the world.

Debbie had done that, although in a strange way from her mom's perspective. Hopefully her mother would eventually get used to her daughter's choices. Her mother likely hoped even now that this phase of her life would soon be over. Well, it wasn't a phase. She was more convinced than ever that Amish life was right for her. Her cooking skills, with Lois's help, were progressing slowly but well. They had a cake and even pies planned for this week. Lois said she'd make the crusts though. That was the hard part about pies, she claimed. And Debbie could easily believe that after she watched Lois's nimble fingers form pie dough into its proper shape. Then she'd formed little creases all along the top edge that looked miraculous. Debbie would learn how to do that someday. She would have to if she wished to be truly Amish. These were things that came more easily if one was born into such a life. Even Verna and Ida could handle pie crust, though neither spent much time in the kitchen.

It wasn't fair really. The few times Debbie saw her mother cook was when she stirred premixed batter from store-bought cartons. It was cheaper that way, her mother had always claimed. But now Debbie suspected there was more to it. It was also faster and easier. But she had much to be thankful for, she told herself. She would have to remind Mom of them if the chance came up, though it was unlikely her accomplishments would mean much to her mom. A wonderful thing like Bishop Beiler's acceptance of her wouldn't signify anything to someone in the world. She wouldn't understand why that was a big deal. Then there was the help she gave the Beiler family with Lois. Lois had almost ceased her talk about the *wunderbah Englisha* life. Of course, Debbie's mom would think that point a complete negative. Neither would she understand her daughter's desire for Alvin Knepp's attention. Not that she'd received any . . . yet. On this, Debbie had been a complete failure. Maybe she'd thought too highly of herself. How did she think there was even a chance she could waltz in and gain an Amish man's confidence?

The Amish believed pride was one of man's greatest sins. And she was, no doubt, guilty of that one. Paul Wagler, on the other hand, teased her every chance he had. She was quite irritated with the man. Verna claimed he acted that way with all the eligible girls. But Debbie wasn't so sure. When she caught his gaze on her during the

Sunday preaching, he would suddenly look away. Yes, there was plenty of interest from Paul. And that was just another failure on her part, although how could she have prevented it? Paul created his own attraction. He was also the one who kept Alvin away, she suspected. In fact, she was sure of it even if there was no way to prove it. Why else had Alvin suddenly stopped his Saturday habit of borrowing tools from Bishop Beiler? Did Alvin's no longer break? She doubted that. The Knepps wouldn't have improved their farming ways that rapidly.

No, the situation lined up too well. Alvin had seen her and Paul laugh and joke together that Sunday night a few weeks ago and had lost his courage. Alvin thought she cared for Paul. In retrospect she should have been more careful. But how was she supposed to know how Amish men thought? And how did one deal with someone like Paul? In her experience, if she ignored him it brought more attention than if she snapped back at him.

Well, she'd better think about something else lest her long face cause her mother to think she didn't like her new life. Debbie turned in at her parents' driveway and knocked twice on the front door before walking in. Her dad caught sight of her first and called over his shoulder, "Callie! Come see what the cat dragged in."

"Oh, Dad!" Debbie gave him a tight hug. "It's so good to see you."

"What have you got there?" He peered at the loaf of bread. "Did you bake this, Debbie?"

"Yes!" Debbie allowed her face to glow.

The approval on her dad's face warmed her heart, so she gave him another quick hug.

He deliberately made a long face. "I thought you might have brought supper with you."

"Oh," Debbie cooed, "I should have."

Her dad laughed. "Now, sweetheart, I was just teasing. Come in and sit down. You're staying a while, aren't you?"

He wasn't teasing on the subject of food. Debbie would have to remember that and cook an Amish supper for her parents again. All by herself this time — once Lois had trained her well enough. They might be the perfect people to practice on.

Debbie followed her dad into the living room. Her mother looked up from her newspaper.

"Hello, dear!" her mother greeted, ignoring the loaf of bread.

"Hi, Mom." Debbie bent over and gave

her a quick hug before sitting down on the couch across from her. She could sense her mother was still uneasy with her new life. But she was still her daughter however Amish she became. And tonight she was wearing one of her "*Englisha* dresses," as the Beiler family called them. She was trying to make things easier for everyone. Someday her complete change to Amish life would arrive and must be faced, but tonight was not that moment.

"I see you still speak English." Her mom looked over her glasses at Debbie.

"Now, Mom, I don't speak Pennsylvania Dutch that well. I still barely understand it."

"So, how are you getting along over there?" her mother asked, motioning in the direction of the Beiler residence.

Debbie smiled. "They're very nice people, Mom. You ought to visit sometime."

"Yes, I suppose I ought to." Her mother glanced away.

Was she hiding a tear? Debbie wondered. "Mom, you *did* want me to move out, remember? It's nice that you do miss me."

Her mother nodded. "A little, but let's not go crying all over the place. I'm too old for that."

"She's quite sentimental . . . underneath,"

Debbie's father offered.

"I know." Debbie got up and gave her mother another hug.

Callie squeezed back this time. "So tell me, are you *really* enjoying it over there?"

"Yes, I do like it. Very much."

"And the new life?" This came from her father.

"I love it, Dad. It's what I've always wanted."

"I thought so." He regarded her for a moment. "Well, I'm glad to hear it then."

"Mr. Fulton says you wear Amish dresses to work," her mother said. "Have things really gone that far?"

Debbie shrugged. "I'm experimenting. And no one is complaining at the office. The dresses are very nice and presentable, although not the latest styles. I'm not scaring off any customers."

"Your mother was just making an observation. She meant no harm," her dad interjected.

Debbie nodded. "I guess I'm jumpy on the subject. The Beilers are accepting me without any complaints. And I've been going to church with them every Sunday in full Amish dress, which includes a head covering they call a *kapp.*"

Her mother's smile was thin. "Any prospects yet? Any interest by that young man you mentioned?"

"Mom! Besides, I haven't joined the Amish church. No Amish man would take a chance on a girl who's not of the Amish faith. And I'm not . . . yet."

"Good-looking girl like you?" Her father grinned. "I'm sure they're lining up."

Her mother smiled. "And a woman with a college education. They ought to line up around the block!"

Debbie laughed. "I'm afraid that's not a plus in their world. In fact, I never hear the Beiler girls mention my education to anyone."

"Surely they don't hold that against you?" Her mother appeared thunderstruck.

"It's just not important in their world, Mom," Debbie replied. "They have other priorities."

"Like having babies every year." Her mother snorted. "That's a really lofty goal."

Debbie frowned. "You don't have to condescend, Mom. They're precious people. And large families are part of their belief system and are needed to help them farm."

"As women's liberation is part of mine," Callie said, shuffling the newspaper in her lap. "Well, now, let's talk about something sensible. I'm sure you didn't come over here to prattle about having babies."

"I'd love a slice of that bread Debbie brought, Callie. We have butter and jam in the refrigerator, don't we?"

Her mother sighed. "Depend on a man to bring the subject back to the 'important' things of life. And yes, Herbert, there's grape jam . . . and plenty of margarine . . . *not* real butter though. Remember your arteries."

"Bread like this," he held the loaf up, "seems to warrant real butter and home-made jam."

Callie sighed. "Now look what you've done, Debbie! He'll want home-baked bread every day of the week."

"Maybe I can bring some more often," Debbie offered.

"You've really learned how to bake?" her mother asked. "You're probably better at it than I am."

"I'm trying, Mom. That's all I can say at this point."

"I imagine that's an admirable skill in your new world," her mother said. "To me it harkens back to caveman days."

"Hmmm. Maybe I'll move over to her caveman world," her father said, returning from the kitchen to wave around his piece of jam-smeared bread.

"He even talks like a caveman!" Callie sounded exasperated. "But here we are, arguing with each other when you've come to visit, Debbie. Here, stand up so I can get another good look at you."

Debbie did a slow turn in front of her. "Mom, I'm still the same person."

Her mother ignored her comment. "There are little changes here and there. Things only a mother would notice, I suppose. But you're happy. That I can see."

"Thanks, Mom." Debbie sat down again.

Her father acted like he hadn't heard the exchange. He wiped his mouth with a paper napkin. "That was really good, Debbie! Thank you!"

"I'm glad you liked it."

He looked at her for a few seconds. "There's something I need to tell you, Debbie. I don't want this to be a great shock, but then I suppose you know that even Amish people have their problems."

Debbie glanced at him. "Yes, I know the Amish have their problems. What's going on? Is there something you think I should know about?"

He shrugged. "You may not even know the person involved since this is a rather large Amish community, but . . ."

"Just say it, Herbert," Callie said.

Her father leaned toward the coffee table and picked up the paper Callie had been reading. He showed Debbie the front page. "I don't suppose you read the newspaper anymore."

Debbie eyes traced the headlines. *Local Couple Under Arrest in Robbery Heist.* Underneath in smaller letters were, *Police expect further arrests to follow.*

Debbie met her father's gaze. "You're not saying these were Amish people? That's not possible."

He shook his head. "No, but the arrests that follow will include at least one Amish man. The girl involved fingered him. Her former boyfriend, she claims. She's cut a deal with the prosecutor for a lighter sentence if she testifies against him. That sort of thing."

"How do you know this?" Debbie asked, suddenly feeling defensive.

"One of the sheriff's deputies came to the garage this afternoon. They picked the man up at noon today, and he was arraigned on the theft charges. He's out on bail now, so I guess the judge didn't consider him a flight risk. The charges are serious enough. Breaking and entering, robbery, all that."

"Who is he?" Debbie tried to still her beating heart.

"An Amish man by the name of Joe Weaver."

Debbie leaped to her feet and steadied herself using the couch. "Joe Weaver? I have to get back right now. Verna has been seeing him. I need to let her know."

"You know this man then?" her mother asked, now on her feet too.

Debbie was already making her way to the door. She called over her shoulder, "Yes, I do. He's Verna's boyfriend. I have to tell her!" With that, she flew out the door.

TWENTY-FOUR

An hour later Debbie sat on the couch with Saloma. Verna was seated between them, her head in her hands, her loud sobs filling the room. As it turned out, when Debbie arrived Deacon Mast was already there with the news. Her race across the fields had been for nothing. The Beiler family already knew about Joe's arrest.

It was only after Deacon Mast and Bishop Beiler left, the sound of their buggy wheels moving out of the driveway, that Verna's sobs had begun. Lois and Ida stood a few feet away, on the verge of tears themselves. No one said anything as Debbie and Saloma clung to Verna's arms. What was there to say? Their world had fallen in because Verna's had.

How could Verna have been so wrong in her judgment of Joe? She'd often said Joe was the only man for her — that he was an honest and caring man. And now this! Joe charged with breaking and entering! Robbery too. Surely there must be some mistake. But Deacon Mast had sounded sure of the charges, and he ought to know.

Verna wailed, "He didn't do it!"

Debbie tightened her grip on Verna's arm. Denial was the first reaction in the face of tragedy. Psychology classes had taught her that much, and Verna was following the norm to the letter.

"There, dear," Saloma soothed. "*Daett* will look into it, and he'll tell us."

What Saloma meant was that when Bishop Beiler came back with Joe's confession, Verna would have no choice but to accept the news. Still, it might not be enough. If Debbie knew Verna, acceptance wouldn't be easy. Verna loved the man deeply.

"I know Joe. He wouldn't do something like this." Verna lifted her face toward the ceiling and continued weeping.

"You should lie down now," Saloma said. "Come . . . it will feel better in your own bed, and maybe you can sleep."

"I don't want to lie down ever again," Verna wailed.

"She's making no sense," Ida whispered.

Saloma shook her head and motioned for both girls to stay away. She leaned closer to Verna. "Listen, girl! You have to gather

289

yourself together. This isn't how we act. Remember that! You've had enough crying. Joe isn't dead. Let *Daett* look into the matter with Deacon Mast."

"This is worse than dead," Verna choked out. "If he were dead, I could mourn at least."

Saloma stood and lifted up on Verna's arm. Ida raced to open the stair door for them, and the two stumbled up the steps.

"*Mamm* will take care of her," Ida said, but she didn't look very convinced.

Debbie listened to the sobs coming from upstairs. Not much was going to help Verna tonight. In the meantime, there was the house to clean up. It was unlikely the supper dishes had been finished while she was gone. Debbie peeked into the kitchen. That seemed to bring Ida and Lois out of their trance. Ida dashed toward the kitchen. Lois shrugged, as if she didn't care one way or the other about the house, and then moved into the kitchen too. Debbie knew enough about the Amish to realize that duty was still duty. And an Amish home was never left unattended, even in times of disaster. She followed the two into the kitchen and began to dry the dishes as Ida washed.

"Were you over at your parents' when you found out?" Ida asked.

"I . . . I was with Mom and Dad. Dad told me. He found out from a deputy sheriff who stopped in at the garage."

"Poor Verna," Ida whispered. "You should have heard her talking to me just the other day. She was so convinced everything was going well."

"I'm sure no one expected something like this," Debbie assured her. "Does anyone know who the girl is who accused him?"

"A girl?" Lois's eyes grew wide. "We don't know anything about a girl. Only that Joe was taken in on charges by the *Englisha* police. That's all Deacon Mast said."

Debbie looked away. "Maybe I shouldn't have said anything. I don't want to make things worse than they already are."

"*Nee,* Debbie," Ida disagreed. "We need to know this. Lois, go tell *Mamm.* She can ask Verna if she knows more about it."

Lois shook her head. "Verna's not in any shape to talk about anything. Listen to her crying upstairs."

The kitchen was quiet for a moment, broken only by the soft sobs coming down through the open stairway door.

"See?" Lois looked very wise. "I wouldn't say a word at the moment. Verna might lose her mind if she thinks there's an *Englisha* girl involved yet."

Ida began to wash the dishes again.

"An *Englisha* girl," Lois muttered moments later. "Who in the world was Joe involved with? And with Verna loving him the way she did?"

"We don't know for sure it's true," Ida said, rinsing a saucepan.

"I wouldn't have thought Joe would have an *Englisha* girlfriend," Lois said. "Would you?"

Debbie shrugged. "If you were talking about Paul Wagler, I'd say yes, but I have to agree with you. Joe doesn't seem the type. But then you never know. Paul and Joe are best friends."

Ida flinched at the mention of Paul's name, Debbie noticed.

Lois gave a little snort. "Paul probably corrupted Joe."

"Sometimes you can't tell by the outside," Ida said timidly.

Lois made a face. "I can't believe you're sticking up for the man, Ida."

Ida didn't say anything, and Debbie understood. Ida had an affection for the dashing Paul. It wasn't surprising. A quiet, inward-looking girl like Ida would naturally be attracted to such an outgoing character.

Minutes later footsteps came down the stairs. Saloma appeared in the doorway and then collapsed onto a kitchen bench. "She's sleeping. I never thought I'd live to see this day. My future son-in-law arrested."

"I doubt if he ever will be your son-in-law," Lois said.

"I know," Saloma said. "Poor Verna. She's liable to get ill over this. O *dear Hah,* we need Your strength. Help us get through this."

Debbie slipped onto the bench beside Saloma. Ida dried her hands on the dishcloth and sat down on the other side of her *mamm.*

Mamm clung to their hands, and whispered under her breath, praying.

Debbie could only catch phrases here and there.

"*Gott im Himmel . . .* help us please. This is too heavy to carry . . . oh please comfort Verna's heart."

Moments later a buggy turned into the driveway. Saloma jumped to her feet. "It's *Daett*! Go up and be with Verna, Ida."

Lois had rushed to the kitchen window. She said, "*Nee,* it's Emery come back from his trip into town."

"We've forgotten all about Emery!" Saloma exclaimed. "He'll be hungry, and the dishes all washed up already."

"I'll get something ready for him." Lois

rushed about the kitchen.

Saloma waved her hand at Ida. "You'd best still check on Verna. She might have heard the buggy come in and shouldn't be alone."

Ida left at once.

Debbie stood up. "What can I do? I want to help."

"You can set the table," Lois told her. "And tell Emery what's going on when he comes in."

"*I'll* tell him." Saloma sighed and sat down again. "He's my son, and he should hear this news from my lips."

Long moments passed. Lois kept up her glances out the kitchen window. "He's coming in," she finally reported.

Before Emery arrived the silence was broken by soft steps on the stairs. Ida appeared with Verna on her arm. Verna's face was white and tear-stained.

"Wait!" Saloma said as soon as the washroom door opened. Emery stepped in and stopped short with his hat in his hand. With a quick glance he took in the room. "So it is true," he said. "I told myself this wasn't possible."

"Then you've heard?" Saloma sounded almost relieved.

They all turned as a soft sob escaped Verna's lips. "You don't believe this, Emery, do you? Joe didn't do this. You know he didn't."

Conflict raged on Emery's face. "I don't know if I really have an opinion on the matter, Verna." He stepped closer to take her hand. "But it doesn't matter what you and I think. This is a matter for the *Englisha* law, and they don't ask what we think."

"Oh it matters, Emery!" Verna's face blazed. "It matters to Joe an awful lot. He must not think that I believe this awful thing."

"I'll guess we'll see." Emery gave his sister a quick hug. "I'm sorry for you, Verna. This can't be easy."

Saloma stepped forward. "Go into the living room and sit down, Verna. Take her to the couch, Ida, before she passes out."

Verna obeyed Ida's tug on her arm and took faltering steps forward. The two disappeared through the kitchen doorway.

Saloma turned to Emery. "Where did you hear this thing?"

"I met Wayne at the feed mill, and he had just heard."

Saloma groaned. "This is a terrible thing. *Daett* will have his reputation destroyed. He was always so careful what boys he allowed to date his girls. And yet this has happened."

Emery gripped his *mamm*'s shoulder.

"The people will understand that *Daett* had nothing to do with this. And Verna wasn't dating Joe that long."

Lois interrupted. "Sit down, Emery. I have the food reheated. But did you have to be this late?"

Only Lois would dare scold at a moment like this, but Emery took it in stride by ignoring her comment.

When Lois placed the food on the table, Emery asked, "Where's *Daett*?"

"*Daett* went with Deacon Mast after he arrived to tell us," Saloma said.

Emery grunted. "I hope they excommunicate the man on the spot."

"Emery!" Lois scolded. "That's not a *gut* attitude. And what if Verna hears you? Didn't you see how much she longs for support? You don't want her heart broken even further."

"*Nee,* I don't," Emery agreed, his mouth full of food. "I'll watch my words, but Joe should not have done what he did."

"Anyone can figure that out," Lois snapped. "See if you can think of something more helpful than that."

Emery chewed, ignoring Lois again.

Saloma got up, and Debbie followed her into the living room. There Verna and Ida clung to each other on the couch, and the two women gathered around them. Debbie slipped her arm over Verna's shoulder and silently prayed again.

TWENTY-FIVE

Several hours later that evening the sun was setting, the long, summer dusk slowly blending into darkness. Bishop Beiler still wasn't back, but it couldn't be long now, Debbie thought as she glanced at the wall clock. It was close to nine-thirty. Debbie stifled a yawn. Beside her on the couch, Verna leaned against her shoulder, exhausted from weeping. Saloma paced back and forth between the kitchen and the living room, and Lois came around occasionally to refill their cups of hot tea.

The tea had been Ida's idea once it became obvious that the evening wouldn't end early. Saloma hadn't objected. Debbie's cup now sat on the footstool in front of her, half empty; Verna's was untouched. None of Saloma's constant urges could bring Verna to take a sip.

Above their heads the gas lantern hissed. Sleepiness crept over Debbie, but the others

— except for Verna — seemed to manage better . . . or perhaps they just didn't show their weariness. The Amish could be stoic in times of crisis, though Verna had also demonstrated the depths to which they felt their emotions.

Saloma paused in front of her daughter again. "Verna, you have to take some nourishment. You have to keep up your strength."

Verna looked up, apparently aroused to action for the first time. "Is *Daett* home?"

"*Nee,* but he will come before long. And how are you going to listen when he speaks if you have no strength?"

Verna sat up and reached for the cup of tea. She took a sip and then another one.

"That's a *gut* girl," Saloma encouraged. "Now drink all of it."

"How long are we staying up?" Lois asked from the kitchen doorway.

"No one has to stay up who doesn't wish to," Saloma said. "Emery's already gone to bed. But I'm sure Verna wants to wait for *Daett,* and I'm staying up with her."

"Me too," Ida chimed in.

"Then I'm staying too, but I do wish he'd hurry." Lois paused to listen. "Is that him now?"

Silence fell as they listened to the sound of buggy wheels in the driveway.

Lois raced toward the front door and said over her shoulder, "I'll go help him un-hitch."

Lois had gone in search of information, Debbie guessed, but if she knew Bishop Beiler, Lois's quest was in vain.

"I hope your dad has a good report," Debbie whispered in Verna's ear. "Should I go upstairs now?"

Alarm showed on Verna's face. "You're not leaving, are you? I want you here."

"But I'm not family."

Saloma stopped her. "Debbie, you're staying. This is something everyone will find out anyway."

"*Yah,* please," Verna begged. "I need you."

Debbie settled back on the couch as the front door opened. Lois came in, followed by the bishop. His face was sober as he took off his hat and hung it on the wall hook.

The news wasn't good, Debbie decided. She wrapped her arm around Verna. Verna began to cry again, so she must have come to the same conclusion.

When silence finally settled over the room, Saloma spoke up. "Sit down and tell us, Adam, please. We've been up waiting for you."

Bishop Beiler shook his head. "You should all be in bed. There's nothing to be done."

"Then tell us what happened," Saloma insisted.

Bishop Beiler sat on his rocker and glanced around the room. "There isn't much. The police arrived at the Weaver place with a search warrant. They went through the house and barn but found nothing. After that, they took Joe to the police station, did whatever they do there, and released him when Joe posted the bond."

"Is Joe guilty of this thing?" Saloma asked.

"Of course he isn't!" The explosion came from Verna, who sat up straight. Her gaze burned into their faces.

Bishop Beiler motioned for Verna to quiet down. "There's no use working yourself up, daughter. Joe continues to claim he's innocent — even after a dozen of his relatives spoke with him tonight. They all took their turn talking to the man. After that Deacon Mast and I had questions for him. Joe will not confess to anything. Yet the *Englisha* police claim they have a solid witness. They also say they have stolen items with Joe's fingerprints on them."

"It's not true!" Verna wailed. "If Joe says he didn't do it, then he didn't do it."

"Verna," Bishop Beiler said, "you will have to face this head-on and understand the

301

meaning of the situation. It looks like Joe has deceived all of us and brought great shame on the community. He was doing things in his *rumspringa* time that even his parents were not aware of. Apparently that is why Rosy cut off the relationship — when she found out."

"Rosy knew about this?" Saloma leaned forward.

"She did not!" Verna exploded again. "This is all lies. All Rosy knew was that Joe had an *Englisha* girlfriend. There was nothing about stealing."

They all looked at Verna. "An *Englisha* girlfriend?" Ida's voice was laced with horror. "So that's true? And you knew?"

Verna didn't answer as she sagged against the couch back.

"I'm afraid that part at least we know is true," Bishop Beiler said. "Joe confessed tonight to having an *Englisha* girlfriend, something his parents already knew about — and Rosy of course. But I did not know of this, and neither did Deacon Mast."

"You can't keep track of what all the young people do during their *rumspringa* time," Saloma came to her husband's defense.

Bishop Beiler sighed. "I'm disappointed in you, Verna. You should at least have

302

waited a while before you saw more of Joe — as I suggested."

"A lot of Amish see *Englisha* friends during that time." Verna's voice was weak. "You said so yourself. And Joe was no different. At least he was sorry and came back to the community. Doesn't that mean anything? Because it does for me. The man has a heart of gold."

"Stolen gold!" Lois exclaimed from the kitchen doorway.

Verna didn't respond, too exhausted for further argument.

Bishop Beiler waved his hand about. "I guess we'll overlook the past. I can understand why Verna was tempted to ignore the man's faults. But I should have stood firm in the beginning when I had my doubts. In this I take full responsibility. So from here on I will be even more careful. And Verna, you are to consider your relationship with Joe Weaver over. I told him so tonight, and he had the decency not to protest. So I have to give the boy that much credit."

"I will not give him up!" Verna's wail cut through the living room. "I'm going down to see him tonight!"

Saloma leaped to her feet. "Verna's overwrought, *Daett*. Don't mind what she's saying. I'll take her up to her room."

303

Verna didn't resist as *Mamm* took her by the hand and tugged.

But there was still fire in her eyes, Debbie thought. This battle wasn't over by any means. She saw the bishop's gaze follow Verna. From the look on his face, he'd drawn the same conclusion.

The bishop rose. "We'll say no more tonight. Already too much time has been spent, and we will not be able to get up in the morning. Everybody off to bed!"

Saloma and Verna were already gone, so Debbie followed the other two girls up the stairs. Saloma met them on her way down. With a weary smile, she said, "Good night, girls. I think Verna will be okay now."

Ida spoke up. "I'll check in on her." Saloma didn't object.

Lois followed Debbie into their room, and the younger girl lay on her bed. Clearly she had no intention of settling down, Debbie thought. Soon Lois's whisper cut through the dim light of the room. "What a night this has been!"

Debbie sat down on the other bed. "Do you think Verna's going to accept your dad's decision?"

"I wouldn't count on it."

"I see trouble myself," Debbie said. "Verna looked quite determined to me."

Lois sighed. "*Daett* will take care of her. He always has before. Look at me. I used to make all kinds of threats about leaving. I even thought I was going to that *Englisha* school this fall. And look what happened. I'm going on with life and — poof! — the thought's gone!" She stared at the ceiling. "I guess I enjoyed watching Verna accomplish a task none of us were able to yet. Getting a man past *Daett*'s sharp eye. Now that achievement is over."

"It does look so," Debbie agreed.

"Much as I feel her pain, I'm also mourning for myself." Lois sat up in the bed as a soft knock came on the door. It opened before either of them could answer. Ida appeared.

"Sorry to interrupt, but Verna wants us to pray with her. Could you both come?"

"Of course!" Lois got up at once and headed out the door. Debbie followed.

Verna appeared hollow-eyed when they entered her bedroom. She whispered, "I'm sorry for the way I've been behaving. I never thought I would react like this . . ."

"It's okay." Lois gave Verna a quick hug.

"Thanks." Verna caught her breath and continued. "Will you pray with me? I'm trying to collect myself, and I need *Da Hah*'s strength."

Ida was the first to kneel beside the bed, followed by the others. Debbie took Verna's hand as Ida led out, "Dear *Hah* in heaven, please help Verna tonight — and even tomorrow and the day after. You know it's going to be hard for her . . . and for all of us. Our hearts are hurting, but Verna's the worst of all. Touch Verna with Your tender love because we know she is even more precious to You than she is to all of us."

Verna clung to Debbie's hand as Lois prayed next. "Please help us. I feel in my heart how much Verna hurts. But I also know what this could mean for all of us. Give Verna the blessing of peace in her heart tonight — difficult as that may be — and also for the rest of us. I ask for the sake of Your great name. And I thank You ahead of time. Amen."

Debbie waited a moment before she began. "I pray too, dear Lord, that You would heal hearts tonight. Give hope to Verna. I know that You will still be with her regardless of what those whom she loves have done. Help me be a comfort to Verna in whatever way I can. In Jesus' name. Amen."

In the silence that followed, Verna prayed. "O dear *Hah,* I ask that You forgive Joe even as we forgive him for whatever he has done. My heart tells me he didn't do this terrible

306

thing. I know Joe told me the truth about his *Englisha* girlfriend back when he wouldn't have had to tell me anything. Now I place Joe in Your hands. That's hard for me to do, but I'm trying. And I promise I will be true to Joe. Soften *Daett*'s heart so that he might also see this thing the way it really is. But if not, help me bear the burden of doing what is right because I will not forsake Joe!"

The room grew quiet as Verna rose to her feet. She gave Debbie a tight hug first, followed by the others. She smiled through her tears. "Thanks for coming and praying with me. It means so much."

"Of course," Debbie said as she squeezed Verna's hand one last time. Then she turned and followed Lois back to their bedroom.

TWENTY-SIX

On Friday morning Verna walked into the barn, threw the harness on Buttercup, and tightened the straps with quick jerks. She'd waited long enough for this visit. It must be done. Buttercup groaned in protest, and Verna gave her a gentle stroke on the neck. "Sorry there. I wasn't trying to hurt you, but I'm in a hurry."

Daett had left for town an hour ago, and he wasn't expected back for some time. Still, Verna wanted to be out of the driveway and down the road a *gut* distance before there was any chance that *Daett* would show up. She would deal with him later. Right now she had to see Joe. *Mamm* knew what she was up to but hadn't said anything so far.

Once she made the trip to see Joe, the deed would be done and her courage wouldn't fail her. Never before had she done anything like this. Rebelling against

Daett's word was unthinkable, and yet she'd not only thought about it but she was acting upon her thought.

Verna pushed open the barn door and led Buttercup outside. She lifted the shafts and swung her underneath. The house lay silent behind her. *Mamm* was probably watching from the living room window, perhaps with tears that threatened to fall. But Verna took her silence to mean she understood her need to speak with Joe — even if it meant defying *Daett*.

Verna fastened the last tug and threw the lines into the buggy. She climbed in and guided Buttercup down the lane. She kept her gaze on the lane as they swept past the house. *Mamm* might change her mind at the last minute and race out to flag her down. But when Verna reached the main road, the lawn behind her was still empty.

She wiped away a tear that stung her cheek. She was glad *Mamm* wasn't involved in her defiance, and so too must her sisters be kept from any association with her deed. Verna had even turned down Ida's offer to help her hitch Buttercup to the buggy. Still, this contact with Joe might bring shame on all of them. The women's chatter at the sewing meeting on Wednesday of this week had made that clear enough. They'd expressed sympathy for her, but they still thought she was the innocent victim. They thought Joe had deceived her. If they found out that she willingly visited him after his shame, all that would change. They would think that one of the bishop's daughters had exercised a terrible lack of judgment. They would wonder why their bishop had not kept his daughter from the contact. "Can't he control his own children?" they would ask, even though Verna was twenty-four years old and capable of making up her own mind.

Verna listened to the beat of Buttercup's hooves on the pavement for a minute or two. Then the thoughts came again. What would she tell Joe once she arrived? The more she considered, the more muddled everything became. What was she supposed to say to him? That she still loved him? That she believed his side of the story? That she would stand with him? She, of course, would even though she wasn't his *frau* — yet. And neither was she promised to him. Would Joe think her forward and out of place? What a fine mess! And worse, what if she drove over to meet with him only to have Joe reject her?

But he wouldn't, Verna told herself. Joe had a heart of gold. He might think of the harm she was doing to her reputation, but he would not reject her. He wouldn't bruise her heart even further.

Some fifteen minutes later, Verna's hands tightened on the reins as the Weaver farm came into view. She'd been here often for the Sunday morning church services, yet the place felt strange, just like so much of life did lately. *A disruptive tragedy must do that,* Verna thought. She decided she mustn't let it bother her. Her Joe lived here. She would find him, and the words that needed saying would come.

Verna slowed Buttercup to turn in the driveway. Should she stop at the house first? *Nee,* that could only complicate things if a long conversation ensued. Joe's *mamm* might feel the need to warn that she shouldn't be here. She would see if Joe was in the barn. That's where he should be at this hour of the morning . . . or perhaps in the fields.

Verna pulled Buttercup to a stop with his nose a foot or so from the side of the barn. She jumped out to tie him to a nail in the wall. The hitching post was behind her, but this felt better — more secluded from the road if people should drive past. If they did recognize one of Bishop Beiler's buggies in the barnyard, they might think *Daett* was here. Verna's conscience twitched at the thought. Here she was practicing outright deception. What a state of affairs things had fallen to — and so quickly! She jumped when the barn door swung open in front of her.

Joe's *daett* appeared. Lloyd touched his hat and glanced around. "Sorry, I didn't mean to startle you."

Clearly he expected someone to have accompanied her. Verna ignored his searching look. "Would Joe be around?"

Lloyd didn't say anything for a few moments. "Why do you wish to see him, Verna?"

Verna shifted on her feet. "Because he's my boyfriend." The words came out much too forcefully, but she couldn't help it.

Lloyd looked pained. "It might be best if you didn't see him until this is over, Verna."

"Why? Does Joe not wish to see me?" The question contracted her throat and caused the words to squeak out. She shouldn't have asked such a thing, but fear gripped her heart.

Lloyd's face showed the answer before he spoke. "*Nee,* he's wishing to see you. That's not the problem, Verna."

Verna had already turned away from the barn door. She spoke over her shoulder. "Then I will go find him!"

She heard Lloyd sigh. "He's racking hay in the back field. Come, I'm leaving to go out there in the hay wagon."

Verna stopped, turned, and followed him without speaking. Lloyd had his team tied behind the barn. Two of Joe's brothers were waiting there. Lloyd motioned for her to get in the wagon. She set her hands on the side of the wagon and swung up as she had done so many times on the farm at home.

"*Gut* morning," she greeted Merlin and Virgil.

They both nodded and murmured greetings.

Verna balanced herself with one hand on the back rack and stood steady as Lloyd drove the team across the rough ground. Once they passed a row of trees, Joe's form became visible. He was riding on the hay rake and glanced their way for a moment then looked down again. A moment later she caught sight of Joe looking up again. This time he waved his hand. He had seen her! Verna waved back and carefully moved closer to the edge of the wagon.

She wanted to jump off the bouncing wagon and run to him, but Lloyd and Joe's brothers were watching her. She could tell Lloyd still didn't approve that she'd come. If she jumped off and ran across the hayfield, that wasn't going to help Joe's family feel better. She'd best move with caution under their watchful eyes. She clung to the hayrack as the bouncing became worse. Lloyd swung the wagon around for the stop a few minutes later. Verna gathered her dress and jumped down. Slowly she walked across the field. Joe had stopped the team of horses and was waiting for her because he couldn't leave the team unattended.

As Verna neared, Joe leaped to the ground and held the team's lines. His face showed conflicting ripples of sorrow and joy. "Verna!" he whispered.

"Joe." She stopped a few feet away. "I had to come and see you."

He swallowed, his Adam's apple moving up and down. "I never dreamed this moment would come, Verna. Your *Daett* said . . . said that our relationship was over. Surely he must have told you. And yet you came."

"Joe." She stepped closer to grab his hands. "It's not right, what's happening. And it's not right that we should cut off the beautiful thing that's happened in our hearts."

"Do you know what is being said about me?"

"*Yah,* but I don't believe it. You told me everything important about your *rumspringa*

314

time. I know you did."

Tears shone in his eyes. "You believe me then?"

"Oh Joe! How could I not believe you?"

He hung his head. "Believing me is a question for which many in the community are finding a different answer. Many now know what only you, Rosy, and my parents knew."

"I told you it doesn't matter, Joe."

He hesitated. "*Yah,* perhaps it once didn't. But now it does. And this makes too much sense for many in the community. Especially since I went out of my way to hide my relationship with the *Englisha* girl."

Verna let go of his hands. "Can't we go on just like before, Joe? Can we let this thing work itself out? It will eventually. Then everyone will see what is the truth."

He glanced away. "I'm afraid I can't put you to that risk, Verna. This testimony of the *Englisha* girl is a strong thing. And I do have my fingerprints on many of the stolen items."

"But, Joe, you have some explanation, don't you?"

A sad smile crossed his face. "I do but it doesn't help much. I was with her. I spent time in her house. That I didn't know those things were stolen at the time is a small comfort now. Who will believe such a thing?"

"I will believe, Joe! I always will."

A slight smile played on his face. "That's so sweet of you, Verna. It warms my heart, but it's what the *Englisha* law says right now that matters." The wagon rattled behind them, and Joe glanced that way. "*Daett* wants this hayfield finished today, Verna. I wish I could speak with you longer, but we have to work."

"Then I'll be seeing you on Sunday night?"

His face fell. "I can't, Verna. I can't even come to the hymn singings until my name is cleared. The shame is too great. And if my name is never cleared . . . Verna, please . . . you don't wish to be associated with me in any way."

"Then I will come here on Sunday nights."

"Verna!" He grabbed her hand. "You must not. The risk is too great. To you *and* to your *daett.*"

"I will not lose you, Joe."

"Verna, dear." His hand trembled. "I promise you . . . once this is over and I am cleared, I will be at your place the next Sunday night, and things between us will be like they were before."

Verna shook her head. "The hours will be

darker than you think, Joe. And your courage will be greatly tempted."

"I know, Verna," he said. "And already I'm missing you so much I don't know if I'm able to stand it much longer."

"Then I must see if I can come." She wanted to kiss him and lean into his arms for a hug, but his *daett* drove closer. He hollered at the team of horses to get in line for the hay loading.

Joe's eyes spoke his love, Verna told herself as Joe climbed back on the hay rake. He took off and hay flew high into the air. Verna turned and began the walk toward the barn. The distance stretched out in front of her. She would need all the time getting back to her buggy to settle her heart and prepare for what lay ahead. *Daett* would not take kindly to this visit. Yet she had no regrets.

As Verna passed the wagon, she waved to Lloyd and Joe's brothers. They lifted their hands in short motions before lowering their heads and bending to their work again.

"Dear *Hah,*" Verna whispered toward the heavens, "help us get through this."

TWENTY-SEVEN

The following Sunday Bishop Beiler led the way upstairs to the ministers' meeting. He tried two doors before he found the ring of chairs in the largest bedroom. After everyone had seated themselves, the bishop nodded and opened with, "*Gut* morning to all of you. We have a long list of things to go over this morning, so we might as well get started."

"*Gut* morning," they all mumbled.

This would not be an easy morning, but Bishop Beiler hadn't expected the community's trouble to vanish overnight. And now with his own household's involvement, the burden had grown even heavier.

The bishop hung his head and continued. "As you all know, Joe Weaver's situation has not improved. And now I have the regretful task of informing you that my daughter Verna refuses to cut off contact with him even when I told her the relationship was over. It's quite plain that the *Englisha* police have evidence against Joe that will stand up in court. Enough, I am told, to easily convict him. Perhaps Deacon Mast can bring us up to date on that situation."

Deacon Mast cleared his throat. "I spoke with Lloyd last night about the matter, and with Joe himself. As we all know, Joe is out on bail. But things are not moving quickly to a trial. Even more so since one of our people are involved. The *Englisha* police I spoke to on Saturday were quite helpful with information. They feel badly about the matter and don't want to shame the Amish community worse than they have to. But they also have their duty, which must be performed."

"*Yah,* we understand that," Bishop Beiler agreed. "And we have our duty, which must also be done. Adding to our burden, we have further problems with Henry Yoder's situation. Why don't you fill us in on that, deacon, instead of me messing up the finer points."

The room was silent as the men waited. Deacon Mast took his time before speaking. "I'm sorry to report that Henry is demanding that we drop all requests that he apologize to the church. He also asked that we drop our request that he take his tractor back to the dealership. He claims he has no further intention of using the tractor's rubber wheels for field work. He says he's taken them back."

Minister Kanagy's face twitched. "Has Henry perhaps been emboldened by the problems with Joe Weaver we're dealing with?"

Deacon Mast thought for a moment before he answered. "My feelings are that he has."

"That's what I was afraid of." Minister Kanagy gripped the side of his chair. "This is bringing nothing but trouble to the community. I think the best route we could take is to excommunicate Joe at once."

"Even before the *Englisha* law proves its case?" This from Minister Graber whose voice squeaked even higher than normal. "What if they should be wrong?"

"You know they rarely make such big mistakes," Minister Kanagy shot back. "Are they not sure of themselves?"

"*Yah,* they are," Deacon Mast admitted when they all looked in his direction.

"But they are trained to appear sure." Bishop Beiler spoke up. "We cannot proceed with such a harsh method if there is any chance they are wrong. We'd lose Joe for sure, and perhaps even his family. And I can't say I'd blame them."

"Is your mind perhaps colored by your daughter's feelings on this matter?" Minister Kanagy stared at Bishop Beiler. "Verna's getting older, my *frau* reminded me this morning. It seems she's hanging on tightly for a reason — even when it's most foolish to do so. Surely you aren't supporting her in this matter?"

Bishop Beiler took a deep breath. "My two eldest daughters have had several offers for their company on Sunday evenings. I am the one who has warned them and held them back until now. As you know, Verna is the first of my girls to date." Bishop Beiler struggled to control his voice for a moment. This discussion had gone where he'd known and dreaded it would. Still, he couldn't sit here and allow falsehoods to be tossed about.

Minister Kanagy snorted. "And your judgment has not turned out that *gut,* if you ask me. Joe is the first man to seriously date your daughter, and now he's arrested for robbery. This is a great shame, as I don't have to tell any of you. I think Bishop Beiler should give way on this matter and allow others to judge who are not as closely involved. Perhaps they can see clearer."

"Are you challenging the bishop's authority?" Minister Graber squeaked, wringing his hands.

"Of course not," Minister Kanagy shot back. "I would not challenge *Da Hah*'s choosing. But that's not the same as questioning a man's judgment when church matters involve his family."

"I think I have always demonstrated my fairness in these matters," Bishop Beiler said. "I told Verna the relationship between her and Joe was over, but they are adults and have the right to make up their own minds — within the *Ordnung,* of course. However, I do understand your concerns and I will stay open in these matters to your judgment. And I will even go further than that. If at any time everyone except me thinks a course of action is wise, then I will not stand in the way. Is that satisfactory?"

"It is," Minister Kanagy said at once. "And *danke* for your consideration. You have my full support."

"And the others?" Bishop Beiler glanced around the room. The other two nodded, their faces sober. "Then we will continue with the question of Joe's excommunication. Do the rest of you think that wise?"

No discussion was needed, Bishop Beiler noticed, before everyone shook their heads. Even Minister Kanagy backed off from his initial counsel. Bishop Beiler sighed. "We will leave Joe Weaver alone until something arises that gives us further direction. In the meantime he should stay back from any communion — should this drag on into the fall — and his membership should be placed on probation. Is everyone in agreement?"

Minister Kanagy hesitated but finally agreed with the others.

"Then what about Henry?" Bishop Beiler glanced at their faces. "I must admit I am at a loss there."

"But what about your daughter?" Minister Kanagy interrupted. "Will she be allowed to cavort with Joe, even with his membership in probation, and perhaps he'll serve a jail sentence before this is over?"

"I have plans to speak with Verna this afternoon on the matter," Bishop Beiler said.

"You have not said anything before?" Minister Kanagy's face showed shock.

Bishop Beiler nodded. "I have, but Verna chose not to listen."

"And you expect her to listen now?" Minister Kanagy's face had grown red.

"I hope so," Bishop Beiler allowed. "But I must admit I don't know for sure. Saloma told me about Verna's visit to Joe on Friday and of her intentions to continue those visits

— to stay in touch, shall we say. I have waited for my feelings to quiet down on the matter before bringing up the subject again with Verna."

"It doesn't sound to me as if your talk with Verna will produce much fruit," Minister Kanagy ventured. "I think we should speak on what our plan will be if Verna continues to defy your counsel. This would make me feel much more confident with our position on the matter. These family matters can get touchy sometimes, as I'm sure you all know."

Bishop Beiler nodded. "It seems to me that harsh measures are not needed here, but the wisdom of your counsel is great, I'm sure. What do the others think?"

He shouldn't have made that sarcastic remark, Bishop Beiler thought. But this wore on his nerves. He'd never thought to stick up for his children, but this wasn't reasonable at all. He had ordered Verna's relationship with Joe to be over in the heat of the moment. That was one thing, but now that Verna had expressed what was her heartfelt devotion for Joe, to threaten her further was something else.

Deacon Mast responded first. "I agree with the bishop on this. My counsel would be that Verna be spoken to for now and hopefully she will listen."

"And you?" Bishop Beiler turned to Minister Graber.

Minister Graber gave a nervous glance at Minister Kanagy. "I can give my counsel to that, with the additional warning to Verna that if Joe is found guilty by the *Englisha,* she will suffer some additional discipline if she does not listen to our counsel."

"Then it's decided." Bishop Beiler settled into his chair again. "And I thank you for your kind counsel."

They all looked pleased except Minister Kanagy, who glowered. He'd get over it, the bishop figured. He had dealt all of them a fair hand in the matter.

"Now back to Henry." Bishop Beiler shifted in his chair. "What is to be done in his case? Shall we allow him off the hook? It would only embolden others, in my opinion, once the word is out. And you know this will come out, especially after the strong warning we gave the last time."

"I agree," Deacon Mast acknowledged. "Henry is challenging us. If we back down, there will be nothing but trouble."

Minister Graber spoke up. "And if we don't back down, there will also be trouble. Nothing *gut* is coming out of this regardless of what we do."

"Let us do nothing right now," Minister Kanagy said. He gave Bishop Beiler a sideways glance. "We should wait until after Joe's problem clears up. Henry might be more open to correction then."

"I don't know," Deacon Mast said. "Henry's right stubborn, if you ask me. Why, I don't know. But something seems to have ridden into his soul. Maybe a strange spirit, even."

"You don't say!" Minister Graber had horror written on his face. "Has Henry been around those wild preachers from Mifflinburg? The ones who claim they are the only true believers left on this earth?"

"Who are you talking about?" Bishop Beiler asked. "Half the world has gone mad it seems to me."

This produced a mild chuckle, but they soon grew serious again.

Minister Graber shifted in his chair. "It's that Plain group I was talking about. Those are the most dangerous sometimes. They run around in sheep's clothing. At least with the *Englisha* world we know what we're dealing with."

"You can say that again." Deacon Mast stroked his beard, lost in thought.

"Are you saying Henry is involved in this group?" Bishop Beiler couldn't keep the stress out of his voice. "It's not like we don't already have enough trouble on our hands."

Deacon Mast shrugged and came out of his contemplation. "I was just expressing my fear. I don't know anything for sure."

The problem was the deacon often guessed things correctly, Bishop Beiler thought. But he didn't wish to share this observation at the moment. Concrete action was what was needed, but such a move might well blow up in his face. But he had to say something. "Shall we warn Henry again then? Tell him we're giving him until next communion time to see things our way? That might buy us some time."

Minister Kanagy snorted. "Henry will be seeing right through that, I'm thinking."

"Do you have any suggestions then?" the bishop asked.

Minister Kanagy didn't miss a beat. "I say we tell Henry outright we'll accept his terms. It will surprise him and perhaps get him on our side for a few months. At least until this thing with Joe blows over. Then if Henry acts up again, we'll have stronger reasons on our side."

Bishop Beiler cleared his throat. "I don't like that option, but what do the rest of you think?" He paused as Minister Graber and Deacon Mast pondered the question.

"I'm with Minister Kanagy." Minister Graber spoke first.

This would put extra pressure on Deacon Mast, Bishop Beiler knew. All of them were tired, and it was past time when they should have returned to the congregation. Below them the singing had stopped some ten minutes ago. They would begin singing again before long. He couldn't allow this meeting to drag out much longer.

Deacon Mast finally shrugged. "I guess I'm with Minister Kanagy. It's a hard question really. But Henry might best be left alone for now. We can't afford to lose him. I really am afraid he will consider jumping the fence for *gut* if we press him too hard."

That was exactly what Henry would do if he *wasn't* pressed hard, Bishop Beiler thought. But the vote had gone against him, and he wasn't in any position to contest the matter right now. Not with Verna continuing to act up.

The bishop bowed his head. "We have unity then. So whose turn is it to preach the main sermon?"

He already knew the answer, but he needed a few minutes to collect his fallen spirit. There was trouble ahead, he was sure. Bad trouble, and they raced ahead of the storm in vain. But now there was preaching

328

to be done, and he wanted his soul calm before *Da Hah.* His will would be done anyway, regardless of how much they struggled.

The voices of the three men rose and fell around him, as they discussed the question. Deacon Mast announced the result. "It's you, Bishop. Minister Kanagy has the opening."

"*Yah,* I think that's correct." Bishop Beiler got to his feet and led the way downstairs. The singing had begun again, but everyone stopped by the time the men were seated on the ministers' bench up in front of the living room. As Minister Kanagy rose to his feet for the opening sermon, Bishop Beiler stilled his mind. He needed peace in his heart right now.

TWENTY-EIGHT

That afternoon Verna carried bowls of white fluffy popcorn into the living room. *Mamm* tried her best to put on a cheerful face. No one really looked upbeat, even when they smiled and offered their thanks for the popcorn Verna gave them.

Ida and Debbie helped by filling glasses of apple cider to go with the popcorn. Their married brothers, Wayne and Reuben, were here, along with their *fraus* and young children. They'd arrived soon after the morning church service and meal had ended. Lois was outside with their children to make sure they stayed in the yard.

Neither of the brothers had mentioned why they'd driven over from their homes a district away, but Verna was certain the trip didn't involve a friendly family visit. Word must have reached them about her troubles with Joe. And perhaps worse — about her stubborn refusal to end the relationship. The family honor was at stake, and if she knew Wayne and Reuben, they would wish to say their piece.

Mamm hovered around the room, now and then shooting off random comments . . . "Your bowl is empty, Reuben.

"Oh how your children are growing — for both of you.

"It's so *gut* to see everyone.

"Shouldn't you eat more? You look so skinny. Men are supposed to gain weight when they're married."

When Reuben's *frau,* Esther, looked up in surprise at this implied insult of her cooking skills, *Mamm* laughed and waved her hand about. "I'm sorry, Esther. I didn't mean anything by that remark. Reuben's always been such a light eater. I often thought he'd wither and blow away as he was growing up."

"Please, *Mamm,*" Reuben interrupted. He reached up to take his mother by the arm. "Sit down. You'll wear yourself out with all this pacing about."

Mamm allowed herself to be seated in her rocker, where she fanned herself with a section of *The Budget* snatched from the floor. "I do declare it's hot in here. Summers always are. Shall I open more windows?"

"We're fine," Bishop Beiler said. "Do

control yourself, Saloma. Worrying isn't going to make anything easier."

Verna fled to the kitchen. She didn't blame them if they discussed her openly. It was the Amish way, but still it made her uncomfortable to listen. Never before had her actions so affected the family.

"You look pale," Ida whispered, her hands full of glasses with cider. "Here, take some nourishment."

Verna shook her head but took a moment to pull in her emotions. She grabbed glasses of cider in each hand and followed Ida back into the living room.

Wayne regarded her with a baleful stare as she handed him his cider. He'd always been decent in his younger years and acted his part as the eldest child of the family. No doubt Wayne expected her to follow his example and, as the eldest of the three sisters, do the right thing. In her case, stop seeing Joe.

"Sit down, girls. Sit down." *Mamm* waved her hands around.

"We still haven't served everyone," Ida protested.

"Ach . . . yah . . . I'm all *ferhoodled." Mamm* appeared close to tears. "But do hurry. We can't keep the children outside much longer."

Verna felt icy stabs of fear run up her arms at this reminder from *Mamm.*

"We'll hurry," Ida said, rushing toward the kitchen with Debbie close behind. Verna forced herself to follow, keeping her gaze lowered as the three of them managed to serve the rest of the cider in two trips. Each girl kept one for herself and found seats among the family in the living room.

Silence fell after *Daett* cleared his throat. "It pains me greatly that things have come to this state of affairs. I do wish to say I did not call for Wayne and Reuben to come over this afternoon. They came on their own accord, but I do give them credit for their concern. This shows a tender heart toward their sister Verna. They have taken the afternoon off and traveled here with their families. So perhaps we will let them have their say first."

Wayne nodded. "I do wish to express my sympathy for what Verna and the rest of the family are going through. This must be worse with all of you living right in the district. We hear things, of course, but it's not quite the same." He shifted on his chair. "I hoped I'd come here today and be able to express my full support for Verna. But from what I've heard, this may not be the case. I hope to hear from Verna herself on what's going on. I wish to have explained why she can't see clearly what's happening with Joe. The man has apparently led quite a secret life, it seems, during his *rumspringa* time. This was a thing Joe has kept well hidden, even managing to join the church without it being found out. We await Verna's explanation before saying more." Wayne folded his hands and stopped though he looked even more troubled than when he'd arrived.

Verna wanted to burst out and say that what they'd heard wasn't true. That Joe had told her everything. But no one would believe her, and she had best remain silent for now. There would be time to speak later.

Daett glanced toward Reuben.

Reuben grimaced. "I don't know if I can add anything to what Wayne said. It expresses pretty much how I feel. Disappointed first of all that Verna has let things come to this state. There's no reason her relationship with Joe shouldn't be history by now, and perhaps Joe should even be excommunicated for the things he's done. People might understand a mistake in judgment on Verna's part when she first dated Joe. We all make those. But this continued stubbornness in the face of the obvious truth is hard for me to understand."

Reuben was being nasty, Verna thought. His words of rebuke cut deep. A tear trickled down her cheek.

Daett looked at her, apparently wanting her to speak. She opened her mouth but no words came. With great effort she finally began. "I wish . . . I had hoped . . . well, perhaps . . . that you would all be understanding of Joe and me and not rush to judgment like everyone in the community seems to be doing. Shouldn't I be the one who understands Joe the best? I'm the person closest to him other than his own family. But even then doesn't a man's *frau* touch the deepest part of his heart?"

"But you're not his *frau!*" *Daett* exclaimed.

"I know, but I will be someday. Already my heart touches his. I don't see why you can't understand that."

"Because you haven't said the wedding vows yet!" Wayne burst out. "There's still time to save yourself from this man."

"And what if I had said the vows?" Verna looked at him. "Wouldn't I stand with him regardless? Why should I do any less now?"

"But you're not even promised to him, Verna!" *Mamm* exclaimed. "Are you?"

"*Nee,* I'm not," Verna admitted. "And yet I love him."

"I see it's useless talking with her," Reu-

335

ben said. "I had hoped for better things."

"So had I," Wayne added.

"We all hoped for better things," *Daett* said. "But this matter is out of our hands anyway. The ministry has decided this morning that Joe's membership will be placed on probation until this matter is settled. And Verna is being strongly encouraged to stay away from him until his situation is resolved. All of us, especially the two ministers and Deacon Mast, hope she will take the counsel given to her."

Verna felt the blood rush from her face. She gripped the side of the chair as a cry leaped from her lips. "*Nee!* You cannot do this! Joe is innocent!"

Daett's voice was firm. "Then time will prove it to be so, Verna. And no harm will be done. Joe understands, I'm sure. In fact, if I have to remind you, Joe agreed with me that your relationship with him was over. You shouldn't be the one to pursue the matter. Accept our counsel this afternoon and let this thing lie."

"I can't," Verna whispered, her whole body now cold. She couldn't even feel her hands that were clinging to the side of the chair.

"Then this is a sad day in the life of this family." *Daett* was extremely serious. "I had hoped you would listen to your elders,

Verna. You're a young woman, and like Eve in the garden, subject to error. Please reconsider."

Verna met everyone's gaze as she looked around the room, but her hands shook. "And if I do and Joe is later found innocent, how will that look to him? And not only him, but to me as well. I would have to live the rest of my life with the knowledge that I didn't stand by Joe in his darkest hour. *Nee,* I-I won't . . . do that to Joe or myself."

Reuben looked ready to say something, but he didn't.

Mamm was crying, as was Ida.

Verna's heart hurt to see them weeping on her account, but what else could she do? She couldn't leave Joe to walk this road alone.

"Then I hope Joe will soon be proven innocent," *Daett* finally said. "You have either great courage, Verna, or you're very stubborn. I'm not sure which at the moment. But know that if Joe is found guilty, you will be held accountable for not following the ministry's counsel."

"Stubborn, that's what she is!" Reuben accused.

You don't know anything about me! Verna wanted to fire back. But she pressed her lips together and held the words inside instead.

337

Mamm had risen to her feet and walked over to give Verna a hug.

Verna wrapped her arms around her *mamm*'s shoulders and allowed her own tears to flow freely. Great sobs came from the depth of her being. She mustn't be totally rejected by the family if *Mamm* still hugged her. Perhaps deep down they admired her loyalty. It was the Amish way, was it not? One stood by her husband . . . except she was doing so before Joe and she married.

If she were proven wrong, there would be horrible repercussions. But she would welcome the pains, Verna decided. The community would welcome her back into the fold after she humbled herself. That option was better than if she were wrong about Joe. And if Joe really was guilty, she wouldn't care what the community did to her.

"Okay, can we dry our tears now?" *Mamm* felt her way back to her rocker. "What's done is done, and I don't think anyone is undoing it. So let's not mourn over spilled milk. The family is together tonight like it hasn't been in a long time. My heart is glad even with this sorrow. Open the front door, Ida, and let the children come in. They've been peeking in the window for the past half hour."

The mood soon lightened as Ida followed *Mamm*'s direction and all four of Wayne's children and Reuben's two raced in. *Mamm* took the smallest ones on her lap. She cooed in their ears. The oldest ones looked around a few times, clearly curious about what had gone on. There was nothing for the children to see except the red, tear-stained faces of the women and the stern faces of the men.

Soon the two eldest children dashed outside again.

Lois went over and tapped Verna on the shoulder. "What was decided?" she whispered. "I have to know."

Verna got up and led Lois into the kitchen. Debbie felt a bit uncomfortable being present with such intimate family troubles being discussed. She excused herself to go upstairs.

"You don't really want to know," Verna told Lois when they were alone in the kitchen. "Everyone thinks I should cut off my relationship with Joe."

Lois huffed. "I already knew that. What happens if you *don't*?"

Verna looked down. "Honestly, I don't know. *Daett* said the ministers and Deacon Mast had discussed it. If I don't heed their counsel and Joe is found guilty, I must undergo church discipline."

Lois appeared indignant. "What if they're wrong about Joe?"

Verna winced. "You know how it works. The ministry will be given credit for being vigilant, which I guess is understandable. If they supported Joe and were wrong, that's what would set tongues wagging."

Lois's face was all sympathetic. "I hope you're not in for a big disappointment."

Verna frowned. "You don't believe Joe's innocent either?"

Lois raised her hands in the air as she said, "I don't know, Verna! Don't attack me. I'm just saying how it looks."

"I'm sorry," Verna murmured. "You're right. And I know how it looks."

Lois wrapped Verna in a tight hug. "You're so brave. I hope I find such a worthy love someday."

"Thank you!" Verna whispered.

Lois held her at arm's length. "Is he really worth this much?"

Verna nodded. "Every last bit of it. Joe has a heart of gold."

TWENTY-NINE

That evening after supper Verna waited as Wayne held the buggy shafts and Reuben came out of the barn with *Daett*'s driving horse, Milo. Her brothers knew where she planned to go — to see Joe. This was something they wholeheartedly disagreed with, yet they'd had their say earlier and were now showing nothing but love toward their sister.

Verna stepped forward to fasten the tugs when Reuben arrived and maneuvered Milo between the buggy shafts. He shooed her away and pointed toward the buggy. "Climb in. We'll get the buggy ready." She did as she was told, and the two men quickly had Milo and the buggy ready to go.

"You're sure you want to do this?" Wayne asked as he threw Verna the lines.

He already knew the answer, so Verna just looked away.

"Get up!" she called to Milo. She glanced

back to see her brothers gazing after her with sorrowful looks. At the last minute, *Mamm* stepped out on the front porch to give her a little wave. Verna clutched the lines. She was a grown woman now with duties beyond childhood loyalties. In her heart she was Joe's *frau.*

Verna guided Milo north at the end of the lane and drove along the empty roads. Her thoughts turned to her younger siblings. They should be at the hymn singing by now. Ida had left with Debbie some time ago with Buttercup hitched to the buggy. Lois had ridden with Emery. Verna had waited until all the young folks from the district were at the evening's activities before she ventured out. The last thing she needed were curious glances as she passed buggies heading in another direction. It wouldn't take many guesses for people to figure out where Bishop Beiler's eldest daughter was bound.

The shame she caused her *daett* bothered her the most. He'd sat on his rocker with his popcorn bowl filled before she left. He'd tried to act cheerful, but all the while his face had been shadowed with sorrow. Verna wiped her eyes on her dress sleeve. This was taking a toll on all of them, and she had her share in the blame.

"Please forgive me, dear *Hah,* if I am

wrong," Verna whispered toward the heavens. There was silence broken only by the steady beat of Milo's hooves. How kind of *daett* to allow her the use of his favorite driving horse. He could easily have forbidden it, and she would have had to use one of the smaller workhorses because Ida was driving Buttercup tonight.

Deep sorrow filled her heart as she watched the hayfields go past the buggy door. She was the eldest girl in the family, and yet here she was the one who broke *Daett*'s and *Mamm*'s hearts first, when all along everyone thought that task would fall to Lois and her love for the *Englisha* world. Minutes later Verna approached the Weaver farmstead. It looked deserted. A few of the Weavers' cows gazed over the barnyard fence at her. The draft horses paused in the pasture to lift their heads as she drove in. Several of them trotted closer to the fence along the road.

Had everyone left for the evening? But Joe wouldn't be out somewhere . . . and certainly not to the hymn singing. Verna pulled to a stop by the hitching post and climbed out to secure Milo. She took quick steps toward the front porch. There she gave the front door a sharp rap. When there was no response, she knocked again. Perhaps she'd been wrong. Maybe Joe *had* gone to the hymn singing. But how could that be?

Verna returned to the buggy but hesitated before she untied Milo. She ought to check the barn yet. Joe was somewhere. Maybe he was working late on his chores and hadn't heard her drive in.

Verna was halfway to the barn when the door opened and Joe appeared. Happiness spread over his face when he caught sight of her. "Verna, you have come?" He hurried toward her, and she held out her arms to him. But he stopped a few feet away, and his face clouded over. "You shouldn't be here, Verna. You're only hurting yourself and your family. Didn't your *daett* tell you this afternoon? My membership has been placed on probation."

"*Yah,* he told me." Verna frowned. "Please, Joe, let's not argue. I have my own choices to make. I believe my heart more than what some people believe using their ears and eyes. Will you hold that against me?"

"But you can't do this."

"Joe." Verna reached out to take his hand. "Joe, aren't you glad to see me?"

"What can I say?" he said softly. "You know I am. I guess I have to gather my wits about me."

Verna pulled on his hand. "Perhaps you

could gather them better sitting somewhere. Maybe in the house?"

"Nee." He stopped her. "I still have chores to finish in the barn. Would you help me? We can talk then."

"Yah." Her face brightened. "You know I will, but I'm afraid we'll only talk about one thing, and it won't do much *gut.*"

"I suppose so." He held open the barn door. "One's mind doesn't stray far from trouble, it seems."

"Then we must make it stray elsewhere." She grasped both of his hands. "Let's see only the future tonight. Let's see only what lies *beyond* this trouble. Is that not what faith does? Believing that *Da Hah* sees us even in our difficulty and has planned a way of escape? Was that not the attitude of the great prophet Daniel when the king threw him to the lions?"

A smile played on Joe's face. "I'm afraid I'm not Daniel, Verna. And we don't quite face the lions. Unless you want to call the *Englisha* law a lion. But they are only doing their duty."

Verna sobered. "There are lions everywhere, Joe. I don't know where exactly or who they are, but they wish to tear our lives apart. If you go to jail it may not be to the lions' den, but it will be the lions' den for our hearts."

Alarm flickered across Joe's face. "That's exactly why you shouldn't be here, Verna. You can still save yourself. Go back to your *daett* and tell him you're sorry, that you made a mistake. That you'll wait until my situation is resolved and then decide what you want to do. That would be so much better for you, Verna."

"And for you?" Her eyes searched his face. "Would that be the best for you?"

He avoided her gaze. "I don't think of myself, Verna, but of you."

"That's why I know you have a golden heart, Joe." She touched his face. "Let's say no more about going back. I will stand with you even if you go to jail. If that happens, we'll make things right with the church when you come out."

Horror crossed his face. "But, Verna, if I'm found guilty that could be twenty years or more of jail time. You and I would be old by then. I can't ask this of you. Your time for bearing children would be gone."

A wry look flickered on her face. "*Yah,* Joe. Did I not say there are lions? That's why you must not be found guilty."

He tried to keep the despair off his face. "I didn't do these actions I'm accused of, Verna. All I can do is depend on that truth."

346

She winced. "That doesn't mean you won't be found guilty, Joe. I don't know much about *Englisha* law, but I imagine innocent people are often put in jail. It's a matter of what they can prove or not prove."

He groaned and sank down on a hay bale. "Then I'm finished. They have the witness's word and my fingerprints on the stolen items. I was seeing her during that time." He buried his face in his hands.

She pulled on his arm, her voice insistent. "Tell me this, Joe — and don't even think of lying! Have you been with her? In that way?"

His head jerked up, his eyes wide. "I would not have done such a thing, Verna!"

Relief flooded her face. "Then she can be driven back. I know it, Joe. *Da Hah* will help us."

"But how, Verna?"

She sat on the hay bale beside him. "I don't know, but I'll talk to Debbie. She knows about such things. I think *Da Hah* may have sent Debbie to us partly for this hour of our trouble. We need someone who understands the *Englisha* ways, Joe. They are so different from us."

"*Yah,*" he allowed, "they are." Silence fell, filled only by the soft rustlings of the barn settling around them. Moments later Joe leaped up from the bale of hay. "I'm forgetting my chores."

Verna managed a strangled laugh.

Joe grinned. "You can tag along. I only have to feed the calves."

Verna stayed close to him while he measured the feed. After the bucket was ready he dropped it within reach of the hungry animals.

"Have they been weaned long?" she asked.

"Only a few weeks. They're spring calves."

"Will you be keeping all of them?"

He shrugged. "The heifers, I think. *Daett* is expanding his herd next year. And these are quality stock."

"I wouldn't expect anything else from the Weaver farm," she teased.

His spirits seemed lifted by the time they were done. Joe led the way back to the front of the barn and lit a lantern.

Verna sat on a bale of hay and waited as Joe hung the lantern from the barn ceiling. Lazy flies soon buzzed around, and a moth banged into the bright glass and tumbled to the barn floor.

Verna watched it flutter downward and a horrible thought filled her mind. Surely she wasn't a moth drawn to Joe's flame of love, only to have her heart burned and destroyed? This wasn't a sign from *Da Hah,* she told herself. Joe was not a flame, and she was not a moth. They were in love, and *Da Hah* would honor their love. She had to believe that or she would lose her mind. Verna glanced over at Joe's face as he sat beside her.

"Hold me, Joe, please," she whispered. "I'm scared."

He looked startled but slowly pulled her into his embrace. His arms were strong. He smelled of clean grain and fresh hay.

Verna turned and buried her head against his chest, willing the fear to leave. Here she was safe and would always be safe. Because Joe loved *Da Hah* and His ways as she did. And *Da Hah* would not fail them.

"Verna?" His voice sounded far away.

"Yah?" She looked up, still nestled against him.

"I know I have no right to ask this of you . . . being in the state I am. I was going to wait until everything is clear, but my heart is moved tonight by your love and by my desire for you. Will you be my *frau,* Verna? When this is over?"

She jerked upright, her heart suddenly pounding at the words she longed to hear. "Oh, Joe! You know my answer to that!"

His arms wrapped around her again.

She clung to him.

"Verna . . ." His calloused hands found her face.

She closed her eyes as he came closer. She held her breath as he kissed her, and she drank in the sweetness of it, her face burning brighter than the lantern flame. But she still met his gaze above his clean-shaven face when he moved back. Their world would be made right. It couldn't be otherwise with the love rising inside her. She would never find another man more *wunderbah* than Joe. There would never be a more memorable night than this — despite their troubles.

He leaned in close again, and moments later, Verna pulled away. She had better go home now. It wasn't *gut* that they were alone too long with no one in the house. They didn't need more whispers in the community about things that were not true.

Verna stood up with Joe's hands still in hers. "I had best be going, Joe. But I will see you again soon."

He rose to his feet. "*Yah,* I suppose you should. I will pray that *Da Hah* soon brings this awful time to an end."

Verna wrapped her arms around his neck, and he pulled her close for another long kiss. Then she slowly pulled back. If she didn't leave soon, she would float home. In a daze, she followed Joe outside and accepted his hand as he helped her into the buggy. He undid the tie rope and put it under the buggy seat.

"Stay on the road," he said with a twinkle in his eye.

"You are a very naughty boy," she said. She clucked and Milo took off at a good clip. Joe had seen enough of her flaming face for one evening, Verna figured. She had touched his heart with her love, and Joe had asked her to be his *frau*! Verna hugged herself as she drove Milo out of the Weavers' driveway. This she would tell no one until they could see what she could see — that Joe was a very *gut* man.

THIRTY

Mid August had set in when Debbie drove her car west toward Lewistown. On this Friday morning it was only a little past seven o'clock. The slight haze that hung along the horizon still hadn't melted away even with the full blaze of the rising sun. How like the troubled clouds that hung over the Beiler household. Debbie was thankful Ms. Hatcher, Joe's public defender, had consented to see her.

The truth was that the trouble with Joe and Verna had stalled things in her own life. Debbie had wanted to approach Bishop Beiler to discuss her plans to join the Amish church, but she decided not to when Lois told her this couldn't happen until the fall classes began right after communion. So there was still plenty of time. But it wouldn't have hurt to broach the subject early, to feel the bishop out about her plan. In his present state of mind, she didn't wish to add further stress.

Lois had also warned her last night, "You have to watch the mood of the community. They might be touchy right now about someone from the outside joining while trouble is afoot. Our people are that way, you know."

Debbie hadn't really known, but it did make sense. When trouble came to a house, everyone's nerves were set on edge. Well, she would just have to wait and see if this would blow over. But would it?

Last Wednesday evening after she came home from work, Verna had raced out of the house the moment the Camry's tires had hit the driveway. "I want to speak to you alone," Verna had gasped, out of breath.

Debbie stepped out of the car and glanced around before she said, "There's no one around, Verna. Has something come up about Joe?"

Verna nodded. "Well, I think it has. But I wanted to ask your advice."

Debbie leaned against her car and waited.

Verna blurted out her news. "Joe has been assigned a public defender — a Ms. Hatcher. She wants Joe to sue the girl who's accusing him of this crime. Sue her for defamation of character. She says it would create sympathy with the *Englisha* people.

353

They would want to see a man defending himself — especially an Amish man."

"Well, yes, that might help," Debbie had agreed.

Verna frowned. "You speak as an *Englisha, yah*. Not as one of our people. And suing someone? Even that is going too far for me. The Amish do not do that. But I do wish Joe could work with his lawyer. His *daett*, though, has forbidden him from taking advantage of any of her suggestions after that awful recommendation. She doesn't understand our people, so no one trusts her anymore. Lloyd says he will go straight to Deacon Mast if Joe does anything but tell the truth. *Da Hah* alone is our strength, Lloyd says, and Joe cannot bring further shame on the community by using the strength of unbelievers."

"I guess that does cause a problem," Debbie had allowed.

Verna had continued. "Something must be done to help Joe. I need to know what the lawyer is telling Joe, and he won't tell me. Maybe it's something that Joe doesn't understand. And you're the only one who thinks like they do. Our minds quickly become caught in confusion when the *Englisha* world is involved."

And so she had been persuaded and

agreed to meet with Ms. Hatcher. Verna had produced the address of the attorney's office in Lewistown, along with the phone number. Debbie had mentioned the situation to Mr. Fulton, who had heard of the case through her father. He'd been appropriately sympathetic and readily agreed to a Friday off for her. Most people — herself included — had that reaction when the Amish were involved. Even ones accused of robbery.

Ms. Hatcher hadn't been happy though. From the sound of her voice, she'd almost refused the appointment. What Debbie had said to persuade Ms. Hatcher she still wasn't sure — perhaps the part about her life with the Beiler family, whose eldest daughter was dating Joe Weaver. That was why Debbie made sure to wear an Amish dress today. If Ms. Hatcher was persuaded by such things, she might as well play them for the full effect. And she supposed it did make sense in people's minds as to why she would be involved.

She wanted to walk in this morning and say, *I'm the sister of the girlfriend.* That would sound good, although it was true only in her heart. She felt like a sister and was treated like a sister. She'd even been allowed to sit in on the family conference that

Sunday afternoon a few weeks ago. It had taken a while to overcome her surprise at their openness as they discussed things right in front of her, but no one from the Beiler family seemed to think she shouldn't be there.

After Debbie had left with Ida for the Sunday-night hymn singing, Verna had gone to visit Joe. Debbie had heard this news after they arrived home, and Lois had gone over to Verna's bedroom to speak with her. There should have been an explosion the next morning at the breakfast table from Bishop Beiler. Lois had predicted it, but instead he seemed more broken in spirit than anything, carrying his sorrow like a man with a heavy burden on his back.

Little was said then. Even Lois kept her ready tongue in check. Verna had done more than speak with Joe the evening before, Debbie thought. The signs were there in the soft glow that crept into Verna's cheeks during unguarded moments.

If this had been her world, she would have guessed something improper had transpired last night. But this was not her world, and Verna wouldn't do such a thing. As to what exactly transpired, Debbie could only conjecture. That something had happened, she was quite certain. She slowed her car as she approached Lewistown and the traffic began to back up. She should have made the appointment further from rush hour, but Ms. Hatcher had said this was the only time she had open.

Debbie glanced at her watch. She'd still make it. She'd allowed plenty of time. While traffic crept along, Debbie's thoughts drifted to her four years of college life in a town similar to Lewistown. She had certainly seen more of the Amish in Lancaster than she did here. That was one of the benefits of the college being there.

Her parents thought she'd thrown her pricey education out the window. But she was still an educated person, so no one had cause for complaint other than for dreams broken — some that had never been hers. And in that department she had her own suffering. If the bishop knew she dreamed of an Amish husband someday, what would he say? But then perhaps he'd already figured that out. Now if only Alvin would do the same. Right now he seemed to go out of his way at the Sundays meetings to avoid her. But was it any wonder? Did she have the heart of an Amish woman? She was just an *Englisher* living in a world she wasn't part of. On Sundays she dressed Amish, but she still drove a car during the week. It was a miracle no one from the community had complained to Bishop Beiler about it.

How strange, Debbie thought, that in her world she had her choice of young men. But here in the Amish community, the man she wanted ignored her. She wasn't ready to admit defeat, even with the doubts that fluttered through her mind. Was she perhaps unattractive to Alvin? Surely that wasn't the problem. Alvin had seemed interested at first, and then — slam! — the door had shut.

Debbie sighed and checked the address before she picked a parking spot. Ms. Hatcher's office was still a block away, but she ought to grab an open space where it was available. Debbie parked and climbed out. A few strange glances came her way. She knew that when a woman dressed Amish and drove an automobile, she should expect reactions. Debbie walked along at a fast clip and soon found the office. Ms. Hatcher might be a public defender, but she kept her office in an upscale area. That might be a good thing . . . at least for Joe's prospects.

Debbie entered the office and greeted the secretary at the desk. "Good morning. Debbie Watson here for an eight-thirty appointment with Ms. Hatcher."

The woman's eyes took in Debbie's unstylish dress before she checked the appointment calendar. "Please go on in, Ms. Watson. Ms. Hatcher is expecting you."

Debbie followed the secretary's directions, found the right office, and entered.

A straitlaced businesswoman in her mid-forties glanced up when Debbie entered. She appeared grim, but said, "Ms. Watson, good morning. Have a seat, please."

Debbie sat down. "Thank you for taking my appointment."

Ms. Hatcher gave her a curt nod. "I understand you are family."

Debbie coughed. "Not really. I live with the Beilers, and have since early May."

"I see. So you're not Amish?" Ms. Hatcher's gaze took in the dress.

Debbie kept her voice firm. "I can't see why it makes any difference, but I'm in the process of becoming Amish. I'm still enough a part of the *Englisha* world that the family wants me to assist with the Joe Weaver matter, so here I am."

Ms. Hatcher leaned forward. "You must know I can't really discuss Mr. Weaver's case with you, even if you were family, without his permission. I'm bound by client confidentiality."

Debbie rose half out of her chair, thinking this appointment was useless. But she changed her mind. "I understand," she said, trying to sound meek — an Amish type of meekness — as she sat back down.

"What is it that you wish?"

"I want to help the family. Joe's girlfriend, Verna Beiler, wants to know if anything could be done that *will* help him."

Ms. Hatcher appeared amused. "I thought the men from the community looked after the family? This ought to be Joe's question, not the girlfriend's, correct?"

Debbie kept her gaze steady. "And has he asked what he can do to help his case, Ms. Hatcher?"

Ms. Hatcher blinked. "No, but I will try again this week. I have a meeting with him this Friday."

Debbie leaned forward on her chair. "And do you expect any better results?"

Ms. Hatcher hesitated. "No, I don't suppose so. He's quite stubborn . . . something about his Amish beliefs . . . and not liking my ideas for his defense. But surely he'll come around. Everyone puts up a defense in the end."

Debbie laughed and then said seriously, "You don't know the Amish very well. That is not how they operate."

Ms. Hatcher frowned. "Yes, that's possible. What do you propose?"

"That you tell me what you need. And I will tell Joe's girlfriend. Between the two of us, we will find the answers if they are to be found. But the burden will be on me because I am still *Englisha* and not subject to Amish restrictions. This way no one can fault the faithful church members. For your part, this will make it a winnable case for you because Joe is innocent."

Ms. Hatcher looked at Debbie. "I see." She hesitated and then whipped out a notepad. She slapped it on the desk. "Let's begin with a list of witnesses and people who knew both of them. Someone who can place Joe Weaver anywhere other than at the sites of the robberies on these dates. Especially here . . . and here . . . and here." Ms. Hatcher's finger stabbed the paper repeatedly. "I've already told Mr. Weaver what I need. 'Alibis' we call them in our world. What are they in yours?"

Debbie gave Ms. Hatcher a quick glance. "I'm not Amish, remember? I do know what an alibi is."

Ms. Hatcher's gaze swept the dress again. "My mistake again. I forgot . . ."

"It's complicated," Debbie said. "I hope to join the Amish community eventually."

Ms. Hatcher gave a sharp laugh. "I can only imagine. Do you think you and Joe's girlfriend can do anything to help?"

Debbie picked up the paper and studied the dates and times. "I'll speak with her, and we'll go from there."

Ms. Hatcher's voice was clipped. "Have Mr. Weaver bring this information to our appointment then. Nice solid witnesses, I hope. With no criminal records, preferably."

"I'll do what I can," Debbie said, but she'd already been dismissed. Ms. Hatcher was rummaging through the papers on her desk, clearly moving on.

Debbie stood and let herself out of the office.

THIRTY-ONE

Thirty minutes later Debbie pulled her car into the Beilers' driveway, driving up until the car was partially hidden from the main road. She was increasingly nervous about the community's reaction to the continued presence of an automobile at Bishop Beiler's place. With all the trouble already, the Beiler family didn't need another note of contention. She might even speak with Emery to see if he could move a piece of machinery and open a place for her car under the barn overhang so it would be even more out of sight.

Verna met her in the middle of the lawn. "Is there *gut* news?" She clutched her white apron, and her eyes begged for a positive answer.

"Come," Debbie touched Verna's arm. "Your prayers may have been answered at least in part, but we need to keep praying. Getting Joe to cooperate may be the hard part. That was Ms. Hatcher's concern."

Verna's face glowed with hope. "Then the lawyer told you what must be done?"

"Yes. She wants witnesses who can testify as to where Joe was on these dates and times." Debbie handed Verna the paper. "Joe may not have been anywhere other than at home, and he may refuse to ask his friends to testify if he wasn't home. Maybe that's why he's not cooperating."

"I don't know." Verna's fingers traced the writing on the paper. "This is a start. We must be thankful for what *Da Hah* has given us."

"We need to gather this information before Joe's appointment with Ms. Hatcher on Friday. Do you think you can get him to cooperate?"

Verna shook her head. "*Nee.* I think it's you that must ask him, Debbie."

"Me? Ask Joe?"

"I think he will tell you what he will not tell the lawyer."

"But, Verna . . ."

Verna's eyes pleaded with her. "You have already done so much, Debbie, and I almost dare not ask for more. But Joe must not go to jail, and this . . . it may be all we have."

Debbie winced. "Do you people always make things this hard?"

Verna appeared troubled. "Now you speak as the *Englisha,* Debbie. I thought your heart was with us?"

Debbie hesitated. "Okay, Verna." She took a deep breath. "I'll do what I can. I have the rest of the day off, and it's at your disposal."

"Oh!" Verna's eyes filled with tears. "It was a blessed day when you came to our house, Debbie. Only *Da Hah* could have sent you. Thank you so much."

Debbie looked away. She understood Verna's emotion, but this much praise was a little overboard. She finally met her friend's gaze.

"Then you will speak with Joe today?" Verna asked.

"If that's what you wish."

"I will go with you." Verna glanced back at the house. "There's not much going on right now. I'll tell *Mamm.*"

"I'll come along," Debbie said as she followed Verna to the house.

Saloma met them at the front door, and Debbie waited while Verna explained their errand. Saloma gave Verna a quick hug. "You know I won't stand in the way of what needs doing, Verna. Just be careful that you don't do anything that's against the *Ordnung.*" Saloma glanced at Debbie. "I thank you for what you're doing, Debbie. We're all very grateful."

"Don't think about it," Debbie said. "You're giving me a place to stay, aren't you?"

A slight smile crept over Saloma's face as she dismissed them with a quick wave of her hand.

Debbie stayed close behind Verna on the walk back to the barn. Though she paid room and board, it wasn't nearly what the amount should be. Perhaps if she helped with Joe and Verna's problem, it would help repay the Beilers in an even greater way than money could. She jingled her keys in her hand and stopped short of her car. "I think we'd better take the buggy, Verna, even though it takes longer."

Verna didn't have to think long. "That's very wise. It will also make it easier for Joe."

Debbie stepped back to allow Verna the lead. They entered the musky darkness of the barn. Inside the summer heat was held at bay. "We'll take Buttercup," Verna decided without hesitation. She called for the horse at the barnyard door and had Buttercup haltered seconds later.

Once outside, Debbie held up the shafts. This she knew how to do. She held them high in the air and brought them down over the horse as she'd been taught. It was easy with two people. The Beiler girls made the maneuver look so effortless when they hitched the horse to the buggy by themselves. Once everything was fastened, Debbie climbed inside. Verna threw her the lines and then pulled herself up.

"You drive," Verna said. "I'm too distracted right now. We might run up a ditch." Debbie laughed, which elicited a weary smile from Verna. "I guess that is a little ridiculous. But I feel so tense I could burst. What if Joe refuses to tell us if there are any witnesses? Or worse, what if he had no one who was with him on any of those nights?"

"There ought to be someone," Debbie offered. She turned onto Route 522. Buttercup knew the way well enough, so Debbie only had to keep slight tension on the lines. She was still nervous about driving a horse.

"I pray you're right!" Verna said letting out a breath.

"Get up!" Debbie called to Buttercup, who was moving forward at an easy walk. The horse paid her no mind. She didn't even switch her tail because Debbie's voice didn't yet contain the Amish air of authority.

Verna's voice was tense as she prayed out loud. "Help us, *dear Hah,* help us help Joe."

Debbie focused on the task at hand — keeping Buttercup on the road.

Beside her, Verna spoke a steady stream of prayer, pausing only to wave at passing buggies. She prayed until they arrived at the Weaver farm.

"Thank *Da Hah*!" Verna exclaimed. "Joe's working with the team close to the barn. I was afraid we'd have to walk all the way to the back pasture."

Debbie pulled Buttercup to a halt by the barnyard fence. Off in the field, Joe waved and came toward them at a fast walk, leading his team. Verna tied Buttercup to the fence.

"You're here again!" Joe came up, leaned over the fence, and touched Verna on the arm. "Do you think this is wise?"

"It's important. Trust me," Verna said, gazing into his eyes.

Debbie glanced away until Joe said, "Hi, Debbie. Good to see you again."

"And you," Debbie replied. "I hope you still feel that way after you hear what we have to say."

"Oh?" Joe's face fell. "Then there is bad news?"

"Depends how you look at it." Verna wrung her hands. "Joe, you have to tell us who was with you on the nights of the robberies. These times." Verna unfolded the paper and handed it to him. "You already know this is what the lawyer needs. Please cooperate."

Joe didn't even glance at the paper. He stared at Verna instead. "Where did this come from?"

"I got it from your lawyer," Debbie spoke up. "Don't blame anyone but me."

Joe met her gaze. "It's not a matter of blame, Debbie. It's what can and cannot be done. We don't believe in doing things the way the world does them. This lawyer already tried to talk me into suing my accuser. I know you come from another world, but suing people is not how we live."

"Joe, please." Verna was close to tears. "This is not about suing anyone. It's only proving where you were at certain times. There's nothing wrong with this."

Joe seemed to waver, so Debbie plunged forward. "Okay, so let me ask the questions of these witnesses — if there are any. You don't even have to get involved. But you can surely tell us who they are — or if there *are* witnesses to your whereabouts at these times."

Joe thought for a moment. "Perhaps I could do that. If you're both agreed that this is right."

"Oh, Joe!" Verna clung to his arm. "We are!"

"There's nothing wrong with this." Debbie pointed to the paper Joe was still holding. "Who would know your whereabouts on those nights and on those dates? Hopefully someone who isn't family and who is reputable."

Joe studied the paper for a long time. His face grew dark. "These are all weekend nights, Verna. Fridays and Saturdays. I cannot do this."

"For us, Joe! Please!" Verna begged.

Debbie saw him weaken and his hand tremble.

"Okay, I will tell you who knows, but I will say no more. If he decides not to speak, you must hold nothing against him. Promise me that."

"He will speak, Joe!" Verna had tears on her face.

Joe said, "The man is Paul Wagler. He's already offered to help in whatever way he can. It's just that there will be trouble for him in the community if he is asked to testify in court. I don't want to ask him, Verna."

"Then *we* will ask him," Verna said, her face glowing. "We need to ask him by Friday morning. That's when you have your appointment with the lawyer, isn't it?"

"It is." Joe looked at the ground. "But you mustn't ask him, Verna. Debbie must. It's the only way Paul will feel free with his choice. He must not be pressured, and you *are* the bishop's daughter."

Verna's face shone. "We must go then. And thank you, Joe. Only Debbie will speak with Paul, I promise."

"I must get back to my work." Joe turned to go and gave a little wave over his shoulder.

Verna didn't wait for Joe to reach his team before she'd untied Buttercup. Soon the girls were driving out of the lane, Buttercup moving along at a brisk trot. Verna took the lines this time.

Debbie's mind was already reeling with what she must do. What on earth would Paul think of her when she went to see him alone? Would he think she'd orchestrated the visit? But she hadn't, and he would have to understand that. She would see to it that no fancy ideas entered his head.

"Oh, Debbie!" Verna held the lines in one hand and squeezed her friend's arm with the other. "Thank you! Thank you! I can't thank you enough for helping us."

"The Amish do make things harder," Debbie ventured. "Why didn't Joe volunteer

371

this information a long time ago? Especially if Paul offered to help?"

"It's his *gut* heart," Verna replied. "And we Amish don't like to deal with the *Englisha* law. But you must not hold that against him. I love Joe even more for wanting to spare Paul from having to testify, especially if, as Joe says, it will cause trouble for Paul."

Debbie nodded. Yes, that was like Joe. For that reason alone Debbie would be glad to help if she could. But seeing Paul Wagler? She sighed. She really didn't look forward to that visit at all.

THIRTY-TWO

Two hours later Debbie parked her car close to the Waglers' barn. She climbed out and closed the car door with care. The silence of the place rushed over her. No one was in sight. Though she'd driven her car, she was still in her Amish dress — at Verna's insistence.

Debbie approached the barn and peeked in. "Hello? Is anyone here?" A few of the horses banged against their stalls. She turned and walked past her car and across the lawn. The front door of the house opened before she got up the steps. Before her the smiling face of Paul's *mamm,* Lavina, appeared.

"Well, if it isn't Debbie!" Lavina gushed. "What brings you out here . . . and with your . . ." Lavina took the car in with a quick glance, but her smile was back in an instant. "Why don't you come in, Debbie? I can get some cold lemonade squeezed right away. It gets right warm on these summer afternoons."

Debbie cleared her throat. "I need to speak with Paul, Mrs. Wagler. That's why I checked at the barn first. I don't wish to take up your time. I'm sure you're busy."

Lavina waved vaguely. "All the men are down at Silas Warners' place, helping with the hay making. You can drive down and see if Paul has a few moments. But first I insist on a glass of lemonade. I couldn't live with myself if I knew Bishop Beiler's Debbie had been here and I sent her away without any refreshment."

"Really, please, it's not necessary," Debbie tried to keep her voice firm, but resistance was useless. The look on Lavina's face said she wouldn't take no for an answer. And it did warm her heart — those few words Lavina had spoken . . . *Bishop Beiler's Debbie.* The sound was like music to her ears. How could she resist? She'd been accepted in the community — at least by some people. This was a delightful moment indeed, and so unexpected in the middle of a hectic day.

Lavina led the way into the kitchen chattering up a storm.

"Oh, Debbie! Paul speaks about you all the time. I hope you don't mind. It's not every day that we get to see such a *wunder-bah* thing happening right in front of our eyes. An *Englisha* person — and a girl at that — coming in from the world to join the faith. I told myself this very week, 'I'm sure Debbie has plans to join the membership class this fall.' I can tell by the way your face looks so peaceful at the Sunday morning services. It's like you've arrived where many of our young people ought to be." Lavina clucked her tongue and barely paused to catch Debbie's quick nod. She hadn't exactly planned to divulge the information about the baptism class, but this deluge of praise unsettled her.

"Yes, I do think I'll join the class — if Bishop Beiler agrees to it. But I haven't talked about it yet. Not even with the bishop."

Lavina now energetically fixed the lemonade. "Your secret is safe with me! Not a word to anyone — not even Paul. Although I think he suspects it already. But there I go, saying things I shouldn't . . . Do sit down a minute," Lavina said, setting two cool glasses on the table. Then she plopped down in the chair across from Debbie.

"This is my own little blend." Lavina beamed. "Just a pinch of salt to bring out the flavor, but not too much or it spoils it.

Paul says only I can pull it off. He says he's never tasted lemonade quite like his *mamm*'s."

Debbie hid her face behind the glass for a moment, as she gathered herself together. "It does look like wonderful lemonade, Lavina." Debbie forced herself to take a long sip, but swallowed with care. Seconds later she made no effort to hide her pleasure. "My, this *is* good!"

Lavina lowered her head modestly. She picked up her glass and took a sip.

"You'll have to give me the recipe someday. Lois is attempting to teach me cooking skills, but I'm a slow learner."

"I'm sure you're doing fine." Lavina sipped on her lemonade and appeared pensive. "My Paul's a hard man to please sometimes. He's seen too much of the world, I think. There were years there when I worried about him more than all of the others put together. I've been on him this last year to make his choice of a *frau,* but he doesn't see a girl who catches his fancy, he claims." Lavina cast a meaningful look Debbie's way.

Debbie stood, the glass of lemonade half finished. She tried to ignore the obvious insinuation. "Thank you, Mrs. Wagler. This lemonade is wonderful. And now I'm sure

I'm keeping you from your chores. I really must go."

"Think nothing of it." Lavina waved her hand again. "The men are down the road about two miles, on the left, with their wagons. You can't miss them. And take the rest of the lemonade with you. Paul can bring back the glass."

Debbie hesitated but finally agreed. Protest was useless, and the lemonade *was* delicious.

"See you again!" Lavina said, waving from the front door as Debbie dashed across the lawn. She must look like a real Amish woman now, Debbie thought with a grin. Lemonade glass in hand, Amish dress flowing behind her. And from Lavina's words, she had the interest of an eligible Amish man — and all before she'd joined the baptismal class. Talk about accomplishments! She ought to practically glow. And she would, if it had been Alvin Knepp's mother who had served her this lemonade. But Paul Wagler's *mamm*? That was a different story altogether.

Debbie climbed into her car, started it up, and made the turn out of the driveway. On the way out, she waved to Lavina still standing on the front porch. Debbie comforted herself. That Paul was interested in her wasn't her doing. She'd never given any encouragement to him.

Now she had a more urgent matter to think about. Did she really want to walk in on a hayfield full of Amish men and ask to speak with Paul? No, she most certainly did not! But duty called, and if she were to come back this evening to talk to Paul, would that be any better? His *mamm* would hang around in the background and read things into her every move. No, she would face the music now and hope for the best. And it was worth the grief if she could help Joe and Verna. So, yes, she would speak with Paul now.

Debbie drove in the direction Lavina had indicated and soon saw the wagons in the field beside the road. A small lane led in, and Debbie turned on it and bounced to a stop. What a sight she must make, she thought as she climbed out. Thankfully someone was already coming toward her so she wouldn't stand here long looking like a dunce. The man hadn't come far across the field before she recognized him as Paul.

He came to stop a few feet away and pushed his straw hat back on his head. "Debbie! What a surprise. What's a beautiful *Englisha* girl like you doing here in a hayfield?"

"I'm Amish," she shot back and pointed at her dress. "See?"

He grinned. "I do see, but it explains nothing. Did the Beilers' house burn down?"

"Would you be serious for a minute?" Debbie scolded. "I wouldn't have come out here over just anything. It's important."

"Okay." He leaned against her car, settling most of his weight on one foot. He waited with a patient look on his face.

Debbie glared at him. "It's about Joe, Paul. His lawyer says he needs alibis for the dates of the robberies." She handed him the paper. "Joe claims you would know about this, and that you've already offered to help. Joe wouldn't say more than that. He wasn't very excited about asking you to help. I take it you two were traveling on the dark side of life at the time."

"And Joe wants me to divulge his secrets?" Paul winced. "I was afraid things would come to this."

"Well, it won't do any good for Joe to say where he was. Who will believe him without a witness? He needs someone to vouch for him. And if there are unsavory details, it might actually make things look better for Joe . . . a hesitant witness on your part, shall we say."

"I see." He squinted into the sun. "An upside-down world. That's what the *Englisha* run."

"You don't have to malign my former life, Paul. I know what it is."

His eyebrows lifted. "Former! I like that. Are you permanent then? Settling in to our life?"

"I would like to believe so."

He nodded. "But back to Joe. What do you want from me?"

"That you verify where Joe was on these dates when called upon. Perhaps you could remember some details about the nights involved. What you were doing, what Joe was doing, and if anything can be verified. I'm assuming the two of you were together. Of course, the prosecution will challenge what you say, so you must tell the truth."

"And Joe wants me to do this?"

"Joe doesn't want you to do anything you don't want to. If you say no, there will be no hard feelings on Joe's part, but I wouldn't say that about myself."

"So *you* want me to do this?" He handed the paper back.

"Of course! For Joe and Verna's sake. And for human decency. What's wrong with you people, anyway?" She hadn't intended to get so fired up, but the words slipped out.

This had been a long day.

"You know what this will mean for the community?" He studied her. "That's the real problem."

"So you'd send a man to jail to spare unsavory details leaking out?"

He grinned. "No wonder Verna sent you."

"Never mind that. Will you do it?"

Paul hesitated a moment and then said, "On one condition."

She squinted at him. "What do you want?"

"Dinner with you, so I can explain what was going on to you first."

"Why on earth should your explanation matter to me?"

He stroked his bare chin. "Converts can be idealistic, you know. More so than we are. I just don't want you hearing about this from anyone else . . . secondhand."

"You shouldn't worry about me. This is about Joe and Verna."

He studied her for a moment. "Is it a deal or not?"

Debbie shifted on her feet. Why was the man being such a pill about this? Wasn't Joe his friend?

When she didn't speak, Paul continued. "Look, this is not the place to talk about this. I've got work to do here. Why don't you and I go out for a meal together . . .

tonight, perhaps . . . so I can explain fully. That way my mind will be eased . . . knowing you already know before it comes out in court."

"You're the limit, Paul. You know that, don't you? I guess I have no choice," she said, deliberately adding disgust to her voice.

Paul took no notice and even appeared pleased with himself. "For Verna and Joe's sake," he said. "I'll pick you up at six then."

Debbie imagined herself in Paul's courting buggy on the drive for all those miles into Mifflinburg. She might as well hang a sign around her neck: *Hey, look who I'm dating.* And if Alvin should hear of it, well, that would be the nail in that coffin for sure.

"Six then?" He was still looking at her, waiting.

"I'll pick *you* up at six!" she snapped. "We'll take *my* car. We can go to Lewistown."

"Okay! See you then." He straightened up, turned on his heel, and walked back across the field.

The nerve of the man! Debbie thought as she climbed back into her car. She'd been outmaneuvered on this one. But she really couldn't say no, and Paul did have a point. She could see where he'd be uncomfortable when she heard of his unsavory life from someone else. With the way he felt for her, Paul would rather spin the tale on his own. Debbie sighed. Well, it was only for one evening. And she knew exactly where she'd take this high-minded young Amish man. The very place Doug had learned his lesson — Andrea's Pizzeria! It was the perfect restaurant in which to bury unwarranted hopes and dreams.

THIRTY-THREE

That afternoon after Debbie arrived home, Verna's horrified whisper sounded in the upstairs bedrooms. "You are doing what?"

"Shhhh! I *think* Paul would have agreed to testify anyway, but it seemed easier to go this way," Debbie said. "And if I already know about what happened, I think it will be easier for Paul to speak up in court. I want to help where I can."

"Oh, Debbie!" Verna wailed. "What horrible things did they do together?"

Debbie shushed her. "I don't think they did anything that bad. Paul's just sensitive about his image and my opinion of him. Of course, if he only knew what I already think of him . . ." Debbie let the sentence hang. "Not that I haven't made things plain enough, but he's blind I guess."

"You'll tell me everything, won't you?" Verna clutched Debbie's arm. "And Joe's got a *gut* heart. He's repented, I know, for whatever it was."

Lois stuck her head in the bedroom door. "I think they're all creeps!" she said.

"Joe's not," Verna protested.

"Give me a break." Lois turned up her nose. "And you're falling for Paul, Debbie?"

Debbie laughed. "I am not!"

"Count me out either way." Lois disappeared from the doorway.

"Like she has anything to do with this." Verna groaned. "Do you mind, Debbie? This extra effort of yours that is needed?"

"I'm fine." Debbie patted Verna on the shoulder. "Now, let me go find Ida before she hears this from someone else."

"Ida?"

"I want her to know." Debbie glanced away. A pained smile crossed Verna's face. So Verna also knew.

"Ida understands. And you're such a nice sister, Debbie. Already you know to involve everyone. That's so sweet of you. Run along and . . ." Verna's face darkened for a moment. "I need to leave at once for Joe's place. He needs to hear this news. And then Joe can tell me himself what Paul's going to tell you."

Debbie gave Verna a quick hug. "Keep at your prayers, dear. Joe has a good heart — like you say. You'll both be okay. I think you'd better just trust him."

Verna took a deep breath. "Thank you, Debbie. You comfort my heart more than you know."

"I'll go look for Ida then." Debbie left and found her way down the stairs. Lois met her coming up, but she didn't comment other than to give her head a quick shake, obviously still thinking Debbie had fallen for Paul.

In the living room, Saloma glanced up from her knitting as Debbie went by. "Is everything okay? It sounds like a lot of ruckus going on up there."

Debbie nodded. "Everything's fine, but I won't be here for supper tonight. And Verna's leaving any moment for Joe's place. I guess she'll get you caught up on the news."

"*Yah,* I suppose." Saloma appeared concerned. "Maybe you could give me some of the details?"

Debbie was ready to begin when Ida came up the basement stairs.

Saloma glanced toward Debbie. "Is it okay if Ida hears this?"

"I was on my way to tell her anyway," Debbie said. When Ida sat down, Debbie ran through a short version of how the day had gone.

"This is a *gut* work you're doing," Saloma

proclaimed when Debbie finished. "*Daett* may have a fit though about these transgressions Joe and Paul have committed. To say nothing of having this all spilled at the trial."

"You know *Daett* will," Ida affirmed.

Debbie took Ida by the arm and whispered in her ear. "Come, I need to speak with you in private."

Saloma didn't object as Debbie ushered Ida out on the lawn. Debbie paused a distance from the house, underneath the tree where the shade fell.

"You're scaring me!" Ida said. "What's wrong?"

Debbie took a deep breath. "I wanted to warn you about what I'm doing tonight. I'm going out with Paul Wagler for supper. But it's not what you might think."

Ida took a moment to absorb the information. "You know I wouldn't stand in your way . . . if you want him, Debbie. I have no claim on Paul."

"Look, Ida. It's nothing like that. I don't care about Paul. But he insisted because he wants to explain himself so that I don't hear the news secondhand or when he testifies. I want to make testifying as easy for him as I can. It's important that Paul testifies. I know he has ideas in his head about me, but I don't care for the man."

"I understand." Ida's hand was on her arm. Her gaze searched Debbie's face. "You don't have to feel bad."

"Ida, please know I don't *want* the man. I never will. What his feelings are I can't control. I'm doing this for Joe and Verna. Honest! I hope you believe me."

Ida's voice was sorrowful. "I do, Debbie. But I'm afraid Paul doesn't share your feelings. And he's used to getting what he wants."

Debbie sighed. "Well, he hasn't run into a former *Englisha* woman yet. We have minds of our own, you know."

"That's what he likes about you," Ida said.

Debbie didn't answer because she knew Ida was probably right. The girl had Paul figured out better than he did himself.

"Maybe you should consider him." Ida met Debbie's gaze.

"And maybe you should be more selfish," Debbie shot back.

They both laughed. And then Ida's face grew serious.

"What a mess life becomes sometimes."

"You can say that again. I've got to change clothes if I'm to pick Paul up at six. I should wear an *Englisha* dress, I think. And here Verna comes. Should we help her get Buttercup ready?"

388

"I'll help." Ida motioned toward the house. "You go change."

Saloma wasn't in the living room when Debbie entered the house. And she didn't see anything of Lois upstairs. Noises were coming from Emery's bedroom, so Lois was probably cleaning it. Debbie changed into her yellow polka-dot dress with the short skirt that came above the knees. She grabbed a black shawl and wrapped it around her waist for walking out of the house. The point was to shock Paul and, thus, discourage his intentions, but this might prove too much for either Bishop Beiler or Emery if she met them. Thankfully they were both still in the fields. When she came back from Lewistown, the hour would be late and dark. If either of them were still up, the shawl should suffice again.

The shawl tangled up on the car seat when she climbed inside, so Debbie tossed it aside. She'd honk the horn at the Wagler farm, and Paul could come out to meet her. If she had to go in the house, she'd park out by the barn and wrap the shawl around herself again. In fact, if she gave Lavina a glimpse of the yellow polka-dot dress her daughter-in-law ardor would probably cool a bit. But then Bishop Beiler would have to deal with a possible ill report that would circulate through the community.

Oh well, they would all get this straightened out eventually. Debbie glanced at her watch as she drove toward the Wagler farm. There was still plenty of time — even enough to indulge in her old habit. She could swing past the Knepp farm, but she decided she'd better not. Alvin would recognize her. Surely there was some positive way to attract his attention. Perhaps Verna could help her with ideas on how to fit into an Amish lifestyle — something that would impress Alvin once this was all over.

Debbie soon pulled in to the Waglers' driveway. She hadn't even paused at the end of the walk when Paul dashed out. He looked spiffy in his Sunday jacket, which wasn't a good sign. Paul had taken the time to dress up.

"*Gut* evening!" Paul settled into his seat and took in her yellow dress and bare knees with a quick glance. "Got the *Englisha* outfit on, I see."

"Do you have anything against *Englisha* girls?"

"*Nee,* but I thought you were turning Amish."

Debbie didn't answer as she turned the car around in the barnyard and drove past the house again. The *Englisha* dress wasn't such a good idea after all, she thought. She glanced toward the house. A face appeared in the kitchen window for a second before it vanished.

"They're just curious." Paul grinned. "By the way, *Mamm* said she had a *gut* visit with you today."

"I suppose she did." Debbie replied. She reached between the seats and produced the lemonade glass. "I was supposed to give you this to return."

Paul slid the glass under his seat. "I hope my *mamm* didn't say too much . . . about . . ."

"Let's just say I got the message," Debbie said.

He met her gaze. "It's no secret I'm quite impressed with you, Debbie. *Mamm* didn't get that wrong."

Debbie grimaced. "You ought to think about Ida or some other decent Amish girl who doesn't carry *Englisha* baggage like I do."

"Ida?" He appeared puzzled and then shook his head. "Surely not, Debbie!"

Debbie rushed out the words. "Ida's just one example among many. She's a decent girl, and you ought to think about her."

"Are you Cupid now?"

Debbie laughed. "Believe me, I don't have

much of a track record in that department. All my girlfriends from college found boys on their own. And look at me . . . not too much success."

He tilted his head sideways. "That's because the right boy hasn't come along. Now look at me, for example. How could you do better than this?"

"Cocky, are we? Where did you learn that?"

He laughed but didn't answer the question. "Where are we going, by the way?"

"Andrea's Pizzeria in Lewistown, where wonderful things happen," she teased.

"You really are something, Debbie." He appeared quite serious. "And refreshing and original. I could live with that."

"And all in a yellow polka-dot dress!"

Paul didn't answer as they approached the edge of Lewistown and made their way downtown. When she had parked and they both stepped out of the car, Paul looked at her intently. "Not bad if I must say so myself."

"That's quite sinful for an Amish boy, Paul."

"Beauty's not wasted on me." He held out his elbow. "Shall we?"

He was smooth, Debbie gave him that. She linked her arm in his and marched up the street. He'd left his hat in the car, she noticed. That pinched the *Ordnung* rules a bit. He could almost pass as an *Englisha* boy with her on his arm, which might well be what he intended. She was clearly at a disadvantage, and the evening was still young.

They entered the restaurant and found a table. Minutes later they had ordered. Debbie was anxious to ask him what Joe and he had done, but she thought he should bring it up.

When the pizzas arrived, she didn't have to. Between bites of juicy pizza, the story came out.

"Well, it's pretty embarrassing to think of it now," Paul said. "We spent a lot of evenings in Lewistown at a pub called Slick's Bar and Grill. We drank beer there, met girls, took them for drives, that sort of thing. Those dates on that paper. Most of those times I was with Joe at Slick's — or we were out with girls."

"Joe had an *Englisha* girlfriend. Did you also have one?" she asked with some hesitancy.

"*Yah.* We stayed away from Amish girls. Too much explaining might be needed afterward — once we came back from our *rumspringa.*"

"I see," Debbie ventured.

He colored for the first time. "You're not like the girls we met, Debbie. And I mean that."

"So you — both of you — were with girls?"

He glanced away. "I was, but Joe really wasn't. That's why Kim's coming after him, I suppose. That was her name, Kim. She was blond, tall, and wanted more from Joe than Joe was willing to commit to."

"So that's why she's accusing him?"

"It must be. That and probably the guys who were in on the robberies with her are making her do it."

"Well, it will be your word against hers at the trial, I suppose. I hope they believe you. I don't understand the whole idea of a *rumspringa.* If you want to stay Amish, why do you have to venture out into the world and make stupid mistakes like this? It just messes everything up. What if you had fallen in love with an *Englisha* girl?"

He reached over to touch her arm, and she didn't pull back. "Maybe I have."

She pulled away from him.

He reached for her hand this time. "Debbie, the past is the past. One can always begin anew. I wanted to clear myself with you. I like you. I'd like to see us spend more time together. But you have to know I would have helped Joe anyway."

"I believe that," Debbie said. "And if you testify, they'll surely let Joe off."

"If they believe me."

A few minutes later, they'd finished their pizza. "I think we should go," Debbie said, standing up. There was no rush, but she needed out of there. Paul affected her in spite of her best efforts. This time could lead nowhere — and she told him so.

"There must be hope for us, Debbie." His gaze pleaded for understanding.

"I'm sorry, Paul. I don't hold anything against you, but as for there being . . . feelings between you and me . . . *no.*"

He fell silent.

On the way home she filled the time with bright chatter. This wasn't over, Debbie reminded herself as she dropped him off and bid him good night. She knew his type.

THIRTY-FOUR

On the Tuesday evening of the following week, Bishop Beiler sat on the couch in Deacon Mast's living room. Outside, the blaze of a summer sunset colored the horizon and heat shimmered across the fields. Above his head, the gas lantern Deacon Mast had lit moments before hissed its low tune. This ministers meeting had been scheduled only yesterday, and Minister Graber and he had been the first to arrive. Minister Kanagy even now was pulling into the driveway. Deacon Mast jumped up from his rocker to rush outside and assist him.

The bishop knew he should offer to help with Minister Kanagy's horse, but it would appear undignified for him to move from his seat at the moment. Minister Graber hadn't budged either. Today had already been a hard day, and now it promised to get worse. A little dignity wouldn't hurt his cause. News of Henry Yoder had dashed his spirits pretty low.

From the other side of the room Minister Graber interrupted his thoughts. "I heard you had a horse down last week."

"*Yah . . .*" Bishop Beiler shook his head to focus his thoughts. "Wouldn't get up, but the vet couldn't find much wrong. Gave her a shot of iron. But I think that was more to make me feel better than anything."

Minister Graber chuckled. "Vets do have their tricks. But that might not have been a bad idea. Horses can get anemic."

"I suppose so," Bishop Beiler allowed. "I think I could use a booster myself tonight. Though I suspect the vet wouldn't dare treat me."

Minister Graber grunted. "So could I. *Da Hah* knows we're all in deep enough trouble with the church problems we're already dealing with. Plus this past week of summer heat . . ."

"*Yah . . .*" Bishop Beiler got to his feet as the front door opened and Deacon Mast escorted Minister Kanagy inside. There were handshakes all around before they took their seats and silence settled in. The only noise for the moment was the hiss of the lantern.

Deacon Mast glanced in Bishop Beiler's direction. "I guess we're ready to begin. The *frau* will have iced tea for us later."

"I could use some about right now." Minister Graber fanned himself with a copy of *The Budget* he'd picked up near the rocking chair.

Deacon Mast made no move to ask for the iced tea any sooner than planned. The men could hear noises coming from the basement where Deacon Mast's *frau,* Susie, had disappeared when the men started arriving. She would bring the tea in her own *gut* time, the men figured. Bishop Beiler clasped his hands. "Let's begin with prayer. Will you lead us, Minister Kanagy?"

They bowed their heads as Minister Kanagy led out, "O great and merciful Father, full of grace and glory. Look down this evening upon this humble gathering of Your unworthy servants. Shed the light of Your wisdom and Spirit into our hearts and minds so that we may see with clear eyes, and hear with open ears, and speak with pure tongues. And for all these favors and blessing we ask and give You thanks. In Jesus' name, amen."

"Thank you." Bishop Beiler shifted on his chair. "As you know, this is an unusual meeting for a Tuesday night. And yet I couldn't see the wisdom of speaking of these things at our next Sunday-morning meeting. The subjects we have to deal with are weighty and shouldn't be rushed, which might happen if we have the congregation waiting on us."

They all nodded in agreement, so Bishop Beiler continued. "I'll let Deacon Mast give us an update on Henry Yoder, which is the main reason for our gathering."

Before Deacon Mast could begin, Minister Kanagy interrupted. "Perhaps you should give us an update on your daughter Verna and her boyfriend, Joe. Seems we haven't been hearing much about that lately, other than the fact that Verna runs over there all the time."

Bishop Beiler nodded. The man had his nerve, but Minister Kanagy was also within his rights. He would have led out with a word on the subject himself if his thoughts hadn't been so befuddled with Henry Yoder.

The bishop sighed. "Verna is finding her own way on the matter, and I've decided to allow her that choice. And from the looks of things, I might have been right. Debbie is involved with Joe's lawyer and keeping her straight on what our beliefs are. Also the lawyer wanted an alibi witness for Joe, and Joe said Paul Wagler could give that. I don't like this, as any such testimony will have to come out in the trial. But this is a man's guilt or innocence we're speaking about, and Paul says he can place Joe at a . . . a bar in Lewistown on the nights in question. Following our ways and counsel, Joe is not pushing his own defense in this matter."

Minister Kanagy's head bobbed up and down. "*Yah,* I've also been troubled thinking about Joe spending time in jail. But this will be a great shame for the community. A public testimony about where our young people are spending their time. I know it was while they were in their *rumspringa,* but in such a place?"

Minister Graber gave a sharp cough. "Surely you're not ignorant on these matters, Minister Kanagy. We all know what some of these boys do during their *rumspringa.* I don't think you've been spending all your time in the hayfields."

Minister Kanagy glared. "We are trying to improve the actions of our young people. Surely you all agree with that. Using their evil deeds to accomplish even a *gut* thing will not help in the least. It may encourage such actions in the future. They will say to themselves, 'See, *gut* can come out of anything.' "

"I think that's a little stretch," Bishop Beiler ventured. "The philosophers among us are not that many."

This produced a laugh from the two of them, but not from Minister Kanagy. He continued, "Then there's the matter of your daughter freely traveling back and forth between your place and Joe Weaver's. Why, she keeps the pavement almost warm with all the trips she's making."

"This is true," Bishop Beiler allowed. "And it has bothered me some, although I could think of nothing further that I can do. Like I said, I have spoken with Verna. I've advised her to allow this to play out before continuing her relationship with Joe."

Minster Kanagy was on the edge of his seat. "Your daughter defies our counsel, and you have thought of nothing else that can be done?"

"Please." Deacon Mast lifted his hand. "If I may say something. We had anticipated that Verna might not agree, but the bishop is right. There are limits to what we can do in this matter."

Minister Kanagy grunted. "Then we need a new plan. The girl is on the road more than a spring calf breaking through the fences. It's a shame, I say. And our bishop doesn't see clearly enough to lead properly. Not that I blame him in full. I might have the same weakness when it comes to my own family."

Bishop Beiler held his tongue for a moment before he spoke. "I'm usually blamed for being too harsh with my girls, not the other way around. Verna may be a little out of hand right now, but she has also had a hard life in the past."

"See?" Minister Kanagy waved his hand about as if in explanation. "I say we impose a separation on the two until this is resolved. I'm shamed by what's going on."

Bishop Beiler glanced around the room. "What do the two of you think?"

They both shrugged, obviously wishing not to get involved.

"I will think about your counsel," the bishop said to Minister Kanagy. "And I will see if Verna can be reasoned with again."

"Thank you." Minister Kanagy settled back into his chair. "That would be something, at least."

Bishop Beiler looked around and then said, "Let us proceed then with Henry Yoder. Deacon Mast was about to give his report."

The deacon shifted on his rocker. But before he could begin, Susie bustled in with glasses of iced tea. The cubes floated on top, delicious looking in the late-evening heat. But at the moment Bishop Beiler wanted no bodily comforts. He wanted this business out of the way. But clearly the others were anxious for refreshment, so he leaned back and said, "Thank you. This looks *gut*."

"There's more out in the kitchen," Susie said as she left the half-empty pitcher on the desk. "Let me know if there is anything else you need."

"I think there's plenty here," Deacon Mast said.

Susie nodded and then retreated.

Minister Kanagy took a long swallow of iced tea and wiped his mouth in a quick motion.

"It's not *gut* news I have to report." Deacon Mast was sober-faced. "Henry's decided to jump the fence. Like in *all the way* over."

Both ministers sat in shocked silence. Minister Kanagy's mouth hung open. The bishop had expected Deacon Mast to break the news with a little more finesse, but then how did one do that? The facts were the facts.

"But I have not heard of this," Minister Graber's voice squeaked. "Is this for sure?"

"I had a long talk with Henry on Sunday afternoon when I visited him to make sure," Deacon Mast said. "Then I came over last

403

evening to tell the bishop . . . and here we are."

"This is unbelievable!" Minister Kanagy's hands twitched in his lap. "We were doing so well."

"It's what comes from compromising." Bishop Beiler tried without success to keep the edge out of his voice. Minister Kanagy had pushed for the light treatment of Henry Yoder's tractor transgressions and the action still stung.

"But Henry Yoder!" Minister Kanagy was almost on his feet. "This doesn't sound like the Henry Yoder I know. He was brought up in the community. I will go and speak with him tonight."

"You'll have plenty of time for that." Bishop Beiler motioned for Minister Kanagy to settle himself down. "No one is rushing into anything, but we do need to arrive at an understanding on the matter. Henry has plans not only to leave the Amish, but to join that new outfit we spoke about — up near Mifflinburg. They have a preacher from the outside, someone told me. It's not the usual Mennonite situation, let me put it that way."

"And all over a tractor!" Minister Kanagy still hadn't absorbed the shock.

Bishop Beiler could understand. He'd

spent a partially sleepless night himself, tossing and turning plenty after he'd heard the news.

"Don't you have more details on what Henry's thinking?" Minister Kanagy asked Deacon Mast.

"Not other than what Henry told me." Deacon Mast shrugged. "How much can you believe once a man starts down that path? They see stars where there never were any before. Henry's all caught up in this spiritual trip. Seems like he visited their revival meetings or whatever they're calling them — maybe a Bible school. I can't remember. Anyway, there was an altar call. Henry went up and had an experience of some sort. He's never been so spiritually satisfied, he claims."

"And I'm sure the new tractor is sitting in his front yard with the rubber tires on." Minister Graber grimaced as if the thought pained him greatly.

"*Yah,*" Deacon Mast allowed. "It was in the barnyard at least."

"We must not speak of things that we do not know," Minister Kanagy got in edgewise. "Henry may have spiritual reasons for what he's doing."

"Now who's going soft?" Bishop Beiler made sure he looked at Minister Kanagy as he spoke. "And Henry's not even family."

Minister Kanagy hung his head and offered no retort.

"*Dah Hah* have mercy on us all," Minister Graber said. "I can see where this one's going. We can't allow Henry to get away this time. If we do, the whole congregation will get ideas. That is, if they haven't already with how easy Henry got off the last time."

"I'm afraid you're right." Bishop Beiler looked slowly around the room. "I have spent a lot of time thinking about this. And I've arrived at my conclusion. I say we give all of you two weeks in which to speak with Henry about the matter. If nothing changes, I don't think we have much choice. If this were a mainline Mennonite church, perhaps things would be different — or if Henry hadn't been making trouble before."

No one protested.

Deacon Mast poured himself another glass of tea, no doubt to calm his nerves. Bishop Beiler felt a similar need. There hadn't been an excommunication in years — at least not in his district.

Minister Kanagy looked like he wished to say something, but then he didn't. Likely, he'd wanted to make a motion for even stricter measures on Joe and Verna.

Bishop Beiler stood. "We can talk some

more about this at the Sunday-morning meeting. But for now we all know the basics."

Deacon Mast followed them to the front door, but he didn't offer to help untie their horses. He looked pale as he stood there in the light of the gas lantern and sipped more of his *frau*'s iced tea.

THIRTY-FIVE

Bishop Beiler shifted on the hard surface of the ministers' bench. All around him the younger children and non–church members were leaving Lonnie Miller's living room. The moment for the vote on Henry Yoder's excommunication had arrived. His heart felt heavy just as it had all night. On Saturday afternoon Deacon Mast had spent an hour at Henry's place trying to talk some last-minute sense into the man's head. The effort had been in vain. Henry was determined to continue his course, and Deacon Mast had reported that Henry had been hard at work with his new tractor clad with rubber tires when he'd arrived. It had indeed come to a sad state of affairs.

The bishop looked up and saw Joe Weaver walk past with his head held low. It was a shame the situation still dragged on for Joe and Verna. Those two at least tried to follow the guidance of the church. Verna had cried for hours the evening he'd asked her again to consider putting a stop to her visits with Joe. He'd explained that the pressure for further measures against her had become difficult to hold back. This had seemed to touch Verna's heart more than any of his earlier commands. She'd rushed over for a talk with Joe, and then hadn't been back for a visit since. The bishop wasn't sure what agreement they'd reached, but Verna's sorrow hung heavy over the house. Her compliance would, for the moment at least, relieve pressure from Minister Kanagy for further action regarding Joe's membership probation.

With the room cleared of nonmembers, Bishop Beiler rose to his feet. Even the murmur of the younger girls in the kitchen had stilled. "This is a sad day for all of us," Bishop Beiler began. "I don't need to make many words over the matter. You all know by now that Henry Yoder and his family have left our fellowship. We now need to vote on excommunication for Henry and his *frau,* Lydia. Henry has not been with us for over two Sundays, and he has refused all our efforts at corrective counsel. As to why this has happened, I don't know all the details. I don't believe much time should be wasted in troubling our minds on that matter. Rather, we should mourn for our brother and his family. And our prayers should be lifted to *Da Hah* that Henry might see the error of his way and return with his family from following the ways of the world. I will now let others express themselves, and we'll go from there."

Minister Graber kept his eyes on the floor as he spoke. "I can add nothing to what the bishop has said. I have perhaps not spent as much time speaking with Henry as I could have, but I find myself weak in such matters. That's best left to others when these complicated things of the faith come up. I ask that you bear with me in my weakness, and that you join me in prayer for Henry and his family. The world is full of danger, and the soul is so easily deceived. We should never take it upon ourselves to walk without the counsel of many brethren at our side."

There were a few moments of silence when Minister Kanagy stood and paused. He cleared his throat. "I too express my sorrow today. I hope no one will take it upon himself to side with the errors of our brother, Henry. Let me assure you that this church group Henry is joining has more errors than we could name. And yet that is not our purpose today — telling you about how wrong other people are, but to take

410

corrective action which may yet save Henry from his error. In this we have the promise of the apostle Paul, who said that the sufferings of the flesh can soon result in the saving of the spirit."

Minister Kanagy fidgeted for a few moments before he continued. "I do need to mention — since I have heard the questions myself — could Henry have been saved if we had taken a harsher hand with his constant tractor use? Especially the last incident in which we had threatened such a thing and then backed off. In this, I confess myself the greatest transgressor. I wish to express my deepest regret in not counseling a firmer hand. We, of course, can never know what would or would not have happened. But I, on my part, wish we had tried. That is all I have to say."

Bishop Beiler nodded toward Deacon Mast. Minster Kanagy's confession was a bit of a surprise, but it hadn't changed anything. They all had regrets, but a cleared conscience never hurt a man.

"I wish only to express my great sadness for this day," Deacon Mast said. "Beyond that, words fail me. I really can't add to what has already been said."

Bishop Beiler leaned forward to whisper to the other ministers. "You may ask the

411

members then."

The three men stood up and began to move up and down the benches, bending over to ask each member if they agreed with the proceedings and listening to each person's reply. Bishop Beiler waited while the votes and comments were listened to. It didn't take long, and that was a *gut* sign. Conflict over the vote would only prolong the agony of what needed doing.

Deacon Mast was back first. He took his place on the ministers' bench. He'd taken the votes from the women's side of the room. He kept his gaze on the floor. The other two ministers soon joined him. Bishop Beiler motioned for them to speak.

"I have found everyone in agreement," Minister Kanagy said. "They expressed their sorrow and wished it were otherwise, but believe the ministry's counsel was the wisest course of action."

"The same here." Minister Graber stared at the blank wall as he spoke. "There were only regrets, but no votes to hold back the excommunication."

Deacon Mast glanced toward the bishop. "One of the sisters did wonder why Henry's *frau,* Lydia, is included since she originally didn't wish to join Henry at the other church. I told her I was not aware of that, but regardless of how Lydia felt at first, she is now in full agreement with Henry. I spoke with Lydia myself last Saturday. Beyond that there were no questions or counsel not to proceed."

Bishop Beiler stood. "This is a sad day indeed, but we will now consider our brother and sister outside the fold until they repent. We will have no dealings with them whatsoever. That is all."

The crowd began to break up even before Bishop Beiler sat down. Deacon Mast rose to his feet and slid onto the bench across from the bishop. He leaned forward and whispered, "I hope I said the right thing to Lydia's sister. She was the one who questioned including Lydia."

"I wouldn't have known how to say it better myself," Bishop Beiler said.

A pleased smile spread over the deacon's face. He was soon in conversation with Benny Beiler seated on the bench behind him. Ten minutes later the men had the dinner benches set up, and Lonnie motioned for the men to take their seats for the noon meal. Lonnie's *frau,* Millie, soon appeared in the kitchen doorway and whispered to her husband.

Seconds later Lonnie tapped Bishop Beiler on the shoulder and whispered in his ear,

"Everyone's ready."

Bishop Beiler lifted his voice so he'd be heard throughout the house. "It's time to eat, so let's pray and give thanks."

When silence had fallen, he prayed, "Now unto You, O God of judgment and mercy. Hallowed be Your great name. Bless this food which has been prepared for us, and allow it to give our bodies strength for the rest of the afternoon. Bless also the many hands who have prepared it. Bless the faithful members who are gathered here today. Strengthen their hearts in the *gut* things which You give both in this world and in Your Word. Amen."

As the men began to eat, Minister Graber leaned toward the bishop. "I'm sure glad this day is over. It tears the heart out when these kinds of things must be dealt with. At least Henry isn't here today. That would have made things even worse — having to see him afterward."

"Yah," Bishop Beiler agreed. He spread a thin layer of peanut butter on his bread. "It makes it easier for us, but I wish Henry had come to express himself. Deacon Mast gave him that option, but he didn't wish to make trouble, he said."

"These are always sad cases." Minister Graber bit into a thick slab of bread slathered with peanut butter. "You did well. This problem finally was dealt with."

"Still it's a shame," Bishop Beiler said. "It just goes to show you where a little thing of the world can soon gain a strong foothold."

Minister Graber nodded. "You should be speaking of this in your next sermon."

Bishop Beiler glanced at him. "It's not like you don't have the chance yourself."

They both fell silent as conversations rose and fell around them. Lonnie's young girl, Betsy, came past with the coffeepot. Bishop Beiler made sure she filled his. He wasn't hungry, but coffee would soothe his nerves. He began to relax even though there was still the afternoon ahead when some members might come up to express reservations they hadn't offered officially. He hoped there were none, but with the way things had gone lately, anything could happen.

The closing meal prayer was soon called, and the tables emptied out. Before Bishop Beiler made it out the front door, the women already scurried to clean the tables for the next round. The men spilled across Lonnie's lawn to sit under the shade trees, setting up benches they'd carried out with them. Bishop Beiler selected a spot that looked like it would stay out of the sun for an hour or so. He bent over to pluck a blade of grass and chewed on it as he settled in.

It didn't take long before Cousin Benny sidled up to him on the bench. "I just wanted to express my wholehearted support, Bishop, for the way things were handled today. Henry has been pushing the fence for years now, and I must say I was a little worried there for a while. You have my thanks."

"You're welcome." Bishop Beiler bobbed his head. "It's not an easy task tending to *Da Hah*'s vineyard. But I'm sure you know that."

"*Yah,*" Benny said and slid down the bench again.

Others soon came and left their appreciative comments before they moved on to give further room on the bench.

"My *frau* and I are glad action was taken today, Bishop."

"We'll now feel much better about the future of our children."

"Yesterday I was talking with my cousin who knows the group up in Mifflinburg well. They are nothing but troublemakers, adding only pain to the body of Christ."

"It's *gut* to see such firm leadership exercised, Bishop."

"Don't worry about ever having to stand alone. My family is with you."

Bishop Beiler listened, and his heart lifted higher with each word given. It was so *gut* when the full support of the brotherhood was behind decisions like this. And no one complained like he'd feared some might. He felt sleepiness overtake him as the last man drifted past, and the conversations around him turned to the last hay cutting of the season and the corn harvest ahead of them.

Someone poked him in the ribs. "Come on there, Bishop. We have to stay awake during *your* sermons!" Laughter rolled across the lawn.

"Maybe if you'd try your hand at preaching we could all stay awake," Bishop Beiler replied.

They laughed harder.

"I heard cousin Benny was fattening up his cows by preaching to them. Improves their circulation, he said."

"Now that's some preaching, wouldn't you say?"

"At least his cows get to benefit even if the church doesn't."

Benny was red-faced from laughter, but he managed to choke out, "I got so *gut* at it, I thought I'd market my skills around. Bring in a little extra cash."

"We'll all have to remember that when our

cattle get close to market," Bishop Beiler said.

"Not to take away from the fine Benny Beiler jokes," another man said, "but I heard of an Amish farmer who had given permission for these hunters to use his land. There was this huge puddle in the middle of the lane, it seems, and the hunters asked him whether they could drive safely across.

" 'Looks to me like you could,' the Amish man told them.

"When their pickup sank out of sight, the hunters floated to the top and demanded an explanation.

" 'Well, my cows could make it with no problem,' the Amish man said. 'It barely came halfway to their bellies.' "

"That's better than a Benny Beiler joke," someone else said, as all the men held their stomachs.

The laughter and chatter continued. Bishop Beiler listened, his mind fading in and out. They dealt with their pain in the only way they knew how, he figured. Laughter was *Da Hah*'s gift, and he was thankful it had come so soon after their great sorrow this morning. This way bitterness would not sit deep in their hearts.

THIRTY-SIX

Verna sat at the kitchen table with her head in her hands. The early-Monday-morning sunlight poured in through the kitchen window. All around her soft noises filled the house as the others worked. The washroom screen door had just slammed shut as *Mamm* and Ida left to check the garden. Ida's last hamper of dirty clothing had bumped down the basement stairs thirty minutes ago. Verna knew she should do something, but she couldn't move after she'd finished the dishes. Her head hurt, and her heart was in worse shape. She hadn't seen Joe yesterday afternoon at the church services, and she hadn't spoken with him for days now. This separation was tearing her apart. Maybe she shouldn't have taken *Daett* quite so seriously. Perhaps she should only have cut back on her visits, not stopped them entirely.

But she and Joe had agreed to take her *daett*'s advice. Were their lives not in *Da*

Hah's hands? That's what *Daett* said. They should trust, and she knew *Daett* was right.

"You're not accepting things," *Mamm* had said this morning at the breakfast table. And *Mamm* was right about that. But how did one accept injustice? Hadn't she determined to stand by Joe no matter what? And yet she'd backed down. Joe had understood. Their love would last this severe trial, he'd told her.

Debbie told her again this morning that she felt positive about Paul's testimony. That Paul's word would prevail at the trial. But what if Paul's testimony *didn't* convince the jury? Paul was, after all, Joe's close friend. That might be a hole the prosecutor would exploit. Debbie had admitted that could happen.

If he were found guilty, Joe would go to prison for a long time. She would wait for him, but she wanted to wait with precious memories of their last days together. Not like this — with separation between them. Even on Sunday morning they were allowed only brief glances. And she hadn't dared serve the unmarried men's table.

She couldn't go on like this — she just couldn't. Yet what else was there to do? Joe wouldn't wish her to disobey.

The screen door slammed again and

voices came into the washroom, but Verna didn't take her head out of her hands. She didn't have the strength to hide this despair from *Mamm* any longer.

When Ida and *Mamm* walked in, they both gasped. *Mamm* and Ida sat down at once on either side of Verna and wrapped their arms around her shoulders.

"Verna?" *Mamm*'s tone was gentle. "Is it too much this morning?"

Verna lifted her head. "*Yah,* but I'll try to get over it. Maybe if you both would pray for me?"

"Certainly," *Mamm* and Ida said in unison.

After a silent moment, *Mamm* prayed, "Dear *Hah,* comfort Verna's heart. We don't know what can be done to help this situation, but You do. Give Verna peace and acceptance of her situation. And help her believe that You always work out things for the best in the end."

When *Mamm* had finished, Verna whispered, "Thank you."

Ida squeezed her hand and added her own prayer. "O *Hah,* we just ask that You shed Your light. Send help for this situation with Verna and Joe. You know how wrongly they are being treated by this accusation, but there seems little anyone can do about it. Even Debbie has tried her best, and it doesn't seem *gut* enough. Amen."

"Thanks for praying," Verna mumbled as she sat up and wiped her tears. "I'm going to speak with *Daett* now."

Mamm sounded weary. "He's not going to tell you anything I haven't."

"I will still speak with him," Verna repeated.

"Hurry then." *Mamm* stood. "The garden needs weeding, and we're starting once the dew is off the ground."

"I'll be right back then," Verna said, standing to leave.

Oh, if *Daett* would only give her some *gut* word, Verna thought. Her heart would soon have warm circles around it. But what wild imaginations did she have this morning? Did she really expect *Daett* to change his mind? *Nee.* It must be *Mamm* and Ida's prayers that had lifted her spirits. And she must not think there was a miracle ahead. Miracles were for special people, and she was just an ordinary girl in love with a very *wunderbah* boy.

Once past the barn, Verna ran along the back lane, the grass slapping against her bare feet.

Daett saw her coming from a distance and pulled his team of horses to a stop. "Is something wrong at the house?" he asked as

Verna came to a stop beside him.

Verna shook her head and took a moment to catch her breath. "Sorry, I didn't mean to startle you, but *Mamm* wants to begin weeding the garden soon, and there isn't much time."

"Time for what?" *Daett* asked as he studied her face.

"Something has to be done about Joe and me," Verna said. "I can't stand being away from him any longer."

Daett stroked his beard. "There's not much that can be done, Verna. Much as I hate to say it. Nothing new has come up, has it?"

"*Nee,* but my heart can't take this any longer. I'm going to drive over some evening before long, *Daett.* I can't help it. None of this is right. Joe may go to jail, and if he does we can't part like this."

"*Yah,* Joe may go to jail," he replied. "And that's all the more reason for you to stay away from him. Before long the hurt will heal, Verna. It always does."

Verna stared at him. "Are you suggesting we break up if he goes to jail, *Daett*?"

Her *daett* looked away before he answered. "I'm satisfied with Joe, if that's what you're asking. But I wasn't the one who got myself into trouble during my *rumspringa* years by hanging out in a disreputable place with questionable people. Joe brought that on himself. But I do believe the man has changed — and from his heart. It's just sad he has to pay such a high price for his sins. But that can be a warning for all of us. Surely *Da Hah* is not mocked. What a man sows, he will reap."

"*Daett,* please don't lecture me!"

He nodded. "I do get carried away a bit, Verna. But what I said is true."

Verna studied his face. "It wasn't your idea to keep us apart. I know that. Then whose was it?"

Bishop Beiler didn't answer.

Verna dug in. "Whoever it is, I'll go speak with him. Today even. Perhaps he's willing to change his mind."

Bishop Beiler sighed. "You're grasping at straws, Verna. It's best that you stay out of these things."

Verna took her *daett*'s arm. "Was it Minister Kanagy? He would do something like that."

Bishop Beiler looked away. "Verna, you have spoken enough. These are not words for you. You are a girl. You must remember that."

"I am also a girl in love." Verna's fingers dug into her *daett*'s arm. "Have you forgotten that?"

He attempted a smile. "I do hope things turn out as you wish, Verna. Joe will marry a *frau* well suited for him, I'm hoping, but in the meantime you must remember your place."

"I'm speaking with Minister Kanagy today," she said, her eyes blazing. "This is not right." For a moment she thought he would forbid her, but his eyes softened.

"I suppose he can't do much to you for saying how you feel. And perhaps it would do some *gut*. You never know."

Verna didn't wait to hear more. She turned and ran across the field and into the lane. *Mamm* and Ida were headed out to the garden when she raced from behind the barn. Neither of them said anything as she joined them, and they began work with their hoes. The silence continued as they frequently stopped to pull the larger weeds by hand. Behind them Ida's wash began to move in the morning breeze.

"I'm going to see Minister Kanagy after we're done here," Verna announced as she dropped down to get the smaller weeds and crawled along on her knees in the soft dirt.

"You're doing what?" *Mamm* lifted her head to push back her *kapp*.

"I'm going to see Minister Kanagy."

"You're crazy, Verna!" Ida stared at her. "Have you taken complete leave of your senses?"

Verna didn't look at them as she pulled weeds. "He's the one who made *Daett* be so hard on Joe and me."

"And *Daett* told you this?" *Mamm*'s voice was horrified.

"*Nee,* I figured it out myself."

"The stress has gone to your head!" *Mamm* said.

"We must pray some more!" Ida whispered.

"*Yah,*" Verna agreed, "I can use all the prayers I can get to soften Minister Kanagy's heart. You can pray that he will listen to my plea and consider how wrong it is that he's keeping Joe and me apart from each other. Especially with the trial coming soon, and no one knowing how things will turn out."

"I will pray for none of those things, Verna." *Mamm*'s voice was firm. "The hearts of our ministers are in *Da Hah*'s hands, and you should not meddle. Have I not taught you girls anything?"

"I'm still going to see Minister Kanagy, *Mamm.* And you can pray for my soul, if you wish."

"Verna, please!" Ida clutched her dress

426

sleeve. "You must not do this."

"What should I do? Stay home and do nothing?" Verna retorted. "How is that right?"

"A meek and quiet spirit will always please *Da Hah*," *Mamm* reminded her. "That is what you must learn, Verna. I'm afraid you're failing the test."

Verna bit her tongue to keep back another sharp retort. Instead she whispered, "I'm sorry if I've disappointed you, *Mamm*. But I am going to see Minister Kanagy. *Daett* didn't forbid me."

"Now I've heard everything!" *Mamm* exclaimed and bent over the hoe to dig at the ground.

Verna gave *Mamm* a quick glance before she continued her work. The argument seemed over and silence had fallen. The late-summer sun beat down on them. Lois came out with lemonade some time later, and they drank from the cool liquid without comment. Lois gave them all puzzled looks before she retreated into the house. Verna didn't feel up to providing an explanation. Right now she was saving her words for Minister Kanagy. She would need all of them she could find.

THIRTY-SEVEN

That evening after supper, the steady beat of Buttercup's hooves on pavement filled the air as Verna drove toward Minister Kanagy's place. Debbie was seated beside her in the buggy, saying nothing. Both of them were lost in their thoughts. Verna was wondering what she would say once they arrived, and Debbie was wondering how she'd allowed herself to get talked into going.

A few wagons were still parked in the fields around them. The Amish farmers looked up upon hearing the horse and buggy and gave them little waves before returning to their work.

Verna glanced over at Debbie. "I know you didn't plan on getting involved in all this, but thanks for agreeing to come with me."

Debbie smiled wryly. "I don't really mind, I guess. I just wish there wasn't so much sorrow in it for you."

Verna looked away as a dark cloud rushed over her face. "Debbie, do you think Joe will really go to jail?"

Debbie thought for a moment before she answered. "It's a jury trial, like I said before. So who knows? I think he has a good chance of being acquitted."

Verna stared across the open field. "I sure hope Minister Kanagy will soften his heart. I couldn't bear it if my last memories of Joe's time as a free man are memories of us being apart."

"It sounds like you're accepting the fact that he may go to jail."

Verna shrugged. "I might as well. If I pose it that way to Minister Kanagy, it might be the only thing that will change his mind."

Debbie looked away. "That seems a little hard-hearted for Minister Kanagy's part, but who am I to judge?"

"Oh, Debbie!" Verna grabbed her hand. "Please don't allow bitterness into your heart. *Daett* and the other ministers have their responsibilities. They have more important things to look after than Joe and me."

"The sacrifice of the individual for the greater cause?" Debbie didn't look at Verna. "I suppose it's noble, but I've never seen this practiced anywhere else but in textbooks. Modern American life has pretty much lost that quality. Well, don't worry about me, Verna. I'm learning. From you. From the others. It's painful and a little hard to follow at times, but I'm still with you."

Verna managed a weak laugh. "Debbie, I'm glad you're with me, but when we get there, I'd rather speak with Minister Kanagy and his *frau* alone."

Debbie nodded. "I'll stay with Buttercup. I'm here to support you, Verna. And you'll tell me all about it anyway. At least what you can."

"You're such a dear!" Verna slapped the reins and urged Buttercup on. "I'll never be able to pay you back."

"There *is* a way you can repay me," Debbie said, her voice low.

Verna's head turned sharply in her direction. "What is it?"

Debbie gave a little laugh. "It's about Alvin Knepp. I wouldn't mind a little attention from him instead of Paul Wagler."

"It didn't help that you went out to dinner with Paul." Verna paused. "Oh, but you did that for me. Sorry."

"You see, it does get complicated."

"*Yah.*" Verna slowed down as they approached an intersection.

"What would *you* do about Alvin?"

Verna gave Debbie a long look. "I don't see why Alvin wouldn't jump at the chance to have your attention. I guess you just need to give him some time."

Debbie winced. "I'm afraid he's insecure."

Verna shook the reins. "He probably is. He doesn't come up to Paul's standards, that's for sure."

"See, that's what I mean. Nobody but me sees any value in the man."

"Mildred Schrock used to."

Debbie groaned. "Great, that's just what I need — competition. Who is she?"

"It's a long story. Didn't Lois mention her to you?"

"She did, but she didn't offer any details. Surely it's not more tragedy?"

"*Nee,* they were school sweethearts — though they never really dated. Mildred hasn't shown Alvin any attention since their schooldays. It kind of broke his heart, I think."

Debbie sighed. "Maybe I can help fix it then since apparently no other girl's willing."

"You can try, I guess," Verna said. "And I'll help out if I can." Verna's heart quickened as Minister Kanagy's place came into view ahead of them. "We're almost there," she whispered. "Now I've forgotten what to say."

Debbie's voice was firm. "You're going to march in there and state your case. That's what you're going to do."

Verna groaned. "That's easy for you to say. You're an *Englisha* girl. I'm Amish at heart and used to submitting."

Debbie touched Verna's arm. "You'll be okay. Just think about Joe and say your piece kindly."

Verna turned into the driveway and pulled to a stop at the end of the walk. "I'm getting off here." She handed Debbie the lines. "You can wait by the fence or at the hitching post."

"I'll take the hitching post. It's closer to the house — in case I have to come carry you out."

"That's not funny!" Verna said, as she climbed down, but she was smiling a bit. At least someone saw humor in this situation.

Verna took a deep breath and knocked on the door. Minister Kanagy answered, one hand stuck in a pants pocket. A toothpick hung from the side of his mouth. Obviously he'd just finished supper. Perhaps he would be in a nice mood.

The words came out of Verna's mouth in a squeak. "*Gut* evening. May I speak a few words with you? And Barbara, of course."

He didn't say anything but swung the door open. The toothpick fell to the floor. His foot shoved it under the rug. Verna stepped inside, and Barbara bustled out of the kitchen wiping her hands on her apron.

"Well, well, Verna! What a pleasant surprise. Did I see someone else in your buggy?"

"*Yah,* that's Debbie. But I wanted her to wait for me with the buggy."

"Of course. We understand," Barbara said. She gave Minister Kanagy a quick glance and he shrugged. "Do come in and sit down, Verna," Barbara continued. "Can I get you something? Apple cider perhaps? The girls can get some from the basement right quick."

Two young faces peered at Verna from the kitchen opening. She waved at them before she answered. "I've just had supper. And I won't take too much of your time. But thank you for the offer."

"Then we can sit right here." Barbara plopped herself on the rocker. "My, it seems like I've been on my feet all day. A body hardly gets to rest with a houseful of children. There's this to do and that emergency. But, of course, you know . . ."

Minister Kanagy cleared his throat and

interrupted his *frau*'s chatter. "Has something happened, Verna?"

Verna glanced at him before looking at the floor. "*Nee,* Minister Kanagy. I've come to make a plea for Joe and myself. I believe it's because of your counsel that Joe and I can't see each other. I wanted to see if I could convince you to allow us to visit. I love Joe, and I really need to see him."

Minister Kanagy didn't look happy. "Does your *Daett* blame me for Joe's situation?"

Verna sat up straight. "Of course not! *Daett* would do no such thing. I took this upon myself. I thought perhaps if you could be persuaded, *Daett* would also change his mind."

Minister Kanagy gave a little laugh. "I think you expect too much, Verna. Your *daett* is the bishop."

He looked pleased though, Verna thought, so she must be on the right track.

"We're all very blessed with your *daett*'s leadership," Barbara spoke up. "He is a *gut* man."

"*Yah,* he is. Yet sometimes he can be persuaded by other counsel. That's why I'm here asking if you would perhaps speak with *Daett* on whether Joe and I could be given some time together. If Joe goes to jail I may not see him for a very long time." Verna felt tears forming in her eyes.

Minister Kanagy's face clouded over. "Do you have information that we do not know?"

"Nee." She tried to keep the tremble from her voice. "It's only what I fear. And my heart yearns to speak with Joe before this should happen. To comfort myself and him, I hope. Would you reconsider . . . perhaps?"

Minister Kanagy's face was still clouded. "This trial will bring great shame on the community, Verna. From what I hear, Joe is having Paul Wagler testify on his behalf. And he will speak of the time they lived in sin. Right out in public for all to hear. These things go down in the records, Verna. The *Englisha* write them all down. And the shame does not go away for years to come."

"I know," Verna managed. "But doesn't Joe have a right to defend himself from something he didn't do? If Paul doesn't testify, Joe would be jailed unfairly. Paul is Joe's only hope."

Minister Kanagy's face reddened. He stood and paced the floor. "No man has a right to sin and then excuse himself, Verna. This is what I'm ashamed of more than anything else. That one of our members is so willing to throw off his cross and seek the easy way out. Our Savior was willing to bear the painful stripes on His back for our sins. Why should we not be willing to bear the punishment for what we have done? This is a great evil that has crept in unawares, and your *daett* is right in not giving in to your pleas."

"But, please!" Verna stood to face him. She caught a glimpse of Barbara's pale face out of the corner of her eye.

"There is no *please* in this matter, Verna." Minister Kanagy stared at her. "The time for please is long past. That's what Joe should have been saying when the temptation to sin came to him. Begging *Da Hah* for mercy. And that's what he should be doing now. Begging for forgiveness from the whole church. Saying he's sorry this thing has even happened. *Nee,* Verna, it cannot be. It's best that you and Joe stay apart. It's the least we can ask for with how things are going."

Verna found the edge of the couch with one hand and sat down again.

Minister Kanagy continued to pace the floor.

"Can I get you something now?" Barbara offered in a whisper.

Verna shook her head. Instead she stood back up and groped her way to the door. Barbara jumped up to support her arm and stayed with her until they reached the front lawn. There, Verna found her own way to where Debbie waited with the buggy by the hitching post.

"Pretty bad?" Debbie asked when Verna climbed in.

"*Yah*, really bad," Verna whispered. "Go! Drive home!"

Debbie didn't say anything as she swung the buggy around in the driveway as if she'd done it many times before. So Verna had only made things worse. She slipped her arm around her friend's shoulder and pulled her close as the tears came.

THIRTY-EIGHT

Friday night of that same week, Bishop Beiler stood on the front-porch steps with *Mamm* beside him. Verna stood behind him at the front door, tears streaming down her cheeks. "Please don't go, *Daett,*" Verna begged. "I know what's going to happen, and my heart can't take it anymore."

Bishop Beiler turned to her. "You know I love you. And you know my heart is also breaking, but there is nothing I can do."

"But you're the bishop!" Verna's eyes pleaded with him. "Don't go to this meeting Minister Kanagy has called."

Bishop Beiler hung his head. "That's the first time in your life you've ever said something like that, Verna. I can't say I blame you, but it shows how low we've all fallen. What with this wild trip of yours to Minister Kanagy on Monday night, everything has changed. I told you that you could go. I shouldn't have, so I'm partly to blame.

But that's the problem, see. We've both let this matter cloud our judgment. Family must not hinder the work of the church. In this case it has, and it sorrows me. That's also partly why I will have to go along with whatever Minister Kanagy counsels tonight. I am at the end of what I can do to protect you, Verna."

"No, you can't go!" Verna wailed. "It's not right!"

"That will be up to what the others say, Verna." *Daett* took her hand in his. "They are also the ministers of *Da Hah* and hear His voice. I'm afraid we must listen to their counsel. I can disagree, and so can you, but in the end peace can only be arrived at by submission to *Da Hah*'s will."

Verna threw her hands over her face.

"Verna, dear!" *Daett* wrapped his arms around her shoulders. "Remember, I will always be your *daett,* and you will always be my daughter. That may not be much comfort right now, but it means more than you may think."

"But I want Joe as my husband!" Verna choked out.

"We will pray about that later," *Mamm* spoke up. She led Verna inside to seat her on the couch. "You have to control yourself now. This has gone on long enough. Soon you will be opposing the ministry outright, and where will that lead you?"

"But it's all so wrong," Verna sobbed. "It's so very wrong. They should be helping Joe instead of punishing him."

"You will speak no more like this." *Mamm*'s voice was stern. "We don't know what Minister Kanagy's counsel will be. And calling a man to repent of his sins and bear the harvest he has birthed is for the betterment of his soul. You know that, Verna. You're forgetting it only because someone you love is suffering."

"I will stay with her," Ida said as she slipped out of the kitchen to sit beside Verna on the couch. "You need to go, *Mamm. Daett* is waiting. Being late for the meeting isn't going to help anything."

Mamm stood up. She wrung her hands before leaving to join her husband on the front porch. When she arrived, *Daett* sighed and led the way to the barn. There the two harnessed Milo in silence. *Mamm* climbed into the buggy and held the lines while the bishop pulled himself into the buggy.

"I'm going to die an early death if this keeps up," *Daett* muttered.

"You must not tempt *Da Hah*." *Mamm* handed him the reins. "His ways are past ours and difficult at times to understand.

Have you not said this yourself so many times in your sermons? Is the fact that your daughter is suffering reason to abandon sound wisdom?"

"You're right," Bishop Beiler admitted. He settled back into the buggy seat.

Mamm stared off into the distance. "And you know you won't be winning any argument with Minister Kanagy tonight. This thing has caused quite a stink in the community."

"I feel like I'm losing my mind." The bishop slapped the reins gently against Milo's back. "I allowed Verna to call on Minister Kanagy. I should have known better."

"What's done is done, Adam." *Mamm* slipped her hand under his arm. "*Da Hah* will use this for His own *gut.* You know He always does."

"And to remind us that we're human." Bishop Beiler's eyes sought the horizon where the sun was setting in a blaze of red and gold. "And to never let us forget that He alone is God. And that man will die someday — return to the dust from which he came."

"Don't speak of such things tonight," Saloma whispered. She pulled close to him. "Is it not enough that we still have each other? And we will still have all of our children, even when this is over? Other girls' hearts have been broken before, and Verna's will heal. She will learn much by accepting *Da Hah*'s will . . . whatever that is."

"You are a blessed woman, Saloma. You comfort my heart more than you know."

Saloma smiled up at him as he turned in at Minister Kanagy's driveway. "Remember, I love you, Adam. And speak your mind tonight but do not act foolishly."

Bishop Beiler pulled to a stop at the hitching post and gave his *frau* a warm look as he climbed down to secure Milo. "You will pray for me, perhaps?"

"You know I always do, Adam." *Mamm* climbed out of the buggy and waited for him until he returned from putting Milo in the barn. They walked together toward the house.

Minister Kanagy opened the door for them, his face serious. "*Gut* evening." He motioned for them to enter.

"*Gut* evening," Bishop Beiler replied. *Mamm* echoed his words.

"The others are already here," Minister Kanagy said as he led the way to the living room.

The others didn't have weeping daughters to attend to, Bishop Beiler told himself, so they could get there on time. He kept silent and took his seat on the couch. *Mamm* disappeared in the direction of the kitchen from where women's voices could be heard.

"We might as well begin," Minister Kanagy said. "It sorrows me to take such measures as to call this meeting, and I did so only because the matter weighs so heavy on my heart. And because the bishop's family is so closely involved."

"I assume this is about Joe and Verna," Minister Graber interrupted. "Has some new thing come up which makes this meeting necessary?"

"*Yah,* you could say so." Minister Kanagy gave a nervous laugh. "More shame for the community, I'm thinking. Verna came by the other day — I understand with Bishop Beiler's blessing — to see if she could talk me into allowing her to have contact with Joe again."

"Is this true, Bishop?" The question came from Deacon Mast.

Bishop Beiler winced. "Verna did beg me to reconsider my opinion, and I told her I wouldn't. She then wanted to speak with Minister Kanagy on the matter, and I did not forbid or encourage her."

"But is this not a little strange?" Minister Graber offered.

"This whole thing is more than a little strange," Minister Kanagy said. "I say this situation with Joe Weaver has caused enough shame and reproach to each of us, as well as the community. Verna's visit just pushed me over the edge. That's why I have called this meeting. It's time that Joe is asked to face the consequences of his actions. It is time he's required to face the things he did while living in sin. It is also time he cease this attempt at defending himself. That's just a sneaky way around not admitting his sin. And do you understand what will happen when Joe has Paul Wagler testify on his behalf? The shame we have known now will be like a child when he spills a glass of milk. At the trial, *Da Hah*'s name and those of our people will be disgraced beyond our imagination. And all of it will be placed in the public record, where generations of *Englisha* can read them."

Deacon Mast coughed. "I'd better say something right here. I don't know what it means yet, but something else has come up."

"Another shameful thing?" Minister Kanagy stared at him in horror.

"Perhaps, but I'm not sure." Deacon Mast cleared his throat. "Joe's *daett* came over this afternoon with the news that Joe's lawyer told him a new witness has been found. A witness for the other side. And Lloyd wanted prayer for the situation. It seems the owner of the place where Paul claims he and Joe were at on the nights of the robberies — this Slick's Bar and Grill — will now testify that Joe and Paul left early on all of those nights. The implication is that Paul himself may be involved in this thing."

"*Da Hah* have mercy on all of us!" Minister Graber squeaked. "This cannot be *gut* news for anyone. Does Joe deny this?"

"Of course," Deacon Mast said. "Lloyd claims none of this is true."

"So why haven't you told me this before?" Bishop Beiler leaned forward. "Perhaps we wouldn't have needed this meeting. I doubt if Joe will want Paul to testify now."

Deacon Mast shrugged. "I didn't know what the meeting was about. And I didn't have time to finish my chores, make the trip over to your place, and still be here on time. Anyway, what's the great urgency? None of us can do anything about this other than pray."

Minister Kanagy's face hardened. "This is yet more reason to have this meeting. Did Joe say he was stopping this defense now that there is a new witness against him?"

Deacon Mast shifted on his seat. "I understand the lawyer still wishes to continue. She thinks Paul's testimony may carry more weight since Paul is Amish. His testimony is all they have, I understand."

"So now we will have an Amish church member testifying up there, telling the whole world about the sins of his youth." Minister Kanagy's voice had risen until it filled the living room. "And then we will have an *Englisha* man going up and calling the two Amish church members liars. Are any of you having a problem with this? And all of this so that one of our church members can draw himself back from suffering for the wild seeds of sin he has sown? How is this being tolerated? Does our bishop have nothing to say?"

They all stared at Bishop Beiler. Silence filled the room. What was he to say? This had clearly turned into an awful situation. All the words he had prepared in Joe and Verna's defense had vanished.

"Do you have something to add to what Minister Kanagy has said?" Minister Graber asked.

"I . . . well . . . I . . ." Bishop Beiler forced the words out. "I admit this news does not sound *gut,* but I must also think of my daughter's happiness. She's deeply in love with Joe, and if Joe really hasn't done these robberies, he shouldn't have to suffer for them."

Minister Kanagy sounded incredulous. "You would wish to bring this shame on the community for one person's *chance* at happiness? How can you say this thing? How can we as ministers lead our people if the individual does not sacrifice his or her well-being for others? And this is so much more than that. Joe has done evil, and he must be called upon to end this shame once and for all. Is this not true?"

They watched him again.

Bishop Beiler shook his head. "You can do what you wish; this is my family after all. But I would counsel that we wait and see if something more doesn't come up. This news has only arrived today, and there may be other things said tomorrow."

"Against a witness of this kind?" Minister's Kanagy's hands twitched now. "I think not. Waiting will accomplish only shame. The people need to see leadership and a clear example established. What better thing than for Joe to bear his shame and accept what *Da Hah*'s will is. Are these not the words by which our people live?"

He was right, Bishop Beiler thought, and he hung his head. "I will not stand in your way if this is your counsel."

Minister Kanagy wasted no time in replying. "It *is* my counsel. And what of you others?"

They nodded in turn, with Minister Graber going first. Bishop Beiler couldn't blame them. If he were in their shoes, he would do no differently. The least he could do was act like the bishop and place the decision into words.

"Deacon Mast will tell Joe our decision then on Saturday. And if he doesn't listen, we will take this before the church. It is our decision that Paul will not testify before this *Englisha* court. If Joe wishes to tell his story, he can. Other than that, his words are to be *yah* and *nee* before *Da Hah* alone." They nodded even before he was done, and Bishop Beiler rose to his feet. "I believe it is time I go home and comfort my daughter. Though Verna may well be like Rachel from the scriptures who could not be comforted."

THIRTY-NINE

The following Friday night Verna lay in her room listening to the tick of her alarm clock on the dresser. Midnight was close, and the house had been silent for some time. She ought to be asleep herself, but sleep wouldn't come tonight . . . like it hadn't come on every night this week. The days had turned slowly since that awful evening last week when *Daett* came home from the meeting at Minister Kanagy's with such dreadful news.

Verna hadn't slept a wink that first dark night. She'd cried until there were no more tears. Ida and Debbie had stayed in her room until she shooed them out. The next day had been a blur seen through sleep-deprived eyes and a pounding headache. She'd never seen *Mamm* look so worried. *Mamm* even insisted she take a nap after lunch.

But the fitful half hour of sleep on the

couch had only made the following night even more restless. To top it off, Verna had lost weight this week. The pins on her dress strap were already inches tighter. Sometime this would have to end. Joe couldn't do anything more about his situation. He had sat in the church services last Sunday with his head low. He never came to the hymn singing anymore, so Verna stayed home herself.

"You can't continue acting like this," *Mamm* had told her. "Life must go on."

And it would go on — though dramatically changed. The trial was a foregone conclusion as things stood now. Joe was going to jail because the *Englisha* court would never believe his side of the story without a witness. And Paul was forbidden to testify. And even if he did, there was that second witness who would testify that both Paul and Joe left the bar early on the nights in question.

Nee, Paul's testimony would no longer do any *gut* even if he could. Debbie herself had admitted that to Verna. Joe might go to jail for years.

There were moments when bitter thoughts overcame Verna despite her best efforts. If Paul had been allowed to testify, maybe the jury would have believed Joe's story even with the bar owner's word against them. But she mustn't think these thoughts. They were the ones that kept her awake at night. They ate at her. She ought to say them to someone so the sting of their barbs would be less effective, but she didn't dare. Such words had never come out of her mouth before. Even Lois, in her most rebellious moods, didn't speak against the counsel of the church leaders. Would she be the one to set the example for Lois to follow? *Nee,* she must not, Verna decided for the hundredth time. Such a path led nowhere she wished to go. And Lois would likely follow her example and use the same excuses. Only Lois would end up in the *Englisha* world and never return.

Nee, she must be strong. She must learn to accept *Da Hah*'s will. But how escaped her grasp. How did one watch a living death and accept it? How did one not scream protests and writhe with the agony of its pain? Joe would never be the man he once was. Not after years spent in a dark, *Englisha* jail. All that time he'd live without the comforting hand of his people to walk with him. And, of course, the *bann* would be placed on him. Minister Kanagy already had his plans in place, she was certain. The *Englisha* jury would no more then hand down its verdict before Minister Kanagy would act.

At least she knew what to expect at the trial, thanks to Debbie's careful descriptions. And Debbie had said anyone could attend. Verna decided no one would keep her away, even if Minister Kanagy took it into his head to forbid such a thing. But surely even he wouldn't go that far. He wouldn't forbid her to share in Joe's final shame. No man of her people was so heartless.

She would sit in the courtroom and listen to Joe tell his story on the witness stand. And she would believe him even when the guilty verdict came back. Even when the whispers of the Amish community rose around her. Already that was happening, although no one spoke directly to her about it at the Sunday meetings. She wouldn't have blamed them if they had. If this had been anyone but Joe, she might have said the same things. She could even imagine the words . . .

"This doesn't look *gut* at all."

"They say there's an upstanding *Englisha* witness testifying."

"I never thought Joe was *gut* at lying."

"No wonder Rosy cut off their relationship."

"Rosy's woman's intuition was working, I would say."

"That Verna's blinded by her fear of being an old maid."

"*Yah,* there are not many chances left for her, you know."

And yet Verna knew Joe was innocent. She would stand by him no matter what. She stared at the darkened wall of the bedroom. From what Debbie said, a guilty verdict could bring a long prison sentence. Longer than even she could imagine. Fifteen or twenty years, maybe. The raw number stared back at her from the darkness. She would wait for Joe. They would be wed after he came out and made things right with the church. Her years of childbearing would be close to an end by then, but perhaps *Da Hah* would have mercy and still grant them a child. Were not *Da Hah*'s compassions new every day? She had to believe they were or she would lose her mind.

Verna climbed out of bed and knelt to pray. "O dear *Hah,* this is a burden too much for me. I can't carry it, and yet I can't let go of it. I see my life with Joe as it could have been. We were so happy with each other. Like we had finally found what both of us were looking for. Surely this was not a sin? Did You not plant this love in our hearts? Why then are You allowing it to be torn away?"

Verna was unable to continue. The pain of what she hadn't dared dwell on throbbed in her heart. Joe's trial would be held very close to the date they had originally chosen for their wedding — the last week of November.

Verna's voice choked as she managed to pray again. "O dear *Hah,* what have Joe and I done to bring this upon our heads? Is this really Your will? How can it be? And yet it must be. You control the world and all that is in it. You name the stars and know the thoughts of every man. How can You not see our pain? You must see it! And You must know that it's for our best. Oh, I cannot bear this, and yet I must believe in You."

Verna pulled her head up as soft footsteps came from the hallway. Her sobs must have disturbed someone. She crept into bed and pulled the covers over her head even as a timid knock came at the door. When Verna didn't answer, it was repeated.

"Come in," she said, trying to sound sleepy.

Debbie's face appeared in the soft starlight that flittered past the drapes on the open bedroom window. "Were you crying, Verna?"

I'm crying all the time, Verna wanted to say.

Her hesitation gave her away. Debbie came in and sat on her bed. "We can talk, you know. Sometimes that helps."

"I think I've found some peace, Debbie. I don't want to keep you up."

Debbie didn't move away. "You haven't been sleeping much lately, have you?"

Verna didn't answer. Debbie didn't need the details of her travails thrown upon her.

Debbie found Verna's hand in the darkness. "I think that's like most nights, isn't it? So why don't we talk about it?"

Verna struggled to sit up. "You know what's going to happen. You told me yourself."

"There's always the hope the jury will believe Joe's testimony. And perhaps I shouldn't tell you this, but . . ." Debbie squeezed Verna's hand. "I didn't want to give you false hope. But my guess is Joe's lawyer, Ms. Hatcher, will subpoena Paul. She's a tough cookie, and she'll do her job. After that Paul will have to testify regardless of what the ministers say. And you and Joe will have a chance, Verna."

Verna clung to Debbie's hand. "I'm sure Joe has told his lawyer by now that Paul is not to testify."

Debbie shrugged. "The lawyer has to act

455

in the best interest of her client. Joe doesn't have final control over the people she calls to testify."

"But Paul will not speak."

"They'll make him." Debbie sighed. "I wasn't trying to make you feel worse, Verna. And I know there are no guarantees."

"Then you must tell the lawyer that she can't call Paul to testify. You're from the *Englisha,* she will listen to you."

"But, Verna, this may be your best chance for Joe to go free."

"*Nee,* you're wrong, Debbie," Verna whispered. "If Paul is called to the stand, he will refuse to testify no matter what the *Englisha* court says. And that will look very bad for Joe. Besides, Debbie, *Da Hah* is my last chance, and I have made my peace with Him. We must not destroy another life trying to save our own. I'm glad you have told me this. None of us know the strange ways of the *Englisha* court. So you must go to Joe's lawyer and tell her that she must not do this . . . this *subpoena* thing. Surely she will respect our wishes. Tell her I will wait for Joe while he's in jail — until *Da Hah*'s will has been accomplished. Tell her that Joe's heart won't fail him because he will know that he's loved."

"But, Verna!" Debbie protested. "This is a

great sacrifice. And Ms. Hatcher might not listen anyway."

"You will still tell her, Debbie. Please? I have prayed tonight, and what *Da Hah* has decided is *gut* enough for me. And I'm sure Joe feels the same way. If you doubt me, you may go ask Joe before you carry my request to his lawyer."

"I'll think about it," Debbie finally said.

Verna pushed Debbie's hand away. "I've kept you up long enough now. The road ahead may be hard and long, but *Da Hah* will walk with us as He has for so many others. There have been those of our people who lost loved ones to death for reasons they couldn't understand. What we are being asked to carry is not an unreasonable load. Go now, Debbie. And thank you for doing this for me. *Da Hah* has you here for a reason. I know that even more now."

Debbie retreated and closed the door behind her with a soft click.

Verna lay back on the bed. Finally peace had come to her heart. She had found acceptance, but at what cost? She had expected joy to come with the peace or perhaps have light cast on the future. But there was none of that. Just the soft stream of starlight that shone through her bedroom window. Her soul felt light and held up by strong arms. *Da Hah has come near,* she thought. And what He would do, she would accept. It was the way of her people, and the way it should be. She closed her eyes and soon drifted off to sleep.

FORTY

Debbie paced the floor at Destiny Relocation Services. She'd been at her desk most of the day coordinating the moving crews. They had a record number of jobs this week, including two long-distance moves. One relocation went into Texas, and the other to Florida. These required arranging motels for the crews and monitoring their progress. The crew bosses were both long-time employees of Mr. Fulton's and reliable, so her stress wasn't work related. Rather it was Joe and Verna and their situation that weighed on her. She'd finally finagled another meeting out of Joe's attorney, Ms. Hatcher. Their appointment was for today after work.

The truth was, she'd put the meeting off for some time even after she'd finally promised Verna she would contact the lawyer. Only Verna's whispered question a few days ago, "Have you spoken with the lawyer yet?"

forced her hand. She had made the phone call.

It seemed such a shame to throw away what little hope there was to turn the case in Joe's favor. And she wasn't certain Ms. Hatcher would follow Verna's request, but it was likely. The weight of her client's wishes, his family, his church, and now his fiancée might be enough to tilt the balance that direction. Debbie would deliver the message to Ms. Hatcher. That was her duty to Verna.

Of all the lessons she'd learned so far from Amish life, this passive acceptance of one's fate was the most difficult to grasp. This surrender of a situation to God when struggle seemed the best response was odd. Did the Beiler family expect a miracle? Some gift from heaven that would make this go away? If they did, they never said a word about it. Lately even Verna walked around with newfound peace on her face, though sorrow obviously still lay heavy on her shoulders. There were moments when a smile would flicker across her face. Sometimes this happened at evening devotions when her *daett* would read a passage. Last night Verna's reaction had occurred when a psalm had been read, the one where King David wrote, "Rejoice in the LORD, O ye righteous: for praise is comely for the upright."

Perhaps Verna's peace came from the righteousness of her soul? Debbie could think of no other explanation for a smile on such a sorrow-lined face. Indeed, the life Verna lived would have to make one feel righteous. She had surrendered the future and her innocent boyfriend into the hands of God. Debbie was sure Joe was innocent. If there had been any doubts in her mind, they had long flown away. Last Sunday at the church service, Joe had also appeared surrounded by peace. No guilty man would look so calm, Debbie told herself. Only the innocent could walk with that depth of humility.

Now she had one last appointment at the office today that must be gotten out of the way. Then she'd be done for the week. Someone had called the secretary two days ago wanting a meeting with Debbie for the last opening on Friday. The odd thing was that the man had given his name as Henry Yoder. But that made no sense to Debbie. Why would Henry wish to see her? But there were many Yoder families in Snyder County. The man could well be someone else who needed advice about moving.

A sharp knock on her office door inter-

461

rupted Debbie's thoughts. Before she could answer, it opened and Rhonda from the front desk peeked in. "Your appointment is here."

Debbie raised her eyebrows. "What does he look like?"

"Some kind of Amish man." Rhonda's gaze swept over Debbie's attire. "Are you dating an Amish man?"

Debbie laughed. "I am not."

"So shall I let him come back or are you coming out?"

"I'm already here," a man's voice said in the hallway.

Rhonda whirled around.

Before Debbie could move, Henry Yoder appeared in the doorway. Or at least she thought he looked like the Henry Yoder she'd known. She hadn't seen him since before the excommunication. His beard was gone and his hair was shorter, but he still wore suspenders and looked about the same otherwise.

"You know who I am?" A hint of his old boldness played on his face.

"Yes, I do."

"May I sit?" Henry motioned toward an empty chair.

The man sure didn't seem shamed by his excommunication, but then he'd always been bold. A vision of Henry when he directed things at his house at that Sunday evening hymn singing flashed through her mind.

"You're the one in the *bann,*" Debbie blurted.

He didn't appear offended. *"Yah,* according to the Amish, but perhaps not according to *Da Hah."*

Debbie stared at him. "I don't know much about such theology. You wanted to see me for some reason? Is there some way I can help you?"

Henry tilted his head. "In fact, I do. I believe I have some information that would be beneficial to the Beiler family. I figured it was useless speaking with them . . . being in the *bann* stands in the way. So I'm speaking with you. You live with them, and I figure you understand these *Englisha* things better than they do anyway. You probably aren't under the Amish church obligation to discard the information as they would be just because, well, since I've been thrown out, let's say."

"You want me to tell them something?" Debbie asked.

He sighed. "What I have may benefit the Beiler family, but the information is not for them. At this time I think it would be best if they don't know what I have to share. The Amish can be strange about such things. I even heard the ministry's cut off Joe's defense completely."

Debbie didn't wait for him to say more. "And you don't agree with that so you want me to do something that would defy their counsel but possibly defend Joe? I'm afraid there is nothing I can do."

"Nee! Nee!" He waved his hand about. "That's not it at all. I have new information to give to Joe's attorney."

Debbie's ears perked up. "New information . . . about Joe's case?"

Henry took a moment to shift in his seat. "It's like this . . . see . . . I now associate with a different church. I'm meeting different people, and they often see things differently than the Amish do. And they don't want an innocent man to be punished. Those of us who know Joe want to help out in this case. We feel sorry for Joe . . . and for Verna too, of course."

"We all feel bad for them," Debbie agreed. "But I don't see how you can help. There are two witnesses against Joe."

Henry didn't move. "You haven't yet heard what I have to say."

"And why would you want to help the Beiler family? Bishop Beiler and the ministry excommunicated you."

Henry made circular motions in the air with his hand. "Perhaps I want to sprinkle a little of those 'coals of fire' on Bishop Beiler's head. But then maybe I'm just acting out of the goodness of my heart put there by *Da Hah.* I'd like to think that also."

"Coals of fire?" Debbie asked out loud, searching her memory. "Oh, the biblical reference on how one should treat the enemy."

"*Yah,* that one." Henry appeared satisfied. "Although Bishop Beiler isn't my enemy — at least not on my part."

Debbie glanced at the clock. "I have to leave in ten minutes for another appointment . . ."

"I'll make this quick," Henry interrupted. He held out a crumpled paper he pulled from his pocket. "Here is the phone number of a member of the church I now attend. One Willis Helmuth. He is willing to testify to repeatedly making cheap purchases of merchandise from the owner of Slick's Bar and Grill. A Mr. Tom Hendricks, I believe. Hendricks is the one who wants to undermine testimony on Joe's behalf. Willis was once Amish himself — from another district. He was in his *rumspringa* around the same time as Paul and Joe. He's discussed this with our church leaders and me, since I know Joe. It's our belief that if this merchandise Willis purchased is checked, it will match some of the stolen goods from those robberies Joe is supposedly tied to. Here's the bottom line. Willis still has these items, and he is willing to turn them over along with his testimony to Joe's defense attorney and the police, if things come to that."

Debbie took the paper, her heart pounding at the possibility. "But this Willis may come under suspicion himself if he knowingly purchased stolen goods."

Henry shrugged. "Willis bought these items cheap suspecting they might be stolen but not sure about it. He asked questions, and Mr. Hendricks assured him they were not. One can hardly go to jail for being an Amish skinflint, huh?" Henry grinned.

Debbie hardly knew what to think. She stood and paced behind her desk. This seemed too fantastic to possibly be true, and it was dropped into her lap on the very afternoon she was to speak with Joe's lawyer! Was this the miracle the Amish had looked for?

"You will pass this on then?" Henry asked, standing up.

"Yes, I think I must," Debbie said. "And thank you!" She held out her hand, and

Henry shook it. Then he nodded, turned, and disappeared down the hallway without another word.

Debbie stared at the paper with the name and details spelled out in black and white. Had God moved right in front of her eyes? She rushed to finish her work and close up the office. As she hurried past Rhonda, she offered a rushed, "See you, Monday!" She unlocked the car, threw her things in the back, and pulled out into surprisingly light rush-hour traffic. When she arrived at Ms. Hatcher's office, she found a parking space right in front and hurried into the building. She took a seat in the lobby after a quick nod to the secretary.

Moments later she found herself seated across from the serious Ms. Hatcher.

"Good afternoon, Ms. Watson. When you made this appointment on the phone, you said you had some bad news for me. I sure hope that's not the case because I'm already about to pull my hair out over this Amish stubbornness. I've been told that Mr. Wagler, my only witness, is refusing to testify. If I'm ever assigned to defend an Amish person again, I do declare I'll have to . . ."

Debbie handed her Henry's crumbled paper. "Maybe this will help."

Ms. Hatcher read in silence for a moment.

"What is this, and where did you get it?"

"A certain *stubborn* Amish man named Henry Yoder gave it to me this afternoon. Only his stubbornness cost him his membership within the Amish community, I'm afraid. I'll spare you the details. Suffice it to say, he has his reasons for coming forward. The paper is a list of items a Mr. Willis Helmuth purchased from the owner of that bar and grill Joe and Paul went to. The owner of that bar is one of the prosecution's witnesses against Joe. Because he was able to purchase the items so cheaply, Mr. Helmuth believes they may have been stolen and might be listed on the police report in Joe's case."

Ms. Hatcher devoured the details on the paper again. "My, this does look good! If the numbers match, I might come out smelling like a rose after all. This ought to send the prosecutor racing off in another direction like a mounted Englishman after his hound."

"That's what I hoped," Debbie agreed. "But I have a request. Can you keep the identity of these witnesses and the source a secret from Joe until the trial?"

Ms. Hatcher rolled her eyes. "You people are certainly strange!"

Debbie repeated, "Can you keep them a secret?"

"If they all don't change their minds about cooperating," Ms. Harper said. "If I go to the district attorney with this, the case might not even go to trial."

Debbie got up to leave. "That would be good news indeed."

As she turned to go, Debbie noticed Ms. Hatcher was already reaching for her phone. She smiled all the way back to her car. Now the question was whether she should tell Verna. She'd been confident enough in the face of Ms. Hatcher's questions, but what if something should go wrong? Would it be fair to raise Verna's hopes only to have them dashed to pieces again? And how would she keep the identity of the people involved a secret? She would wait, she decided as she climbed into her car. She would tell Verna she'd been to the lawyer's office like she'd promised. Verna wouldn't ask any questions beyond that.

FORTY-ONE

The following Tuesday night it was late when a buggy pulled into the Beilers' driveway. Supper and the evening devotions were finished, and the family was sitting in the living room visiting.

Verna glanced over at *Mamm.* "Perhaps I'd better go upstairs?"

The peace that had entered her heart the night she'd prayed had stayed with her, but there were moments when its hold wavered. If Deacon Mast had come for a talk with *Daett* on some church trouble or, worse, if this was a new trouble that concerned Joe, she didn't wish to see him.

"You'd better stay," *Mamm* replied and gave Verna a quick glance. "We don't know who is here. And you can't go running away from problems. You don't even know what this is about."

Mamm was right. Trouble was better faced head-on. *Daett* was already on his feet and headed out the door. Any conversation between him and Deacon Mast would occur outside by the buggy. Verna could surely handle that much stress. And if this concerned her, *Daett* would break the news afterward whether she fled upstairs or not.

Verna nestled down on the couch and gave Debbie a pained look. "My nerves are a little raw, I guess."

"Mine would be worse than raw," Debbie said. "You're a perfect saint in my opinion."

"Hey! What about me?" Lois asked from the other end of the couch. "Am I a perfect saint too?"

"No comment!" Debbie teased.

They all laughed, the soft sound filling the living room.

Life was slowly returning to normal, Verna thought. Despite the added pain of Joe's almost certain future imprisonment. This was how *Da Hah* worked when one trusted Him. She would make it through the years ahead with *Da Hah*'s help. She would travel with the same grace He was giving to her now. *Yah,* it would be shaky at times, but there would be help available when she needed it.

Joe's trial would occur soon, and sorrow might overwhelm her soul then. But *Da Hah* would not fail her. She would always believe that truth. She glanced up and saw Debbie regarding her with a worried expression.

"Are you okay?" Debbie asked.

Verna forced a smile. "Just thinking of the trial. Yes, I'll be okay."

Debbie glanced at the floor. "There's something I should tell you . . . I mean . . . I hope things turn out okay, and they might yet, you know."

"Thanks for the encouragement." Verna gave a strained laugh. "You're such an optimist, Debbie. You always see the bright side. I wish I were more like that."

Debbie almost spoke again, but Bishop Beiler reappeared in the doorway, looking shaken.

"Daett!" *Mamm* leaped to her feet. "What's happened?" She took him into her arms.

He briefly hugged her and then said, "Please, everyone, sit down."

They all sat down except *Mamm,* who stayed beside *Daett.* Everyone in the room stared at him, waiting. What horrible news had Deacon Mast brought? Would Verna be able to take it?

Finally *Daett* sat down and asked *Mamm* to do the same.

Mamm complied, her gaze still on his face.

"I'm trying to recover myself." Bishop Beiler glanced over at Verna. "Will someone please sit beside her before I share what I have to say?"

Verna felt the blood leave her face and the room began to spin. "What's happened to Joe? Is he dead? He's dead, isn't he? There's been an accident? Something worse has happened than Joe going to jail? What did Deacon Mast say?"

Mamm was already beside Verna, holding one hand, while Debbie wrapped her in a tight hug from the other side.

Above the flood of emotions roiling inside her, Verna heard *Daett*'s proclaim, "*Nee*, daughter! It's nothing like that. Verna, that wasn't Deacon Mast come calling. It was Joe! He's outside now, and he claims it's all over. All the charges against him have been dropped!"

"What?" Verna tried to focus.

"It's over!"

Her *daett* appeared within her vision. "And I think the boy is telling the truth."

"It is true!" Debbie declared. "I was hoping it would turn out this way! I just didn't want to say until I was sure."

Bishop Beiler regarded Debbie for a moment. "You had contact with the *Englisha* lawyer, did you not?"

Debbie nodded. "I was aware of a new development, but I was waiting to see . . ."

473

"Then perhaps we *can* believe this." He sat back in his rocker and let out a long breath.

"What is this you're saying?" Verna clutched Debbie's arm. "I don't understand."

"New evidence came up that I hoped would help Joe's case . . . and it sounds like it did," Debbie said.

Great hope rose in Verna — one she couldn't control. She wanted to believe a miracle had happened! And she wanted to see Joe! She wanted to believe *Da Hah* had seen it best to restore Joe's life and their happiness. But was this possible? Did *Da Hah* really come through? *Daett* didn't sound that convinced even with Debbie's assurances. And neither was she. Someone didn't just show up and say a problem of this magnitude was solved.

Debbie's hand moved on hers. "You should go speak with Joe."

"Joe?" Verna stared at her.

"Your Joe is outside waiting for you, Verna," her *daett* said.

Debbie pointed toward the front door. "I'm sure Joe will tell you!"

Verna looked around the room. Suddenly she jumped to her feet. She looked at her *daett,* and he didn't shake his head so it must be okay to go see Joe!

Debbie rose and stood beside Verna. She took her friend's arm and together they went out onto the front porch and down the steps.

"Can you walk from here on your own?" Debbie whispered in her ear.

Verna didn't say anything. Her gaze was focused on Joe, who was standing beside his buggy like a statue. She felt Debbie's arm leave hers, and her body seemed to float down the walk. Joe was running toward her now, and when he arrived his arms wrapped around her.

She buried her face in his chest for what seemed like an eternity before pulling back and looking at him. "Is it really true?" Her fingers reached up to trace his face.

"It's a miracle!" he said. "Yes, it's very true!"

"How did it happen?"

He didn't answer. Instead he drew her close again. "Oh, Verna!" His lips found hers, and she was ready to drift right up to the skies and never come back.

"I have to breathe," she said as she pulled away and laughed at the same time. "And they are seeing us."

"Do you care?"

She blushed and pushed him away. "You

have to come in and tell us all what happened. We will have time for this . . . later."

Joe followed her up the steps, all the while holding on to her . . . only letting go when they walked inside.

"Joe's come to explain! I wanted all of us to hear it together," Verna said.

Mamm ushered them to the couch, and when they were seated *Daett* cleared his throat. "Start talking, Joe," he commanded with a smile.

Verna snuggled tightly against Joe and looked up at his face.

Joe seemed flustered now. He took a deep breath. "All I know is what the lawyer told me. She called our phone shack with a message for me to call. When I called back, she asked me to make sure I was available. Some new information had come up. It was important information that might pan out. I didn't want to know any details, and she didn't offer any. She said I was supposed to stay on standby in case there were questions that needed answering. She asked me to come to her office late today."

Joe took a moment to take another deep breath. "Today when I walked into her office she told me it was all over. She said *all* the charges had been dropped! A witness came forward who had purchased merchandise from the nightclub owner, Mr. Hendricks, and it turned out the stuff was some of the stolen loot. This evidence has tested out. It appears that . . ."

Joe glanced around and then hung his head. "Well, it appears that Kim, my former *Englisha* girlfriend, and her buddies stole stuff and used Mr. Hendricks as the clearing house to sell the items. The prosecution dropped charges against me! Here I am! I'm free and no longer in danger of going to jail!"

The bishop stared at him. "You didn't tell us who this new witness was."

Joe shrugged. "The lawyer said there was a request to keep it quiet unless necessary. I decided that was okay. I mean, I don't care as long as . . . as long as the truth was revealed."

Bishop Beiler thought for a moment. "*Englisha* people are always into secrets. I suppose it doesn't matter if you're out from under suspicion. Debbie, can you confirm that this is all aboveboard?"

"It is," Debbie said at once.

"I don't care how it happened!" Verna declared, struggling to keep a quaver out of her voice. "I have Joe back! We should all be thankful!"

Beside her, Joe stroked Verna's arm in-between quick glances at her *daett.*

"I suppose so," Bishop Beiler allowed as he stood. "I'll need to pass this information on to the other ministers. I'm sure they will rejoice with us."

"Just be thankful!" *Mamm* tugged on her husband's shirt sleeve. "Sit down, *Daett,* and let's take this all in. And Verna and Joe can go somewhere they can talk. They have plans to make."

The words weren't even all the way out of *Mamm*'s mouth before Verna was on her feet pulling on Joe's arm.

He got up and smiled in the bishop's direction. "I guess we do have some things that should be taken care of. Do we need to wait for the ministers to lift the probation and the counsel to not see each other?"

The bishop smiled. "*Nee,* I believe I can authorize your time together."

"Go!" *Mamm* waved her arm toward the front door. "Don't let us hold you up at a moment like this."

Verna took Joe's hand and led him outside and across the lawn. "We can sit inside the buggy since you didn't bring your courting rig."

Joe helped Verna up, then climbed in beside her.

Verna allowed her eyes to trace the

weather-beaten lines on his face. He was so handsome, so *gut* to look at. "Oh, Joe! Am I having a dream?"

He looked dazed. "If it's a dream, I hope we never awaken."

Verna allowed herself to melt into his arms again.

Joe took off his hat and tossed it onto the shelf behind the seat. Then he leaned back in the seat, his fingers entwined in hers. "I've suffered, Verna, through these longs weeks. But I think you've suffered the worst. And yet you never forsook me. How can I ever thank you enough?"

"By making me your *frau* this fall yet," she whispered.

He sat up straight. "Then we'd better start making plans fast!"

Verna laughed softly. "But tonight we talk only sweet nothings. I want to soak up the joy of your presence. I think I'll pinch myself every few minutes to make sure I'm still alive."

He pulled her close. "Those were dark days, Verna. I hope we never have to travel such roads again."

"Yet *Da Hah* was with us, was He not?" She looked up at his face. "And He gave me peace in the darkest hours. I obtained a trust that He would do only what was for

479

the best. And now He has. None of that will change whatever the troubles lying ahead. And we will have each other as long as He allows it. Is that not enough, Joe?"

He gazed down at her for a moment. "You shame me, Verna. Not only am I getting a beautiful woman — but one filled with such faith. My heart is stirred deeply."

Verna hid her face under his chin. "You must not say such things."

"I will if I wish to because they are true."

"Then I will plug my ears when they become too much."

He laughed. "You may have to wear earplugs all day long then."

Verna peered up at him. "You haven't seen my faults yet."

"Faults? You don't have any!"

Verna chuckled. "You poor, deceived fellow."

He was serious now. "Doesn't it bother you? What I did on my *rumspringa*? The whole community knows now, and I am ashamed."

"And the whole community will forget soon enough." Verna wrapped her arms around his neck and kissed his protest into silence.

FORTY-TWO

The weeks rolled around, and the last Thursday of November had arrived. Joe's case had died away slowly within the community. No whispers circulated regarding who the mysterious witness had been though. It was as if Bishop Beiler wished to banish the whole situation from his mind, and his wish had been granted.

Clearly Henry Yoder hadn't babbled things around which, Debbie thought, was much to his credit. Perhaps the man wasn't so bad after all, even with his self-aggrandizing statement about heaping coals of fire on Bishop Beiler's head. Apparently Henry was content to allow the good work to simmer without a claim of credit for himself.

Debbie was thankful that the day of Joe and Verna's wedding had finally arrived with no outside distractions to ruin the event.

The Beiler house had been scrubbed and cleaned to within an inch of its life. Verna had threatened to use the Beiler's barn for the services since she was the first daughter to wed from the family, but her *mamm* would have none of it. There was room to spare in the house, she claimed. That was if they moved all the furniture out plus used the first-floor bedroom. The guests seated there wouldn't be able to see all of the ceremony, but they could hear it. The meal afterward would be served in the upper hayloft of the barn, accessed from the "bank side."

Verna had eventually given in, and now everyone was crammed into the house so tightly they could hardly breathe. All faces were turned toward the kitchen doorway where Bishop Beiler was concluding the main sermon. Alvin Knepp was sitting only inches from Debbie, his black pants and white shirt pressed so well the creases stood up on their own. This wasn't exactly how Debbie had envisioned the first hours they would spend together, but it would have to suffice.

She didn't need romantic regrets in her head now that she had access to Alvin for the day. He was her partner in serving the food after the service. Thoughts on how to charm him would be a more worthy goal, she decided, although how that would be accomplished she wasn't certain. The rules for relationships with Amish boys seemed quite different from what she was used to. Here a person was cautious before giving any attention that wasn't asked for, which should have placed her at Paul Wagler's side today. But she had turned that option down flatly when it had been proposed.

Paul was currently seated across from Ida, who was the witness for Verna's side of the family. Ida had been blushing all shades of red ever since the service began. The poor girl! Ida had wanted this badly. This was her chance to do something with Paul since he clearly had no plans to ask her home from the hymn singings.

Today any couple could be paired up and no one would draw inferences. Verna had assured Debbie of this, but during the planning stage she had still refused to be seated with Paul. This probably also explained why Alvin was comfortable with the arrangement today . . . and why he sat beside her right now. Debbie wished Alvin *would* draw some conclusions, but his actions so far indicated he had no special interest in her. They'd met earlier in the hayloft with the other waiter couples, and beyond a smile and a *gut* morning, he hadn't made any attempt at conversation.

She would have to dig deep and find her charming skills, Debbie decided. There was no question about that if she was ever to get past the walls Alvin had built between them. There had been a time when things had been much more open, but then Paul had come along and messed everything up.

Why couldn't Alvin put two and two together? Why couldn't he see that she could have chosen Paul for this day if she'd wanted to? But that likely wasn't how Alvin's thought processes worked. Ida was Verna's closest sister in age, and Paul was Joe's best friend. The two went together as naturals for Verna's wedding day.

At the moment, Alvin had his gaze on Bishop Beiler's face as he wrapped up his sermon. Debbie wished the boy would steal a glance at her once in a while, but he hadn't so far. She would find a way to thaw him out before the day was over! Surely somewhere inside of him Alvin held an inkling of interest in her. Why else didn't he date some Amish girl? Sure, his options were slim in the community, but he could visit other communities if he felt desperate enough.

Debbie drew her thoughts away from Alvin, and focused on the bishop as he finished his sermon and turned to speak to

Joe and Verna. "Now if both of you still wish to enter into the holy state of matrimony, will you please stand to your feet."

Joe stood first, with Verna right behind him. Verna dazzled today in her dark-blue wedding dress. The color deepened her skin color until it seemed to glow in the soft sunlight that came through the living room window. Joe's face was full of joy as he looked first at Verna and then at the bishop.

Bishop Beiler asked Joe, "Do you, our brother Joe Weaver, believe in your heart that this, our sister Verna Beiler, has been given to you as a *frau* by *Da Hah*?"

"Yah!" Joe's voice was firm.

Bishop Beiler repeated the basic question to Verna.

Verna reply was a softer *"Yah."*

Several other questions and answers followed, and then Bishop Beiler joined Joe and Verna's hands. He proceeded to proclaim them man and wife.

Debbie waited for the kiss and almost laughed out loud when it didn't come. This was her first Amish wedding season, and the ceremony still wasn't totally familiar. At an *Englisha* wedding there would be a long and passionate kiss right now. Alvin stole a quick glance at her. She must have let some of the laugh slip out. This was just great.

Now Alvin probably figured she couldn't be respectful in services. And what Amish man would want such a *frau*? Well, she would have to work all the harder to overcome this bad impression.

Joe and Verna sat down again, and a song began. At its conclusion, the couple stood and filed out first. The bench full of table waiters was dismissed next, and they spilled out into the yard. Several of the boys yawned and stretched their arms skyward, obviously bored with the whole thing. Alvin marched straight ahead, on his way to the barn where the meal would be served. Debbie kept up his fast pace. They were one of the first couples to arrive in the serving area, which was curtained off at the back of the hayloft. One of the cooks glanced up and smiled. "Did they get married off okay?"

"Yep!" Alvin said crisply. "Where can we begin work?"

"Hold your horses there," another of the cooks told him. "Dinner's not served for a while yet, but I guess you can wash the pots and pans if you have all that energy."

"Why not?" Alvin glanced at Debbie. "Are you willing?"

"You think *Englisha* girls don't know how to wash dishes?" she shot back at him. That wasn't what she'd intended to say — at least not in that tone of voice, but it had slipped out.

Surprisingly, Alvin appeared amused. "So you have learned how to work at the Beilers'?"

"Like I didn't know how to before?" she asked.

He didn't respond this time.

She followed him over to where the pots were piled high. Once there, she plunged her hands into the bowl of soapy water.

He cleaned scraps from the pots and handed them to her. "I guess you did grow up around the Beiler family."

"You're more conceited than you look," she told him. "I'll have you know that my parents taught me how to work. And I have finished college — and debt free at that. With Mom and Dad's help, of course, but I worked summers."

"Sorry. I didn't mean any disrespect," he said, sounding puzzled at her defensiveness.

She was supposed to charm him, Debbie remembered. And here she was practically in an argument with the man. She took a deep breath. "I'm sorry myself. Isn't this a beautiful day for Joe and Verna's wedding? I'm so happy for them! After what they had to go through with those false charges and all."

"They did go through some rough spots," Alvin allowed, his attention fixed on the spot where he was scraping a pan. "But all's well that ends well. That's what our people say."

This was *not* going well, Debbie thought. She stole a glance at his face. She might as well make the plunge. It really couldn't get any worse. She blurted, "There's nothing between Paul Wagler and myself. I wish you'd stop thinking so."

He gave a short laugh but said nothing.

Debbie kept going. "I used to drive past your place for a reason. I didn't stop doing that because of Paul. I stopped because I thought it might no longer be appropriate since I'm living at the Beilers' place."

His face showed a flicker of interest. "Then why were you cavorting in town with Paul at Andrea's Pizzeria?"

"Did Paul tell you that?"

He shrugged. "I don't see that it makes any difference who said it. It did happen, didn't it?"

She took another deep breath. "The fact happened. But I was working on Joe and Verna's case. Paul requested the meeting."

He seemed to process the information.

"Well, then it's *gut.*"

Debbie pressed her advantage. "I'm planning to stay Amish, you know. Maybe I'll even join the spring baptismal class, now that Joe and Verna's problems are past."

"I see."

Debbie continued to wash as the noise of the crowd behind them increased. Alvin should be impressed with her work if nothing else. And perhaps she'd reached him with her direct approach. He looked less stern than he had at the morning service.

He didn't say anything more though.

Moments later a cook appeared. "Time to get ready, you two. My, you've done some work! But get those soap bubbles out of your hair, Debbie."

Debbie wiped her hands on the offered cloth. She dabbed her face and hair with gentle touches. Were all of the offending bubbles off? There was no way to tell without asking, and the cook had vanished. Alvin solved the problem. He stepped closer and took the cloth from her hand before she even thought to ask him.

"Hold still," he said. He touched her forehead in several places with the dishcloth. "There! All done." He stepped back to give her a once over and smiled with satisfaction. "You look perfect now."

A quick retort sprang to her lips, but Debbie kept it inside. "Thank you, Alvin."

"By the way, I always liked it when you drove past my place in your car."

"You did?" she whispered.

"Maybe you should do it again sometime." His voice stopped as if a surprising thought had just occurred to him. "I suppose it's up to me now?"

"Alvin . . ." Debbie caught her breath. "Please understand that I . . . I . . ." She couldn't say the words. They seemed inappropriate now that the moment had arrived. She should let him take the lead. That was the Amish way. But, oh, this was hard. What if Alvin never fully understood the depth of her affection for him?

"We'll have to see then," he said as he turned to lead the way back to the other waiters. They were milling around and peering out through the curtain at the long tables of seated guests. It was just as well they all were busy, Debbie thought. Someone might notice her blushing face otherwise. But what did she care if they did? The advancement of one's love life on a wedding day was just about perfect. And she'd taken hers forward by great leaps and bounds, she was sure.

If Verna could think about anything other

than Joe for a moment, she would be thrilled. Perhaps Verna would even notice her glowing face when they served the corner table. Why, she almost had a date lined up once she joined the instruction class! Alvin hadn't said so for certain, but he would get there before long. Debbie was sure of that. Her thoughts were interrupted by Bishop Beiler's voice calling for prayer.

When the bishop finished praying, the waiters filled their arms with bowls of food and spilled out from behind the curtain. Debbie led the way to Joe and Verna's table, which was set up at the far end of the hayloft.

Verna had insisted on a marvelous array of fresh fruits and vegetable arranged on the table around her — the only decorations allowed. Now with Verna and Joe beaming, the whole place seemed lit up with light and joy. The scene couldn't have been more perfect, Debbie thought . . . except for the sight of Paul, who winked at her.

Debbie set the bowl of potatoes down and gave Paul a quick glare before she spoke to Verna. "Congratulations! You finally made it."

"*Yah,* we have. By *Da Hah*'s grace." Verna's face glowed. "And thank you, Debbie, for everything. You have been so *wunder-bah.*"

"And congratulations to you!" Debbie told Joe while ignoring Verna's gushing praise. "Just tell us if you need anything. Alvin and I are at your beck and call."

Alvin had set down his dishes and joined her, sharing his own congratulations with the happy couple.

Debbie turned momentarily when Paul sang out "living on love" in her direction. Then she tried to ignore him.

"They sure are a charming couple," Alvin whispered as they left to pick up another round of filled-to-the-brim food bowls.

And so are we! Debbie almost said. She gave Alvin a sweet smile instead. "Thank you for serving the tables with me today."

His face also glowed despite Paul's inappropriate remark.

Debbie felt as if Verna's grace had overflowed onto her. Love was finally taking root in the right places!

"I was delighted to accept, Debbie." Alvin reached over and brushed her fingers with his. His gaze lingered long on her face.

DISCUSSION QUESTIONS

1. How do you feel about Debbie's mother wanting her to move out of the home now that she had finished college?

2. Is Lois's fascination with the *Englisha* world a wise choice to make for an Amish girl?

3. What is your reaction to Callie's concerns that Debbie will "wither" if she boards at the Beilers?

4. What do you think of Bishop Beiler's reasons to accept Debbie as a boarder at the Beiler home?

5. What are your feelings about the Amish practice of *rumspringa* for their young people?

6. Do you think Debbie's influence on Lois

to remain Amish will last?

7. What lies at the heart of the Amish's reluctance to deal with lawyers and the law?

8. How could Paul have approached Debbie with his attentions that would have won her heart?

9. What do you think of Debbie's handling of Paul?

10. Should Minister Kanagy have taken such a strong stand against Joe and Verna in his attempt to keep the congregation pure?

11. Did Bishop Beiler do the right thing as he became more sympathetic towards the plight of his girls?

12. Was Debbie wise to continue her pursuit of Alvin Knepp?

ABOUT THE AUTHOR

Jerry S. Eicher's bestselling Amish fiction (more than 500,000 in combined sales) includes The Adams County Trilogy, Hannah's Heart series, The Fields of Home series, Little Valley series, and some stand-alone novels. He's also written nonfiction, including *My Amish Childhood* and *The Amish Family Cookbook* (with his wife, Tina).

After a traditional Amish childhood, Jerry taught for two terms in Amish and Mennonite schools in Ohio and Illinois. Since then he's been involved in church renewal, preaching, and teaching Bible studies.